THE WALL

THE
WALL

JOHN MARKS

RIVERHEAD BOOKS

A MEMBER OF PENGUIN PUTNAM INC.

NEW YORK

1998

Mar

RIVERHEAD BOOKS
a member of
Penguin Putnam Inc.
375 Hudson Street
New York, NY 10014

Library of Congress Cataloging-in-Publication Data

Marks, John, date.
The wall : a novel / by John Marks.
p.   cm.
ISBN 1-57322-122-8 (acid-free paper)
1. Berlin Wall, Berlin, Germany, 1961–1989—Fiction.   I. Title.
PS3563.A66655W35   1998   98-3717 CIP
813'.54—dc21

Printed in the United States of America
1   3   5   7   9   10   8   6   4   2

This book is printed on acid-free paper. ♾

Book design by Marysarah Quinn
Map by Jeffrey L. Ward

FOR DEBRA

BERLIN 1989

NORWAY

Atlantic Ocean

UNITED
KINGDOM

North Sea

FRENCH SECTOR

THE WALL

BORNHOLMERSTRASSE

EAST

BERLIN

BRITISH SECTOR

INVALIDENSTRASSE

FRIEDRICHSTRASSE (CHECKPOINT CHARLIE)

WEST

BERLIN

AMERICAN SECTOR

THE WALL

GLIENICKER BRÜCKE

Potsdam

DREILINDEN

to West Germany

0 *Miles*   10
0 *Kilometers*   10

PORTUGAL   SPAIN

Mediterranean Sea

Atlantic Ocean

ALGIERS

MOROCCO

RABAT   ALGERIA

©1998 Jeffrey L. Ward

EUROPE 1989

And it shall come to pass, that when they make
a long blast with the ram's horn, and when ye
hear the sound of the trumpet, all the people
shall shout with a great shout; and
the wall of the city shall fall down flat,
and the people shall ascend up
every man straight before him.

JOSHUA 6:5

From this place and from this time forth commences a new era
in world history, and you can all say you were present at its birth.

GOETHE AT THE BATTLE OF VALMY

ON MY WATCH

CHAPTER ONE

1.

A T DUSK ON NOVEMBER 9, 1989, in the chief Allied listening
post in West Berlin, Captain Nester Cates eavesdropped on a telephone conversation between two members of enemy intelligence seated in
an office building on the eastern side of the Berlin Wall. Nester checked the
hammer and sickle hands of his watch, 1838, Central European Time, and
began to take notes. The enemy, it seemed, was talking about him.

"You've heard something about this officer—?" Nester looked over at
Corporal Jerome Tunt, an ambitious young American from Jamaica who
had alerted him to the conversation just moments before and was listening
too on his own headset. Tunt gave a nod of acknowledgment. With a stub
of pencil, Nester translated the conversation into English.

"Well, yes, something."

"Black—"

"That's him."

"Speaks German like a native." Nester pressed too hard on the pencil,
and the nib broke. Tunt rolled him another one. The conversation would be
recorded, but Nester wanted the words in his immediate possession, in case
security considerations and red tape prevented him from getting a copy.

"Better than a native, supposedly, but I'm skeptical—"

"Jet Kraut, his own people call him." One of the men had broken into
English, for an instant, to pronounce "Jet" incorrectly as "Yet," using the
German sound for the letter J. "You know what it means—"

"It's meant as an insult, of course."

Nester caught a look of embarrassment on Tunt's face. It was a well-
known nickname around field station.

The East Germans turned to questions of translation. "The black weed, it means, I think—"

"The black *German*. Much worse than weed."

"Anyway, as I said, I'm skeptical. Africans can't speak German well. Too many consonants—"

"He has a German mother—"

"*Ach ja*—"

"She's from Hamburg. Pale as a Beelitz asparagus."

Shaking his head at the low grade of the information, Nester scrawled in caps: "Checotah, Oklahoma, black as Turkish coffee." Only the dead looked as pale as Beelitz asparagus.

"He's blue-eyed—"

A wretched little mistake, Nester thought, for one of the world's most effective covert agencies. He was brown-eyed, as even the most basic description of him would have told them. They must be slipping. Still, Nester was disconcerted that they had collected anything at all on him. He lived an obscure life in an even more obscure world. No one should know about him, not even such trivia as the color of his eyes, the quality of his German, or the race of his mother. It suggested a leak.

"So what about him?"

Exactly, Nester thought. What about me?

There came a long, significant silence, in which the East Germans appeared to wait for a comment, and in that instant, Nester experienced a rush of heat. He smelled the burning of human skin.

2.

H E GLANCED LEFT. The man beside him, a civilian computer programmer from Bad Aiblingen, had caught on fire. Nester gripped the arms of his chair. For an instant, he could not move. The programmer had come that very day to transfer the contents of Terminal Sixteen, an old Japanese computer, onto a master disc. He was one of the very few civilians Nester had ever seen allowed into field station.

Clasping two hands that were flames to his beard, the programmer shrieked. His beard ignited.

Nester flung away his headset, leapt from his seat, and grabbed at the man's head.

"Jesus Christ!" he heard from the crackling lips.

"Motherfuck!" he heard around him, as the other soldiers in the Box comprehended.

The flames stung Nester's fingers. He reared back. The programmer writhed onto the linoleum floor and kicked at the underside of the desk as his pant legs blazed.

Nester snatched Tunt's phone, dialed a security code, and dropped the receiver.

Then he noticed Tunt, who had not moved an inch.

"What?!" he cried over the screams of the civilian. Tunt shook his head. There was a very specific panic in his eyes. "Do something, goddamn you! Help me!"

But Tunt froze. So did the others. Fifteen signals traffickers pressed back against the walls of the Box, a cramped space packed with computer consoles, fax machines, and telexes, and stared at the burning man in paralyzed fascination.

Nester wheeled on them: "Goddamn, people! Move!"

He took Tunt by the sleeve: "Get a fire extinguisher!"

Then, throwing one arm over his face, he tried with the other to grasp the programmer by a foot and pry him away from the cubicle, to no avail. The man had thrust himself as far beneath the desk as possible, as if to douse himself in darkness. Smoke and flames and moans of pain came from the underside of the cubicle. Nester knelt, closed his eyes, and muttered a surah for the dying.

3.

SECURITY THUNDERED IN. The squad leader reached Nester. "What the hell—?!"

Weapons swung. Tunt came running. The fire extinguisher gushed.

"The guy just went up," Nester heard himself say.

The squad leader shook his head, uncomprehending. Nester knew it sounded insane, but he had no better explanation. Either the programmer had spontaneously combusted, or something had gone fantastically wrong with his machine, which had also been incinerated. The squad leader kept shaking his head back and forth as his men hustled the rest of the signals team out of the Box.

Terminal Sixteen was special. Tagged SCI, Sensitive Compartmentalized Intel, it was off limits to most people in the signals unit. Nester, an occasional visitor to the Box, did not have clearance. Coogan, his commanding officer, did, as, obviously, did the civilian. But Corporal Tunt, Nester's underling, who sat adjacent to the machine, could not have used it without a special dispensation.

A soldier tried to muscle Nester out of the area, but he resisted. He did not want to leave until he knew more.

The programmer's corpse sent up a vapor, a stinking mix of scorched meat and plastic. Nester tried to recall the man's name. Terry, Larry, Don? He realized he had never known it. The man had come from the intelligence outfit at Bad Aiblingen, that much Nester distinctly remembered. They had encountered each other in the field station lounge, exchanged a greeting, chatted about a bistro on Savignyplatz, nothing more.

Medical staff poured into the room. A few signalers peered through the door of the Box, murmuring among themselves. Nester realized he should get out of the room too; as an analyst, he did not really belong there, and someone might make much of this fact, especially if the destruction of the machine had been intentional, which, now that he thought about it, made sense. What would better explain the flash inferno?

But Nester couldn't bring himself to leave. A stretcher came bobbing between two medics. The man was pronounced dead. His eyes were covered.

With alarming speed, security sheathed the remains in a lead-lined bag. This being field station, and deeply covert, no one would ever hear of the programmer again. God's cigarette butt, Nester thought, stubbed out and trashed.

Now came a new unit, more security people. Tunt was among them, talking to them. These men focused on the computer. They crouched, muttered, glanced over at Nester but asked no questions. Tunt appeared to supply whatever they needed.

The other members of the signals team were to be kept out for a while. A bomb detail would come through. Despite the necessity for these precautions, Nester knew, Major Coogan would hate the thought of interruption. The Box functioned twenty-four hours a day, eight days a week, gathering information from East Berlin to Moscow, snatching from every frequency and every language, tapping telephone conversations, satellite transmissions, anything that moved within a thousand miles east of the station. And in this moment, of all moments, they could not afford to waver, not with East German citizens stampeding out of their own country, not with Gorbachev undermining his satellite governments . . .

Who knew what had already been missed in those few minutes of initial shock, much less what would be lost if the Box had to be shut down for a bomb sweep?

Nester gazed intently at the wreckage of the computer. Yes, he thought, the agent of destruction must have been a bomb, Semtex, most probably, the size of a pencil eraser.

A scenario would be developed. A technician would take blame for a breakdown in the computer's maintenance schedule. Theoretically, no one would know otherwise, but only fools would believe the story. It left the door wide open for speculation.

Nester was the ranking officer in the room at the moment of explosion and nominally in charge, though he was well out of his area of expertise. His office lay two floors below, but he ventured into the Box every now and then to steep himself in the nuts and bolts of data gathering. This time around, he had been invited. Tunt had tipped him to the transmission between the East Germans, and he'd run upstairs. Had he stopped to go to the bathroom, had another assignment beckoned, he would have missed the fire.

Tunt glanced over at him, and Nester was shamed. He had been wrong to lose his temper in front of the others, wrong to use curse words, to have shown such a lack of composure.

When he allowed himself to indulge in a little immodesty, he felt that he was the most courteous and alert American officer in the walled city of West Berlin. He had memorized every line of the service etiquette, and those under him marveled at his heartfelt finesse and had told him so. He squired around visiting brass as if they were secretaries of state. He never lost his temper, never used obscenities, and never treated his inferiors as less than equals. He had even been known to open doors for enlisted men, though his superiors frowned upon the practice.

He was so well spoken, so impeccably uniformed for every occasion, so mindful of protocol in all he did, that he might have been born with the service etiquette in his blood, and etiquette meant more than manners. It amounted to unceasing vigilance. No man should suffer on Nester's account. No job should go undone. Nester's father, who had immigrated to America from British Guiana in the 1950s, was a stickler for good behavior too, a pedant when you got right down to it, who took as much offense at an inappropriate word as a bad grade in school.

Nester's superior, Major Coogan, strode into the Box. With a dull whip of his head, he remarked on Nester's presence.

Fifteen minutes earlier, the major had left the room to attend a meeting—with whom, Nester did not know—and in that whisper of time, the computer had blown up. For those fifteen minutes, as luck would have it—after endless twenty-four-hour cycles during which Nester never showed his face in the Box—he had been the ranking officer in the room. What were the odds?

Corporal Tunt requested permission of Coogan to leave the Box. Coogan denied it. Instead, he looked over at Nester.

"Captain?"

"Yessir."

"Vamoose."

For a second, Nester contemplated defending himself, but against what? He could not say. With a salute, he left the Box.

4.

AS SOON AS THE DOORS SHUT behind him, he tore off the Commie wristwatch given to him by his best friend, Lieutenant Stuart Glemnik, for his thirty-fifth birthday, and shoved it to the bottom of his pocket. Just an hour before, it had seemed a clever gag gift, an honorary timepiece from the People's Army of the German Democratic Republic. Now it felt like some kind of horrible mistake, an admission of laxity.

A vision of the fire-engulfed man returned to him. He clasped his left wrist with his right hand and waited for the revulsion to subside. He concentrated on something else, a minor worry, but sufficient to divert his imagination.

Where was Stuart? He had not been around in well over forty-eight hours. In fact, Nester had calculated, it was more like seventy-two. He had not answered the telephone when Nester called, had not come to the door when he knocked. Nester needed Stuart now, needed to talk to him, to sort this sudden mess out.

A marine guarded the sector elevator. He gave Nester wide berth. Nester pressed the button for free zone, the declassified area two floors down. For ten seconds, he was alone. He took deep breaths. Another marine monitored his exit from the elevator. The free zone corridor echoed beneath his footsteps. It seemed especially quiet all of a sudden, but then field station always had a deserted quality, even when at full alert.

Truth be told, Nester didn't like the place. He had been at the post about a year and had never become accustomed to its silences and pressures, as palpable as the treated air rushing through its vents. The listening station perched at the summit of a 115-meter-high artificial mountain known as the Teufelsberg, the Devil's Mountain, a pile of Hitler's war rubble. Thirty-seven years of landscaping, what the Germans called *Begrünung,* had disguised the rubble beneath the scrub, and now the construction looked more or less natural, an upsurge of bluff on the wide Brandenburg plain. In the winter, though, when the cold air stripped its leaves away, Nester could tell that the Teufelsberg didn't conform to its surroundings, and the recognition of a geographical lie made him uneasy. Maybe because that lie elaborated on another: that the field station did not officially exist.

In the lounge, a rectangular space with six red tables, six pairs of matching benches, a sink, and a soda machine, he made some coffee. In a corner, over the sink, hung a defaced centerfold. Nester gazed at the lace-cradled blonde in irritation.

When the coffee was ready, he flipped a first cup down his throat. A mote of energy shot up his spine. He was trembling.

It was now 1900 hours, which seemed impossible. Only twenty-two minutes had elapsed since the fire. If Nester remembered correctly, darkness had fallen at about 1720, but the exact moment hardly mattered. There were no windows at field station. Sunsets came and went without trace.

The chrome of the sink showed him a dim reflection. His bifocals were crooked. He adjusted them. He needed a shave. His skin took on some of the redness of the room and the silver-gray of the basin: plum, blood, metal. You're the color of the Rhine in thaw, his mother had once lyricized, when the creeks and streams of the Black Forest come ripping out of the mountains, spilling their mud, torn branches, and ice gravy into it. And in truth, Nester felt like an agitated river, as if all the strange, unseen rivulets of field station had poured into his soul and made him spill over his banks. He noted with chagrin how little hair clung to his head. In the course of two years, two of the worst of his life, he had practically gone bald.

Face facts. He had been kicked out of the Box, and that meant trouble. Coogan personally despised him of course, didn't like the mastery of the German language in a black man, loathed the combination of black skin and supergrade designation, a rarity in his tight little universe. But that was routine.

He also despised Nester's institutional origins. Nester came out of the Defense Intelligence Agency, a troubled bureaucracy that inspired derision among other branches of the service, and within that bureaucracy, he had worked for a particularly ill-regarded section, the UFO Working Group, a team of specialists chosen from every sector of the intelligence community and tasked with the sole purpose of addressing questions about extraterrestrial life. Nester had not volunteered. He had been drafted because of his association with a high-ranking Communist from Romania who had been exiled for admitting to a close encounter. The work was top-secret. It involved contacts across all branches and agencies and made him an insider far beyond his years. Coogan hated Nester for it.

But that too was *pro forma,* nothing new. Nester seated himself on a bench and concentrated on the detonated terminal.

Sixteen was old, he knew, and scheduled for removal. The rest of the Box had been upgraded the previous year, but for some reason, this terminal had not been addressed until now. The programmer, as Nester understood it, would have transferred the files from the hard drive onto a master disc, so that nothing would be lost during the upgrade, and by the following week, Sixteen would have been gone. Now, in high Wagnerian style, it was.

So what required its destruction? Had someone wanted to send a message to the Americans in their mountain retreat, or had the terminal itself been the point? Had the civilian been the target, perhaps? Nester could answer none of these questions with certainty.

A last question, more frightening than the others, crept into his head. Did the disaster have anything to do with him?

That did not seem likely, given his lack of access to the computer. He could not possibly have been sitting in front of Sixteen at the moment of detonation. But still, after days of absence from the Box, he had managed to appear just before the computer exploded, and the coincidence made him deeply uncomfortable. Why should he have been listening to a couple of East German buffoons at that precise instant? Jerome Tunt might have an answer to that question.

Nester shook his head. One way or another, he shouldn't have cursed the corporal like that. To a watchful eye, like Major Coogan's, such a breach of conduct would hint at panic, and panic might suggest guilt, though guilt over what, Nester could not begin to imagine; for being in the wrong place at the wrong time, perhaps, a Cold War crime par excellence. Suddenly, he felt exposed.

There had always been a downside to Nester's reputation for courtesy, and he knew it well. People thought him distant. He'd never understood it, but they did, as if hiding behind the manners lived a different man entirely, one who didn't take much comfort in interactions with other human beings and who substituted courtesy for genuine human warmth. His reputation for mastery of the German language accentuated the myth. Hence that despised nickname: "the Jet Kraut."

With his histrionics in the Box, he had just given everyone a new annal in the saga. The Jet Kraut had launched a blitzkrieg. That's how it would be related throughout field station. He had taken the Lord's name in vain! The thought lingered a moment, made him angry at himself. He must get some sleep. But Sixteen troubled him more with every passing minute. He could not shake the feeling that he had been summoned to its destruction for a reason.

5.

HEELS SNAPPED. Nester looked up. Major Coogan stood in the doorway. Nester made a salute. The major returned an extremely formal one, a bad sign.

"Cates."

"Yessir."

"In my office."

Coogan wore his khakis tight as a parade boot, and as he strode down the first subbasement corridor ahead of Nester, his entire body had a ceremony about it, as if he were not a man, but a foot planted and jerked by a marching leg.

The major, like Nester, was the son of a vet, an army brat through and through, and that allowed room for dialogue between the men. Nester's father wasn't Citadel, but he'd fought at the battle of the Ia Drang in Vietnam and had returned to Southeast Asia much later in the midst of the Tet Offensive, where he'd been wounded badly enough to receive oak clusters and a cushy desk job in Heidelberg. Nester had spent his formative years in that city, falling in love with German philosophy and the girls who liked to talk about it between smooch sessions on the Rhine. Here, the two men parted ways. Coogan disliked the Germans. He disliked every people on the earth but Americans, preferably white, and the Filipinos, whom he admired for their friendliness, their housework, and their readiness to speak English. But it didn't matter. The soldiers had a common heritage. They could hate each other's guts and still suffer a truce.

Nester entered the office and stood at attention until Coogan offered him a seat in a worn leather chair beside the desk. Another chair waited opposite. They were expecting company.

"Cigarette?"

"No thank you, sir."

"That's right. Don't drink either, do you, Captain?"

"No sir."

"Nor do you eat pork, as I understand it."

"That's correct, sir."

The major found a pair of keys in the cupboard to his right and unlocked a file cabinet in his desk. Two images hovered on the wall behind his
head. One was an aerial photograph of Berlin just after the war, blocks and
blocks of gray, blasted building husks, at their center a single standing
church, its steeple beheaded; the church, Nester knew, had functioned as an
orientation point for bomber pilots in the air. That's why it had been spared.
The other image, shining behind glass, was a vintage movie poster for a
Marlene Dietrich film about the black market. Both had been bequeathed
to the major by his father, who had been stationed in Berlin right after the
war. Nester kept his eyes on Dietrich's chin. She kept her eyes on him.

"No pork, huh? Is that a religious conviction, Captain? Are you a Mus-
lim or a Jew?"

"No sir."

"Sammy Davis, Jr., was a Jew, wasn't he?"

"I believe so, sir."

Coogan pulled a bottle of whiskey from a drawer, unscrewed the cap
and poured a slug into a coffee mug decorated with an 82nd Strategic Reconnaissance insignia. He drank, swirled, closed his eyes. "Then why?"

"The undiscovered country, sir. I fear it."

It was bad to quote Shakespeare in front of the major. Nester knew it.
But he'd done it anyway. His superior suppressed a wave of disdain. Ven-
omous light flickered in his eyes.

"Tell me what you saw, Captain, and be quick."

Nester crossed his arms. He could feel temper tensing his muscles. His
mother had a temper too, and she'd always told him to tap three times on
his wrist whenever it arose, and that would reverse the charge. He'd tried,
but over the years, the three taps had turned into a propensity for scratching
until the skin broke and his wrist bled.

Nester related what he had seen. Coogan poured himself another
whiskey. All the time, he kept a clinical demeanor, as if he were dispensing
medicinal tea into the coffee mug.

"And all this means what, Cates?"

"Sir?"

The major chewed on his lower lip. Rumor had it he was just weeks
away from admission to the Battle Command Training Program at Fort
Leavenworth, Kansas; weeks away from a career track to the heights of military rank. The thought of this man as a general depressed Nester.

"It was a bomb, we can assume. So? You're the expert on our neighbors."

Nester thought it over. He was not yet prepared to say anything about
the conversation he had overheard between the East German bureaucrats.

Their words in reference to him could mean a leak of some kind, but not necessarily, and he did not want to provoke hasty judgments at that moment. Anyway, the notion that some branch of the East German government had tried to bomb field station, which the tone of Coogan's question implied, struck him as absurd. Such an act could serve no purpose. Before he could formulate a reply to this effect, the major changed the subject.

"Where is Glemnik, by the way?"

Coogan pulled a cigarette-making kit from another drawer in the desk, rolled one, lit it with a spare match, and dragged once. The brand was harsh, and its fumes clouded the room.

"I have no way of knowing that, sir."

The question rattled him. The hammer-and-sickle timepiece clicked in his pocket, as if its pulse too had quickened. Under the circumstances, anything could be used against him, including a friendship.

In many ways, Stuart Glemnik was Nester's opposite, and that had created a certain chemistry: two misfits at opposite ends of a behavioral pole. Stuart had grown up civilian with neither manners nor discipline. He had run away from home at the age of seventeen, received his high-school degree from the army but had never earned a college diploma. Though he spoke passable German and was nearly as well-read as Nester, he was self-educated and had risen through the ranks in spite of it. There would be a ceiling to his promotion, Nester knew, because many of his superior officers, while recognizing a certain genius for intelligence in Stuart, did not like him. He was a bit too anarchic for most military intelligence personnel, never quite able to conceal his contempt for the practical uses of the material, always theorizing about the ultimate meaning of his work; and it had to be said, he did not make much effort to endear himself to his fellow officers, except for Nester, who was a kind of mentor to him.

Beyond this, Coogan hated Stuart, as he did Nester, because of certain "affiliations" which protected Stuart, which were secret and, everyone assumed, quite powerful. Nester believed them to be real. Stuart had worked on the Syrian border, a highly classified sector of operations, and he still received the occasional visit from an old Company hand who had known him there. Whatever their actual status, these ties to other organizations made Stuart autonomous. He could leave town without much notice, unlike the other men in the command, who were bound by orders to stay in West Berlin. Even now, he might be on some confidential mission. That would explain his absence.

"Are you telling me, Cates, that you find nothing suspicious in the coincidence?"

"What coincidence is that?"

"Playing stupid will only get you into deeper shit, Captain. The coincidence I'm speaking of is the one between Glemnik's disappearance and this matter in the Box."

Nester shook his head. He had not given much thought to the coincidence. Now, unnerved, he did so. "If you don't mind my asking, Major, why exactly am I in 'deep shit'?"

"Do you know a man named Styles over at the consulate?"

Nester motioned with his head. He knew the name.

"You know what they say about him?"

"He's CIA. Goes by the name of Rick Doyle. Got caught in an explosion in Lebanon a few years back. Jiri Klek's work, I believe. State Department hates him and has him stashed in a little office near the Zoo train station. In the Amerika Haus, if I'm not mistaken."

Coogan's face reddened, and his annoyance, which he had never been able to hide, not even from his enemies, spilled out. "I knew that sonuvabitch was an owl the minute I laid eyes on him."

Nester was surprised. In field station parlance, owl meant CIA, an ambiguous reference both to the agency's supposed wisdom and to its infinite foolishness. He'd never heard his superior use the term before, and it struck a false note. For whatever reason, Coogan, who most of the time liked to distance himself from the lowly minions of field station, and their slang, now wanted to emphasize his distance from this owl.

The major took another drag on his cigarette. "He's been asking questions about your buddy Glemnik. Now he's here, and he wants to talk to you. To me, that qualifies as some deep shit."

Coogan mashed the cigarette out in a piece of aluminum foil. He plucked up the phone receiver and punched three numbers.

"Come on, if you're comin'," he said.

Nester's eyes wandered through the maze of war-broken streets on the wall. He braced himself. The doorknob turned.

In sauntered a man with a shattered jaw. He was six feet four inches tall, or thereabouts, clothed in a black turtleneck, olive wool blazer, and black jeans, and his eyes pierced Nester right through. In them, with suspicion and rage, lurked ruefulness. Nester tried not to stare. From the crown of his head to his nostrils, this owl—Carlton Styles—had a normal, even handsome face, with dark, intelligent eyebrows, high cheekbones, and a full head of wavy chestnut hair. But below the nose, right where the face narrowed, the bones crumpled. Teeth protruded, three of them, like the exposed girders of a building struck by earthquake. It had happened three years ago on the Green Line in Beirut. The blast had almost killed him.

Styles took a seat in the other chair and clasped its arms with great purpose. "Stuart Glemnik's your friend. When did you last see him?"

Nester thought back. "Must have been a week ago."

"He's got a civilian visitor. Is that correct?"

"I believe so, sir. A brother."

"And a girlfriend with political ties?"

"She's been checked out, sir. Thoroughly. Far as I know, she was cleared. Sometimes she has tidbits for him about the local chapter of the Communist Party. Nothing too interesting lately, but she has been known to produce good things. It's in his dossier."

"I see. Does he pay her anything? Is she that kind of source?"

Nester realized he'd already said too much. The owl might reasonably ask why he was so well informed. "Not to my knowledge, sir. I do know Glemnik even made a note of her affiliations with someone at the Pentagon. Like I said, it's all in his dossier."

"I've read the dossier, Captain. Many times."

Nester tapped once on his wrist, and it helped. Coogan locked fingers together on his desk and gazed into the space enclosed between his hands as if deciphering hieroglyphs on the face of a rock. Nester prepared himself for the next question, for the owl to ask him about the connection between Stuart and the explosion in the Box, but for a while, no one spoke.

Then, Styles's left foot began to tap at an alarming rate. He ran a hand through his hair and cleared his throat.

"This is between the three of us, soldier. Understood? You never saw me here."

Nester nodded.

"Tell me what you know about Jiri Klek."

Nester shot a glance at Coogan, but the major averted his eyes. So he recited a short bio of the world's most elusive terrorist. In the all-time sweepstakes for political murder, Klek ranked second only to Carlos in his range of exploits. As an apprentice, he may have had a hand in the slaughter of Israeli athletes in Munich, circa 1972. He was said to have supplied the gun fired at Pope John Paul II in 1981, and the poisoned cane used to murder a Bulgarian dissident in London in 1985. He was attached like a clothespin to Lockerbie, stapled like a memo onto the car bomb that decimated American troops in Lebanon, thumbtacked to the heart of the La Belle Disco bombing in West Berlin a couple of years back.

No one had ever seen Klek's face. No one knew his approximate age. Some believed he did not exist.

Finally, after an internal deliberation, Nester mentioned the Beirut bombing that had damaged his interrogator's visage. At that point, Styles cut him off.

"To your knowledge, has Klek surfaced in Berlin since the disco bombing?"

"To my knowledge, admittedly scant, he is in the Bekaa Valley in Lebanon. But I have heard rumors, none confirmed, that he is in East Berlin. Are you suggesting that Klek blew Sixteen?"

Styles and Coogan looked at each other, as if Nester's words had settled some argument between them. Nester tapped his wrist again.

"Not exactly," Styles replied. "What if I told you I had seen Klek myself, Captain? A little over a week ago, sitting in a cafe. I spoke with him, in fact."

Nester could not conceal his incredulity.

"You spoke with Jiri Klek?"

Styles dipped his head in affirmation.

"But no one has ever spoken with him," Nester stammered. "No one has even seen his face. How could you know it was him?"

The owl ignored the question.

"I have something else to ask you, Captain, an appeal to your particular expertise. In your opinion, have the East Germans any means of access at field station? Currently?"

Nester pressed his hands together to keep them from shaking. This was genuine trouble. It sounded to him as if something concrete had been uncovered, and Stuart was implicated. If so, Nester could be implicated too. With an effort of will, he stopped his mind from racing and reminded himself that this consular man Styles, this owl, might be jumping to conclusions. No one in the world was more paranoid than a CIA hand under diplomatic cover. It was their job to believe the worst of everybody.

"The East Germans?"

Styles moved his wreck of a jaw up and down.

"Do you have some specific authorization . . . ?"

"Just answer the question."

The phone conversation overheard between the East Germans had become crucial, Nester realized. But he must talk to Tunt first. The Jamaican would tell him what he needed to know, and then he would tell these men. "No sir, I have no reason to believe we've been infiltrated. Technologically, as you know, East German intelligence is still light-years behind us. If the East Germans are inside, they've done it the old-fashioned way. Either with wiretaps—which I seriously doubt—or with people."

Styles coughed into a fist.

"Well? And is there someone inside?"

"Does this have something to do with Sixteen, sir?"

"Answer me, Captain."

That did it. Technically, Styles had no jurisdiction over field station, and yet Coogan was indulging him. Nester had had enough. If need be, he would go over Coogan's head. He would go to Colonel Redding or even General Haddock. This whole thing had been conducted in a slapdash fashion. The military had its appropriate channels, as Coogan well knew, and they must be respected. "If you're curious," Nester replied in a dismissive voice, "you should launch an official inquiry."

Styles held him with that rueful stare. Nester tried not to blink.

"Captain." Styles reached a hand to the arm of Nester's chair. "I don't know why you were in the Box when that terminal was destroyed, and I really don't care, but I have it on good authority that you seemed particularly interested in getting to the man before he died. No one else moved, but you were all over him—"

"That's because he was burning alive, sir. Any soldier would have done the same."

Styles pulled himself still closer, leaning across the space between the two chairs until Nester could see the medication in his mouth, crumbs of Percodan or some other painkiller in the fissures between teeth. "Any soldier didn't. *You* did."

Nester felt perspiration break out on the back of his neck.

"*You* are Stuart Glemnik's best friend, and Stuart Glemnik has gone missing at a curious moment. In fact, he is our prime suspect. So you see, I have more than enough evidence to get you thrown into the stockade right now. But I'm going to cut you a break. I'm going to give you twenty-four hours to locate Stuart Glemnik and bring him in. If you do not, I will have no other recourse but to finger you as an accomplice in the bombing of a highly sensitive military installation."

"An accomplice? I know you can't be serious."

Styles settled back into his chair. He turned his face to Coogan, who said, very slowly and deliberately, "That's an order, soldier."

Nester realized the conversation had ended.

6.

A MINUTE LATER, he was out of the room, racing up the stairs to the field station exit.

He tried to put the pieces together. A computer programmer had burned to death. Stuart was a suspect; Jiri Klek too.

The sky above West Berlin dangled close and dark, but Nester felt a rush of brightness. It was the first time he'd been outside in twelve hours. A chilly Baltic wind blew. The city's lights glittered like ice through the branches of trees. He took a path running along the outer perimeter fence of the compound, which separated it from pine woods. Off in the distance, helicopter blades juddered. He came to a bench overlooking the city and sat. He dug a finger into the softness of his left wrist.

The events that had just occurred had to be connected with the rising chaos, his gut told him. They had to be. The Warsaw Pact was crumbling; four decades of tension were building to an explosion.

Nester thought back to China, six months ago. In May, students had hijacked Tiananmen Square, and after a brief pause, the Chinese government sent in tanks. Some of the students had been killed, others imprisoned. A few had fled. Nester had experienced a dull revulsion at the familiarity of it all.

Revolt followed by tanks: that's how the game against the Soviets in his part of the world had been played for half a century, and Nester had thought back then, during the China suppression, that the world as it was would never change, not in any serious way. Russian tanks had been in Eastern Europe too long to go back home. They had been there ever since World War II when the armies of Stalin had penetrated into the heart of the continent, entering Hitler's Berlin before the Allies, liberating death camps, rolling into Warsaw, Prague, Budapest.

After the war, Moscow had squatted on the region, like a fat old peasant with a panzer-plated rear. Hundreds of thousands of her soldiers lay buried in the wretched ground between the Vistula and the Spree, planted in the dark earth like seeds. These men, numberless, faceless, moldering in countless military graveyards, had saved the world from Fascism, according to Soviet ideology. Their consecrated ground could not be left to the Poles, Czechs, Hungarians, and other quaint nations living on top of it; no, it must be defended against sacrilege. So in the years following the armistice, puppet regimes had taken the place of democratically elected bodies. Freedoms had been suppressed. Villages, towns, cities, and countries, half of Europe, had fallen into a bland darkness, becoming merely strategic, a buffer zone against the West.

That's why Nester was here, wasn't it? That's why his father had been stationed in West Germany. To wait, watch, and listen, to observe the Soviets with binoculars across the Wall, to listen for the heartbeat beyond the barbed wire and mines and border guards, beyond all the nauseating bric-a-brac of undeclared hostilities.

There had been moments of near conflict. In 1953, the East Germans revolted; in 1956, the Hungarians; in 1968 and 1981, the Czechs and the Poles. Each time, Moscow sank her ass upon them.

But after China—yes, definitely, Nester thought, right after that—things had begun to change. A geopolitical screw had loosened. In June had come the Polish elections, which were supposed to mark a gradual transition to a free vote. Instead, the Polish United Workers Party, Moscow's proxy, had been devastated by the results. Its leaders' names had been crossed off lists. None of them had been able to take power. For years, the Kremlin had been relaxing its muscles, taking ideological salt baths, using words like "openness" and "reform" to lower its own blood pressure, but these elections— they were something else. Nester found them deeply troubling. He did not trust the man who, finally, was responsible for them, this man with the strange birthmark on his forehead, this Soviet leader, Mikhail Gorbachev.

Gorbachev seemed to be relinquishing power and territory without much thought to the consequences. That made him dangerous, as far as Nester was concerned. The Polish elections had brought an end to the monopoly of the Communist Party in that country. The party had always been the tool used by the Soviets to excuse their presence among the Poles; now it was smashed. What could Gorbachev be thinking? Didn't he grasp the implications? Nester was glad for the Poles, and like any other American soldier, he wanted to see Communism gutted, but God help him, when Nicolae Ceausescu, the Communist dictator of Romania, posed the question whether Moscow should invade Poland, Nester himself felt that the words had been taken right out of his mouth. He felt a deep need for suppression. It would have been ugly, but might have bought time for a reasoned negotiation, for a measured and more reliable step toward democracy.

Later that month, on June 16, the day Stuart Glemnik's brother showed up in West Berlin, something even more extraordinary occurred. The Hungarian government reburied a freedom fighter it had executed back in the 1950s, and masses of people, two hundred thousand, gathered to pay homage. This was a clear provocation to the Soviets, who had backed the regime that had murdered the man. But Gorbachev had approved.

It could not continue. Someone in the Kremlin would wake up. Or one of the Kremlin's stooges, Milos Jakes in Prague, Janos Kadar in Budapest, Erich Honecker in East Berlin, would fight back. War loomed. Nester could feel its approach, and in his worst moments of irrationality, he felt that only his vigilance could keep it at bay; if war broke out, a demon voice whispered, he alone would bear the responsibility.

Late summer had been tense. In August, Gorbachev had called up the head of the Polish United Workers Party and told him, in so many words, to let the anti-Communist opposition take power; the opposition leader fainted as he was being sworn in. Meanwhile, instead of going on vacation, thousands of East Germans decided to obtain West German passports. They flooded West German embassies in Hungary, East Germany, and Czecho-slovakia, vaulting over walls, begging for help, until the embassies had to shut down. In May, the Hungarians had begun to dismantle the barbed wire and barricades along their border with Austria, and since then, East Germans on holiday had been sneaking over it. One day, two hundred of them went on a picnic near the border. When no one was looking, they hoisted up their picnic baskets and crossed into the West.

In September, the Hungarians made it official. They opened the border, and East Germans began to spill out by the thousands.

Now, in early November, West Berlin had filled with refugees, waiting for something. What did they know that Nester had not? What had made them so sure it was time to leave their country?

A mere month ago, in October, on the fortieth anniversary of the founding of East Germany, the East German dictator, Erich Honecker, had lifted a glass of red wine between clenched fingers and toasted the friend-ship of the Soviets and the East Germans against his will. In private, Gor-bachev had already told Honecker he must reform his government or depart, just as he had told the Pole. The Soviet leader had grown tired of these dinosaurs. They had embarrassed him with their antiquated forms of repression for the last time. Consequently, Honecker's toast had been one of utter despair, as if the old revolutionist had been lifting a cup of his own blood to drink.

Nester had watched this moment with rising panic. On television, Ho-necker's voice had been timid. His words, for the very first time Nester could ever remember, dripped fear. At that very moment, outside the walls of the congenitally ugly Palace of the Republic, television cameras had shown in the darkness of East Berlin a small gathering of dissidents, two thousand or so, calling for their savior "Gorbi." They seemed harmless enough, but under the circumstances, of course, they weren't. They chal-lenged the very foundation of the state, just as the students in Tiananmen Square had done, and the police descended on them with truncheons. That night, the representatives of the East German people, *das Volk,* scattered like rats, but the day after Gorbachev went home, they returned, seventy thou-sand of them in Leipzig alone. Did the Soviet leader have any idea what he had unleashed?

Nester needed no more proof. Civil war would descend. The horror of his own immediate experience in the Box felt like a foretaste of it, the first clean outbreak of fire, blood, and terror. After Gorbachev's departure, after those first demonstrations, the dictator Honecker had wanted to kill the agitators. He had wanted to send in the tanks, like the Chinese, but his own followers ousted him instead.

Now they must be having a change of heart. Ever since they had dumped Honecker, as October gave way to November, as the demonstrations swelled, as one half of the East German population rose against them in disgust and the other half abandoned the country for the West, these men too must have seen the sense in bloodshed. Nester was certain of it. To keep power, they would have to shoot their people, and when they did, the Soviets, with their hundreds of thousands of troops surrounding the two Berlins, would return their fire. Gorbachev's credibility with the West depended upon it.

That's how it would begin, this war. The seeds had been sown with Monday-night demonstrations following Gorbachev's visit. Hundreds of thousands of people had occupied the streets of Leipzig, Halle, and Dresden, bearing candles, waving banners, and singing "The Internationale" in the darkness. Hadn't World War II begun with Nazi parades, with mass demonstrations, long before Hitler's troops invaded Poland? Crowds were a prefiguration of armies, nothing more. His father disagreed, of course. When Nester told him that in the little city of Suhl, East Germany, a crowd of thirty thousand had sung "We Shall Overcome," his father had replied, "There's a step in the right direction, son. Even you can't deny it." With great respect, Nester had ventured to correct him: "We're talking about Europe, Daddy. Dr. King would have been shot before he ever reached Selma."

Wind rattled the razor wire atop the fences behind him. Beyond the wire rose antenna casings, billowy white spheres that boomed with every gust.

Treason, Nester thought. At a moment like this, I have been accused of treason against my country. The thought made him so bitter he had to spit the taste of it from his mouth.*

7.

WALTRAUD SIKORSKI, Nester's girlfriend, was tending bar at the Narkose, not too far from the Teufelsberg. As he wound his used gray Renault down the road leading away from field station, he wondered if her crowd of Yankee groupies were keeping track of political events as they sucked down oceans of beer, schnapps, and seltzer water. He doubted it. They'd be playing cards, watching a soccer match, brooding as Elvis Presley tunes thumped from the jukebox.

*For the reader's benefit, a chronology of historical events in Eastern Europe from 1917 to 1992 is offered at the back of the book.

He parked the Renault, stepped around a pair of Harley-Davidsons and into the amber light of the bar. A miasma of odors met him at once— boiled pork, burped beer, body odor. A dull haze permeated the place. Lampglow sank in nicotine murk. Back at the pool table, two thick-bearded, big-boned men in laced-up leather pants and Hell's Angels T-shirts played eight ball and puffed on what smelled like Polish cigars. At the cash register, Waltraud disputed a bill with a customer.

She saw Nester and waved. He motioned her to the far end of the counter. She excused herself from the argument, drew a half-pint of beer, let it sit so the foam could settle, and hurried to Nester. They kissed. Her breath tasted nice. It had a flavor of Turkish cigarettes and apple juice.

She was not a conventional beauty, but like West Berlin, she had grown on Nester till all other female faces seemed dull by comparison. She had a slender nose with a bump in the middle, where she had broken it as a child. Her curly hair was short, cut above her ears, and she had dyed it that favorite color of the middle-class German woman, a flagrantly artificial maroon. Around her eyes were lovely wrinkles, crow's-feet that altered every message sent by her face, making her smiles a little sad, her frowns amused, and her moments of stillness somehow animate.

Tonight, she was dressed for work in a yellow cotton shirt with rolled-up cuffs and blue jeans, very Yankee.

"You want something to eat?" she asked.

He squeezed her hand. "I need help."

She ran her fingers across his bald pate. "You look tired, *Maus*. I make you something to eat first. Take a nice glass of bitter lemon with ice. When I come back, we talk. You want goose? It's nice tonight."

He couldn't resist, though he would have preferred a plate of his father's chicken curry and fried plantains right at that moment. She poured two small bottles of bitter lemon into a wide-mouthed glass, loaded the glass with seven or eight ice cubes, squeezed a lemon into the mix—as he liked it—and hustled to the kitchen to get the food.

Even in his panicked state, Nester marveled at her industry. She owned a one-third share in the Narkose, but ran the place alone, without interference from the other two partners, one of whom was a retired U.S. Army colonel with alleged CIA connections. Her personality, partially shaped by a spiteful Polish-German marriage that had endured ten years before bursting apart, laid the foundation for the bar's wild orderliness. No one was unwelcome until they broke a glass, and the more Yanks the better. Twice a year, she held costume balls. People came as their favorite American celebrity. At Thanksgiving, she served up turkey, mashed potatoes, and stuffing to homesick soldiers and their German mates.

The goose came. He devoured it.

Waltraud served a beer to a customer, its foam long settled, then dragged a buxom girl from the darkness of a phone booth and told her to tend bar. She guided Nester to an empty table at the back of the room.

"So tell me."

He took her hands and whispered, "Have you seen Stuart?"

Waltraud shook her head.

"Uta?"

Emphatically, again, Waltraud shook her head. "You know I have nothing to do with that pinko bitch."

"Stuart hasn't shown up for work in three days, and now some guy is asking questions about him. And about me."

"What guy?"

Nester released her hands. "Central Intelligence Agency." He put his arm around her and drew her close, lowering his voice even further, till he could barely hear his own words. "A computer blew up tonight at field station, and a man was killed. They suspect Stuart had something to do with it. This dude from Langley is making me an accomplice—"

The fingers of Waltraud's right hand dug into the skin of his forearm. She shook her head in disbelief. "Go on."

"Have you seen Stuart's brother?"

"No." She glanced at the bar to make sure her girl was working. The place was filling up. She excused herself, drew a line of beers, then roused a young man from the kitchen to begin taking meal orders. Upon her return, she took him by the arm.

"Why don't you go sleep a little in my office? You could use it, *Maus*. In the meantime, I'll do some thinking."

Nester didn't want to sleep, but knew she was right. He needed rest if he was going to be worth a damn.

"Go."

8.

TWO HOURS LATER, after a nap so sound and deep that Nester felt his soul had coursed out of his body into the night, Waltraud hurried into the room and switched on a lamp.

"Come on," she said. "There's something on television."

On the screen, the spokesman for the Central Committee was finishing his nightly press conference.

Nester rubbed his eyes. "You woke me for this?"

"A new travel law. Anyone can cross the border with proper identification. Not just special cases. *Anyone.* Inside Berlin too. It goes into effect tomorrow."

Nester shook his head.

"It's not a law, Waltraud, only a draft. They've been working on it for days."

She appealed to Trude, the cook, who had also been watching the TV. The spokesman had announced a new law, and it seemed, to both of them, to be immediately valid.

Waltraud's eyes brimmed with emotion. "Dagmar."

She was speaking of a cousin, a woman who, like so many others, had been lost on the other side of the Iron Curtain. For ten years after the construction of the Wall, Waltraud had sent Dagmar packages, and Dagmar had written effusive letters in response, recalling their days in Treptow, making mud pies in bomb craters and playing princess in peril. Then, for no clear reason, Dagmar had stopped writing; she had dropped off the face of the earth.

Nester fished the watch from his pocket and snapped it on his wrist. Dagmar would have to wait. Twenty-two hours left to find Stuart. He had no idea where to start looking, but he made an imaginative leap. If his friend was indeed an agent or a terrorist of some kind, and if he had any inkling at all that his cover was blown, then maybe, just maybe, he'd make a run for the East. The question was where. Which exit would he take? He pulled Waltraud away from Trude.

"If I were going to defect tonight, and I wanted to avoid as much hassle as possible, where would I do it?"

Waltraud thought about it.

"Bornholmerstrasse, maybe? No tourists. Mostly diplomats and locals. But if he doesn't have the right papers—?" She shrugged.

Nester bowed his head in frustration. He might as well search the trash cans of West Berlin for a detailed map as try to second-guess Stuart's plans.

"Careful," she whispered.

He kissed her and left through the kitchen door.

9.

FIRST, FROM A PHONE BOOTH on Heerstrasse, the closest major thoroughfare to the Narkose, he tried Stuart on the telephone. Still he got no answer. At the very least, he'd hoped Stuart's brother, Douglas, would pick up.

Next, he called a central military packet-switching service, gave his code number, and was transferred to field station. He asked for Tunt. He had to know more about that conversation between the East Germans.

"Evening, Captain. What can I do for you?"

First, Nester told him to check on the alleged TV announcement about travel. The corporal put him on hold, then came back on the line after a few seconds.

"That's affirmative. All private citizens can travel, but there seems to be some confusion about when. West German television says it starts to-morrow morning. But the East German press guy seemed to think it's right away."

Nester picked at his torn wrist.

"We have something else too. Real strange. For the last thirty minutes, we've been monitoring telephone conversations between the Bornholmer-strasse checkpoint and Main Directorate Six. Apparently, people are lining up—over a hundred, at this point—asking if they can cross the bridge, but the officer in command hasn't got a clue. He keeps calling his superior and complaining about these new travel regulations, asking what he should do, but his superior doesn't know either. It is my impression, sir, that they are utterly baffled."

Suddenly, Nester realized that he must get to Bornholmerstrasse. Instinct told him so. Whether or not Stuart crossed there, he must go. Something was happening.

"We got something else too. Seems for some people the travel visas are one way. You can leave, but you can't go back."

"Anything else?"

"That's it, sir."

Nester swallowed. "Listen, Corporal, about that phone conversation we heard earlier tonight. I'm curious about something—"

"Excuse me, sir?"

"The conversation, Jerome, the one between the two idiots who thought my mother was white—"

Tunt didn't speak for a moment.

"Corporal? Are you there?"

"Yessir, but I'm not following you. Your mother is white?"

Nester lowered the receiver. He closed his eyes and swallowed again. Keep calm, he told himself. With wet palms, he lifted the receiver to his mouth again.

"Now, Corporal, you know very well which conversation, the one you told me about. It's the reason I was in the Box tonight—"

Again came silence. "Honestly, sir, I'm at a loss."

"Jerome, we may be sitting on top of a civil war here. Don't mess around!"

Tunt didn't speak. Nester slammed the receiver down. He returned to the Renault and locked it. He could not drive with shaking hands. What the hell was going on? Why would Tunt lie?

He hailed a cab and asked the driver to take him to the bridge at Bornholmer Street. He had to think, for God's sake, had to try and grasp the thing.

The taxi driver took him into the working-class district called Wedding, through violet-gray streets dense with slow ruin. Nothing seemed extraordinary about the evening. Old women carried the day's last basket of bread home. Drunks crawled into amber-lit bars. Long past the official closing time of six p.m., a Turkish grocer shouldered the last crate of Moroccan tangerines back inside his store, anxious at the sight of a suspiciously approaching police van. Young men with indignation on their faces stood alone at bus stops and stared at the taxi as it passed. The police van sped up, blue lights whirled, it was gone. Nester grabbed the back of the front seat and wondered for a silly instant if this was it, if the fighting had begun on the other side. The cabbie sensed his animation and told him to relax. They were in Wedding. Police sirens could mean anything.

Suddenly, unbelievably, Nester saw a familiar face.

"Stop!" he cried. The cabbie swerved the car to the right, pitched it over a curb, avoiding a Litfass advertising column by inches. The wheels came to rest. Nester dropped thirty marks on the front passenger seat and leapt from the back seat. As far as he knew, they were about five kilometers from Bornholmerstrasse, and it could be no coincidence. The man seated on the curb beneath a glaze of cold streetlight, head clutched in his hands, was Stuart's brother, the exterminator.

CHAPTER TWO

DOUGLAS GLEAMING HELD A HEAD in his hands; his own, he thought. The cold northern air pried at his fingers. The wind came from Siberia, a voice had told him once: Stuart's, perhaps. Same wind that once blew on political prisoners in the camps.

Douglas could not remember anything much about his brother, not mouth, hair, shoulders, or skin; he could not remember anything coherent, like where he had come from just now, where he was going . . . One thing, though. He'd been walking and stopped. His rib cage hurt. Someone had hurt him. Thumbs had pressed against his temples and made him vomit.

He gazed down into the asphalt at his feet and saw an absurd trail of dust, plant fragments, and mayonnaise culminating in his feet, the end of the line. He followed the trail backwards with his eyes—chewing gum wrapper, dead ant, plastic straw, spittle . . . The trail that had brought him to this place, this curb in Europe, in a city like an insectarium, with a reinforced glass roof, artificial vegetation, and stretches of empty space, an insectarium with contours sharp as kitchen knives, which had no place for him, where the women appeared and vanished like beetle shadows on a summer night. He did not want to be in West Berlin.

Nester Cates was calling to him. "Douglas?!"

Douglas tightened his arms around his legs. Nester had a bad habit. He scratched his wrist too much, the way other people checked their watches. Douglas noticed things like that, and they irritated him. People had always felt comfortable displaying their worst habits to him. Why was that?

"Help me," he said. "They tortured me."

Nester knelt, reached out to touch Douglas's face but stopped short. Douglas was remembering now. The man's presence brought things back.

"Who, Douglas? Who tortured you?"

Douglas found he trusted Nester. This tall black soldier had been gentlemanly to him from the very beginning. He had made an effort to be polite and welcoming. He made efforts to explain things.

Nester reached for him again, and this time, Douglas relented. He allowed himself to be lifted off the curb. "I'm hurt, Nester," he said. "My entire body hurts."

"We'll get you some help."

Nester was in trouble too, Douglas figured. What Stuart had done would be bad for him, because he was Stuart's friend. Had Stuart thought about that?

"I want you to tell me what happened to your brother," Nester said. "Is this something to do with your brother?"

"I don't know."

"Sure you do, man. Think."

Douglas became nauseous. "Let me sit back down again." Nester lowered him to the curb.

"Just tell me one thing. Where is your brother?"

Douglas let his arms fall between his legs. His fingers brushed the cold stone of the gutter. Cars zipped past. Things crawled at his toes. He didn't know where to begin.

"Can I ask you a question first?"

A dart of Nester's eyes betrayed impatience. "Go ahead."

Douglas recalled a conversation with Stuart a while back. It had to do with Nester's old job. The matter popped into his head now, itched at his brain. "Is it true the army is trying to locate extraterrestrial life?"

The impatience left Nester's face, replaced by another emotion, hard to decipher. He waited for the question to pass, as if it were a sneeze.

"You have something to do with that?" Douglas persisted.

"No," Nester finally said. "It's not true, but it's a common rumor."

Could he be lying? If Nester was lying about this, Douglas surmised, he might be capable of more profound deceptions. He might be in league with Stuart. But it didn't seem likely. Douglas wanted to trust him. He needed to.

"Satisfied?" the soldier finally asked.

"Yes."

Nester crouched. Douglas wiped moisture from his eyes. He had been crying without knowing it. Nester steadied him with a hand. Douglas remembered now. The past loomed up in his mind, and he found he could escape into it.

BOOK I

THE LAST COLD SUMMER

CHAPTER THREE

1.

His life had become infested, that was the thing, and the infestation had been like all the plagues of Moses combined, a literal and figurative assault which had begun with the destruction of his insectarium—when had it been? Over a year ago. His ex-wife had done it. A year ago, in early November 1988, just before the presidential elections, she had shattered the wire-reinforced glass roof of his insectarium with a baton once twirled at college football games. Fire ants, gypsy moths, and blister beetles fled into the cracks of the house, never to be seen again; his wife fled into the night.

At work, there had been trouble. A forklift driver, Daddy Chelms, removed "Entomologist" from the door of his cubicle in quality control and stenciled in "Exterminator," a reference to a dead puppy. Truck drivers whispered tales behind his back, "Motherfucker poisoned a dog," and one of them actually dropped a dirty diaper from a cab window onto his head. He had not meant to kill the puppy. When you worked with poisons, such things happened. He told this to Nester, but the man didn't care. He wanted to know about Stuart. Just hear me out, Douglas told him, just listen. Otherwise, he would never be able to get where he needed to go.

He had been swept from Dallas to West Berlin like a crab on a tide. Dark, segmented things came scuttling at him in dreams, divorce papers slithered under the front door. Then, when he'd most needed her, his mother died, the last living relation—but one—with whom he'd had any contact.

He was forced to admit a hard truth—he was a wrecked man. The company therapist agreed. Douglas looked back at the five years of married life, at the professional promise he had shown in college and afterwards, and he could see it all pouring into an abyss. This realization had come in late spring, 1989, long after the destruction of the insectarium. Toads wandered in the weeds. The mail piled at the doorjamb. The phone stopped ringing. Linda had been gone for months. Their bungalow beneath the trees of Oak Cliff, the one they had purchased together in the first blush of married life, had started to resemble an unused garage. Bugs teemed. He had lost an entire life.

No alternative, he told himself, standing naked before a mirror five months ago—even now, as he sat on the curb, he could see himself reflected in that mirror—a skinny six-foot man with eyes dull red beneath thick, dark brows, a blotch of black at the top of his left cheek from a coal tar accident (the "housefly," he called the blotch, because someone had once tried to swat it off his face), and a mat of black hair streaked by premature silver. The looks of a father he barely remembered lived on in him: a Slavic gloom, olive skin that had known little sunlight over the years, handsomeness of a kind that might have been seen as exotic had he ever tried to cultivate it. A single stray dimple was the last evidence of the young man he'd once been, the bug-crazy kid who never made trouble in school, always made his mother happy, never cheated on his wife, despite all the pitfalls in his life . . . Sleep-deprived eyes, prominent ribs, and a love-starved dimple—they told him what he already knew. He must act.

Either he accepted his brother Stuart's invitation to West Berlin or turned the pesticide on himself. He requested three months' leave from Fleischmann's Refrigerated Warehouses, put the bungalow on the market, and bought a round-trip ticket to West Germany. It was his first vacation in seven years.

Now he was remembering in fine detail. That first moment in Germany had been a good one. He had burst away from America and wafted down in Europe, free of ballast. His life fit into an old blue backpack. Necessities were there—T-shirts, jeans, a field guide to the insects of northern Europe, the collected essays of Henri Fabre, and an old pair of field glasses once used on field trips to find scorpions in the Hill Country. Lately, his passion had been dragonflies, and he was hoping, in his spare time, to locate and obtain a certain indigenous species known as *Cordulegaster catani*. That would remind him of better days, he hoped, of why he had bothered to become an economic entomologist in the first place.

No one had come forward to meet him at the gate. He searched the tunnel of people before the entrance for long blond hair, blue eyes, and dirty corduroys. In high school, that would have been an apt description of Stuart Gleaming. No one at the gate fit it. Douglas grew upset.

Ten minutes passed, and the terminal thickened with bodies. Stuart had left home at the age of eighteen, and for a long time, Douglas and his mother heard nothing. Douglas assumed Stuart was dead, his mother suspected prison. They speculated now and then over dinner, but mostly kept their thoughts to themselves. After all, their family had begun as four, dropped to three, then descended to two, as if hit men had been hired to take them out, one by one, over the course of years.

Three years after the vanishing, about the time Douglas finished his second semester in college, a postcard without return address arrived. Stuart, it turned out, lived and worked as an air force technician in Turkey. His mother was overjoyed. Douglas didn't know what to think. Once a year, at Christmas, the brothers exchanged platitudes over the telephone, but a shadow lay between them. Stuart would not come home. He refused to have them visit. He never felt obliged to explain what happened, why he'd left or why he'd stayed silent so long. Until their mother's death, small talk had been the sole conversation between them; small talk concealing enmity.

The crowd around the gate closed in. A man in tangerine slacks and lavender jacket raised a placard bearing the name "Doktor Egg," and a thick-maned woman slashed Douglas with a rose thorn. He began to panic, negotiated a path around the thorn, and stepped on a dachshund's back. The animal yelped. Its owner regarded Douglas with hatred. A man in khaki uniform emerged from the crowd and told him—in stilted English—that he was under arrest. The fine for assaulting a dachshund was five hundred marks.

His elder brother grinned, absurdly white teeth set in a head red as a match. There was little resemblance between the picture Douglas had maintained in his mind and the man standing before him. Stuart Gleaming, the misfit in the army-navy greatcoat, steel-toed boots, and hair tangle, had been washed away by the years, leaving behind a chiseled figure in a buzz haircut and a real soldier's uniform. His brother now had a deeply plunging widow's peak, a high, sun-crimsoned forehead, and ears that Douglas could not recall ever seeing before. The shoes were polished and plain, with no hint of steel, and there was even a belt with a simple brass buckle. His voice had a touch of high school principal in it, of trivial authority, underscored by a pair of gold-rimmed glasses with tiny circular lenses that glittered across the same uneasy eyes. But there was a sense of humor too, which recalled vaguely Stuart's old malicious wit toward the world. They backed away from each other and shook hands.

"The prodigal brother!" Douglas blurted. "Shorn, no less!"

Peering at the patches of cracked skin on his brother's nose, and into the quicksilver blue of his eyes, Douglas could not escape an odd thought. Stuart had been baked at high heat for all the years of their separation.

"So what do you think?" Stuart replied in a shy voice, running his hand through the bristles on his head. "Does it suit me?"

Douglas was surprised at the earnestness of the question. "It does. It suits you fine. It's a change, though. Not exactly the Stuart Gleaming of Azalea Hill High School."

"Glemnik." Stuart took his suitcase, and they moved away from the gate. "My name's Glemnik now. Don't tell anyone here about Gleaming, okay? I changed it when I joined the army."

"Glemnik?"

"Remember? Old Vink Glemnik. Our ancestor. Grandpa Lou used to tell us about him. I didn't want to be twilight's last Gleaming, if you know what I mean."

"You didn't want to be twilight's last Gleaming. I see. That must be military humor."

Douglas resented his brother for dropping this kind of detail right at the gate, but didn't lose his temper. Stuart had not wanted them to find him, so he had changed his name, it was obvious. But Douglas refused to let their new relationship begin badly. "You're Glemnik now. I'm Gleaming. Fine. Nice to have these things clarified. I assume we're still related?"

"Of course."

"And can I still hug you?"

Stuart nodded. They stopped at the glass door leading outside, set the luggage down, and embraced. Douglas broke into tears. It was the flight, he explained; it had been long and hard.

They patted each other on the back. Douglas wiped his eyes. Stuart took Douglas's backpack and led him outside to a Volkswagen Beetle parked on the curb in front of the terminal. High blue sky stretched away from the airport. A sweetness touched his nose, not so much a scent as a presence, a deep, tasty summeriness carried light on the air. Stuart tossed the backpack into the trunk of the car, motioned for Douglas to get into the passenger seat, and they sputtered down a ramp into the summer coolness of West Berlin. Stuart asked questions about the flight, and Douglas inquired about the location of the Berlin Wall. Stuart pointed off to the east of the highway.

"Over there," he explained. "I'll show you all that stuff later. You hear about the Hungarians dismantling their border?"

Douglas replied, with embarrassment, that he hadn't followed Hungarian politics very closely, but he had seen the tanks attack the Chinese students on television. "That was scary," he offered, trying to think of something relevant to say. His job, his troubles, his entire life, had kept his attention diverted from politics. After all, if there were any profession more distant from the turmoil of governments than economic entomology, he could not imagine it. The subject turned to dragonflies.

Douglas asked about parks and water sources. Two rivers and lots of small lakes, Stuart told him; plenty of northern European Insecta.

Douglas rolled down the car window and sniffed the sweetness again. Away from the highway, he could see the tops of trees heavy with pink bloom.

Stuart smiled. "Gorgeous, aren't they. *Kastanien,* they call them here. Chestnuts. The blooms always remind me of cupcakes."

A gust of wind brought petals onto the highway. "Exactly," Douglas agreed, "cupcakes."

Stuart cleared his throat.

"By the way, Doug, I just wanted to say that I'm sorry I couldn't make it to Mom's funeral—"

"Stuart—"

"It was just—"

"Stuart—"

"Yeah?"

"There are a lot of things I want to discuss with you, okay? But as a favor to me, never bring up her funeral again. You should have been there. Period."

After that, the conversation dropped off. Douglas began to feel the exhaustion of the transatlantic passage. Outside the car, sprawling away from the highway, West Berlin didn't look like a city surrounded by a wall and hostile soldiers. Red-tiled roofs undulated between the fat heads of the chestnuts. Church steeples rose between apartment blocks. Billboards advertised roast meat, chocolate, and cigarettes. Breasts bared nipples.

"Is that allowed here?" Douglas asked.

"Hell, it's encouraged."

The car passed the breasts and something that looked like the Eiffel Tower. Stuart clicked on the radio. A man with a British accent talked about the reburial of a famous Hungarian politician, and Douglas stole one last glance at the dwindling aureoles. The two disparate entities—the story on the radio and the billboarded mammaries—became one large, opaque thing, an imminent strangeness.

2.

THE BROTHERS CAME TO KNOW each other again. In high school, they had been more guardian angels than friends. Stuart had never liked Douglas's crowd of anemically gifted misfits and had never once come to an assembly of the Hemiptera Club, which Douglas ran as his own fiefdom. Douglas, on the other hand, never had much patience for Stuart's Nietzsche-quoting, drug-hazed cabal of outcasts whose greatest intellectual efforts were wasted on games of Dungeons and Dragons. Still, the brothers had talked every day at lunchtime, and if ever Stuart had problems with a class, if he skipped one, for instance, or produced lackluster homework, Douglas tried to persuade the teacher to give his brother, a bright but wayward student, a second chance. Stuart reciprocated by protecting him from the humiliations of being too smart and too bony in a Texas high school devoted to football. There had been understanding, if not affection, between the brothers, and the contempt of the student body for both of them strengthened the bond.

There was also the matter of their father's disappearance, which gave them a common mystery, never discussed but ever present. One day, their mother broke the news to them. They were in the backyard weeding, a chore mandated by their father. Douglas liked it. Stuart complained. She had sat them down beneath the patio awning and explained. Dad was gone. She didn't know where. She didn't know why. She was sure he still loved them all. She had no doubt of that. But for a time, he would be away, and they should pray. Nothing came of it.

Eight years later, when Stuart flew, the bond between the brothers, such as it was, dissolved.

Now in Berlin Douglas didn't know exactly how to revive it. He waited for his brother to give him a cue. One night, after days of a one-sided conversation in which Douglas complained and Stuart listened, it happened. Stuart opened up and scared the holy shit out of him.

They were drinking beer in his brother's apartment. Music videos played on the television screen in the bedroom, sound turned down. Stuart liked the images, hated the music. He was showing Douglas the book collection in his bedroom, handing him copies of old editions. Besides the television, the room contained Stuart's mattress, a clock radio, a bag of golf clubs, three footlockers placed side by side against one wall, and books from floor to ceiling against the other. The bulb in the overhead light was burned out, so the alternating colors from the videos glimmered across the bindings and the irons. Light pulsed with the rhythm of a tide. Douglas glimpsed fragments of German words embossed in a black Gothic script. He fingered the grooves of names: Lenin, Marx, Du Bois, Einstein, Freud, Nietzsche, Musil, Hegel, Schelling, Fichte, Novalis, Hitler . . . on and on and on, old books with strange titles, and something which, in the various emanations of light, looked like a Koran.

Stuart reached for an edition on the top shelf, and something around his neck caught Douglas's eye. He asked about it. Stuart lifted a necklace of leather over his head and handed it to Douglas.

"It's nothing much," Stuart told him. "Just a piece of old wall."

"Berlin Wall?"

"Unh-unh."

"Basalt, is it?"

Stuart had the book he'd wanted in his hands now.

"Very good. It's a piece of the old Byzantine wall around the city of Diyarbakir in Turkey."

Douglas bounced the stone in his palm.

"So why do you wear it?"

Stuart shrugged. "It' s a kind of talisman, I guess. Wards off shit. A lot happened to me in southeastern Turkey. I needed all the help I could get."

Douglas handed the stone back to him, and Stuart replaced it around his neck. "Where exactly were you?"

"A place called Pirinclik. In the desert."

Stuart grabbed another two books off the shelf and beckoned for Douglas to come into the apartment's other room, a den occupied by a second and even bigger television set. With the remote, Stuart turned it on, found the music videos, and muted the sound.

He sat at one end of the only piece of furniture in the room, a couch. Beside the couch sat an open cooler, clicking with ice and beer cans. Breezes clattered through the venetian blinds.

"I saw a lot out there."

Douglas sat beside him. His brother had clearly become upset. "Want to talk about it?"

Stuart ran the back of his hand across his eyes. "Women and children died before my eyes. I mean, before my binoculars. They were Kurds, and the Turks shot them. That was . . . December 1987, my last month in Turkey. Not so long ago, maybe two years, but it sticks with me, you know. A lot of times, my mind is just swimming with stuff on the surface, all kinds of things, ideas, images, arguments, jokes, but that—those dead people—that's at ground zero. It never leaves me."

He made a gesture at his chest.

"I slept with Kurdish whores. They were practically dead. Their mouths were coffins, but I kissed them, you know, the whole deal. At the time, it seemed like a good idea, like walking on top of the walls of Diyarbakir, even though they were narrow and high. I could have killed myself."

Douglas nodded. He had never been to a prostitute, had never even considered the prospect.

"It's a dark corner of the world, Doug. People fear the night. It's your birthplace of man, your Tigris-Euphrates, your basic hell on earth. I guess—" He flipped through the pages of one of the books from the bedroom. "I guess what saved me was this German I met named Günter Talibor. He gave me this old copy of Goethe's *Faust*. I was just out of my mind and terribly lonely when I met Günter, and he was a man of the world, a Communist who flew with the Condor Legion before he changed sides during the Spanish Civil War, and he seemed so complete, you know what I mean? I mean, whatever else you wanted to say about Günter, the man was linear. He knew what he thought about the world, and he tried to convey some of that to me—"

Douglas took a deep breath. "I don't know exactly what you mean by linear."

Stuart flipped another page, to a drawing of Faust with an astrolabe. "Have you ever seen a real astrolabe? Supposedly, they have a real one in one of the history museums in East Berlin. I'd love to see it."

Douglas didn't give a damn about astrolabes. "Linear, Stuart."

"What do I mean by linear? Well, I guess I would start by saying that you are linear. Everything you do and think has a line in it. You study bugs or you kill bugs or you hunt for bugs, and can give reasons for that. 'I study bugs, because they interest me.' Like that. You have classification systems by which you understand the various kinds of bugs, and all the mysteries of the universe can be fitted into this classification system. Some things may remain mysteries, but you know the approximate radius and diameter of whatever it is you don't grasp. Does that make sense?"

Douglas said it did.

Stuart pointed to another drawing. "That's Gretchen, Faust's lady friend," he said. "You ever read Faust? Günter taught me to read in German with old newspaper clippings, and now I read *Faust*. Pretty good, I'd say."

Douglas admitted he had never read *Faust*.

"Not that it matters," Stuart went on. "Nothing tracks with me. Like Nester says, I have all this stuff up here, out here"— he gestured at his skin, his eyes, his head—"on the surface, I mean, but at the center, at bottom, it's like I'm anoxic, you know, like the Black Sea. There's no dissolved oxygen, so nothing can live. I'm sterile. I can't conclude. So what if I can read *Faust*? I'm an intelligence operative, not a literature professor."

To Douglas, it made no sense, this idea of anoxia. Water could be anoxic; a person could not.

"But you've come so far in the army, Stuart. Look at you, you spent all those years in intelligence in Turkey, and now you're a lieutenant. That means something. You've constructed a line, maybe without knowing it, and it runs to here, to West Berlin."

His brother inhaled from the book with great deliberation, as if he could smell the desert in it.

"No. The line you're talking about is an illusion. Eight years I was at Pir-inclik, Douglas. Eight years. I could have done anything. I could have married, had a family, started a business, gone back to school. Instead, I spied on the Syrians and the Russians. I learned German from a dying old man who had fled his own country. I lost contact with you, with Mom. I saw the most horrible butchery. And for what? I don't know. My life seems impelled along a course. It seems to be moving without me, and that's a line, but it's not mine. It's the longitude, maybe . . ."

Douglas didn't know what to say. Stuart took off his glasses and rubbed his eyes.

"Deal is, I've reached kind of a crisis, I guess, a crisis of spirit. I'm anoxic inside, and even when I tell you all this stuff, it's like I'm not really telling you anything, because the real problem is hidden from me. If I could think in a linear fashion, if I could say to myself, okay, I know A,B,C are normal and E,F,G are abnormal, then I could put two and two together and come up with the real problem. But no letters have values for me, Douglas. I have no nomenclature, except the nomenclature of intelligence, where every value is random, unless you believe in good and evil. That's the hell of it. I could not tell you the name of a single thing that is wrong with me, and yet I know everything's wrong."

Douglas heard childish self-pity in all this. He could not help it. On the other hand, whatever the true nature of his problem, Stuart needed to talk to someone, and why not to Douglas? Perhaps, against all expectations, Stuart and he might one day have a real friendship, and that would be a precious thing indeed, should it come to pass.

"I see that look, Doug, but you're wrong. I'm not just feeling sorry for myself. I *am* doing something about my problem. Günter Talibor gave me good advice. He introduced me to ideas and ways of living that involved coherent action. When he was in Spain, he bombed a village, and he was so horrified at what he had done that he changed sides and became a Communist. I mean, that's decisive. Wouldn't you say?"

Douglas had no way of knowing.

"Truth is, my superiors at field station think I'm a land mine, and even though I can speak and read German fluently, even though I've had more experience in real, hard-core intelligence gathering than anybody on that fucking mountain, they think I'm crazier than I am smart, and maybe they're right. Maybe there's no helping me."

The music video flushed bright red, the red of the hammer and sickle, of Red Square. A samurai slashed at darkness. A red bikini became a flag.

"I'm glad you came." Stuart's eyes were watering.

He reached into the cooler, uncapped his fourth beer of the night, and let his speech blur away in the cathode rays. "I mean it."

Douglas felt a rush of emotion. He took a beer too, and the alcohol made him blunt.

"Why did you leave home?"

His brother gave a sigh.

"Was it Dad?"

Stuart looked deep into the TV set. "In Dallas, I saw him. He was living there at the time, with a woman in Oak Cliff. I ran into him one night when I was out on the town—"

"You saw him? No way. I don't believe it."

Stuart didn't answer. There had been a time when his words made an ever rippling curtain of lies. But that was the past, Douglas told himself. His brother had been transformed from a sociopathic outsider to a man serving his country in an area directly linked to its national security, to an intelligence operative.

"Did you talk to him?"

Stuart shook his head.

"Nope. There was nothing to say. The very next morning, I went down to the army recruiting station on Commerce Street and gave myself to the United States military."

Maybe Stuart was drunk and dreaming. Douglas's gaze wandered through video thighs, incurving and sleek.

Stuart put a hand on his leg, "I am terrified of myself, bro."

3.

FOR THE TIME BEING, Douglas refrained from further questions. Almost as a distraction, he got to know Uta Silk, Stuart's girlfriend. Together, Uta, Stuart, and he wandered the city.

West Berlin was a strange place; at first, it reminded Douglas of a putt-putt golf course he'd once seen. His mother and he had taken a trip to Virginia Beach, Virginia, many years ago. For emotional reasons, one February, she had wanted to get away from Dallas, and a friend suggested she rent a bungalow somewhere deserted, where she could have some time to herself. Virginia Beach was closed down for the winter, but a few denizens remained: beach bums wrapped in wool, waiting for the summer to come again, sailors down from the naval port at Norfolk, and evanescent locals who spent the empty months behind shuttered windows. What Douglas remembered best was the putt-putt golf course. Right on the main drag, a grand old hotel had been scorched black by a fire, gutted and never rebuilt, and next to it, looking through its windows, reared grotesque plastic things: *Tyrannosaurus rexes*, maniacal clowns with bloody axes, demons with fifteen-foot wingspans, rebel pigs, space lions, and octopods. Beneath the creatures, dragging on cigarettes or sucking at hip flasks, had been sailors and beach bums, playing their bored way through endless games of mini golf. The locals watched from secret slits. That was West Berlin.

Activities were bucolic. Often, the three of them, Stuart, Uta, and he, went on picnics at the Schlachtensee Lake, and these lasted far into the evening. Stuart liked to gather insects and have Douglas name them. Often, Nester Cates and his girl, Waltraud, came along and, when they thought no one was looking, went skinny-dipping. Douglas saw kisses in the dusk between the trees. The sight embarrassed him, though the lake was full of skinny-dippers, bright and naked as minnows in the twilight. Uta laughed when she saw him staring, his lips parted in disbelief. Douglas thought of silver. The late-rising moon wrapped the lovers in a deep moist silver. At midnight, a church bell tolled, shaking all four of them from somnolence and following them home through streets as empty as abandoned movie sets. Their footsteps echoed on cobbled stone.

They tossed Frisbees, hiked along bike paths, listened to AFN radio play Golden Oldies as a million gnats swarmed on their faces. They ate honey cakes, cream pies, *Wienerwürstchen,* and *Eisbein,* things so delicious and fattening that Douglas got sick one minute and craved them the next.

It was a world of listless pleasure, like nothing he had ever experienced. Young Germans seemed to have no inhibitions. They drowned each other in kisses on the subway, lolled nude in the parks, and spent the rest of their time in cafes where they smoked, sipped coffee, argued with each other, or lost themselves in newspapers or South American novels. They didn't seem to know or care that his brother was in West Berlin to defend them, that a hundred thousand Soviet troops surrounded the city, or that they were prisoners within a wall. Douglas had climbed atop the wooden platform near the Brandenburg Gate and seen the towers, the guard dogs, the machine guns, and the wasteland between the two walls where the East German government had sprayed the most malevolent insecticide he had ever sniffed. It seemed to have killed everything but the rabbits. The danger was more than apparent to him, and yet the students, people like Uta, acted as if these irrefutable boundaries were a historical exhibit they could occasionally visit. Their eyes were more focused on the Nazi monuments in West Berlin.

Once, at the beach on Wannsee Lake, Uta had pointed out a two-story manor across the water. "That's where our people decided to kill the Jews once and for all," she explained with more emotion than Douglas had ever heard directed at the Communists. "It was the culmination of all our wonderful German culture," she told him. When Stuart suggested that not all German culture led to the Holocaust, she silenced him with a glance.

The older people were different. Now and then, an old lady with a shopping bag would stop Stuart and ask if he was American, then proceed to thank him for protecting the city. In addition to his brother's top-secret installation, Douglas knew, there were several military bases crammed with thousands of American, French, and British troops in West Berlin, and their job was, indeed, to guard democracy against the East. Stuart would listen with a grateful but artificial smile, and after the person left, he'd glance at Uta with embarrassment.

She was tough on his brother, Douglas thought, a little on the overweening side, but he was developing a slight crush just the same. Three things made a big initial impression on him. One, Uta had blond hair as luminescent as glass. She had chopped it short, close to her head, and it seemed to Douglas, at times, as if she wore a dazzling gold cap. Second, her last name, which was spelled like the English word "silk," was actually pronounced "zilk," with a *z*. The surprise sound of the word delighted him, and he liked to repeat her name in private: zzzilk, zzzilk, zzzilk. Last, and perhaps most irresistible, she had brownish blond hair in her armpits and never shaved it. Though he would not have admitted such a thing to anyone, Douglas found them arousing in the extreme and wondered what it would be like to kiss them.

But it was more than just these exterior attributes. Two incidents deepened his appreciation.

Once, after midnight, coming down the steps of an elevated subway deep in a part of the city called Kreuzberg, the three of them saw a fire break out in the window of a Turkish department store. No one else was in sight, but a lone violin played from the tunnel of the elevated subway. Above the store rose an apartment building. Its windows were dark, its inhabitants asleep. Uta dashed to the entrance and rang the bell of each dwelling; she warned the inhabitants one by one about the blaze while Stuart ran to a telephone booth and called the fire department. Douglas marveled at this sudden adventure in his life. There he stood on a deserted street in West Berlin while a violin played, axes chopped into glass, and men hosed back flames. "Arson," Uta observed with a tinge of moral outrage. "You mean you want it to be arson," Stuart countered. "So you can enjoy your anger." Douglas did not see why it mattered. He watched Uta's golden silkiness in the flickering light, admired the way the fire and shadow played upon her limbs, and was entranced.

Another time, they went to a laundromat so Uta could wash her sheets and underwear. A family of Gypsies—or as she called them, Roma—came into the establishment, and in a matter of minutes, the Germans cleared out, all of them except Stuart's girlfriend. The Roma children scrambled on top of the washers, climbed into dryers, and tried to steal coins as Douglas placed them into slots. Before long, Uta's patience withered. She grabbed a naughty boy who had tried to snatch a cigarette from her mouth, threw him over her knee, and slapped once with a rigid hand. The boy wailed and dove for his mother, who was rubbing the grime out of carpets and tossing bright pink skirts into the maw of a giant machine. She sang at the top of her lungs and ignored him while her elders, prehistoric Gypsy women, dragged on fat cigarettes and regarded the scene with measured amusement. But a man in a gray suit, the patriarch of the bunch, did not take it so lightly. He wandered into the laundromat, listened to the boy's loud complaints, and strutted up to Uta with a demand for apology. She rebuffed him. The man began to shout. Uta asked Douglas to hand her a couple of coins and proceeded to do her laundry. The man cursed her, then stormed out of the laundromat. The women raised fingers of imprecation at Uta for humiliating their man, but Uta didn't mind. She had won.

One morning, as Stuart polished boots and buckles he'd taken from one of the footlockers, Douglas used the subject of Uta to broach the question—once again—of his brother's disposition toward the world.

"So how did you two meet?"

Stuart rubbed black wax into the leather of a boot and replied with a fond smile.

"It's kind of weird. We met in a country-western dance class in a West Berlin community college."

"No shit."

"Yeah, Uta's father started listening to country-western music after the war, when the GIs showed up in Marburg, and because of that, even though she is a totally extreme Marxist, she always had this thing about Buck Owens, Kitty Wells, Johnny Horton, and especially Faron Young. So she didn't tell any of her friends, and she enrolled in this course and I was feeling homesick at the time and also trying to meet women, I have to admit, so I enrolled, and that's how we met."

"So who asked whom to dance?" Douglas sprayed water from a plastic bottle onto the toes of the boots, as Stuart had requested, and his brother slapped them with a rag till they shone. For a man who lacked conviction, he thought, Stuart polished his boots with principle.

"It was pathetic. Neither of us knew the first thing about country-western dancing, you know, two-step and all that. But everyone else seemed to have been practicing at home, because once the music started, they would just go nuts. I couldn't keep up, and neither could Uta. So this one song started, I remember exactly, it was 'If I Ever Fall in Love with a Honky-tonk Girl,' a Faron Young song, of all things, and both our partners got disgusted with us at the same moment and gave up. And there we were, looking at each other with these stupid grins on our faces, like, uhhh, do you really want to dance with me? She was the one who broke the ice. She grabbed me and away we went, not knowing a single goddamn step but having a helluva time to-gether."

"Uta grabbed you?"

Stuart nodded. Done with the boots, he took up a belt buckle. "Let me tell you something about old Uta. She knows what she wants and goes for it. I admire that. I admire it very much. She's linear as hell, like her father. But sometimes it makes for trouble."

Douglas carried the boots over to one of the footlockers and set them on top.

"I mean we can go weeks without speaking to one another, because she gets so mad at me. She wants me to believe in something, anything, and I do—up here . . ." He indicated the surface regions of his body. "But down here, in the anoxic regions, which make up ninety percent of me, I am committed to nothing. I am dead. Whether the desert killed me, or all the dope I smoked in high school, or whether I was born anoxic at birth, I don't know, but it's a fact, and when I tell her this, she goes into a rage. She doesn't believe it's possible for a person to be dead who just showed up at a German class on country-western dancing without knowing a soul. She just flat-out doesn't believe it."

"Do you?"

Stuart lowered the second buckle, which sparkled, and pondered a moment.

"Eight years is a long time to think about yourself in the desert, Doug. When I walked the walls in Diyarbakir, I thought about jumping—"

"Not really."

"Sure. But I truly believe the German language saved my life, because German is a language of exactitude, and it's like a drug to me, because my mind is so inexact. As long as I can read it and hear it and speak it, then I have a reason to think I might reach some kind of final result in my life, something to live for, even if this is only an illusion created by the sound of the language. Something Günter once said has always stayed with me. 'We all have a second home, where everything we say and do is innocent.' That's what he said, and in some odd way, it's the only thing I've ever heard that points me in a direction I can understand. A second home, where everything we say and do is innocent. Exactly. That's logical. That's what I want."

Stuart was done. He placed the buckles beside the boots. Douglas put away the shoe wax and rags. His brother's attention was diverted back toward the television screen, where a child's whirlwind breath scattered sprites and angels across the top of a pink-frosted birthday cake.

"I am a better soldier," he announced, "than anyone believes me to be."

4.

SUMMER WANED. Now and then, Douglas felt the need to be alone, and on those days, he stalked the dragonfly.

One Sunday, in a far corner of West Berlin, he found what looked like a country village—Heiligensee, it was called—an hour north of where his brother lived. He made his way down a cobbled street through the middle of the village to a spit of land pointing across the Havel River at East German guard towers and beyond them to a grim gray building with copper windows. On this side of the river, West Berliners had built homes and planted gardens, and there was no obvious place to begin the search for *Cordulegaster catani*.

For lack of a better plan, he meandered down the bike path on the riverbank. Minute creatures whined at his feet. On the water, thin boats with snapping flags sliced past. Binoculars scrutinized his progress. The men in the boats were halfway across the river, or Douglas would have been nervous. As it was, he had the strange sensation of being protected by an invisible field of force.

The bike path turned landward. Douglas kept to the shoreline, but the way grew difficult. To his immediate left, private gardens appeared behind green wire fences. Their beds overflowed with languid color—milky white lilies on manmade pools, teetering scarlet hollyhocks, and geraniums of clownish red. Their blooms drooped in the heat, and bees dangled from their tips. Douglas glimpsed dragonflies here and there in the moist shadows, but they were inaccessible. Once, he put his nose to a fence, and a woman in a sun hat menaced him with a trowel. Her poodle snarled. Out on the river, the men with binoculars continued to track his movements.

After an hour, the embankment widened. Water striders shot like sparks through the air. He fought across a terrain of thorn, fern, and stunted tree and came upon a pool of stagnated water left behind by the withdrawal of the river. It was shielded from the intensity of light by branches of a wild apple tree. The atmosphere of the spot—secluded, ripe with mosquitoes and hover flies, still as time—suggested the imminence of dragonflies.

Douglas daubed a fresh layer of homemade, chili-scented bug repellent on his exposed skin, dropped his backside into the grass, and waited for a sign from the heavens. He daydreamed in the heat that he was back in a Devonian landscape. Out of the sky came a terrible whirring, and the sun was eclipsed by two and a half feet of iridescent wing. The leaves of the wild apple tree trembled, and Douglas was snatched like a mosquito in the claws of *Cordulegaster catani*'s most distant ancestor. The daydream was not scary but sweet. It reminded him of the most innocent days of his life, when he had wandered alone through the farm country of East Texas and believed himself to be another Henri Fabre, the famous, impoverished French entomologist who had given the world its most stirring depictions of insects in the wild.

In those days, in direct contravention of his hero's methodology, Douglas had cared nothing for the trees and the flowers, for the seasons and how they determined the various life cycles of the animals; for him, then, each bug had existed in a vacuum of its own fabulousness, even the most mundane of them, like fantastic forms described in a wizard's book. He had hunted bluebottles with a net, a killing jar, and a dog-eared field guide. Ignorance had been bliss. He closed his eyes and tried to recall the feel of Indian paintbrush against his heels.

A telltale sound jolted him back to the present. He rushed to the edge of the pool just as two mating *Cordulegaster catani* hummed in tandem into its radius. He raised his field glasses. The male had grabbed the female behind the head with the small hook at the tip of his abdomen and was dragging her through the air as she lifted her sex organ to his. They bent down toward the water with the double load of copulation, and their humming had an angry quality. By any human standard, the yellow-striped creatures looked hopelessly contorted. An untutored eye might even have taken them for a single entity, a bizarre, bifurcated freak of nature.

The sight moved him. Passion, effort, and intimacy elevated this feat to something like a work of art. They were such delicate creatures, and he had found her, after all, out of many hundreds, even thousands, of strange species whirling around him, and their copulation would be successful and bring forth life. Their naiads would grow up in the water, emerge into adults, dine on mosquitoes and die, just as they would, all beneath the shadows of this unremarkable wild apple tree. It was an idyllic life; perfect, Douglas would say, and he had witnessed its genesis. He, who had failed to achieve anything remotely as sublime in his own marriage.

Later that afternoon, at Stuart's apartment, he yearned to recount the event. No one had ears. They had all been listening to the radio and getting irritated with each other. Uta slumped into a corner of the couch. Anger scrunched her face; she refused to look anyone in the eye. Waltraud had insulted her, evidently, by saying that all the governments of all the Communist countries, especially the Chinese, should be lined up against a wall and shot. Uta had told her that since she spent all her time working in a bar that catered to American ass-kissers, it was no surprise she would think that way; then she'd said, with a forced smile on her lips, you have to break a few eggs to make an omelette, to which Waltraud had replied, right, but it's all a question of which eggs, and besides, she announced as a final coup de grâce, you've never made an omelette in your life, you spoiled little swine. The man on the radio spoke with resignation of a Hungarian pastor under house arrest in Romania.

5.

THROUGH DRAGONFLIES, Uta and Douglas grew close. Three days out of the week, she took time off from classes at the Free University to drive him to parks to look for the insects. On the way, they killed time with discussions about all kinds of things. Uta was not effusive on any subject. Instead, Douglas talked while she smoked a cigarette and considered his words with chin up and eyes gazing into the distance. Occasionally, she offered comments, and these were by and large gloomy.

"I am not a fan of marriage," she informed him. "It destroys love."

At first, she would hunt with him along the littorals of the ponds, but as the weeks wore on, she got bored and decided to use the time to sun herself and read. In the beginning, she did the former with her clothes on, but the more often they went, the less bashful she became. Until one day Douglas came back from questing and found her lying on a light pink towel in nothing but a pair of black panties. He feigned disinterest and rushed back to the pond. Afterwards, in the car, Uta asked him if he'd been bothered by her nakedness, and he confessed it had taken him by surprise, but by the next time, she'd see, the shock would have worn off. His ex-wife, Linda, would never under any circumstances have removed her clothes, he told her, but in West Berlin, he'd come to see this attitude as prudish and unhealthy.

Uta told him this was an enlightened opinion. Stuart didn't like her to strip in the parks, she confided with a conspiratorial grin, so they'd have to keep it a secret. From then on, she brought wine and cheese to their outings. Douglas began to take off his shirt and pants too, and they would have heart-to-heart talks about their dreams.

As it turned out, both of them had grand ambitions. After her university work ended, Uta planned to write a provocative study of the poet Rilke. She intended to knock him off his high horse. He had completely abused his wife, who had been a great artist in her own right, abandoned her with child, and lots of other things. Poets were bastards, she said, and he was the worst of the lot. Furthermore, she insisted, his poems were so apolitical they were almost Fascist; once, in Paris, the Nazis had held a symposium about Rilke, and one of his old friends had shown up. The great poet of the metaphysical had been used as a national symbol. She was sure the academic world was ripe for this reassessment.

Douglas spoke about living like Henri Fabre on a plot of three acres, which would be a laboratory out in the open, what Fabre had called his harmas. He confessed, almost in tears, how ashamed he was to have become nothing more than an exterminator in his job at Fleischmann's, when all his life he'd dreamed of being a practitioner of pure research. When Uta pressed him to explain why this had happened, he admitted he didn't know but thought it had something to do with his ex-wife and his demanding mother. She scoffed, but he didn't mind. At least she listened.

Once, he found a May beetle that had died of natural causes and brought it to her. She told him how important the creature was for Germans, how every year the children waited to report a sighting of the year's first May beetles and how the newspapers reported it on their front pages. As a little girl, Uta had associated the beetles with something magical and indeterminate, but now the whole thing had become commercialized. Every year, come spring, the bakeries sold little chocolate candies called *Maikäfer,* she said, and it was almost as bad as Christmas. Together, they buried the corpse Douglas had found. Uta dropped a final finger pinch of dirt on the grave, and said, "I pronounce you the last May beetle of the year."

"You rip up the animal and I study it alive!" he quoted Fabre to her one day while they were lying exceptionally close and gazing into each other's eyes. "You turn it into an object of horror and pity, whereas I cause it to be loved; you labor in a torture chamber and dissecting room, I make observations under the blue sky to the song of the Cicadas . . ."

Uta put one warm hand on his shoulder, lifted herself on an elbow, and kissed his dry lips. He pulled her close and smelled the dampness along the tendons of her neck. She whispered in his ear that they should go somewhere. They didn't speak in the car. Douglas didn't know where she was taking him, but it hardly mattered. Before long, they came to a graffiti-smeared apartment building across the street from a graveyard. Together, holding hands like sweethearts, they climbed three flights of stairs to an apartment that smelled of coal, soap, and day-old spaghetti. She put a kettle on the oven, lit the gas stove with a frantically whispering match, dropped two tea bags into chipped mugs, and led him down a corridor with a high ceiling. Cherubs grinned from the molding, lost in afternoon darkness. She opened wide her arms, and he kissed, at last, the trackless paths within them.

CHAPTER FOUR

1.

TWO WEEKS AFTER the affair began, on the day the Hungarians opened their border with Austria, Uta received a surprise visit from her Tante Greta.

It was a warm afternoon, flies buzzed against the windowpane, and Uta cleaned house as she listened to the latest on the radio. With the opening of the border, a tiny exodus had begun, East Germans heading west through Hungary by the dozens. The news made her so nervous she almost knocked a flower vase off a dresser. Why couldn't they stay home and try to solve their problems, she thought, instead of making things worse for everyone and giving the reactionaries an excuse to gloat? She eyed the telephone, half expecting it to ring.

Instead, the door buzzer sounded, and there before her, looking moist and pink, stood Margarete Silk, her father's sister, come all the way from Uta's hometown of Marburg on urgent business. She wasted no time. Removing a canary-yellow scarf from her head, glowering at Uta's ragged curtains, she insisted on buying lunch at a fish restaurant she knew. They must go immediately.

"And oh." She turned with an afterthought, just as they were hurrying out of the apartment. "Bring identification."

A chill of suspicion touched Uta. She had always trusted her aunt, who had been banned from her brother's house after taking part in a demonstration against American missiles. But identification? Uta could not risk any brushes with officialdom.

"Why?"

"You'll see."

She decided her aunt was incapable of playing spy for the West German government.

"He isn't here, is he?"

"Oh no, my dear." Tante Greta seemed pained. "He couldn't possibly be."

At lunch, over plates of trout sautéed in butter, she stated her business. Two nights before, while completing work on his twenty-first book, a treatise on the foliate masks of the Rhineland cathedrals, her father had collapsed at his desk. He had sustained a brain hemorrhage. Uta put her head in her hands.

"*Ach,* my dear, you know, this was inevitable at his age." Tante Greta dabbed at her lips with a napkin. "But you must make your peace. That's the way of wisdom."

Uta wiped away tears, angry at herself. Her aunt paid the bill, and they returned to the car. For a while, they drove in silence, southwest into the American reaches of West Berlin, where the Yankee soldiers and the very rich lived.

Uta had adored her father once. For eighteen years, she had been companion, student, and acolyte, everything but a lover, she realized in sad amazement. From the trivial to the profound, they had liked the same things. They had shared musical tastes—Bach and country-western, except for Johnny Horton, whom her father dismissed as "too black"—and food, especially the heavy German dishes at a restaurant they nicknamed "the schnitzel ranch," just a few kilometers from Marburg. Together, they toured great cathedrals, like the Münster in Strasbourg, and explored ancient crypts, like the coin-operated one in Marmoutier where they had seen the skull of a young girl adorned with lace; her father had wept like a child. Every spring, they had both looked forward to plucking sun-warmed fruit off the cherry tree in their backyard, and every winter, they had delved through antiquarian bookstores till their bags overflowed with old paper.

And finally, as a consequence of all these pursuits, in full solidarity, they held in contempt the petit bourgeois materialism and self-satisfaction of most other West Germans they knew, including her mother, who had always been the outsider in their home, the bemused object of their scorn. Even in school, among her peers, Uta had been her father's emissary—a little martinet on the subject of the universal Catholic Church, the inevitability of the unification of Germany, and the importance of national pride. Her father, a famous Catholic theologian who had made his name writing modern commentaries on Saint Augustine's letters, had made her an ardent disciple. God, how long ago that seemed!

She rubbed her eyes and recalled their last meeting a year and a half ago in the French city of Metz. It had been her mother's idea, a last trip to-gether, just the two of them, like the ones they had taken when Uta was a girl. The arguments over religion and politics had been going on for months at that point, and each time, they became worse, as Uta deepened her polit-ical commitment, formally quitting the Catholic Church and joining the Communist Party, among other things. For the sake of family, she had agreed to her mother's plan. Her father and she would take the train to-gether to Metz, where he wished to research a foliate face embedded in the stone above a fourteenth-century doorway. Afterwards, they would rent a car and drive around the countryside. From the beginning, the plan had failed. In Metz, they had wandered along the river Mosel, beneath the shadow of the gold-stoned cathedral, attempting to talk about things that would not hurt either of them. But at eighty-five, her father was too old to play that game. When he had a thought, it came out.

They walked past a Palestinian in a head scarf, and the old man's temper burst. He should not be walking around in such garb, her father had said within audible distance of the Palestinian. It was unseemly. His kind used Western Europe as a staging ground for cold-blooded murder. The Israelis had every right to shoot him down like a dog. Uta had not been able to bear it.

"Shoot them like we shot the Jews, you mean?"

"We?" he had screamed at her. "Who here has ever shot a Jew!"

And then he'd come out with a line she'd never heard him utter before. "Listen, my girl, if the Jews had demonstrated even a fraction of the spirit they've shown since the war, no one would have shot them."

That was the end. She had denounced him to his face, insulted the church, the nation, his books, everything he held dear, as the long, wrin-kled, silvery head, with its crest of white hair, had loomed over her like one of those foliate masks he so detested, a slab of limestone carved in the like-ness of a plant; a thing of livid eyes and dead lips, an ecclesiastical vegetable. When she was finished, he pronounced her fate: "We are finished, my daughter. Forever."

Tante Greta pulled into a narrow street overhung by chestnut trees. To their right, in the shadows of the chestnuts, Uta saw a German soldier in a guard box. She stiffened.

"What's this?"

"It will all be clear in a moment."

At first Uta refused to get out of the car, but the guard in the box looked over at them, and she decided it would be better to go along until she knew what was happening. It's probably nothing, she told herself, but began to wonder. What had her aunt done? The guard asked to see identification, glanced at the documents without much interest, waved them through. Tante Greta led the way down a cinder-block path between saplings to a thug of a building topped by an American flag.

Uta stopped at the door. Tante Greta gestured at the entrance. Evidently, she had made an appointment. A clerk behind a counter took their documents and gave them passes, which they attached to their shirts. For a moment, they waited.

"I'm leaving," Uta said, "unless you tell me."

Tante Greta's eyes narrowed to slits.

"It was your mother's wish. As soon as she understood that your father would not recover, she said to me, Greta, it's time."

At that moment, a woman emerged from a door and beckoned them to follow. In bewilderment, unable to gather much sense from her aunt's words, but growing curious, Uta gave in. They entered a room of wooden tables and chairs, like a seminar at the university. In one corner, a youngish couple searched through a folder, hunting for something specific. In another, a man who looked like a scholar lifted papers to a magnifying glass.

Uta sat. The woman brought a gray folder and asked her to sign a form. "These materials have been gathered from a great many sources," she whispered with deep somberness. Her eyes gleamed with moral light. Uta looked to Tante Greta for an explanation, but her aunt had already left the room.

Twelve hours later, Uta was submerged. The bathwater trembled around her neck. She closed her eyes, clasped her favorite strawberry soap in her slick hands, and listened as Johnny Horton wailed about the Rock Island Line.

A wick of incense burned in a wine bottle at the foot of the tub, casting the shadows of her African violets against the bathroom wall. The sun had set, shining a deep red from a far window. After begging Uta in vain to come to Marburg with her, to sit beside her father's bed and tend to him as an act of Christian forgiveness in the spirit of Saint Elizabeth, her childhood patron, Tante Greta had gone. Uta would be happy never to see her again.

Later, Stuart had called, then Douglas. She told them she was ill and didn't want to be bothered. She telephoned the headquarters of the DKP, the German Communist Party, of which she was an active member, and told Rolf, the confused, guitar-playing boy who ran the switchboard, to leave a message with Renate, her district supervisor, that they must speak. He informed her that the leadership would be meeting at eight p.m. in a

Turkish restaurant on Kottbusser Tor to discuss the latest developments. Uta told him she would not be able to make it, but repeated that she must see Renate.

That had been hours ago. Now she held the strawberry soap against her chin. The tears came again. Johnny Horton wailed to her in that voice of doom and sex she could never get out of her mind, that voice like moonlight on train tracks, calling from the grave. Of all the times to discover this, why now? Things were insecure enough as it was, what with governments changing, people fleeing, borders opening. The gray file had contained more of her father's past than she ever wanted to know.

It changed everything. It cut Uta off from her past, from her future. It was a judgment.

In her mind, she heard her father's voice. Ever since the war, he had revered Saint Augustine above all other church teachers, even above Jesus, she suspected. His first family had been killed by the bomb that destroyed the Marburg train station, and the moment he heard, he died to this world, or so his story had gone. He had been in Croatia at the time—the file bore that out in gruesome detail. He had been in Croatia, a devoutly Catholic country, and he had thrown himself at the feet of the Virgin of Zagreb and begged forgiveness for his entire life, for all his actions, and the Virgin had directed him to Augustine, who taught against the spirit of the age, who taught the highest kind of faith, a faith that beggared the claims of reason. The church had become weak, her father maintained. That's why it had not resisted Hitler. That's why it had locked itself up inside the Vatican while Europe burned, because it had lost its sense of divine authority over the affairs of men. It had succumbed to all the little demons of the *Unterhimmel*—in his famous formulation, "the lower air," where people lose their way, where prevarication, weakness, doubt, and greed feed on us like pigeons on crumbs, where politics, money, and sex mock us like the impassive faces of the foliate masks on the great cathedrals.

When they first argued, Uta tried to persuade him that she had not abandoned her faith entirely. Father Ernesto, a Salvadoran priest guest-lecturing at the Marienkirche, had told her about how faith led to liberation in his country—

The mere mention of this name sent her father into a rage! A Latin American?! A mere child of civilization, whose forefathers had been savages in the rain forest a generation before?!

Father Ernesto taught a spirituality of the earth, of practical means, Uta persisted, and it was based in the end on the truths embedded in Marx, who had seen that God existed, if anywhere, then in the machines men used to produce goods, in the transactions between laborers and capitalists, in the underlying economic forces that drove human beings into suffering and poverty. That's where Uta had found God. She too believed in the demons of the lower air, she told her father, only her demons were religion, ethics, fashion, and art, all those things that distracted the mind of the downtrodden from the truth about earthly power. Saint Augustine had believed in a City of God, as opposed to a city of men, a perfect city, where perfect justice reigned; well, so did she, but it must exist on earth! It must!

Her father pounded his fist on his constant companion *The City of God* in frustration. There is no God in Marx! There is nothing permanent in Marx! No justice, no law, no economy! Marx declared the end of everything. He left no room for belief in a higher principle. That was the point of his philosophy. All things, even the means of production, change from one age to the next, and so nothing was fixed—not money, not trade, not philosophy, and certainly not God. Marx had proposed a classless society, that was true. But in doing so, he had betrayed his own deepest insight. He cannot have it both ways, her father cried, and neither can you! Either God or Marx, but not both! Please see that, Uta, please—

For a year and a half, these arguments had run through her brain. I am fulfilling your vision, she cried to his disembodied face. Traitor, he replied. But it didn't matter anymore. The file had intervened. Her father was one of the murderers, and this ended the argument. This was the final word. Before, she had detested him. Now she feared herself.

The phone rang again. She knew somehow it was not Renate. For a time, she stayed in the tub, refusing to be summoned, but the bell rang on and on, until long after Johnny Horton's voice had faded and the crickets could be heard from the cemetery across the street. Finally, in despair, she wrapped a towel around herself and went dripping into the den.

2.

THE NEXT MORNING, after a night of lashing dreams, Uta found herself at the zoo, seated on a bench across from the seal pool. Her contact was five minutes late.

The morning feed began. A flock of children flapped and shrieked along the sides of the pool. As their little bodies bumpered back and forth, jockeying for place, a green kidney of water appeared for an instant, and out of it rose the jet-black eye of a seal, which locked on Uta. She sat up. The eye lingered a moment, blank and dark and shiny. She swallowed. The eye gleamed. A wall of schoolboy bottoms closed off her view.

A woman with a pail in one hand climbed to an artifical outcrop of rock above the heads of the children, where she stood like a prophet delivering a sermon. She plucked a dead fish from the pail, dangled the silverness by the tail for a ghastly moment, then flipped it into the air. A slick, wiggling seal who had followed her up the rocks leapt after the bait, snagged it midair, and belly flopped into the pool. A wave of water rose like a giant hand and slapped down upon the crowd. Giggles of delight and gasps of shock mingled in the aftermath.

How perfect, Uta thought. Ostensibly, these children were being introduced to the marvels of nature. In reality, the woman with the pail had just taught a how-to lesson in enslavement. The thought made her tired. She closed her eyes and wished herself back into the bathtub. She plucked a paperback from her purse of Guatemalan hemp.

The same dream from before, the one she'd been having ever since the Polish elections last June, had plagued her all night, waking her in a cold sweat, creeping back as soon as she fell asleep. She was a teenager again, bicycling in Marburg; sometimes her father was there, other times she was alone. She always began at the highest point in the city, at the old castle, and ended up at the bottom of a long, steep, winding road, at the Church of St. Elizabeth, a trip she had made countless times. As she cycled down the incline, she squeezed the brakes on the handlebars to keep from going too fast, but the cobblestones made her wheels bounce, threatened to shake loose her grip. The sun shone through leaves of thick dark oaks. Friends waved. She saw Douglas, Stuart, Renate. There were children everywhere, children like little pigs scurrying away from the wheels of her bike. She kept landing on them, breaking their toes and fingers. Her father flickered in and out, like an image on a broken television screen, until they came to the church, and he was utterly gone, and she began to scream as the doors opened wide.

A heavy body thumped down onto the bench beside her.

"*Grüss Gott*," greeted a beer-soaked Bavarian voice. She opened her eyes, lifted herself off the seat without looking at the man, and headed across a tree-darkened pavilion to the path running in front of the lammergeier cages. The Bavarian followed. She passed the lammergeiers without a glance and headed up a flight of stone steps. These ended in a step bridge overlooking an artificial lagoon, where ducks, seagulls, and lame heron congregated. Halfway across, she stopped, leaned on a rail, and waited for the Bavarian to catch up.

It was her contact, Herr Mundung, wearing a Tyrolean cap with a boar brush in it, a heavy wool jacket that hid the two massive loaves of his behind, and cheap plaid pants that sagged over brown-heeled chunks of shoe. As always, he tried too hard to be the Rosenheimer on vacation, and every time he did—she had told him this a hundred times—he gave away his East German heritage. One, most people in Bavaria didn't wear that stuff anymore. Two, if he insisted on clothing himself in this style, then he should make a genuine investment. As it was, his pants were threadbare and smelled of gasoline, and the boar brush in his hat resembled a stuffed rat.

He settled next to her on the rail, not close enough to be mistaken for an acquaintance but near enough to be heard. "The park beyond the canal. Five minutes."

He departed whistling. She waited a few minutes, then followed.

Arriving in the park, she saw he'd picked a spot beneath an oak tree at the far end of a grazing lawn. Alpacas, pigs, and red deer roamed at will. She took the path skirting the edge of the lawn, and at its end, seated on a bench, was Herr Mundung. The only animal in the vicinity was a woodchuck splayed aross a boulder. Autumn yellowed the first of the oak leaves. In groups of three, they spiraled down.

As she sat, he gave her a sideways look of concern.

"What's the matter?"

She shook her head.

"You knew I would call, of course."

Yes, she had known. She had known as soon as the Hungarians opened their border, but had hoped against hope he would not.

"You didn't want to answer your phone."

"No."

"Why?"

That was all she needed, an interrogation on top of everything else. The suspicion in his voice bothered her even more than his lateness. She studied his face. Its small eyes, nostrils, and mouth reminded her of cinnamon cloves pressed into the side of a honeyed Christmas goose. A drop of perspiration fell from his left temple. He removed the Tyrolean hat and ran a hand across the matted swath of brown-silverish hair.

"What do you want?"

He patted heartburn out of his chest. She did not look at him, but stared at the alpacas grazing in the sunlight.

"We're going forward."

Uta put all her concentration into the crossing of one leg over the other.

"The time has come to activate your friend on the mountain. It will be a very simple affair, nothing at all to worry about. Routine to its toes. Are you ready?"

She nodded. The man wiped his forehead.

"I have mapped out everything, and when it's done, I am through. I retire. So it will succeed, and succeed brilliantly."

Never before had he talked like this. All the time, from the moment of their introduction at a Rilke symposium in Göttingen until this moment, it had been ideology and jokes, as if their relationship consisted of nothing more than a flirtation between an older man and a younger woman. Action had been a possibility before, but in the same way the final stage of Marxism was a possibility—for all intents and purposes, an ideal. Now, in the beat of a heart, it was a matter of logistics.

"Arrange a meeting."

"All right."

"He doesn't want money. Is that correct?"

She answered in the affirmative.

"That raises suspicions in this day and age, of course, especially when it's an American. So I want to take his measure. You make the introductions and leave the rest to me."

She turned to face him now. Her left arm rested on the back of the bench. He patted her knee, a fatherly gesture that sent a shiver of horror through her body.

"There is a slight problem," she said. "My friend has a brother here. If possible, I would like to get him out of Berlin before we begin."

Herr Mundung fanned himself with the brim of the hat. "Is he leaving anyway?"

"Not that I know."

"Then he stays. A sudden departure might arouse suspicions. Perhaps I can find a way to keep him out of our hair. What does he do for a living?"

"Bug exterminator."

An affected yawn burst from the man's face, revealing teeth neglected for decades. She wondered, not for the first time, how old he actually was. "I can think of one possibility," he mused. "At the Zoo train station, across from it, there is a cafe, a little place without any distinct feature, just a way station for travelers really. This cafe is owned by a man named Grams, and he is a friend of mine. Perhaps, he can help. Perhaps he needs a fumigation."

Uta's gaze ran down the canal behind them to the place where decades ago Fascists had dumped Rosa Luxemburg's body into the water. A small metal plaque on the bank said so. No matter what Herr Mundung wanted, she must get Douglas out of West Berlin at all costs. That was one good thing she could do. A leaf rustled down on his hat. She drooped her head and wished for a few minutes of unconsciousness in which to gather courage.

"Why did the Hungarians open the border, Herr Mundung? This is an impossible situation they have created."

Herr Mundung shrugged. "Who knows?"

"Surely you have an idea."

The man's eyes shut, and the face before her became a slab upon which nothing could be read. An evil thought passed through her mind: If you know something and won't say so, your government deserves to fall. If you truly know nothing, then it will fall, whether it deserves to or not.

"What sort of information do you want from my friend?"

A couple walked along the canal, hand in hand, in the direction of Rosa Luxemburg's demise. Herr Mundung waited until they had passed, then spoke.

"That's between him and me. But you may tell him that his information will not be acted upon in any specific way. No one will be hurt. It's all very, very routine."

He sighed and removed his hat again. "That woodchuck has not moved once. Do you suppose it's working for Washington?"

When she didn't laugh, his somberness returned. Uta crossed her arms and focused on the woodchuck, which, as Herr Mundung had correctly observed, had not moved an inch since their arrival. The agent put his hat on with a certain finality, closed his eyes and inhaled the cool autumn breeze. "It's going to be a nice autumn," he said. "I can feel it. Lots of sun and clear skies."

She rubbed her right temple, which was still throbbing. "Have you told me everything?"

"No." He stroked his round chin. "Get out of the party. Now."

She resisted. Her party work was a source of great pride and comfort, especially now. "Must I?"

He frowned. "It won't do to be affiliated with Communists, however insignificant."

"It might work in my favor, Herr Mundung . . ."

He chuckled. "Trust me. It will not."

His smug conviction struck her like a hammer. It sealed her lips.

He regarded her mournfully. "Do you want this, my dear?"

Uta didn't, but she denied the thought its expression.

"Come, this is a minor thing. You act as if someone is going to be kidnapped. We are all acting in the name of a higher good, I assure you."

He gave her a warm smile and rose from the bench. "Remember what you once told me about your father's beliefs—"

"What about them?!"

The words spat out of her mouth before she could stop them. He gazed at her a long time.

"You knew." Uta's voice cracked. "Didn't you?"

Tears streamed from her eyes.

"Yes."

She could have torn the skin off his face. Rage coursed through her. She lifted a finger to his face and scooted as far away from him on the bench as possible. "Never mention his name to me again. Never throw him up to me or use him in the context of our work. If you do, even once, we're finished."

For the first time that day, his expression betrayed true concern. His mouth sagged. His eyes squinted.

"I will arrange the meeting," she told him, getting up.

They exchanged cold kisses, one on each cheek, mocked a familial hug of farewell.

Herr Mundung straightened his hat.

"I want to meet both brothers. You understand me? Both."

He waited for a token of accord. She nodded. That satisfied him. He waddled off. In front of her, behind its fence, the woodchuck stirred. One of its eyes opened, surveyed the nearness of the human. Without a sound, it slipped away.

3.

THE NEXT EVENING, she prepared dinner for the Glemnik brothers and Herr Mundung—ratatouille with a salad of sliced avocado, apricot, and millet. A Nubian stick dance played on the stereo; her contact knew nothing of her love for American country music, nor did any of her party friends. It was a passion shared with only two people, Stuart and her father.

She listened to the evening news. East Germans were hemorrhaging out of the East through Hungary by the thousands, and the numbers were expected to climb. They had overrun West German embassies in Prague and Warsaw. She still didn't understand this exodus.

Like everyone, she knew that the government had erred on the side of repression. She did not approve, but no government was perfect. She also knew that the East Germans craved the things they saw on West German television, but surely they were not stupid enough to believe they could change their lives by merely crossing a border. Her father had always said that the country was a disaster because the smart ones had escaped, leaving only the stupid behind. Maybe, in his own twisted way, he had been right.

In her first year at the Free University, Uta had spent two weeks at a labor union resort on the Baltic coast of East Germany. She had been pleasantly surprised to see the prejudices of the West, as enunciated by Ronald Reagan and his cronies, one by one refuted. There were goods on the shelves and plenty of people who could buy them. People had nice little houses, some had cars, and a few even had sailboats and motorboats. They did not seem to be suffering. The people she met criticized the government much like their counterparts in West Germany might have done over this or that policy, but they chuckled at the suggestion of an Evil Empire.

The ratatouille simmered in a skillet on the stovetop. Uta cut slices into the sides of three avocados and stripped away the skins.

She refused to take Herr Mundung's advice about quitting the party. Surely he knew how much that affiliation meant to her. The day she joined the university chapter of the DKP had been the dawn of a new life, and she couldn't just renounce it, not now, not after what she had learned about her father's wartime career, his "intervention" in Croatia, as the file put it. All these years, she had despised him for trying to airbrush German history, when it was his own personal history that he'd been most concerned to hide.

She heard the words of a poem in the back of her brain, words familiar from a dozen May Day demonstrations but never fully grasped until now: *"Der Tod ist ein Meister aus Deutschland, sein Auge ist Blau."* Yes, she thought, death is truly a maestro from Germany, and his eye, like my father's, like mine, is blue.

She thought of Douglas, whom she had absentmindedly bedded and now must account for. The day they had begun, in the park, seemed to have occurred in another millennium, a time in which nothing had mattered and very few of the things she had done or thought held weight. Now everything was changed, and she must jettison this relationship quickly and safely, with as little damage to him as possible. One means of doing it would be cruel but effective. She could tell Stuart about the affair, and within a few days the entomologist would be back on a plane to Dallas, where he obviously belonged. Superficially, it would be painful, but in the end Douglas might be spared worse.

Herr Mundung arrived, dressed in a checkered coat and dark green pants. His belly protruded between suspenders, and like a fat country suitor, he produced a bouquet of lavender. She was grateful for the flowers but thought the gesture incongruous—like cloaked death handing out marzipan candies. The lavender smelled overly sweet. He took a seat on her couch, and she brought him a wheat beer in a glass mug.

"I am your father's cousin from Würzburg, Herr Dampfer. I just dropped in. You haven't seen me since you were a little girl."

Uta nodded. He lifted his glass and drank. "That's my world," he said, a toast in appreciation of the beer. She returned to the kitchen.

Ten minutes later, the brothers showed up. Douglas sulked, but his eyes brightened when Uta took his hand. Stuart gave her a kiss on the lips, then noticed the fat man. Uta made introductions, and before long, the three men were sitting around her wicker table, cradling beers and speaking in German about the European Cup finals. Even Douglas participated, which astonished Uta. He had picked up enough German in the last few months to hold a stammering conversation with Herr Mundung.

Dinner was served. Stuart helped to bring dishes of ratatouille to the table and congratulated her on a beautiful meal. The other men murmured agreement. The lavender shimmered on a windowsill, Balinese monkey chants screeched from the stereo. For an instant, sadness overwhelmed Uta. She wished that these three men would disappear. She wished her Tante Greta had never come. A year ago, her university friends would have been here, gathered to talk about lives, loves, rent increases. Uwe, her previous boyfriend, would have been bragging about his latest fistfight with a skin-head, Renate would have gone on about affairs with revolutionaries, new and old, and Rolf, the melancholy guitarist, would have plucked his way through the latest Billy Bragg tune. Uta wished she'd never met Stuart Glemnik. He pulled out a chair for her, and she sat.

Herr Mundung was very chatty. Eyeing Douglas, he told a whopping lie about an export-import business, which involved Persian carpets, South African ostrich eggs, and Japanese lanterns. Stuart was reading him as he would have a tabloid, with skepticism and amusement. Douglas showed interest. He was a very polite man, so one never knew. The talk turned to politics.

Stuart railed about Oliver North and the Iran-contra affair. This visibly pleased Herr Mundung. They agreed on disliking the current American president, George Bush, shook their heads at Tiananmen Square, lauded Gorbachev. Both saw a future for a more relaxed and humane Communism. Yes, she thought, it's going well.

Normally, she would have asked the men to clear plates, but this time, she welcomed the respite. In a matter of minutes, she rushed plums, chocolate candies, and coffee onto the table. The room had grown quiet. The guests were sucking on plum stones and unwrapping candies. Douglas excused himself to the toilet, and as the door clicked, everything was settled.

Herr Mundung and Stuart shook hands. Douglas returned. In a few minutes, the coffee had been sipped, the last pleasantries dispensed. Stuart made it clear he would be staying with Uta. Herr Mundung offered to give Douglas a ride home. Uta let both men kiss her cheek.

4.

STUART ENTERED THE KITCHEN and put his arms around her waist. He kissed her neck and whispered into her ear.

"I'm doing the dishes, and then I'm going to draw your bathwater."

She tried to resist, putting things back on their shelves, wiping crumbs off the countertop, but he pushed her out.

Later, the dishes done, the wineglasses polished and placed in the cupboard above the stereo in the den, Stuart sat beside her on the couch, hummed "Mama Tried," and administered a back rub. He had strong fingers, and she sank under their mastication. In her mind and soul, she wanted so badly to tell him what she had learned, but she could not bring herself to. What might he say? It was one thing to sleep with a Communist, quite another to sleep with the child of infamy.

"*Bleib sitzen,*" he ordered. "I'm going to get the hot water going, and then I'll give you a shave. What say?"

She said yes; she always did. He walked down the corridor toward the bathroom, singing a snatch of the chorus: "I turned twenty-one in prison, doin' life without parole . . ." She heard the spigots rumbling in their sockets. Water thundered into the basin, such a lovely sound.

A few minutes later, he came back into the room, undressed her, wrapped her in a thick towel, and led her to the bathroom, where she climbed into the steaming liquid. He followed. They sat awhile in contemplation. He massaged her temples. Then he sat on the lip of the tub, his feet in the water. She lifted her legs, one by one, so he could soap and then shave them. It felt delightful beyond words. She wouldn't let him touch her armpits, which Douglas seemed to enjoy inordinately, but for this sensation, for this rapture of cleanliness, she would allow herself to be an *amerikanische Frau* from the thigh down.

As he shaved, they talked.

"I know you're worried about all this," Stuart said. She looked down into the soapy water. "I know you're worried about Douglas, and believe me, I appreciate everything you've done to look out for him this last couple of weeks. I would have felt guilty otherwise."

She stayed calm.

"But he'll be fine. I've decided he should stick around a little while, just so my routine isn't disturbed while I'm getting started on this project, just in case someone is keeping an eye on me."

Uta saw the matter was beyond her control, and she was ashamed. With Douglas, she had betrayed Stuart, and now with Stuart, she would betray Douglas.

Her father, the great Catholic thinker, that universal lover of mankind, had left her a share of his mendacity, an unforeseen inheritance. I am his daughter, she thought. I am his flesh.

He had been a cultural officer in France, as he'd always told her, working on the dissemination of "good" German literature, making sure Jewish writers like Franz Kafka and Heinrich Heine were not totally eliminated from memory. But then he had been reassigned, according to the documents, meaning there had been two wars, the benign one and the malevolent one. There was the beginning of the war and the end of the war, and the end of the war looked very different. But then, really, so did the beginning. His National Socialist Party badge numbered 473,481. On March 31, 1931, two years before Hitler created the dictatorship, he had become a Nazi. He had been a true believer. At this, she should have felt vindication. She had been right about him, so right! But she experienced only shame, deeper than any she had known possible, as if she herself had joined the party.

"Shit!"

Uta opened her eyes. She saw a smear of blood on her leg. A drop of it hit the water and dissolved. Stuart looked at her with his wide apologetic blue eyes and blurted out: "That wasn't on purpose."

She swallowed.

"I know what you did with Douglas, and I forgive you." He ripped a piece of toilet paper from the roll and stanched the blood with it.

"Don't be mad"—Stuart continued the razoring—"I try to do everything right, to please everybody. Isn't that right? *Erinnerst du dich?* I told you I was dead, but I'm not, and I'm proving it, and you're going to be very proud of me."

Uta put a hand on his thigh. "I'm so sorry, Stuart. One gets mad at you. But that was another Uta in another time."

Stuart stopped with the razor. He took up the hand and bent to kiss it. He gazed into her eyes. "That's all right, my dearest *Schneckli,* my love. We've all done things we've been ashamed of. Me too. Just promise me it's over with Douglas, and you'll leave him alone. If anything were to happen to him, I could never live with myself. He's an innocent. *Verstehst du? Ein Unschuldiger.*"

She nodded. Stuart was wise and good. That's why she loved him, though she had never told him so.

"Promise?"

Fear engulfed her shame. She promised.

CHAPTER FIVE

1.

D OUGLAS ROSE EVERY MORNING around six a.m. and had a quick breakfast of cinnamon toast and orange juice. Then he put a few pieces of fresh fruit, a killing jar for collecting specimens, two thermoses—for coffee and homemade tickicide—and a vial of ethyl acetate into a shopping bag and caught the subway from Oskar Helene-Heim into the center of town.

The cafe, a narrow bar space jammed with gambling machines and stools giving onto a loose collection of dining tables, occupied a trash-strewn corner across from the train station. Vagrants slept against its sides at night and were just waking up by the time Douglas arrived. The waitresses grew to recognize him. Sometimes, they offered a roll for breakfast, but he always declined. The job turned out to be pleasant, mindless, and well paid.

He had been hired to kill ticks, and once a week, on Mondays, Wolfgang Grams, the proprietor, called him into the office to ask for a progress report on the eradication campaign. Sipping cheap Hungarian sherry and smoking a French cigarette, Grams would listen, but not attentively. His nose was red from drink and sneezes, and he'd peer at Douglas as if he were miles away. Douglas would repeat a request for a light source, and Grams would sigh. The answer never changed. The friend who normally rigged up the generator suffered from a debilitating disease of unknown origin. Until he recovered, Douglas must be satisfied with the flashlight.

Week after week, Grams would inquire whether Douglas had vanquished the ticks, and the entomologist would produce the killing jar containing the carcasses of a few creatures exterminated by ethyl acetate fumes; no pigeon ticks, as of yet.

If Grams was impatient, he didn't show it. Douglas went on to tell him about the natural insecticide he'd finally settled on—a stinking mixture of citrus peel extract, chili pepper, and sulfur. Grams would pull an envelope with the week's payment from a drawer, whip it across the desk, and turn his attention back to the sherry. Douglas counted the bills, whispered an uncertain *"Danke schön."* Then, without a word of parting, he'd gather his things and leave. Most of the time, Grams didn't even notice his departure.

This sequence of question, answer, and payment operated like the ritual of an extinct church. It had no meaning beyond itself. For weeks, Douglas did not exterminate a single pigeon tick. Grams behaved as if this was irrelevant.

"You know, this business is weird," Douglas had told Stuart one night as they did laundry. Stuart folded underwear. Douglas stuffed a sock.

"Grams is paying me an awful lot of money, but he doesn't seem to give a damn."

Stuart seemed cross. "So? It's *his* money."

After that, Douglas didn't speak of Grams again. Without telling his brother, he wrote Fleischmann, his old boss, and asked about the status of his former job. For the first time in months, he was homesick.

2.

TICK HUNTING CONSUMED HIS DAYS. He always took a deep breath before descending into the darkness of the air raid shelters where they supposedly lurked. Grams's establishment sat on top of a five-layered bunker abandoned since the war, a place that weighed on the proprietor's mind, both because of the parasites and because he had never been able to make profitable use of the space. At their first meeting, Grams admitted to Douglas that he was superstitious about the shelters. He believed skeletons in SS uniforms might be clicking around. For a monthly fee of one thousand marks, Douglas was hired to go where his employer would not set foot and destroy every last pigeon tick he uncovered.

"It's curious," Douglas remarked, "ticks who presumably use pigeons as their hosts, that is, creatures that fly in the air, infesting an area so far underground. Doesn't make much sense, does it?"

Grams bristled and stubbed his cigarette in an aquamarine clamshell.

"You're calling me a liar?!"

So Douglas searched. Work clothes consisted of jeans, a flannel shirt with sleeves buttoned to the wrist, and a pair of cotton gloves on his hands.

As a precaution, he attached the hems of his jeans to the ankles of his boots with electrical tape so that, from neck to toe, he was encased.

During the first week, he did a thorough rec of the upper level, which was half the size of the office above and easy to tackle. There were no ticks. Just to be sure, Douglas did a routine check around the entrance and gave the floors a good sponging with the tickicide.

The following week, he went down a level, and right from the start, stirred up *Blattella germanica*—the good old German cockroach, what a surprise! The roaches were not his concern, of course, but they were a nuisance, and he decided to expunge them.

It was simple work. Douglas began by dusting the place with pyrethrin easily obtained by Stuart from the base commissary. This would flush the insects out and reveal the extent of the problem. In the event, there were only two significant roach patches, one along the stairwell leading to the door of the first shelter and one at a corner adjacent to moist pipes.

At home in the evenings, while Stuart studied German and went over paperwork from field station, Douglas sat at a table in the kitchen and made roach traps. He collected seven mason jars from the commissary, wiped the insides of the jars with Vaseline, then dropped a piece of white bread soaked in beer into each jar. By the end of the week, he'd captured thirty-seven *Blattella germanica,* which he proceeded to drown in soapy water.

That week, he began to feel uneasy. He sat on the steps leading down to the second level, stillness gathered around him like a blanket, and waited for vermin to appear. Thoughts crept into his head from the walls, the floors, the ceiling. Forty-five years ago, human beings had packed into this darkness, trembling as bombers blew their city apart, as the ground shook and sirens wailed. Grams said old civilians had died of heart attacks and been buried at the bottom. At the end of the war, SS men had fought a last stand in the shelter until they were sealed off and drowned with an influx of water by the Soviets. The bodies had not been found until a decade later.

A roach scuttled across his fingers, and he nearly tumbled down the stairs in surprise.

3.

UTA WOULD HAVE NOTHING to do with him. He tried to catch her before a lecture at the Free University. She escaped. He called her apartment four times a day. She never picked up the phone. Now and then, he went by her apartment, but no one answered the door. As political events gathered speed, Stuart spent more of his time at field station. Gorbachev was coming to East Berlin for the fortieth anniversary of the German Democratic Republic, and everyone was nervous. Nester came over on occasion, to have a beer and watch a televised jazz concert, but these visits ended after a while. Douglas found himself increasingly alone.

Finally, he wrote Uta a letter, a long missive describing his feelings for her and the difference she had made in his life since his divorce. Before the infestation, he explained, he had existed with bugs on a single cosmic plane. They glittered around him, infinite as stars, and he revolved in their midst, a planet at ease. Linda had broken that orbit. She had nearly destroyed him. But over the course of the summer, he wrote, Uta had given him back the old confidence because she understood in a way Linda never could what motivated him to seek out truth in the smallest of creatures. Yes, he assured her, Stuart made the situation awkward. There were ethical questions that had to be answered. But her actions toward him, her loving caresses, would not leave his brain.

Then he delivered his ultimatum. Fleischmann had written him back and offered him the old job at the warehouse, as long as he promised to stay away from strychnine. He was forgiven for the blister beetle episode and for the dead puppy. Once again, his star was rising. He would be back on salary, at the head of his own department in quality control. He would walk like a king through vast dark halls, shining his flashlight into corners, running fingers through spilled meal to check for larvae. That was autonomy—something Uta understood. His orders would come from the top, from the clean, bright offices where decisions were made. Money for projects would pour back into his hands. He would win awards for developing environmentally sound pesticides, and these awards would elevate him to new heights. In a fit of fancy, he even told her that he imagined himself at the Smithsonian in five years, back in pure research and free of extermination. But he was willing, he said, to give this up—every last bit of it—if she would have him. Never in his life had he made such a commitment.

He sealed the letter, put a stamp on it, and slipped it into the mailbox. She didn't reply, and he lost himself in drink. The cockroach job was finished. The second level of the shelter had been purged. Grams didn't care.

On the third level, Douglas stumbled across the droppings of a Norway rat. He could have been negligent. Grams had not hired him to exterminate mammals, a task which he had performed successfully but reluctantly at Fleischmann's. *Rattus norvegicus,* the world's most common rodent, had overrun the cheese bay at one point, and Douglas had bowed to pressure from the front office to employ the most virulent chemical onslaught. The cheese had been removed, the hydraulic doors had been shut, and the place had been packed with a rolled-oat bait laced with an anticoagulant from somewhere up north. Afterwards, it looked like Jonestown in there.

This time around, Douglas had something far less dramatic in mind. On the evidence of the droppings, which were two or three days old, and a few gnaw marks on the wooden threshold of the door to the fourth level, he guessed at a population of no more than twenty rats. In all likelihood, they did not spend much time in the room, but used it as a conduit to get to food sources elsewhere. He found several telltale chinks in the wall, large enough for the passage of a rodent skull. These he closed with a mixture of mortar and crushed glass. He bought five spring-operated traps, baited them with chunks of cooked bratwurst, and waited. By the end of the week, he had killed twelve of the animals. By the middle of the next week, the droppings had vanished. The third level was clear.

4.

HE SAW HIS BROTHER for the first time in weeks. Most of the time, Stuart was immersed in work at the Teufelsberg, leaving the apartment before dawn and returning after midnight. When home, he slept. But on an evening in late October, a few days before Halloween, he asked someone to work his shift, and the two of them went to a small Oktoberfest celebration put on by the German-American Friendship Society. Men in lederhosen wandered about, sausages drooping from their fingers. A Ferris wheel whirled. Doughnuts hissed in fat.

After eating, they found a table away from the noise, and Stuart made an odd declaration.

"I've never been able to grasp this Cold War thing, as you can imagine."

Douglas could not even remotely imagine. "This Cold War *thing?*"

"You know what I'm talking about. It's so well defined. Someone like Nester can actually believe in one side or the other, but I have never been able to sort it out to my satisfaction. I mean, here in West Berlin, it's possible to see the thing in terms of black and white, but out on the Syrian border, it's just rock and sand and scorpion, and you have only barbed wire to make distinctions, which doesn't exactly inspire one to thoughts of light and darkness. Truth is, I was never able to believe in the absolute rightness of any proposition. You follow?"

Douglas shook his head. He didn't see any point in trying to follow. Unfazed, Stuart resumed.

"Nietzsche says it would be better for us to live in untruth, to accept our need for falsehood, and I do, I do. I understand that Nester needs to believe in a good side and a bad side, so he can put up with all the bureaucracy and bullshit of the army. But I can't. I simply can't. If I can get it, I prefer something vaster."

For the first time, his words hinted at something specific, and Douglas became attentive. "What are you saying, Stuart?"

"Nothing really. More bullshit."

"No, tell me."

Stuart pointed at a fat, full harvest moon above the bunched chestnuts. "I actually wanted to talk to you about something else. Would it be— No, let me start over. What would you think about going back to Texas?"

"*That's* what you were driving at? Hell, Stu."

Stuart squeezed his shoulder. "I know it's kind of out of the blue, but hear me out. I'm a mess right now. Just like you. I may not look it, but I am, and I guess I'm asking you a favor. I'm asking you to let me sort out my life here. Let me sort out Uta. Get myself together, and then you'll see, I'll be a better brother to you. I've told you about my psychological problems, about my anoxia of the soul?"

Douglas rubbed his forehead. "Right."

"Well, I think we may be on the brink of psychological oxidation. And I need to concentrate."

Douglas had an odd sensation of listening to words in an Esperanto containing one comprehensible idea for every three alien.

"I could get you on a plane day after tomorrow? It's a little abrupt, I know, but it would make things easier. I've got so many things to do. There's a big barbecue coming up for my unit at field station, and I'm on the steering committee. I mean, you can stay, Doug, if you want, but it would help me a lot if you would just think about going home."

"Shit, Stuart. I never knew anyone to dodge the point like you. Just spit it out. This is about Uta, isn't it?"

"Uta?!"

So he knew. She had told him. Douglas had thought as much. "I'm terribly sorry for what I did, and I would understand if you hated me for it. But just tell me the truth. No more of this metaphorical wheeze. It's insufferable."

Suddenly, Stuart grabbed Douglas's hands with his own. "You're forgiven. You're forgiven. Now please go home."

Douglas shook his head and pulled his hands away. Somewhere in that confused, sun-scarred head, Stuart meant well; but Douglas found his words offensive. He had considered going home. He wanted to go back to Dallas, in fact. But, like any other human being, he didn't want to be rushed. It made him feel unwanted.

"I'll go, Stuart—next week—"

"Tomorrow."

Douglas shook his head.

"I promised a man I'd do a job, and I'm going to."

Stuart wiped an eye. He did not appear satisfied, but he relented. Douglas stood up. Nearby, a small orchestra had established itself on a dais. Violins tuned, and horn notes rose to the sky. He tossed dregs of beer onto the ground.

"Relax, for God's sake. I told you I'm going."

An ancient diva in fur and rhinestone took the stage. A sparse crowd cheered. Someone struck a match. Beneath the autumn moon, she sang *"So schön wie heut', so müsst es bleiben."* "Every day should be like today." Douglas hoped not.

5.

ON HALLOWEEN DAY, without warning, Grams went on vacation. He pinned a note to Douglas's backpack saying he would return in a week.

"Suits me," Douglas murmured on his way down the steps of the shelter.

Aside from a distant stench, the fourth level was fine. It needed no cleansing. This might be easier than he thought. Stuart might get his wish. But he unlocked the door to the fifth level of the air raid shelter and saw immediately that something was wrong. For the first time, he entertained the reality of pigeon ticks in the basement. Odd noises bounded up the steps to meet him. The vague odor of rot detectable in the fourth level became overwhelming.

The noises were unidentifiable; they might have been the distant moan of subway trains on their way through the earth, they might—it was not inconceivable—have been human beings, homeless people. Holding his nose, he ventured down.

The steps were moist; so were the walls to his left and right. From the water of a busted sewage main, he surmised. At the bottom of the stairwell was a landing. He put pressure on it to make sure the stone was sound. To his left, a corridor with a low ceiling opened up. Its walls were unpainted, and the bricks were larger, cut in a different era perhaps. They had the gray of limestone, not of paint. His flashlight found the far end of the tunnel, a jagged black hole which, if he was not mistaken, led out of the shelter and into some other space. As Douglas drew farther away from the landing, the noises grew louder, and the temperature dropped by several degrees. He came to the end of the shelter, took a deep breath, and peeked through the hole to make sure there wasn't a drop-off.

A great space soared above him. He aimed the flashlight up. In the chiaroscuro, masonry jutted, crisscrossed by pipes and surrounded by what appeared to be metal scaffolding. Very high, far away, daylight spilled through grates the size of postage stamps. He could reach out and enclose them in a fist. Now and again, shadows crossed the grates, as people walked over them. Wings fluttered. That would certainly explain Grams's insistence on the pigeon ticks.

Douglas looked down. The ground seemed firm, so he stepped onto it. At his feet lay a patina of debris: rock, stick, cloth, glass. His shoes crunched upon the material, the refuse of some process, presumably mechanical— trash compaction was a possibility—but he could not ascertain much in the darkness. Though the space above him stretched far, the actual circumference of the floor area was cramped and indeterminate. Walls barred his way in three directions. He made his way across the debris toward the grate light. He allowed himself to breathe through his nose again and caught a great stench of death.

Lots of things had decomposed down here. He hunted for an explanation, wondered if the corpses were dead civilians buried under the debris-strewn floor during air raids. The stench could also have come from dead SS men, he supposed. Was he treading on graves? He came to a spot in what he presumed was the middle of the space. The light shone above and off to his right.

Birds, he thought. I hear birds.

There was a gentle, insistent cooing. As his eyes adjusted to the darkness, Douglas glimpsed them: beaks, eyes, and the curve of fowl torsos in dim hollows. He began to understand. One of the grates above him must have a hole. He couldn't tell for sure; the grates were five floors above him. But he believed a hole must exist, and pigeons had found their way through it into this underworld, where they had roosted. Their murmuring suggested generational habitation, comfort, familiarity. They had been colonizing this domain for a long time.

Douglas stopped, knelt, and gave the floor a closer inspection. What had first seemed like shreds of paper were bird feathers. Could Grams have known about this place? Surely not, Douglas concluded. Otherwise he would never have been so mysterious. This was clearly the source of the parasites. Evidently, at least one pigeon tick had made it up all those levels to the office. The breed had been identified, but no one had ever bothered to ask why it might be around, not until now. Douglas felt proud but horrified.

He plucked a rounded object from the ground and smelled. The thing was fetid in odor, and as he turned it between his gloved fingers, he comprehended. It was a cranium. Douglas's stomach lurched, and the birds in their aviaries began to rustle. He tossed the cranium away. A sensation of presence came over him, of sentient creatures close by, and as he looked closer at the walls around him, he realized they were full of holes, and in those holes were Norway rats, dozens of them, peering at him with red eyes as they gnawed on bones.

And around him in the darkness, he saw what he thought were other kinds of remains, larger and more suggestive. Grams was right. Ticks and SS corpses were everywhere. He had walked into an infested ossuary. And now, as quickly as possible, he must get out. In his haste, he tripped and flew headlong into a pile of bird charnel.

He got to his feet, feathers and bone bits clinging to him. In his fingers, the flashlight trembled. Its beam was scanning the wall ahead of him for the exit when it landed on an object that rooted him to the ground. At first, he believed that it must be a trick of his eyes. The object, he noted, attempting to maintain an empirical calm, could be described as round, or rather spherical; pale—that might be the glare of the beam; and the approximate size of a football. Futhermore, if he was not very much mistaken, it hovered in midair, about six feet off the ground, hovered in the darkness like a white balloon a few yards ahead of him. But it wasn't a balloon, he knew, because balloons didn't have eyes. Under other circumstances, he might have called out, but these eyes did not require a greeting. They regarded him from an immeasurable distance, from a platform humans did not occupy. Douglas wanted to run, but where? The thing barred his way. He refused to go the other way, back into the depths of the fifth subbasement.

Besides, the more he saw of the object, the more astonished he became. He took a step forward, studying one particular feature of what appeared to be a face. It could be no mistake. Beneath the left eye shone a mark, *his* mark, the housefly. The skin of the face had aged. Shadows pooled in vertiginous wrinkles. But Douglas recognized himself well enough. At last, gathering courage from recognition, he spoke.

"This is what I am then?"

The head did not respond. It gazed at him. Its eyes did not blink. They might have been the backs of two glittering ticks.

"Is that what you're telling me? This is my true face? I have become *this*?"

If anyone had asked him to identify his interrogator at that moment, he would have answered with utter certainty: my mind. I am talking to my mind.

And that thought sparked another, which scared him so badly that he almost dropped the flashlight. He was losing his mind. It had all been too much. The exit must be near at hand. He had not ventured very far from it. With a quick sweep of the beam, he would be able to find the door to the upper world. But he did not want to let the head out of his sight. He held the beam, which seemed to keep it at bay. But without the beam, he could not find the exit. He quickly shone the light around, located the exit—a dark gulf just to the left of his head. Relief flooded him. His hand twitched. He darted the beam back to the right to locate the apparition. He found nothing. A presence descended on him. He ran for it.

6.

HALFWAY OUT THE DOOR of the cafe, he realized how cowardly he had been. My God, he thought, have I lost every ounce of sanity, not to mention professional brio?

A dark corner of the cafe beckoned. He removed the backpack, which emitted a faint fume of the underworld, stuffed it under the table, and ordered a whiskey. He flicked feather and bone off his shoulders. A woman in a cobalt-blue turtleneck sweater wrote postcards at the table next to him. She was attractive in a very American way, fresh-faced, dark-haired, and unpretentiously serious. The deliberate movements of her hands, the way they finished one postcard with a determined signature, placed that postcard at the bottom of a stack, methodically and gracefully addressed the next, dispelled the madness in him. At some point in her life, he mused, she may have baited a spring trap. Her hands were that deft. A waitress brought the whiskey and a menu. He ordered pea soup and drank.

He studied the young woman shamelessly. She had dark, thin eyebrows and deep brown eyes that implied a melancholy submerged in humor. She wore no makeup, as far as he could tell, but her cheeks had a red blush, perhaps from the cold. Her black hair fell curly to her shoulders, neat without being manicured, which he liked. Her age? Mid-twenties, he guessed. She looked up, and he glanced away.

His nerves calmed, Douglas placed his hands over his eyes and contemplated the situation. Leaving aside the question of his mental health for the moment, he focused on the pigeon ticks, which, after all, had turned out to be genuine. But were they his problem?

Douglas saw no reason to continue working for Grams. A team of specialists would be required to clear out the fifth level. Furthermore, they should not waste their time with fancy solutions. If asked, Douglas would recommend a Drione storm for the entire space beneath the third subbasement. The living pigeons would have to be evacuated, the dead shoveled out. And, he advised to an invisible note taker, this should happen as soon as possible. He opened his eyes and found to his dismay that the woman at the next table was watching him with a troubled expression on her face. Yet the look contained something of human mercy too, for which he was grateful in the extreme. She probably smelled the stench.

Douglas decided not to wait for the pea soup. Taking his backpack from under the table and dropping a twenty-mark bill into the ashtray, he rose to leave. Just then, someone addressed him.

"Excuse me."

Douglas looked up. He jumped backwards, jiggling coffee cups on the table behind him. For an instant, he thought the head from below had followed him up and was poised to bite. The stranger's mouth had cracked open like an egg. But he came to his senses. A normal man stood before him. The mouth might be misshapen, but otherwise, the man was dressed in a navy blazer and glum burgundy tie, which made Douglas ashamed of his own appearance. As the stranger approached, his eyes burned with an emotion akin to shock.

Douglas addressed him. "Can I help you?"

"Maybe."

The man pulled a seat out for himself, glanced over his shoulder at the woman writing postcards. She was no longer staring. He gestured for Douglas to sit.

"I was just going—"

The man didn't seem to hear. He ordered a mineral water, unbuttoned his coat, and became pensive, as if about to pose a philosophical question. The eyes were large and humiliated. He put a hand to his left cheek.

"How did you get that?" he asked. Douglas shook his head in disbelief. The man was referring rudely to his housefly.

Seeing Douglas's discomfort, the man made an attempt to explain himself.

"I am with the American State Department, political section. My office is just around the corner in the Amerika Haus." He reached a hand across the table. "Carlton Styles."

Douglas took the hand.

"How did you get that scar?"

Something about the tenor of that word "scar" struck Douglas as unhappy. The mineral water and the pea soup arrived together. Nervousness dampened Douglas's appetite.

People had stared at the housefly before. A few had asked about it, though in far more delicate tones. In fact, the housefly wasn't really a scar. A few years ago, Douglas had been hunting dermestids in a newly built warehouse bay and happened to crawl behind a stack of pallets. On top of the pallets had been a barrel of hot coal tar to be used in sealing the floor. Without seeing Douglas behind the pallets, an incompetent forklift driver had lifted them, bumped too hard against the adjacent wall, and sent the barrelful of tar down onto him. Most of the stuff came off, but on the spot where the edge of the barrel had cut his cheek, a blotch of black had remained, and Douglas had never taken the time to have it surgically removed.

He told a short version of this story and prepared to leave the table.

"You live here?" the diplomat then inquired, his tone unhappily menacing.

A tremor ran through Douglas.

"No. I'm visiting my brother."

"Your brother?" The man Styles seemed daunted by this.

Douglas took courage. He should have mentioned Stuart before. That would have settled the matter quickly. "He's an officer in the military. His name is Stuart Glemnik, if you wish to pursue the matter."

This news did not have the desired effect. On the contrary, it appeared to enrage the diplomat.

"Stuart Glemnik, you say? You're his brother?"

Styles brought the water glass to his lips and tried to drink, but in his agitated state, most of the water dribbled to his chest. Suddenly, Douglas felt sorry for him. Styles spoke again, this time with a deep malevolence in his voice.

"You resemble someone I once knew. In Lebanon. Ever been there?"

Food mounted in Douglas's esophagus.

"No."

"Are you doing some kind of work here? Your outfit would suggest it. Do you have a work permit?"

"Um—"

"Does your brother know that you are working here? So close to the Amerika Haus? Is he helping you?"

Douglas steadied himself. This conversation nauseated him. Styles downed the last of his mineral water in a gulp, as if to prove his prowess. Half the glass drenched his shirt, but the man affected not to notice. Douglas dropped his spoon. A searing pain struck him in the left temple. His body shook, and soup flowed from his throat.

"I'm sorry." Douglas wiped his mouth. "I just saw something terrible downstairs."

The waitress regarded him with alarm and disgust. Styles went stiff. He seemed to have come to a conclusion. The restaurant went silent as travelers looked over their shoulders. The woman in the cobalt-blue turtleneck scribbled away. The waitress hurried over with napkins and a bowl.

"I'm sorry if our conversation has upset you." Styles offered his napkin. "Is it my face? You're a bit disgusted by my deformity, aren't you? Ah well, that's the result of a terrorist incident, and I can do nothing about it. Jiri Klek is responsible. Do you know about Jiri Klek, Mr.—Glemnik?"

"Gleaming. Douglas."

Douglas wiped an eye. Styles broke into the most bizarre smile he had ever seen. It had nothing to do with humor or glee or affection, the usual impulses for smiling, but appeared to have more in common with murderous rage. His proud front teeth made a single fang.

He leaned forward and whispered, "I don't believe a word of your story. I know exactly how you got that mark. It's not coal tar. It's a powder burn."

Styles pulled back, shelled out coins for his mineral water, and put his hands on the tabletop, as if getting ready to spring.

"That's incorrect," Douglas stammered.

The bizarre smile vanished.

"Is it?"

With that, the diplomat left.

Two sensations gripped Douglas at once. In the first place, he felt that he had just had a conversation with a seriously unhinged—he might even say dangerously unhinged—person, someone who made his own mental state look harmless. And at the same time, he had an unquenchable conviction that the man's words foretold some apocalypse. To his dismay, he noticed that the woman in the cobalt-blue turtleneck had stopped writing.

CHAPTER SIX

1.

JODIE BLUM CONGRATULATED HERSELF on the greatest eavesdrop of her life. As a reward, massively deserved, she took out the aromatic new American Express charge card she'd been hiding from herself for a month and bought a pair of rose-red Italian dress shoes with gold-filigreed buckles. At the moment, she couldn't afford the shoes and had nowhere on earth to wear them, but by the time the bill arrived, life would have changed.

What she'd heard transpire between the two men at the cafe was genuine. No question about it. And not just any reporter would have perceived that, she told herself. Not just any reporter would have had the sense to write down every word of the conversation on the backs of a series of postcards. Her fingers hurt from scribbling.

You have to give yourself points, she coached in her mind, as she sat on a bus overcrowded with depressed, staring East German refugees. Just like Pansy Buckner would.

By the time she got home to her sixteen-square-meter room in the far outer suburb of Lichtenrade, she was more depressed than she had ever been in her life, and Esperanza "Pansy" Buckner loomed over her like a fierce, unforgiving goddess, seated in her assistant's chair on the tenth floor of the *New York Times*. Even at journalism school that girl had struck Jodie as sacred in some way. Good looks, a command of Arabic and French, a way with older men, and yes, a modicum of talent; right from the start, Jodie could see she was headed for the fast track, to the three-part byline on the front page of the world's greatest newspaper. Meanwhile, Jodie Blum was headed to Iowa City, Iowa, to slave away on school board stories.

She threw herself on a makeshift bed and skinned a tangerine. The former occupant had evidently been a long-term chain-smoker, and his habit haunted the air. At night, when she turned out the lights, she could almost imagine him, the ghost of a German punk standing in the doorway, puffing on a butt in black-leathered ugliness. That image fit her mood.

She looked around with brooding eyes. Her sixteen square meters bore an inevitable resemblance to the confinement cells she'd seen at juvenile delinquent homes in Iowa. A pint-sized refrigerator hid beneath the sink, and the cupboards above it were made of a light, loose polymer; the slightest weight sent them toppling. Her bed was a series of couch cushions lined against a wall. The couch itself no longer existed. At the foot of the cushions sat a color television set that, she regretted, spoke no English. Then there was her laptop computer in its carrying case, and lined against one wall, novels, histories, journalistic accounts of central and eastern Europe. She'd packed one suitcase full of these books, and they were her dearest companions.

One final item of importance, a rotary telephone with its digits buried at the bottom of deep circles, completed the room. One month ago, Jodie had sent the phone number to twenty-five different editors around the United States of America. Not one had ever returned her calls.

Pansy Buckner now worked as an assistant to one of the most powerful editorialists in journalism, Hammond J. Stamps, and she, Jodie, moldered in the most remote corner of West Berlin, practically up against the Berlin Wall, with no contacts, scant knowledge of German, and a pair of four-hundred-dollar shoes she could in no way afford. She flipped the rose-reds into a corner.

Above all, Jodie demanded honesty of herself. She was willing to make mistakes, a lot of them, in fact, but she didn't want to play games with herself. If she made mistakes, she must acknowledge them.

As a journalist, she was flailing. The conversation between the two men in the cafe had been incoherent and meaningless, like a catchy tune with garbled lyrics; it reminded her of that song "Band on the Run" which she'd sung over and over as a child but never understood and still did not grasp. She'd only eavesdropped because the first man had made such an impression on her. Like the diplomat, she noticed the livid black mark on his left cheek. At first, in the darkness of the cafe, it looked like an open cut. Then she saw his clothing. His pants had been taped to his ankles with electrical tape, his shirt was spattered with coffee and tufted with what looked like bird feathers. And a smell had come off him . . . it had been frightening. Like an outhouse on an oil spill.

He'd been nervous too, and at first, she had pitied him. She thought he was a homeless person who had come into the restaurant to bum change.

The impression didn't last, though. He'd caught her looking at him, and she could see he was not accustomed to being seen in such a foul light. That made her curious. And as she studied him, the curiosity grew. There was horror in him, evident in the fumbling of his hands as he produced his wallet, the furtive looks he gave on every side, the speed with which he downed his whiskey.

Then, at a table near the door, she had caught sight of the other man, the one with the deformity, not just staring but visibly shocked. From then on, she had been mesmerized. The diplomat had terrified the other man, already badly scared, and Jodie was sure he meant to do so. At the end, he leaned forward into the guy's face and spoke louder than he probably realized. "I don't believe a word of your story," she read again off one of her postcards. "I know exactly how you got that mark. It's not coal tar. It's a powder burn."

Which was provocative, but so what? What did that amount to? American diplomats, as far as she knew, did not make a habit of threatening American citizens. Still, she thought, it's not enough.

"I should never have come to this place," she muttered to herself as she flipped the postcard aside and plucked a book on the Cambridge spy circle from the wall. Rain began to pelt her windows.

The previous May, after spending a year in Iowa City, writing stories about school board meetings where the chief topic was the enrollment of students who didn't exist—of phantom students, as they were called—Jodie had decided to take a chance. Pansy Buckner might have landed a clerkship at the *New York Times,* but Jodie would trump that. She would go to Europe, where things were beginning to happen, and become a stringer, and then a foreign correspondent. Other people had done it, up and gone, then landed jobs. And Jodie had been considered one of the most talented in her J-school class, more talented even than her nemesis, by some lights. Even if she didn't get a job, the experience would be invaluable.

Within a month, plans were made. She asked her favorite relative, Aunt Rachel, a rich widow living in Manhattan, to help buy her a laptop computer, promising to pay the money back when she got work. All her savings had been swallowed by a student loan, so she borrowed more money from her folks and bought a round-trip ticket to West Berlin, which would function as a base in Eastern Europe. She set herself a deadline of one year. If after one year, she'd screwed the pooch, Jodie would lay down her laptop and get a job in an advertising agency. That was the bargain; not just with her parents and Aunt Rachel, but with herself.

A month before her departure for West Germany, a good omen had come. A wire service wanted someone in West Berlin by early September.

Grasp of the German language would be especially helpful, the letter said. She bought tapes and feverishly began to teach herself.

Then it was time. She quit her job in Iowa and went home to Minneapolis. She bought books on European history, a new correspondent's bag, exchanged cash for traveler's checks, and received her first passport. On the night before her departure, her parents revealed their true feelings. They regretted her decision; in fact, they despised it and had only given in after Aunt Rachel, in her usual high-handed manner, had chewed them out. Bitter arguments ensued. How would Jodie live without a job? How could she pay the rent? And who did she think would foot the bill if the entire thing went south? Not Aunt Rachel. That was for goddamn sure! Another question arose which struck Jodie as hypocritical for two people who had raised their child with very little religion. Was it ethical for a young Jewish woman to live in Germany? Her father demanded an answer. Was it appropriate? After all, distant relatives had died in the camps.

Finally, after midnight, after tears had been shed and feelings hurt, Jodie's mother convinced her father to give up the fight, and on a cool morning in late August, the two of them drove her, their only child, to the St. Paul airport.

Within a week of arrival, the wire job fell through. Someone within the company had taken the position. She realized now that her parents had been right about her rash decision to come here. Three weeks ago, for their sake, she had gone to Yom Kippur services at a synagogue in the middle of town, but among the German Jews she felt her loneliness even more profoundly. The service, in Hebrew and German, was incomprehensible, and to make matters worse, the people were not very welcoming. Never again, she'd told herself, leaving the synagogue, and that made her feel even worse, as if, through these emotions, she would shame her family, especially Aunt Rachel, whose husband had survived the Holocaust in a root cellar in eastern Czechoslovakia and later committed suicide.

Eavesdropping on an inane conversation between two strange men in a sleazy cafe near the train station only confirmed Jodie's worst suspicions about herself. Before, she had always been fearless, unafraid to confront total strangers with their own bad conduct, unafraid to ask the hard questions, unafraid to venture out at any hour of the night to get a story. Now, all of a sudden, she was professionally crippled.

It had started a few days after Yom Kippur, on the weekend Gorbachev had come to East Berlin for the fortieth anniversary of the German Democratic Republic. On that Saturday, there were supposed to be antigovernment demonstrations on Alexanderplatz, and Jodie resolved to go.

She took the subway to Kochstrasse and came out on a narrow street that ended in Checkpoint Charlie, the Allied checkpoint flanked by the Wall and overshadowed by an East German guard tower. In the weeks since her arrival, Jodie had not accustomed herself to the towers. They had glassy slit eyes, flat skulls, and blank square trunks. The men in them were flitting shadows, immaterial but threatening. On either side of this tower stretched the Wall itself, which made a far less harrowing impression on her, perhaps because of its status as a tourist attraction on a par with Disneyland or the Pyramids; she'd seen it on television shows, in travel brochures, and in countless magazines and history books. To the left and the right, vandals had sprayed "Happy Birthday" in hot-pink letters on the concrete slabs, and from the subway exit, she could see the curlicued letters of the birthday greeting much more clearly than anything else at the border. Somehow, the letters calmed her nerves. This was not the portal to the underworld. It was a highly visible, half-farcical scrap of a geopolitical squabble. Normal people from places like Terre Haute, Indiana, and Iowa City, Iowa, crossed it every day of the week to give themselves a thrill unavailable anywhere else in the world. They imagined themselves crossing through the valley of the shadow of death and returning, to tell their friends back home of an adventure on the very edge of the civilized world; on the dividing line between light and darkness. Well, Jodie wasn't buying it. She inhaled cool October air, drew strength from her gut, and marched up to the checkpoint. She showed her passport to the American soldier in the booth.

"You'll be lucky to get through today," he warned her, but caught up in her own thoughts, she didn't listen. She entered the no-man's-land between East and West.

A few yards beyond the Allied station, she had to stop. East German border guards loomed. They wore pine-green uniforms and caps. Most were shaven, pale, and young, bland as artificial Christmas trees.

In German, Jodie asked to get by. She stammered the word *Journalistin.* The head guard, a man with a pale blue sheen on his skin, gave her a doubtful look and asked for some kind of identification. He was blond and broad-shouldered and decorated with East German insignia. No trace of humor, no recognition of their common humanity, came from his eyes. She took the passport from her purse and thrust it forward. The guard unhooked his hands from behind his back, raised the right one, and wagged a single finger back and forth.

"*Presse,*" he insisted.

Humiliation made Jodie blush. She didn't have real press credentials, because she did not work for anyone. Only journalists with full-time affiliations received accreditation. But she couldn't possibly tell him this.

Despairing, she took out her ID from the *Iowa City Press Citizen,* a green piece of laminated paper with her photo and a police stamp on it. It didn't wash. The guard stepped back, his hands folded behind his back. The matter was ended.

To make matters worse, she would have to go back through a crowd of tourists already turned away.

The incident made her despondent. For the first time in her life, surrounded by strangers, submerged in a foreign language, overwhelmed by the risk she had taken, she lost faith in herself. Since then, two weeks had gone by, and she made no more effort to cross the border. Even when the Monday-night demonstrations started, when the checkpoints opened up again, she stayed away. She did not even inquire about accreditation, because she knew it would get her nowhere.

She was a nobody. A real reporter would be on a first-name basis with the senior American diplomat at the general consulate in West Berlin. But why should such a diplomat bother with Jodie Blum?

It was time to get a grip, she told herself, or get out. Depression kept her in bed for the next twelve hours.

2.

THE FOLLOWING DAY broke with names repeating like busy signals in her head.

Douglas Gleaming, Stuart Glemnik, Carlton Styles, Jiri Klek . . .

The names prodded Jodie from sleep. I have seen something, she thought. A secret has been revealed to me.

The rain had stopped. Gray morning light seeped through her window, autumn leaves traced whispery circles across the glass; far away, someone knocked.

She made coffee. Then she tried on several outfits and finally opted for a black skirt, black wool stockings, a red cotton blouse with gold buttons up to the throat, crescent-shaped gold earrings that suggested vaguely the hammer and sickle, and on her feet, the rose-reds with the burnished buckles.

To her, the shoes felt like hands. They possessed body heat, and Jodie imagined it came from the human who had made them, an Italian artist with a ball-peen hammer, toothpick-thin nails, and a paintbrush as small as an eyeliner. Those hands gave her strength. They held her firm.

An American diplomat had menaced an American citizen. That was the nut of a story. The whole thing could be a personal matter, a contretemps among friends, but it didn't seem likely. She gathered the postcards from the previous day, slotted them inside a journal of notes, and raced down the steps of her apartment building.

Just in time, she caught the bus. It was almost empty. She hurried up steps to the top deck, to her favorite spot, the front-row bench above the bus driver with its panoramic view of the street. She sat at the aisle end of the bench, retrieved the postcards from her backpack, and began laying them out in front of her. She concentrated on names. One by one, she wrote them into her journal. Each name got its own page. Douglas Gleaming (as in twilight's last gleaming?), Stuart Glemnik, Carlton Styles, and Jiri Klek. She knew the least about Stuart and the most about Douglas. Under the latter's name, she scribbled a series of facts: "brother in the military," "visibly scared by something he had seen (where?)," "nervous stomach (vomit)," "drinks whiskey, inexpensive brand (six marks per glass)." What else? "Powder burn or coal tar?" "Birds." And then it occurred to her too, remembering the way he had looked at her: "single."

Then she moved on to Carlton Styles. On one of the postcards, early in the conversation, she had written down Styles's occupation. She found it again. He had almost certainly said, "U.S. State Department," and then something like "political section." His office was in the Amerika Haus, a few hundred yards from the cafe. She wrote this down, then added: "deformity (from a terrorist act? committed by Jiri Klek?—see entry)," "burgundy tie, navy blazer," "drinks coffee regularly at the cafe?" "'I don't believe a word of your story, etc.,' to Douglas." But why not? Why in the world not? What did he actually suspect?

It was not much of an entry, but that hardly mattered. The entries didn't have to be comprehensive. She was just trying to organize her thoughts, to figure out where to begin. As an afterthought, at the bottom of the page, she scratched down the word "impostor?" Just because a man said he was a diplomat didn't mean he was. For all she knew, he had just fled the asylum.

Next up was Stuart Glemnik. She put "Gleaming" in bold letters and parentheses beside his last name. "Changed it?" she wrote. The bus bounced. Her pen jabbed into the seat. Back a few seats, an old woman glared with disapproval. Under that same name, she wrote down, "West Berlin?" and underlined it twice, "brother of Douglas," then "military?" Then, on a whim, inspired by her reading the previous night, she scrawled a last faint thought: "spy?"

3.

STEP ONE WAS STYLES. First, she went to the Amerika Haus, a rather ugly, two-story building intended as a bastion of American democracy in besieged West Berlin, a place where the locals could find month-old newspapers, magazines, and books from the States, hear whole-some lectures by famous Yankee authors, artists, and celebrities, and revel in the culture of the Occupier. Aesthetically, the building reminded her of an abortion clinic in suburban Minneapolis.

Stepping up to the main counter, Jodie asked the woman at the desk if she could see Carlton Styles. At first, the woman ignored her. She put checks beside names on a list, including the name of the American ambassador to West Berlin. At the top of the list were the words "51st Anniversary Commemoration of the Jewish Pogrom—Kristallnacht," followed by a date, November 9, 1989.

Jodie repeated her request. The woman, a German, did not look up. She said she had never heard of the man. When Jodie described his looks, she received an expression of cold indifference. "Try the embassy," the woman suggested.

That meant a trip across town. She bought a döner kebab with yogurt sauce and boarded another bus. At the U.S. embassy in Dahlem, she inquired again. In order to do this without getting herself into trouble, she concocted an elaborate lie, which she proceeded to tell to a youngish press attaché.

"And you work for . . . ?" The attaché clasped his fingers.

"The *Sacramento Bee.* I'm freelancing." Jodie considered using her Iowa City press card, but it would have been either laughable or suspicious, the idea of a midwestern university town of that size with its own foreign correspondent.

This did not impress him, she could tell. He gave a cool nod. "And how may I help you?"

Jodie made it up as she spoke. "I am doing a piece on how American diplomats are responding to the changes in Eastern Europe, and one of my editors in San Francisco mentioned that an old college acquaintance was working for the mission here."

The assistant's face became more attentive. "Oh really? Who might that be?"

"A Mr. Styles."

The attaché scooped up a directory and leafed with concentration through several pages. "Ralph Styles?"

"Ralph or maybe Carl."

"We have a Ralph in commercial. I don't recall a Carl. And you want to talk to this person, you said, about what it's like to be a diplomat in Europe with all the changes and what not? And you want to talk to him . . . when?" The attaché paused, locked on her with eyes too august for his age. "Now?"

Jodie nicked her head. "Why not?"

The attache picked up his phone. While it rang, he cupped a hand over the receiver. "Do you have a card?"

"Ran out."

"I see," he said. A voice emerged from the receiver. "Hey, Jan. It's Ted. Mustermann. USIS. Is Ralph Styles around?"

Jodie's heart thumped. She hated telling a lie to an official of the United States government, but there was no other way.

"I've got a reporter down here. A young woman from the Sacramento paper. . . . Yes, I believe that's the one." He cupped the receiver again. "From the *Bee,* you said?" She nodded in the affirmative. "That's right, Jan, the *Bee*. She's doing a piece on diplomats in Europe right now. . . . Apparently, yes, the good people of Sacramento are actually interested in our profession. . . . It *is* nice. Do you think he'd talk to her?"

A long silence followed, during which the attaché's face shifted textures. Its bland surface became taut, then wrinkled, then smooth. She detected dismay. He hung up the phone. "Um, there is a Ralph Styles over in commercial," he said. "But he's away in Hamburg today. There is one other possibility. I don't know if it will interest you, but we do have a gentleman who often talks about general diplomatic affairs, a Mr. Doyle. Rick Doyle. He usually isn't in this office, but he's over for a conference. Jan tells me he's free for the next half hour. Can you give me some idea about how you want to do this?"

Jodie followed him up a flight of stairs.

"Deep background suits me."

"Fine. That's how Rick likes it too."

They stopped at a door without a number. The assistant tapped twice with two knuckles. "Rick?"

A muffled voice asked them to enter. Introductions were unnecessary. The man before her was the diplomat from the cafe, Carlton Styles. As they shook hands, a faint flame of recognition trailed across his eyes. He offered her a seat and coffee. She accepted the first, declined the second, and decided not to reveal the true reason for her visit. Here, in the sedate banality of an office, she found the diplomat terrifying. He was tense. His hair had been blow-dried into a malevolent turban.

The attaché took a chair beside him, and before she could get out a word, Doyle-Styles launched into a rote but energized speech about his experience as a diplomat. He looked more statesmanlike than the day before. The suit had a nicer cut, and he wore glasses. But the overbite was worse.

The three front teeth lunged forward, as if attempting to jilt the head. The farthest to the left was crooked. Its side showed, and a pink space appeared between it and the other two, which shot in erratic directions from beneath the lip. He talked about a time in Cairo that he had cabled his superiors that Anwar Sadat would be flying to Israel, then slapped his hands together in self-congratulation. "True story."

She scribbled words on a notepad and screwed up her eyes to convey attentiveness. At the end of ten minutes, Doyle-Styles came to a full stop, and it was clear he'd completed his speech and had nothing more to add. More than anything, Jodie didn't want this man to recall her face from the cafe. It was a completely irrational instinct, but Jodie felt, in his presence, an extreme danger.

The attaché betrayed her. "Say, who was that friend of yours at the paper who knew Ralph?"

"A friend knew Ralph?" The diplomat was curious now.

"Except you thought the name might be Carl, didn't you, Ms. Blum?" the attaché said, to her horror. "Do you know of a Carl anywhere else in Germany, Rick? In Bonn, maybe? A Carl Styles?"

Jodie swallowed. "I think it was Ralph, now that you mention it. I don't know why I thought it was Carl."

That was a bad thing to say. Doyle-Styles sat up in his chair.

"Who at your newspaper?"

Jodie stammered out a fabrication. "Her first name is Ann, I know that much. It's kind of embarrassing, honestly, because I haven't been working for them very long, and it was one of those things where your main editor is on the phone and another editor hears someone is going to West Berlin and just rushes in with, hey, go see my friend so-and-so when you get a chance and tell him I said hello . . ."

Thick eyebrows met above his nose as he processed the explanation. The fangs thrust forward from dry lips, eager to fly at her, and Jodie recalled what he had said in the cafe. An act of violence had wrenched the teeth forward. Faint scars around the mouth confirmed the fact.

"Ralph has never mentioned an Ann to me," he sniffed, "but that doesn't mean anything."

Screw this, she thought, I've got to get out of here. "She's the science editor. He should call and ask for Ann who edits science and they should put him right through. She'd love to hear from him, I'm sure, or it seemed that way. Maybe he doesn't want to talk to her, though. Maybe she's some old girlfriend or something. *Anyway.*"

Styles raised the watch on his left hand. "Time to go."

The attaché coughed out an apology. "She doesn't have a card yet, but perhaps, Ms. Blum, you could write out the details on a piece of paper. And put down the phone number of the newspaper in Sacramento, please."

"Yes," the diplomat urged, "and please do send me a copy of that article you're writing on diplomats."

The last two words of the sentence came out of that vampiric mouth a beat or two slower than the others. "On dip-lo-mats." Each syllable insinuated doubt. Jodie wrote the fake numbers on a piece of paper, popped out of her chair, and reached to take the diplomat's hand, which held her fingers a beat longer than necessary. The attaché hustled Jodie out of the room.

4.

S HAKEN, SHE HURRIED to the Staatsbibliothek, her favorite place in the city and the most wonderful library she'd ever seen, a vast incubation chamber for West Berlin eggheads.

She found a wide wooden table in a sunny spot, and laid out her materials. She looked in a periodical guide for the years 1987 through 1989 and found a dozen entries on Jiri Klek. With a librarian's stern help, she retrieved extracts and took copious notes, filling up several pages.

Klek, Jiri. No extant photograph. Born in Dalmatia, village of Klek, date unknown, possibly in 1920, according to one source, or in 1941, according to another, or in 1954, claimed a last, under Tito. For each date, there was a different version of his life.

In the first and most detailed, the one beginning in 1920, his parents were ruined after the collapse of the Habsburg Empire. Father committed suicide. Mother raises Klek till he leaves home. Ends up, at sixteen, fighting in Spain, in the Civil War, on the Communist side. Imprisoned by his own side, then released. Disappears. Now, she wrote, he would be sixty-nine.

In the second and most widely accepted version of the story, Klek was born in 1941, right before the German invasion of Yugoslavia during World War II. His parents are partisans hung by Italian soldiers. Nothing more known. In this scenario, he would be about her parents' age, forty-eight.

In the third, and to Jodie most believable, account, he is a relatively young man, born in 1954, a Croatian nationalist student radicalized in 1968, then thrown into jail, a kind of terrorist hippy, thirty-five years old.

She made a note on the Douglas Gleaming page. "Klek connection? Last name sounds vaguely Slavic."

No wide public familiarity with Klek's name exists until the Palestinian attack on Israeli athletes at the 1972 Olympic Games in Munich. Klek is credited with elements in the plan. At the time, no one believes he is real; the name's a cover for a Palestinian extremist grouping. A series of actions follow, making him notorious. Hijacking of plane to Entebbe. Klek-inspired assassination attempt on the Pope. Car-bombing of marines in Beirut. Klek traced once more. Bombing of La Belle Disco in West Berlin. Klek yet again. Lockerbie. No proof, but a distinct possibility. His last suspected action, not surprisingly. Current whereabouts unknown. Speculated: Bekaa Valley, southern Lebanon; Damascus, Syria; Diyarbakir, Turkey; Sofia, Bulgaria; East Berlin, Germany."

Hair stood on the back of her neck. She could just barely remember the horror with which her parents had spoken of the murder of the athletes in Munich. But she remembered the assassination attempt on the Pope. And Lockerbie was very close; the friend of a friend of a friend had been on the plane. And the man responsible for all this suffering might be near, just a few kilometers away, on the other side of the Berlin Wall. In a sense, in the presence of Styles, she had been face-to-face with him, with the dearest work of his hands and mind, and the thought jolted her with twin emotions, a distant sorrow for the diplomat, and a very personal hatred for the terrorist.

One detail struck Jodie as clearly significant. Among several other possibilities, Jiri Klek could be in East Berlin. That meant, despite the differences lying between these four men, they shared—or might share—one thing in common. They had ended up here. That had to be the key.

Still, leaving the library, notes mashed in her hands, she realized she had learned virtually nothing.

5.

BY NOW, it was early November. The last of the summer had faded, and on the air, with the cold wind, came a scent of lignite, brown coal burning in the ovens and heaters of old buildings in East and West. It was a harsh smell, a much larger, more diffuse version of the odor left in her room by the chain-smoker, but she liked it somehow; it was, to her, a first real taste of the Europe on the other side of the Wall, where on Mondays now, people were demonstrating by the thousands. Something was coming, the smell said, an enormous fire.

She turned her efforts to Douglas Gleaming, and finding him turned out to be easy. Leafing through the West Berlin phone book, she found a number for an S. Glemnik. No address was attached to the name.

That night, from a phone booth, she called. The phone rang several times; then a sleepy male voice picked up.

"Uta?"

"No, this is Betty. Have I reached Stuart?"

A long, troubled silence ensued. "No."

"Um, is this Douglas—?"

She could feel the man growing impatient on the other end of the line.

"Yes, it is. Are you calling about the barbecue?"

Jodie swallowed.

"Yes, as a matter of fact—"

"You want the address?"

She grabbed a pencil.

"They changed the venue. It's going to be at Colonel Redding's house."

He read the information.

"And what's the date again?"

"Same as before."

"I lost my invitation."

Douglas sighed in irritation. He wasn't the nicest guy. "Tomorrow evening. Monday, November sixth. Bye, Betty."

He hung up.

6.

COLONEL REDDING LIVED IN A BUNGALOW at the final loop of a dead-end street. Jodie didn't need to knock. The door was open.

To a loud strain of country music, courtesy of a stereo, she wandered down the front corridor through the kitchen, where a woman in an apron unwrapped lemon squares, out the back door to the least populated corner of the yard, where she caught her breath and devised a strategy beneath a gold-maned chestnut. From her vantage point, she could see the eighteen holes of an American military golf course, a flat expanse of green turf, broken by a pond or two. A halfhearted sand trap glimmered in the dusk. Off in the distance, a man in pink teed off, the last round of the season. She placed her elbows on the top of the fence. The metal was cold. She cast a glance at the yard behind her and wondered how in God's name she would find one of the brothers without giving herself away.

It was a very American scene. On the back porch, someone had installed a boom box, and its speakers throbbed with the noise of a prerecorded college football game, Notre Dame versus somebody. The cheers of a crowd rose above the remote din of pedal steel guitars, still playing within the house. Not far from the porch, placed against the fence line opposite Jodie, was the eats table. Soldiers milled around it, in and out of uniform. A few of them cocked their heads in Jodie's direction, even though she'd dressed down for the occasion.

The woman from the kitchen placed the lemon squares in the soldiers' midst, and their attention momentarily shifted.

At her back, the tree dropped its chestnuts. One of them hit the ground and cracked open, revealing a nut as green as spring. She bent and plucked it up, dropped it in her pocket for love, luck, and whatever else might pass her by.

Beyond the ball game and the country music, she began to hear something else, a rustling of low voices reminiscent of static. She concentrated on it. In the backyard, two dozen people were all talking at once, murmuring to each other, not about football, but about the Monday-night demonstrations, about the five hundred thousand people expected to march that night in Leipzig, about the dictator of Bulgaria, Todor Zhivkov, who was about to be ousted, and about everything else occurring beyond the horizon of the dislocated American golf course.

The sun fell. Jodie drifted forward to a clutch of men gathered around a barbecue grill. Bratwurst, hot dogs, and pork chops gleamed in wrappers on a cooler beside the grill, and one of the men—the colonel, she guessed, by his age and manner—held tongs. Mercifully, the drinks table lay near the grill. She could eavesdrop while making a tequila sunrise.

The conversation centered on one man, dressed in the khakis of a uniform. He had close-cropped blond hair and a sunburn painful to behold; in the evening glow, he looked irradiated, the orange of the dusk setting alight the crimson on his skin, pooling like grill embers in the crystal of his glasses. He seemed to be explaining himself in an apologetic manner. Beside him, a head taller, listening intently, stood an austere black man in civilian clothes: a rich brown turtleneck, a black vest, and jeans. His face was large and bookish, she thought, an impression reinforced by a pair of thick black bifocals resting on the tip of his nose. He was all but bald, this man, and Jodie detected a proprietary element in his relation to the sunburned speaker. He hovered as a tutor might over a child making a point before a teacher.

"You're a reader of history, aren't you, Colonel? We were talking about Gibbon the other day—"

The man with the tongs dismissed the charge. "Oh well, I read here and there, you know, when I have a little time."

Jodie dropped ice into her cup and searched through bottles for tequila and grenadine.

"Well, I have this theory that I wanted to tell you about, that's a little out there, I admit, but it intrigues me, and I know you'll be intrigued, because you can't fool me, you think more about history than most people around here—"

The black man watched his sunburned friend with growing alarm. No mistaking it, Jodie thought. This was an unwelcome conversation.

"What theory is that?"

Other men joined these three, beers in their hands. One of them had brought buns. Jodie felt suddenly conspicuous. The party's other women huddled on the back porch, holding their wineglasses, watching a pair of guys, one white, one black, toss a nerf football. She drank her tequila sunrise, sans grenadine, and stared at the lone golfer on the course, hoping no one would notice her.

She wanted to hear a name. The sunburned man was speaking again.

"I was reading a biography of Allen Dulles the other day, sir—you know Allen Dulles?"

"Of course, Lieutenant, that much history I do know. You'll forgive me while I put the brats on. The ladies just gave me the high sign."

"Let me help you, sir," the black man said.

"Go on, Lieutenant."

"Well, Dulles's father studied theology in Leipzig in the 1880s, around the same time the philosopher Friedrich Nietzsche was there—"

Jodie saw the black man's head shaking in unhappy disbelief. He was laying the hot dogs and bratwurst side by side and muttering under his breath.

"Unh-hunh." The colonel did not seem the least bit interested.

"Well, I had this theory that the two of them met, you see, and that Nietzsche convinced him of the relativity of all things, of all values and principles, and that he passed these on to his son Allen, who went on to become the father of modern American intelligence—"

"You're pulling my leg, Lieutenant."

A troubled silence descended on the men around the grill. The black man interjected, "Yes, he is. He's just trying to show off how much he's read. He's showing off his knowledge of German."

Hot dogs whistled over the heat.

"Sir, I am not pulling your leg. I am just trying to point out certain valid connections between our work here and the history of ideas—"

"Good for you, Glemnik." The colonel turned his attention to the meat. "I can take it from here, Captain."

In that moment, as Jodie exulted in finding her man, Glemnik caught her eye. He knew she was eavesdropping. Drink in hand, she hurried away from the barbecue grill, back to her corner beside the chestnut tree. She turned and found him at her elbow.

"Who are you?" he asked.

Jodie pointed at herself.

"You were listening just now, but I don't recognize you."

The darkness beneath the tree thickened. She wondered if anyone else in the backyard could see them. He was pushing her back into the shadows.

"Answer me."

"I'm supposed to meet Douglas Gleaming here."

She had barely stammered it out.

"Douglas Gleaming? My brother? That's a lie."

She gave him her biggest smile.

"You must be Stuart then."

She glimpsed the black man over his shoulder. He was scrutinizing them.

"Douglas isn't invited to this party, so he couldn't have invited anybody. Who are you?"

He grabbed two fingers of her drinkless hand and bent them down. His voice lowered to a whisper.

"Who *are* you?!"

Her fingers hurt.

"I'm a reporter. I need to talk to you. Your brother's in danger."

He bent harder. "I *know* that. Now tell me the truth. Who do you work for? Styles?"

"God no."

"I see. You know who I'm talking about, but you don't work for him."

She tried to stutter out an explanation. He interrupted.

"You've got some nerve coming here. This is a military intelligence barbecue. I could have you arrested."

"I'll leave."

He loosened his grip. "You tell Styles something for me, sweetheart. You tell him if he comes near my brother again, I'll kill him. No matter what else happens. No matter what he thinks, if he touches Douglas, he's a dead man."

Someone gave a wolf whistle from the other side of the yard. "I'm telling Uta!" a deep voice called.

For an instant, Stuart was distracted. Jodie jerked her hand away.

"Stop manhandling me. I told you who I was. It's true. I'm here to get a story. From you."

Then her heart stopped. He was either laughing or beginning to cry, she couldn't tell.

"A reporter. You really are a reporter. Oh my good God, of course. That's just what I need, on top of everything else. Beautiful. Thank ya, Jesus. Listen to me. You have walked into the full, dead middle of danger, sweetheart—"

She was fondling the chestnut in a fist inside her pocket. If need be, she could hit him once in the face, then jump the fence before anyone caught her. Stuart Glemnik removed the glasses and wiped the tears from his eyes.

"Oh Christ, you're not going to write about me, are you? This is all too much."

"Where is your brother?"

Stuart rested a hand on the fence. She tightened her fist around the nut.

"He's here. I begged him to leave, but he won't, for his own reasons. But you can't write about this. I'm asking you, as one human being to another. I'm begging you. I will get down on my knees and beg, sweet sister."

She said nothing. He lifted his hand away from the fence and put the glasses back across his eyes. "All right then. Whoever you are, whatever you want, I've abased myself enough. Get out of here."

7.

THAT NIGHT, when she got home, her phone—miracle of miracles— was ringing. She snapped it up.

The line was fuzzy. A distorted voice reached her ears.

"Excuse me?"

"I said I'm looking for Jodie Blum. That you?"

Distance fuzzed the line again. The caller was far away.

"You still want work?"

She dropped back on her bed of cushions.

"God, yes."

The caller cleared his throat.

"Good. This is Dick Chubbs. I'm running the world desk at *Probe*. We lost our man in Germany last week, never mind why, and we need two thousand words on the situation in East Berlin by Wednesday. Think you can file by then?"

She barely stammered out an affirmation. *Probe* magazine was one of the biggest newsweeklies in the country. She had sent a résumé to them weeks ago and expected nothing.

"This is on the ground stuff. Vox pops. But with some good hard political analysis too. Use your best sources. Be honest with you, if we weren't so desperate, we never would have called you. But your clips are good, so what the hell. Here's my fax number. When we know you better, we'll get you hooked into our computer."

She nodded and then remembered to answer him. She would use her best sources. That's right. All those beautiful sources she had cultivated while parading through the highest diplomatic circles in West Berlin.

"If this works out, we may want you to go to Prague in a few days. You got your papers in order?"

"Prague." Jodie's mouth was dry. "Yes," she replied, "I could go to Prague."

"Good. How's your German?"

"Fluent," she lied.

In a few minutes, he was gone. Jodie pulled the chestnut from her pocket. That was it then. Her luck had changed. No more chasing bedeviled Americans. No more diplomats with bad tempers or pretentious soldiers. It was time to kick ass.

CHAPTER SEVEN

1.

IN THE CAFE, Douglas swizzled down a final whiskey. Glints of sunset faded from an abandoned champagne glass at the next table. West Berlin grew dark. Across the street, the windows of the Zoo train station, last terminus of the West, gave off a sad gloom. Douglas was going home. That evening, Stuart would drive him to Frankfurt and from Frankfurt, next morning, he would catch the plane to Dallas. He had put his return off long enough.

He descended to Grams's office and peered through the milky panes. Beyond swam darkness. He unlocked the door with the keys Grams had given him, then laid them on a desk beside the door.

"Ho there."

No one answered. Grams was either gone for the day or still on vacation. Douglas flipped on a light, moved down the central corridor. Radiators tinkled. A Swiss clock ticked. He knocked on the door of Grams's personal office. The room was locked and still. He came to the end of the corridor, to the shelter. Now a moth fluttered. Its wings beat down the hall behind him. At the shelter entrance sat a box containing most of his extermination equipment.

He rummaged through it. Twine was there, matches, mason jar, ethyl acetate. Most important were a backpack sprayer, courtesy of the U.S. Army, and two one-gallon canisters of Kenyan pyrethrum, all of which had to be returned before his departure.

He retrieved the keys and checked his watch. As Grams had already paid him, and as he really didn't want to return the cash unless he absolutely had to, maybe he could do a little work on the door to the horrendous fifth level of the shelter, seal its entrance or something. That would be easy enough.

He took a small mortar-making kit from the box, along with a trowel. This might not solve the problem, but it was a gesture at least. Grams would have a barrier of sorts against the ticks, and Douglas could depart with an easier conscience. Besides, he had a little time.

It was now five-thirty, Thursday, November 9. Last night, after returning unexpectedly early from work, Stuart had told Douglas to have his things packed, to have everything ready, by seven tonight. Since then, Douglas had not seen him. In order to get leave for a full day, his brother forewarned, he would probably have to work overtime at the Teufelsberg. And he had, which was fine. In his absence, Douglas had been able to say his goodbyes to West Berlin, to load up on German chocolates and central European insect guides. He had written Uta a goodbye letter and posted it. He had packed. This was the last obligation.

He jangled up the master key to the shelter, inserted the key in the lock. The noise of the insertion struck against the silence of the office. The moth shifted its flutter. He clicked on the high beam of the flashlight, took his usual deep breath. The terror of bones, ticks, and disembodied heads had faded. Douglas had regained his professional composure. He propped the door open with the box and smelled, to his surprise, eau de rosewater and sherry.

The aroma gave him a start. Grams never came into the basement. Douglas whipped the flashlight beam around, found nothing out of the ordinary. In an empty room, he told himself, a problem is either visible or it is not. And Grams was not visible.

The second level reeked of rosewater and sherry too. Grams had obviously been down there. Maybe he'd checked on the work. Any good businessman would have. Maybe he had returned to find Douglas gone and had angrily stalked through his basements. With dismay, Douglas saw that the roaches had returned.

Rosewater and sherry persisted on the third level too, but otherwise, the space was as it had been: empty and unremarkable, no sign of rats.

He inserted the key into the next door. He nudged it open with his foot. Two bodies, one prone, one crouched, came up in his light.

2.

DOUGLAS WAS TOO STARTLED to speak. He focused the light on a face. Human breath echoed.

"Stuart?"

"Yeah. Christ, you scared me."

His brother's eyes blinked in the glare. He knelt at the foot of the stairs, perpendicular to a corpse. The body was covered by an afghan Douglas had seen thrown across the back of a couch in the offices above.

Stuart was dressed in clothing he had never seen before: a blue windbreaker, black trousers, and a lavender shirt. His hair had grown out from his head and turned black. The buzz had been replaced by a black mop. Douglas took one step down the incline of the stairs. His brother was wearing a wig.

Stuart lifted the blanket off the corpse. Patent leather shoes appeared. Douglas knew the identity of the corpse, and a question sprang out of him before he could stop it.

"Did you kill him, Stuart?"

His brother sneezed and wiped his nose on his shirtsleeve. Douglas trained the flashlight beam on the shoes, which he recognized as the last Grams had worn in his presence. The rosewater and sherry began to nauseate him.

"Did you?"

With these words, Stuart dropped the blanket. He put a hand over his eyes. "Mind getting that light out of my eyes?"

Douglas obliged.

"He wasn't killed here." Stuart glanced around the fourth level. "There's no blood. Someone hit him, then dragged him here."

"But *you* didn't?"

"No, Doug. But I know who did."

Douglas thought of things his brother had been telling him all summer long, about Turkey, about their father and the desert and the military. The implications of those words arrived at last from a great distance.

"What is this?"

Stuart rubbed an unshaven chin. Douglas made a closer inspection of him. For a moment, in the exaggeration of shadows created by the flashlight, he wondered if the man before him was indeed his brother. But no, he saw the impudence in the eyes, the weariness in the mouth, the arched-back shoulders concealing a mental slump. It was Stuart Glemnik, all right, and he'd been sitting in the dark with the corpse of a man he wasn't even supposed to know, sitting in the dark and waiting for something.

"What you have to understand, Doug, is that Styles never recovered mentally from the bombing episode in Beirut. That's how he could have made this mistake with you and Klek, that's the only goddamn explanation for any of this shit—"

"What the hell are you talking about?" Douglas braced himself against the wall to his right.

Stuart's hands were gloved, Douglas realized. His brother knelt over the body as if about to eat it. "I was in Turkey right before the bombing occurred," Stuart continued. "Styles came through Pirinclik on his way down to Lebanon. Back then, he was okay. Normal, I mean. But afterwards, when I ran into him again, I could see he was gone. Up here." Stuart tapped his head. "The Company kept him aboard, for security reasons, I guess. A couple of years ago, they shipped him here, and now he's a walking hallucination. He thinks his own people are out to destroy him. He thinks *I'm* his enemy now."

Douglas recalled the conversation with the diplomat, which he had filed away as nonsense, which he had not mentioned to Stuart for fear his brother would use it as another excuse to get him out of the country and away from Uta, and for the first time, bits of it made sense. "Are you saying that Styles killed this man?"

Stuart gave Douglas a long, meaningful stare, and Douglas nodded. That was fine. He required no further explanations. He was willing to leave the entire thing to whomever it might concern.

He reached behind him for the frame of the door. The best thing would be to turn around, to lock the shelter and go. His life seemed to make sense as long as he stayed away from the shelter. It might have been troubled, but it made sense. The minute he crossed its threshold, a whirlpool of disorder sucked him down. That had been the case from day one. Ticks, pigeons, rats, diplomats . . .

Before he could leave, Stuart bounded up the stairs and grabbed his arm. "You should have told me, Doug," he said in a low voice. "You should have told me that you ran into Styles. He has identified you as Jiri Klek, which sounds absurd, of course, but makes a tiny bit of sense, because of this mark on your face. Because of your 'housefly.' If you had told me a week ago, I would have been able to get you out of here easily."

"A powder burn," Douglas whispered, touching his cheek.

Stuart went on. "Styles thinks I have double-crossed him. He believes I have smuggled Jiri Klek into West Berlin and that the two of us are planning an act of terrorism with the help of the East German government. Right now, he's waiting for some last shred of proof to execute us both. Not even Styles is crazy enough to kill an innocent American citizen without evidence. But his patience must be wearing thin, or I'm wrong about our dead friend here. I figure Styles tried to get him to confess to some involvement, and when he didn't, the fucker wasted him. He means business."

Stuart took the flashlight and went back down the stairs to the body. He had some further business with it, evidently.

Douglas didn't care. At that moment, he only needed to know one thing.

"What happens now?"

From the bottom of the stairs, Stuart gestured.

"Sit for a second—"

Douglas had lost the will to run. He sat.

"We have to get out of West Berlin," Stuart began.

Douglas grasped it then. In keeping with tradition, his brother had not told him the whole story. The thing about Klek was preposterous, of course. Douglas must wrench the truth out of his brother.

"You're a traitor, aren't you?"

Stuart winced, as if the suggestion were too naive to be worthy of comment.

Douglas persisted in the thought. "That's why Styles is after you, and that's why he thinks I am a terrorist. Because you are a traitor. That's what I'm missing here. That's what you haven't said."

Stuart didn't answer, and Douglas didn' t require it. He didn't want details. His brother might explain, but the details were immaterial, because what mattered were consequences. There must be some quick and easy way to discern consequences. Jail. Death. Deportation. He was the brother of a man who had betrayed the American government. Didn't treason qualify as a capital offense? He grew afraid as he had never been in his life. The silence spoke around him. It gave advice, offered the possibility of madness. If he burrowed into one of the far shells of his own consciousness, the silence said, some inaccessible place where pigeons never fluttered and rats never gnawed, he would be safe. No one would find him.

With his gloved hands, Stuart took Grams by his ankles. The corpse crawled in his brother's hands; it crawled along the floor toward the open door of the fifth level of the air raid shelter, toward the well of dead pigeons. Douglas was in a fucking air raid shelter with a corpse in the year 1989. Grams rose for an instant. The blanket fell away as Stuart lifted him. The sherry drinker's sagging lips made a last pout. His eyes rolled in the beam of the flashlight. Then he collapsed back into darkness. Stuart had his own set of keys, courtesy of whom? He locked the door to the fifth level behind him.

Douglas had never seen a dead man before. What impressed him most was the immobility. A dead man has no more character than a dead cockroach, and he wondered whether there was much difference between the two species when you got right down to it. After all, the Russians called cockroaches Prussians, the Poles called them Swabians, and on the Rhine— hadn't Uta herself told him so?—they were "French."

"We have to *go*," his brother urged, peeling off his gloves. "There's a lot to say, I know, but we have a situation of great delicacy here, an equilibrium I am trying to maintain for your protection—"

Something on Douglas's face made him continue.

"Fine, Doug. Since you've brought it up. I am not a traitor. I mean, we could debate what that word actually means, because a traitor, abstractly, is someone who lives on both sides of a given but arbitrary line. But fine, we are not dealing in abstractions here, and for our purposes, let's say I am not a traitor. Because a traitor must, theoretically, betray his country, and I have worked in tandem with mine, for the most part, up till now. We're talking here about a perfectly reasonable little project, a minor test of the Cold War, gone haywire. It was a thing I could devote myself to, a project with an honest, decent application that would also advance my career and help me to do something for once, to square all the circles in my life, and at the same time, to take an action, to make up for what was lost. I met a man once in the desert, an East German—I told you about him once—and he was a good man, and he asked me for help, which I relayed back to my superiors, and they agreed I should help, for their own reasons. Which has now got me into trouble, because one of these superiors has, quite literally, gone mad."

Douglas gave a nod of sympathy. It was the only thing he knew to do.

"Now we have to go."

This finally prompted Douglas to speak. "We're not going in the same direction."

Stuart backed him up the stairs.

"Yes we are, for now."

"Get away!" Douglas heard himself shout.

Stuart hoisted him up. Douglas did not recall how he came to be sitting on imitation leather behind the driver's seat of a four-door Volvo. The driver pulled away from the curb. He saw fingers clasping a steering wheel and heard his brother's voice utter a single command: "Bornholmerstrasse."

3.

DOUGLAS'S CHEEK BURNED against the windowpane. His eyes escaped through glass to the outside, to the darkness and color of West Berlin, to passing police vans and Mercedes-Benz taxicabs, to gas stations and fruit stands, theaters and bookstores. They hurtled down Hardenbergstrasse, around the traffic circle at Ernst-Reuter-Platz, then north, in

the vague direction of the Wall. Lights in skyscrapers gleamed and shimmered.

His brother spoke to the driver, a woman with shiny black hair. She
replied in German. Douglas understood every word. It was Uta, wearing a
wig. Had they purchased these wigs together? At a party store? Why not
rubber noses too?

"Are we okay on gas?"

Uta nodded.

"And you've got his stuff?"

"Na klar."

Uta glanced back at him. Douglas hated her guts. The bitch had betrayed
him. She had known all along. She had seduced him, blinded him to his
brother's duplicity, by involving him in one of his own. She reached beneath the passenger seat. Something rustled. Stuart took a plastic shopping
bag from her and handed it back to him.

"Clothes, Doug," he said. "Put them on."

Douglas kept his left cheek pressed against the pane and began to unlace
his shoes. Stuart got impatient. He reached into the back seat and tugged
them off.

"We're in a hurry here," he said. "Unbutton your pants."

Douglas did so. Stuart tugged them down. The bag rustled. A pair of
damp gray trousers appeared. They were a size too small.

"You do the rest." He turned around in the seat and muttered, "He's
lost it."

Uta, of course. They were both in on it. She was Stuart's accomplice,
and— Suddenly, with a brilliant clarity, a dinner party came back to him, a
gathering in her apartment presided over by a fat old man in suspenders . . .

Douglas reached for the door handle to his left. It had been broken off.

"Too late," his brother said, watching him from the front seat. "If you
get out now, you'll be arrested for treason, at best. More likely, Styles will
put a bullet in your brain."

Uta asked why they were crossing at the Bornholmer Bridge. Stuart said
it was just a hunch. Bornholmer was the most obscure transit point in the
city, a crossing for diplomats and others with special passports. Styles could
not know they were in possession of such documents, which they owed to
East German counterintelligence, so he probably wouldn't look for them at
Bornholmer. He would expect them, if anything, to cross at Friedrichstrasse, with the tourists, or by highway at the western exit.

Stuart was silent then. Douglas shed the rest of his work clothes, buttoned down a dull orange work shirt, zipped up a lilac windbreaker. The
car pulled into traffic again, passed a sign for the neighborhood called Wed-

ding. Douglas had always thought it an odd but nice name for a place. Wedding, pronounced in German with *V,* like Vedding, though he preferred the English way.

He closed his eyes. In the darkness, he saw the disembodied head again. With its sleepy eyes and withered skin, the head had conveyed a warning. It had told him to flee, like a ghost in a fable, but he'd paid no attention.

"Listen up," his brother announced. "There are three separate divisions guarding the border. Customs, which we won't have to worry about. Soldiers, who will not be a problem unless we're very unlucky. And Stasi under Main Department Six of East German intelligence, the very same department that issued these documents of mine. They'll be dressed in military uniforms, but they are definitely our guys, so don't panic if you see a soldier coming at you. Understood?"

Uta honked her horn at a pedestrian. "What about the *Volkspolizei?*"

"The police have a guard station beyond the checkpoint. If we make it through the border okay, we should have no problem with them."

She sighed. "The second thing is this," Stuart continued. "Since Douglas doesn't have a passport yet—"

"Ach nein!"

"There wasn't time, Uta. Just listen. This'll work. When we get to the East German checkpoint, you hand the guard our passports. When he asks for the third one, say the man in the back is our cousin from Friedrichshain and he's ill and has to be rushed to the hospital. He was in West Berlin on a short visit for dinner, we'll say, and ate something bad. A bad piece of herring. And he has to be treated immediately. Our own stamps should tell the guy we're on his team. If not, I'll have to throw a screaming fit. Douglas, you lie down back there and put your hands on your belly. Like that. Yes. Groan, if you can."

Douglas refused to groan. Stuart turned back to Uta. "If the East Germans don't cooperate, be ready to floor it."

"But aren't they expecting us?"

Stuart continued to watch in the rearview. "No. The operation's too classified. If Mundung had told the *Grenzpolizei* about us, he would have given himself away. To his own people and to whoever else is watching. And he'd be in worse trouble than we are."

"So Mundung knows? He is expecting you?"

Stuart didn't answer immediately. Douglas knew his brother well enough to know this silence portended a lie.

"Of course he's expecting us."

"Wedding," another sign said, and Douglas thought of his six years ago—in retrospect, a relatively happy moment. Linda had worn a gauzy blue gown and an amethyst acanthus leaf around her throat. She had believed in the mystical properties of acanthus. For the first and last time, he had worn a tuxedo. Linda had not been a bad woman, after all, not compared to Uta. And their marriage, for all its ups and downs, had not been quite the hell he'd imagined.

Suddenly, the car slowed. They came to the Allied checkpoint, a box in front of a bridge. A metal fence blocked the right half of the road. Uta pointed at Douglas, made explanations, said she had accidentally left her cousin's passport in her aunt's apartment when he got sick. The guard didn't seem overly concerned. He took a peek at Douglas, flipped through their two passports one more time, returned them. He said something to a guard behind him, waited for an answer. Cold November air pierced the car. The guard waved them through.

They ascended a bridge. In the windowpane at his feet, Douglas saw an engineer's artfulness, curling metal skeins, the last vestiges of West Berlin vanishing behind him like a surf withdrawing from shore. Between the skeins were bars. He had counted twenty-three when a chunk of white concrete broke the pattern. It filled the windowpane. Light flooded the back seat. The car veered to the right and slowed. An urge to laugh swept through him. They touched the lip of the East.

4.

A DARK GREEN UNIFORM APPROACHED the window on the driver's side. A chin lowered into view. The face had a terrifying geography. Nose and chin obliterated every other characteristic.

The man spoke. He requested identity. Uta gave him the two passports. A pause followed. He fingered the two East German documents without opening them and waited. The driver spoke up. She said her cousin was sick. He was from Friedrichshain. He had been visiting for the evening, to a birthday dinner for a mutual aunt, and someone had brought spoiled herring. He was in a bad way, she explained, and must be taken immediately to the Charité Hospital. Nose and chin shifted to the back seat window. Eyes glimmered out of caverns. The man opened the back door.

"*Ausweis,*" he said. Douglas knew the word. It meant identification.

He froze in blank terror.

"*Ausweis!*" the man insisted.

Uta muttered something to the guard. Didn't he see her stamps? This man had a very high position in the personnel office at the Narva lightbulb kombinat. He was a ranking member of the party. There would be hell to pay if he didn't get to the hospital in time. The guard reached for Douglas. Uta's voice rose. She demanded to see the guard's superior officer. She told him he would end up at the Polish border if he wasn't careful. Douglas kicked at the man's hands. Abruptly, Nose and Chin backed away.

Douglas sat up. Stuart glanced back, his eyes widening behind their round, desperately intellectual lenses. No amount of prevarication would get him out of this one. Douglas looked around for the first time and saw where they were—in a kind of narrows, like the entrance to a parking garage. Buildings flanked them on either side. Floodlights illuminated the checkpoint, so everything had a marbled sheen to it. The walls shone white, the road gray, the uniforms dark green. The building to the left consisted mostly of windows, like a tollbooth, and Douglas glimpsed uniforms inside. To the right was a kind of barracks without windows, beyond it the top of a guard tower. At the barracks door were two guards, one with a weapon slung over his shoulder, another restraining a German shepherd. The ramifications were obvious. His brother was a Communist—his lover too. They were defecting without advance warning. These guards were unprepared and suspicious. Douglas saw his chance.

With a certainty he had not known in ages, he grabbed the bag containing his clothes, reached for the right door handle, and lifted it. The door loosened, Douglas kicked it open and sprang out.

Stuart whipped around in his seat and through the window gave Douglas a look of profound agony, a look that, despite everything, struck Douglas with sorrow. Douglas looked back at him and shook his head. He was not a Communist, would not defect, no matter what. Across the roof of the car glowered the guard, Nose and Chin. Douglas dropped the bag of clothes and raised his hands.

"*Ich bin* entomologist *aus den* United States of America!" he cried. "*Ich habe keinen Ausweis!*"

"*Was?*"

"En-to-mo-lo-gist!" Douglas repeated with a German inflection, enunciating at the top of his lungs. "Don't shoot!"

Nose and Chin backed away from the car and called for assistance in a heated voice. Guards in green parkas came running. Pistols leapt from holsters. Bodies surrounded the car. Douglas kept his hands up. Voices buzzed behind him. Nose and Chin made explanations, repeated what Douglas had said to the others—that he was an American of some kind.

A hard point jabbed Douglas in his lower back. It had to be a gun. He fell. At the same time, he heard Nose and Chin order Uta to remove the keys from the ignition, hand them out the window, and await further instructions.

Still in pain, Douglas got up on one knee and crouched at the right rear fender of the car. He saw the tip of a boot to his left. A guard reached for the door handle on Stuart's side.

The car roared into reverse. He flung himself backwards. Men scattered in all directions. In disbelief, Douglas saw Uta speeding away from the checkpoint in reverse. He stood up.

Uta put on the brakes, spun the car round, and faced west, at exactly the point where the bridge rose to a soft summit. They are leaving me behind, Douglas thought, they are going back. But the car idled where it had turned, twenty yards west of the checkpoint, taillights gleaming east, headlights shining west.

Seconds passed. Nothing happened. Behind the steering wheel, Uta waited. She waited, and Douglas prayed for them to come back and settle this matter in a logical fashion. After all, they *were* defecting. Surely there must be procedures for this sort of thing. The guards clicked the safeties off their guns. Uta was screaming at Stuart now. Douglas could just make out his name through the open windows. An officer in charge heard too. He yelled at the guards. *Nicht schiessen!* Don't shoot! There came a moment of extreme stasis, as if all of them—the guards, Douglas, Uta, and Stuart— were reconsidering. Reason must prevail. These were intelligent people. Neither side wanted bloodshed.

Uta floored it. Douglas smelled the burn of rubber. Goodbye, a voice inside him said. But she didn't head west. She wheeled around east and came back for him. The guards let loose a volley of fire, then burst apart in chaos. Douglas stayed close to the road, waiting for them to stop. The car didn't even slow. Hubcaps spun an inch from his knees. She reached the narrows between the buildings at a hundred kilometers an hour, her front fender scooping up a German shepherd. The dog shrieked. Fur, blood, and bone spewed before Douglas's eyes. The car lurched right and smashed through a road bar. One minute, taillights were there; the next, gone.

A gun butt slammed into Douglas's ribs, and he went down.

To his left lay the dog. Its head was crushed between its forepaws. Not another one, he thought, not another dead hound. They seemed to mark the path to his own final destruction. In that moment of confusion, he saw before him the puppy he had poisoned in the candy bay at Fleischmann's. "I would trade all my life for your death," he whispered to the corpse, but he knew that he didn't mean it. He didn't deserve to die for killing the puppy at the warehouse. He didn't want to die. The tongue of the dog before him drooled blood. A single unlidded white eye gazed at him.

Bootheels clacked around him. Guards made a ring. Machine guns glittered in a curtain of blinding white light. A gesture told Douglas that he was expected to lift himself off the ground, and he tried. Pain shot through his ribs, but he staggered to his feet. A guard caressed the destroyed head of the dog.

Douglas raised his hands again. "You saw," he said to them in trembling English, his voice booming around in the light-flooded space between walls. "I got out of the car of my own free will."

The ring of soldiers didn't move. Their bodies might as well have been stakes. Now Douglas remembered what his brother had said in the car. Some of these men were spies. Others were soldiers. He wondered who was who, and which might be more sympathetic to his case.

"This is a misunderstanding," he stammered out. "I am an expert in pest control."

The man who had been caressing the dog got to his feet and came through the circle of mute guards to Douglas. His rage made him demented. His words burst with spittle. Douglas tried not to blink. A man in an oak-clustered cap appeared from the barracks, shoved aside the other man, and issued a series of orders. Most of the guards broke into two groups: those who would take care of the prisoner and those who would deal with the dog. The rest resumed their duties at the checkpoint. *Ordentlich benehmen!* someone called out. Behave yourselves! Guns poked at Douglas, and he was forced to limp into the barracks. He bumped his head on the top of the door, which was too low. A gun butt shoved him over the threshold. He passed through an office made too warm and moist by a massive heater. He was led down a flight of stairs and into a cell even more humid.

"Entomologist?" a man behind him remarked in a German as blithe as Douglas had ever heard. "What's that mean?"

"Bugs," replied his colleague. "The study of bugs."

5.

DOUGLAS WAS SUMMONED to a table. Already, he saw a problem. The barracks, which housed as many dogs as men, was infested with fleas. The men scratched themselves and asked questions. They wanted to know why Douglas disguised himself, who he really was, who the man and the woman in the car really were. At first, Douglas thought the problem was body lice, but no, when a German shepherd reclining outside the cell rose to paw itself, he grasped the truth; the dog left a trail of "salt and pepper," a telltale mixture of flea eggs and dried blood, which fleas digested, crapped out, and fed to their young. His wallet was taken, its contents spilled on a table. One soldier ogled Linda's picture, which he'd kept against his own better judgment in the deepest crevasse of leather. The man ogled and scratched, and Douglas felt all his instincts as an exterminator come to the fore. In all likelihood, the problem could be solved with a few kilos of sorptive dust and a good bath for everyone involved.

Several phone calls were made. The interrogation faltered, started again, paused. They were trying to reach somebody at a ministry, but apparently the lines were jammed. Several times, a man mashed fingers into a phone, screamed incoherently into a brownish-white receiver, and hung up in disgust. He slapped his arm. Fleas made people bad-tempered. It was a fact. They pierced the skin. They induced allergies. Some of them were vectors of disease.

"I am an economic entomologist from the United States of America," Douglas reminded them again and again. "I demand to speak with a representative of the United States government. Surely one of you has the telephone number!"

"Name, rank, and serial number?" Nose and Chin would demand in reply, his voice metallic. The dog's owner sat nearby with an unpleasant air of expectation. Did he know that his beloved partner, man's best friend, had brought a plague of *Ctenocephalides canis* down upon him before dying? Would he be so distraught if he understood that?

Douglas was accused of all kinds of things he didn't understand, as well as animal torture. He was told he might well face charges of high treason, if he were found to be a spy, and that he would be shot if he did not cooperate. But somehow, and this had always been the case for him, the presence of the fleas, of a population of unleashed insects, possessed a far greater reality than the human beings and their threats.

After about an hour, he was taken from the holding cell up a flight of stairs, through two sets of doors, to a room that looked, at first, like a laboratory storage facility. It contained row after row of jars set upon shelves and conveyed less evidence of infestation, maybe because dogs were not allowed in there. A single yellow light steeped the jars in a urinous glow. Douglas was shown to a wooden bench set against a wall and told to sit. He didn't like the look of the place. It suggested crustations. An arachnid's web clouded the wall above the bench. He scanned the floor for dried blood, flea eggs, anything to tell him what he could expect. For a man who'd spent his life around insects, the idea of becoming infested himself with some virulent East German flea was chilling.

An officer gave strict orders—*Ordentlich benehmen*. Behave yourselves—one more time, and left. Of the three remaining guards, two were familiar: the man who was upset about the German shepherd, as well as the venerable Nose and Chin. Both were most likely Stasi, Douglas thought. A third had the uncertain eyes of a rookie soldier. The wedge of blond hair on his upper lip weighed down his head. The soldier scratched at his armpit. Poor soul. Douglas wondered if these men had wives and children. The question struck him as profoundly relevant.

"You have a dire flea problem," he ventured. *"Ein Flohkatastrophe."*

"Mund zu! Das war mein Hund!" the offended man hissed. *"Ich habe es selber dressiert! Scheiss-Amerikaner! Selber gefüttert!"*

"It was my dog," Douglas believed the man was saying. "I trained it myself, fed it myself!" Yes, and look what it got you, he wanted to fling back, a case of the itch and an allergy and maybe worse. But he refrained.

A knock came at the door. Cups of hot coffee were ushered in. Douglas received nothing. The door was closed, and a viciousness rippled through the room. The rookie looked away. He scratched again. Nose and Chin tipped his head toward the dog owner, who came forward and spat on the ground. He gazed down at Douglas, one hand gnawing at his leg, and Douglas wondered if they had flea shampoo in East Germany. Maybe they didn't. Maybe technology had not given the countries behind the Iron Curtain adequate protection against vermin. Of course, that was still no excuse for the situation in the barracks. The real problem lay with that enormous heater in the front room, which created an accommodating temperature, and all those dogs. The entire building was a spa for Siphonaptera.

Then things got worse. The dog owner, whose mutton chops must have been crawling, took off his cap, and with a flick of his hand, flung hot coffee in Douglas's face.

It burned, and he cried out. The rookie continued to scratch, and the other two communicated the result of this experiment to one another without words. They seemed pleased. Douglas knew this kind of thing was forbidden—*Ordentlich benehmen!* Behave yourselves!—and he knew, in the very same moment, that rules made in places like Geneva didn't necessarily apply on cold autumn nights in East Berlin. He also knew that a man who flung coffee into another man's face for no reason at all could easily commit murder.

Coffee trickled down his chin. Against his will, tears burped out. Douglas did not want tears. They would be more precious than blood to his tormentors. But it was too late. The dog owner saw it and stuck a thumb into it, into the soft spot beneath his left eye, as if he meant to gouge out the eyeball. His nail dug into Douglas's skin.

"My dog," he growled. Douglas saw things wriggling in his facial hair. The man would infest him.

In the meantime, the rookie had come to attention. He stood behind one of the shelves of jars, and Douglas saw an eye, white and wide, bulging through the refraction of the glass. The uniforms of the three men stank. Outdoors, Douglas hadn't noticed it, but in the last few minutes, as the four of them shared the small room, he became aware of a meat-flavored stench. Sweat had poured and dried in these uniforms dozens of times since the last cleaning. The odor and the fleas tortured his senses worse than any fingernail. Perhaps cleanliness was not next to godliness in the Communist state; or maybe it was a German thing. West Berliners did not wash very often either. The smell nauseated him, and he began to fear the worst—that he would vomit the next time anyone accosted him. And if he vomited, they would find a way to kill him. He was certain of it. The man removed his fingernail. Douglas felt a trickle of warm liquid down his cheek.

Something else began to happen. As the rookie watched, the two torturers positioned themselves on either side of Douglas on the bench. He saw their bodies from the corners of his eyes but pretended to ignore them. He cast a glance at the rookie, who watched with the forced enthusiasm of a soldier who knows the chief virtue of a young recruit is camaraderie. The pressure came gradually, applied to his temples by two thumbs on opposite sides of his head. A shrill note sounded in his ears. Blackness seeped from the sides of his face. It swelled across his brain, like a trash bag full of hot water. Oh Jesus, he heard himself say aloud. This is it. The pressure eased. The second time, he did not realize the thumbs were back until he had almost fainted. A copper taste hit his mouth. Blood slammed through his temples. The room spun loose. The jars whirled.

Before he could stop it, a gout of hot chocolate, ham, and stomach acid burst from his lips onto the floor. The pain at his temple, the compounded reek of vomit and body odor, the fleas, the strange winking jars—it had all been too much. The men cursed and jumped back. One slapped Douglas on the back of the head. The rookie receded farther into the shadows beyond the jars, his facial expressions unreadable.

Just in time, relief came. A hand rapped on the door three times, then three times more, and the dog owner answered it. The farther away this man stood, the better Douglas felt. Words were passed through a crack in the door. With a nervous glance, the dog owner left the room.

Nose and Chin sidestepped the brownish-pink pool of vomit, gazed down into it as if to catch a glimpse of his reflection. He flicked a finger at the rookie to make sanitation detail. The latter scuttled from his repose like a surprised cockroach, made a delicate, somehow poignant leap over the puddle, and also left the room. Douglas stayed in convulsion mode, head bent forward, mouth open. Strings of saliva connected him to the floor. The terror of waiting seared his stomach. He vomited again.

The rookie returned, knelt with gray toilet paper and cleaned up the mess. The dog owner still hadn't come back when another knock sounded on the door. This time, Nose and Chin answered. He listened, just as the dog owner had. His eyes squinted. He seemed to be hearing something un-palatable. Douglas sent up a prayer of gratitude. The rookie was told to watch Douglas and keep his mouth shut. The bastard left.

The rookie seemed relieved. He wiped his own chin with a scrap of the toilet paper, then tugged a wet cloth from his coat pocket and wiped the vomit and coffee from Douglas's mouth. For an instant, Douglas recoiled, but the rookie, who could not have been more than twenty, patted him on the back, saying he should, it sounded like, relax. *Ausruhen.*

Douglas lost track of time. For long stretches, nothing happened. Then a knock would come at the door, the rookie would answer, more words would fly, the door would close again. Hours could have passed between these conversations. At some point, Nose and Chin returned, but a com-motion of some kind in the next room sent him away again. This was the last thing Douglas remembered for a time. Consciousness slipped away from him, like another guard off to destiny.

He jerked up in his chair, and his first thought was: Fleas are feeding on me. His eyes took a moment to readjust to the yellow drizzle of the light. The jars glinted at him. Each had a single pissy eye. Douglas turned to ask the rookie for another bit of toilet paper and discovered, without trusting his senses for an instant, that the man had gone. The room, but for him, was empty. Douglas's temples hurt. He massaged them. Someone must be ob-serving him through a secret panel.

He counted half an hour, then made up his mind to stand. What could it hurt? The effort nearly paralyzed him. He doubled over and managed to stop another convulsion.

The door snicked open a crack. Douglas dropped back onto the bench. He blacked out for an instant. When he came to, he was still alone.

"Hello!" he called out.

No one came. Outside, at a distance, came an indistinct noise, a com-motion. Something had happened. Something had drawn the guards away from him, and it must be serious. It began to look as if a draft of wind had blown open the door, which meant—he guessed with a wildness closer to hunger than curiosity—it must be unlocked. Must be. He got off the bench, tiptoed across the room to the crack and peeked outside. The adjacent room had become an impromptu kennel, full of German shepherds. Tearing at themselves with maddened claws, the dogs hardly noticed as he peeked around the corner. Now he saw the fleas. They made a kind of haze around the animals. My God, did no one know? Certain fleas carried bubonic plague.

Beyond the dogs, in an adjacent room, a radio droned folk music. He made a snap decision. As long as the dogs were distracted by minute attackers, they might not care if he sauntered through, particularly if his scent, thanks to the open door, had become familiar. He took a step forward, ready to leap back into safety if they objected. But the dogs plunged deeper into their own bitter warfare and left him alone. They whined in agony. He pitied them, but thanked their tormentors.

He entered a dark corridor. Down it, to his right, he heard movement; behind a closed door, someone flipped through a newspaper. A knee bumped against a wall, a toilet rim creaked. In the other direction, the radio continued to play. And right ahead of him, directly across the corridor, lay another door, slightly ajar.

He found himself in a familiar room, one he'd seen on his way through the barracks. A complicated electronic device, some kind of computer attached to a radio dispatch, dominated one end of it; the massive heater, the real villain in the flea invasion, the other end. A microphone sat on the desk beside the dispatch, but the chair at the desk was unoccupied. A cup of steaming liquid rested against the mike. The man in the toilet had been sitting in that chair until moments before, Douglas suspected, and would be returning at any moment. He cocked his ear back toward the corridor, listening for a flush. The room was dimly lit. He made out metal detectors, stacked in a corner to his immediate left. A few old rifles slumbered in a gun rack above them. Here and there, beneath desks, were dog beds. And then, right in front of him, he saw the door.

A guard stood in it, gazing out into the night, kneading his itchy buttocks with long fingers. Douglas retreated into the corridor. He had maybe ten seconds to decide, then a flush from the john decided for him. Pants were being pulled up. Douglas reentered the room. The guard at the door continued to pry at his nether fleas as he watched whatever was happening at the checkpoint. God knew what it was. Some new political development, a troop movement maybe. The bathroom door slammed in the corridor. Douglas took a gun off the rack.

He walked across the room on tiptoe. He counted three and lifted the butt of the gun to strike. And then the fleas struck. He felt them all over his body, sucking, piercing, scrambling. They had been waiting for the perfect moment.

The guard wheeled around. Douglas was caught up in a dance of Saint Vitus, and as he danced, he saw it was the rookie, watching him in terrified fascination. Their eyes locked for a single moment of mutual recognition. The gun dropped from Douglas's fingers, hit the floor, and exploded with a burst of fire. The rookie tumbled with a groan, grabbing at his feet.

Whirling in agony, Douglas saw another man, the crapper, enter the room and clutch at his holster.

"*Hilfe!*" the rookie cried.

Douglas made his move. Overcoming the horrific sensation of animal presence on his body, he leapt over the rookie and into the night. He sprinted west, his burning legs hurling him forward. Tears flooded his eyes. A clap came. He thought it must be a shot. He screamed out: "*Nicht schiessen!*" Don't shoot! But the words got all tangled in his throat. His arms were pumping. He was heading up the rise of the Bornholmer Bridge toward freedom, toward West Berlin. Fleas were swarming. They surged upward toward his mouth.

He tripped, and now it was all he could do to get the things off him. He didn't care about freedom anymore. Men were shouting. Boots were stomping. Douglas dragged himelf across the concrete. He wiped his eyes.

As they cleared, he realized he was staring up at the blinking confusion of a middle-aged woman. He grabbed a leg and begged for mercy. He pleaded for his life in gouts of English and German. *Bitte*, please, *bitte, bitte!* The fleas! They're all over me! A hand steadied him. The fit dwindled. He recognized the surroundings. He lay on his side at the approximate summit of the Bornholmer Bridge, a few dozen yards west of the East Berlin checkpoint. He had come that far before stumbling.

Above him, still staring down, the double-chinned woman in a mauve scarf, lilac-blue jacket, and pajamas was shaking her head. She frowned. People had been waiting all night, she told him. He refused to let go of her leg, so she pried his fingers off, one by one, and helped him up. Something *had* happened. They descended the western slope of the bridge, away from the summit toward West Berlin. She asked him if he'd been drinking. He told her he had sipped a whiskey earlier in the evening, but that was all. He asked her if it was all right to go home, and she asked him where that would be. "Dallas, Texas," he replied. He wanted her to take him by the hand and lead him there, but she said, those guards will give you a hard time when you go back tonight. They may not let you through, an awful drunk like you. She pointed back east. Behind them, the bridge swarmed with people; not guards, but people, like the woman. Douglas peered at them.

He blurted out: "What is this?"

"Ach," the woman replied, breaking into the English of a disappointed high school teacher. "If you were sober, you'd know. The Wall has opened. We're making history."

BOOK II

A MEANINGLESS CONFIGURATION

CHAPTER EIGHT

1.

NESTER TOOK ONE OF DOUGLAS'S ELBOWS in his hand and tried to lift him off the curb, but the man would not budge. He was crouched, feet in the gutter, arms clasping knees. The left eye puffed out. Beneath it, blood dribbled from a cut. Nester let go of the elbow. When he did, Douglas unclasped his arms and began to scratch his groin and ribs.

A police van slowed. Nester flashed military identification and told the cops his buddy had drunk too many bottles of *Weizenbier*. The men tipped their caps. The van drove on.

Douglas licked his lips, touched the torn spot beneath his left eye. Nester pleaded with him to rise, and after a moment of indecisive defiance, he did. Pain screwed up his face.

"I'm infested," came again the constant refrain of his tale. "The northern rat flea, I'm beginning to think."

His elbows were skinned, Nester saw. He had been badly handled, tortured, he claimed, by East German *Grenzpolizei*.

More important, Douglas confirmed that his brother had defected. Stuart Glemnik had run to the East. Nester was not surprised. Perhaps he had always known Glemnik would do something of the sort. He was a misfit, after all, one of life's prodigals and prey to whatever vulture happened to be swooping. But if he'd really known, Nester wondered, if he'd seen this coming, then why had he revealed so much of himself to Stuart? Why had he confided in Glemnik about his UFO job at the Pentagon? Why had he been weak, when for years he had been so strong?

Douglas sat back down on the curb.

These mistakes galled Nester, but he must accept them now and try to make sense of what he knew. He sat down on the curb too, and began to cull through the events of the last few hours, analyzing them as he might the troop strength of the East German Interior Ministry or the political future of a Polish apparatchik.

The strangeness of the evening had begun with the phone conversation between the two East Germans, so Nester started there. At first, during his interrogation by Styles, Nester had thought the conversation itself important. But this was a mistake. Tunt's lie was the important thing. Tunt's lie led him, oddly, to the truth. Why had the corporal lied?

Because the point of the conversation had not been to eavesdrop on a couple of low-level East Berlin bureaucrats. In all probability, that conversation had been fabricated. The point was to lure Nester into the Box. He was certain of it. The corporal's lie over the phone about the conversation—that it had never existed—was his second of the evening. The first had been the one summoning Nester to the scene of the crime.

Nester nodded. That's right, he thought. The computer exploded, and I was there. Mission accomplished, as far as Tunt was concerned. Two hard conclusions could be drawn from this. Whatever was going on, Tunt was involved. And, more to the point, he had been unafraid to tell a blatant lie to a superior officer, so he had some kind of formidable backing.

Fine, Nester concluded, and he set these two facts aside for the moment.

Next came the fire. He did not believe for a moment that Jiri Klek or any other terrorist had planted explosives in the computer in order to send a message or make a point. The target had been limited and very specific; the programmer's death was probably accidental. This seemed an obvious point to Nester. Why, then, hadn't Styles raised it? Why hadn't he wanted to know anything about Terminal Sixteen? Why hadn't the owl asked him a single question about the detonated computer or the man it had killed?

Nester could draw but one conclusion here. Styles hadn't asked about the computer because he didn't require the information. He knew everything already. He knew what was on the hard drive of Sixteen, who had bombed it, and why. That meant a near miracle had been achieved. It meant the investigation into the bombing, which began less than an hour before Nester's conversation with Styles, had been so thorough, so exhaustive in its findings, that the testimony of an eyewitness—*the* eyewitness, Nester—had become irrelevant.

That, of course, was absurd. No bureaucracy operated so fast, certainly not the United States Army. Depositions would have to be taken, files sifted, stories checked. No, reflected Nester, if Styles knew what had happened by the time of their conversation, then his knowledge was proprietary. It came from a personal source.

Nester set this aside too for the moment. He turned to Douglas's account of Stuart's defection.

The details had been jumbled. Elements of the story did not cohere. But Nester had debriefed enough people over the years to piece together a loose version of the truth.

Just before crossing the border, according to Douglas, Stuart had tried to explain himself. He was not a traitor, he'd said. Rather, he'd embarked on a mission sponsored by his own government, and Douglas had the impression the mission involved at least one other American. It also involved Uta Silk, Stuart's Communist girlfriend, and her German uncle, a man whose name Douglas couldn't remember.

Nester placed a mental bracket around these facts.

According to Douglas, Stuart had panicked. Douglas could not recall all his brother had said, but he knew that the panic had been caused by one of the other people involved in the mission. This other person had suddenly become paranoid, according to Stuart. He had become paranoid after stumbling across a man who had nearly killed him a few years before.

That American was Carlton Styles. Nester shook his head. He had trouble digesting this piece of information. Stuart maintained that Styles and he were partners in the mission? Douglas nodded. Had Stuart explained the nature of the mission? Douglas said that he had not. Nester scratched his wrist. Douglas continued.

A week ago, this man Styles had accosted him in a cafe. Nester interrupted. Styles had *accosted* him? He was absolutely sure the man had been Styles? Yes, Douglas said, it had happened at a cafe not far from the Amerika Haus. Uta's German uncle had found Douglas a job as an exterminator in the basement of that cafe, and Styles had *accosted* him there. That was the only word for it. In the basement? No. Douglas slapped a hand on the curb. In the cafe itself. Styles had asked him about the mark on his face. He had called Douglas a liar.

As Douglas talked, Nester began to whittle out a theory. Styles and Stuart had been working together on a covert mission. There had been a falling out. Styles had become dangerous. Stuart fled. He took Uta and Douglas along in order to protect them from his former colleague, who, according to Stuart, believed Douglas and Klek were the same person. And why?

Nester glanced at the exterminator's black mark and shook his head in horrified disbelief. He wanted to buy the story. It would explain so much. It would certainly explain why Styles had been more interested in Jiri Klek than in the computer. It would allow him to believe in Stuart's innocence.

Logic told him it was a lie. Not even Douglas believed it, Nester could tell. True to form, Stuart had constructed a tale exonerating himself from any responsibility. In this tale, he had been serving his country, and Styles had broken faith. Styles was responsible for the defection. Stuart had defected to protect his loved ones from the murderous rage of a spook run amok.

Perhaps it was a lie with noble intentions. Maybe Stuart had sought to protect his brother. One way or another, he was a traitor. Styles had discovered him, and Stuart had run. This didn't cover everything, Nester knew. It did not quite account for the encounter between Douglas and Styles in the cafe. But it made a very simple sense, and Nester placed the highest value on simplicity, always had.

The hard drive in Terminal Sixteen must have contained an incriminating piece of evidence. Stuart had no doubt destroyed it to cover his tracks, and in the process, had killed a man. Nester could now answer an earlier question. Styles had not asked about Sixteen because he knew unequivocally that Stuart had done it.

Which brought Nester to Tunt, and the conversation between the two East Germans, the unbelievably well-timed conversation that had carried him right to the very brink of the disaster. He didn't know quite what to make of it. On the one hand, he could see why Styles might suspect him of collaborating with Glemnik. They had been best friends. He could see why his presence in the Box at that very moment further suggested his guilt. But Nester had been *lured,* quite clearly; he had been set up. That's what he could not understand. If he was a suspect, why would anyone *need* to set him up?

He scratched his wrist. Suddenly, he found a glaring implausibility in Douglas's story.

"You said you were on the East German side of the border, right?"

"That's right."

"So how did you get back here?"

Douglas pointed back east.

"See for yourself, man. They're walking right through."

2.

AT THE BORNHOLMER BRIDGE, several pedestrians milled about. Nester tapped one of them gently on the back and asked what had happened. The man told him he didn't know exactly, but a few hours ago, on television, he had heard that the border was open, so he grabbed a couple of friends on a lark and came to Bornholmer. And now he was here.

"Here?" Nester asked. "As opposed to where?"

"As opposed to there." The man pointed eastward across the bridge, toward East Berlin. "*Wahnsinn, nicht?*"

He was going to see a West Berlin girl who had come to visit him in 1975. Her name was Issie Martin, and she'd claimed to be a famous rock star in the West. Had Nester ever heard of her?

Nester approached a woman with a child wrapped around her legs. The child gazed with dark, excited eyes at his face. Nester asked her what she was doing there, and the woman answered just as the man had. She had been sitting home when her ex-husband called and told her to go next door, to the neighbor, and look at the television. She had not believed the news, but had been taken with a sudden, overwhelming urge to come to the bridge nearby and see for herself. She woke her daughter, already fast asleep, and rushed through the dark streets, where she saw neighbors, like herself, who had heard what she heard. She started to cry.

At the base of the bridge were others, standing with a West Berlin camera crew in a circle of light. They talked into a microphone, telling the same kinds of stories.

"No," Nester murmured to himself, still not believing, too skeptical after all these years to buy it. "Can't be. Cannot be." There was the Wall, for God's sake, and guns and police, who had shot more than a thousand people for doing what these people had just done.

He joined Douglas at a Litfass column a few meters away from the base of the bridge. "I told you," the exterminator said. "I wasn't lying."

The bridge, a marginal checkpoint used by diplomats and pedestrians, was getting crowded. Beneath a line of border lights, people walked from East to West. Nester saw their legs first, thin black shadows obscuring the gray of asphalt. Around them, like stylized cobwebs, hung spans of the bridge. The sky glittered bright and high. They were coming by the hundreds.

Nester could hear them, their padding, clicking, clomping, shuffling. At the western end of the bridge, away from the crowd, police vans had parked, and in them sat the dim shapes of men in beige uniform. Beyond the vans were taxis, drivers huddled in one cab and passing around a cigarette.

The footsteps touched his ears from a distance, like signals reaching through static. They came closer. He could sort out footwear—the softness of tennis shoes, an intimate quality, as of slippers coming down a hallway at midnight, the clomp of heavy winter boots, the uncertain pattering of children.

"This can't be." His own words sounded trite in his ears. He had expected war.

Faces appeared. They emerged from the darkness between the lights. Amazement touched them—concrete amazement, a mixture of grief, astonishment, and extreme joy. It looked to him like a state of religious ecstasy. The oldest of the people crossing the bridge had waited nearly three decades for this moment. He heard them talking. They were whispering their own disbelief. It was 1989.

Twenty-eight years struck dead in the blink of an eye, he thought, twenty-eight years, damn near all my life; twenty-eight years since that day in 1961, in an August hot as the griddle, when he'd stretched out on the floor of his parents' house at Fort Sam in San Antonio, in a den ruffled by fan breeze, sucking on a Popsicle and watching Edward R. Murrow on their new Zenith. His dad had been in Asia, but his mother had been right beside him, leaning forward with bright eyes, shaking her head and saying, "This'll mean another war for sure," as the East German Reds sealed their own people within a wall. Seven years old, he had been.

He covered his eyes. "Lord have mercy," he said.

"Mein Gott," rustled voices in the darkness.

Nester believed history could not be experienced as one experiences most things. It could not be seen, felt, touched, or tasted. Neither could it be entered as one enters a marriage or endured as one does a sickness or abandoned as one does a house. Nevertheless, all his life, against his own best convictions, he had wanted history to be closer to him, to feel more like a marriage, a sickness, or a house, or like a destiny, a flowing river of light, ending in a delta of goodness. If it could not be touched, Nester decided, it should at least be visible from afar. Of course, the older he became, the less he was able to sustain such a naive yearning; but it had never really left him, not in all these years of disappointment.

Now a sensation of joy came over him, deeper than any he had ever known. What, he asked himself, was this line of people coming out of the East if not that very river of his imagination, if not history itself? Or was it something greater, more profound, that would later be reduced to history? What *was* it?

Douglas tapped him on the arm. "Excuse me, Nester, but is this what I think it is? Is it possible that my brother fucked up this badly?"

Nester didn't know how to answer the question, but he remembered something Stuart had once said, a quote concocted out of his experiences in southeastern Turkey and passed off as a line from his favorite novel, *The Man Without Qualities,* an obscure but great Austrian work. "We all have a second home," Stuart had babbled through beer breath, "where everything we say and do is innocent."

Nester had not understood the meaning of those words until tonight; he still did not know exactly what they meant to Stuart Glemnik. But he grasped what they might mean for a mass of people. As he watched the East Berliners cross the bridge in the bright coldness of the night, as he thought back on the associations the Wall had held for him through the years, he perceived a spell being cast. He and every other man, woman, and child in Berlin were about to enter an unexpected realm where nothing made sense as it had in the past, where all things blazed with the energy of transformation, where magic and divinity and miracle became, for a brief moment, the commonplace facts of existence, and the blandness of ordinary life, with all its mistakes and desolations, passed away. They were about to enter their second home, which they had known of since childhood and in which they had never actually believed, and for the duration of their stay, Nester understood, they would all be perfected creatures. They would be, in some profound way, innocent.

"Your brother has done something terrible," he answered, "but how terrible remains to be seen. I don't know what this means, Douglas. I don't know what a defection means in light of this thing we're both seeing. Does it mean the defection is null and void? I don't know. This changes everything."

Douglas cleared his throat. "Stuart said Styles would kill me if he caught me. Do you believe that?"

Nester's awe gave way to anxiety.

"Not really," he replied with confidence. But he left it at that. He did not want to be the one to break the news to Douglas, if he did not know already, that his brother was nothing but a traitor. That was not Nester's job, thank God.

He forced himself to concentrate on the business at hand. They must first go to Stuart's apartment. There, Nester might find a few clues, anything to support his theory that Stuart had been involved in a conspiracy against his own government. It was too late to hand Stuart over to Coogan, of course. The defection had taken care of that. But Nester could hand over Douglas, and if he did, he would need evidence to refute Stuart's account of himself, as filtered through Douglas; he would need something to demonstrate to Coogan that Stuart had acted alone. Nester's career, and maybe even his life, depended on it. If Coogan believed him, then he might be vindicated. If not, he was sunk. They found a cab.

Nester asked to hear the most important elements of the story again—Styles, the meeting in the cafe, Uta, the crossing. In the front seat, the taxi driver yelled into his shortwave radio that the Wall was open, and the dispatcher yelled back that he was drunk or lying and should get off the fucking radio.

The cab pulled up in front of Stuart's apartment. The door to the building was open. An army jeep had parked on the grass.

Someone came out of the apartment. It was the man himself, Styles, with a pair of MPs. Douglas ducked down in the seat. Right then and there, Nester wanted to confront him with what he believed; he wanted to tell Styles that he had been right, Stuart had been a mole. But it wasn't time yet. He must go to Coogan first. Even if his superior officer hated him, he was still a soldier, and as a soldier, he would be Nester's best defense against the owl.

First, they would go to Waltraud's. For the moment, her place would be safer than his apartment, which would be watched and probably bugged. Their relationship was no secret. Every soldier at field station had to report his or her romantic affiliations. But Waltraud had listed her address and phone number at the Narkose. Very few people knew her private address, a precaution she had taken after splitting up with her ex-husband, who had announced his violent intentions in the wake of the divorce. At the very least, it would take the owl some time to find out about her place, and that might be all the time Nester needed to think through his next move.

The cab pulled away from the curb. After a while, he peered back into the darkness of the street, checking for pursuit. No one had followed.

Doubts nagged at him. One could play devil's advocate and say that Styles's supposed confusion of Klek with Gleaming was not entirely ludicrous. Rumors had fixed the terrorist on the outskirts of East Berlin in a dacha provided by the Central Committee, but they had remained rumors. Maybe Styles knew different. Maybe he had evidence.

Still, of all people, Douglas Gleaming? How could he possibly be the man? That notion seemed a piece of the night's sorcery, which turned everything upside down, the upright man into the fugitive, the entomologist into the terrorist, the philosopher into the traitor.

"I am supposed to be on a plane to Dallas tomorrow morning," Douglas remarked.

Nester did some calculating. It was eleven o'clock on the nose and moving toward midnight. The Wall had opened an hour and a half ago, at approximately nine-twenty. By his best estimate, Stuart Glemnik had crossed the Bornholmer Bridge three and a half hours before that, at six o'clock, which meant that, at the time he crossed, he could not have known the Wall would open. He had defected three and a half hours before defection became obsolete, the poor dumb bastard. A last, obvious question arose. Five hours had passed since then. Where was Stuart now?

Waltraud's apartment lay a few blocks down from the Rathaus in old

town Spandau, one floor above a restaurant that served Yugoslavian special-
ties. The noise from the restaurant and the smell of grilled meat followed
them up three flights to her door. Nester knocked twice. She was wrapped
in a yellow terry cloth robe. As soon as she saw Douglas, the gleam in her
eyes dimmed. The wrinkles around her eyes conveyed a sudden mistrust.

Nester led Douglas to the couch and asked Waltraud to make a pot of
chamomile tea. She turned on the electric stove, filled the teapot, then ran
to the bedroom to dress. Nester cast a hurried glance around the room,
more from astonishment than suspicion. Things were as usual. Her burnt-
sienna carpet rested comfortably at the foot of burnt-orange walls. Above
the liquor cabinet hung the likeness of a rifle-toting John Wayne, a
bleached cow skull, and a photograph of the cabin where Muddy Waters
was born, his contribution. Somehow, he expected an alteration in the very
fabric of things; but this room held its ground.

By the time Waltraud returned in a sweater and jeans, Douglas's teeth
were chattering. He continued to scratch himself for fleas, though Nester
had not yet seen one.

"Wait," she said. She brought a bottle of Finnish vodka and a couple of
iced shot glasses to a square-topped table in front of the couch. "This is for
me and him," she told Nester. "He obviously needs it, and I believe I will."

She poured two shots of vodka and lit a cigarette. This done, she announced her readiness.

He told her about the Wall. Blood rushed to her cheeks. "Dagmar!"

Yes, he agreed, there was a chance her cousin Dagmar would cross
tonight, if they continued to let people through. He explained the situation
as best he could. As he did, she gained control of her emotions and hastened
to apologize. "I'm sorry. I can't help it. I must do something."

Douglas watched them, exhaustion, annoyance, and sorrow darkening
his face. The cut beneath his eye had started to scab over.

Waltraud wiped her eyes, lit another cigarette. "Do you mind? I really
must call Trude."

Nester waved her toward the phone. She dialed, relayed the news, and
ordered her cook to haul every last knuckle, nackensteak, and sausage out of
the freezer and prepare as many pots of goulash as she could; four emergency kegs of Warsteiner could be found beneath a tarp in the basement. In
ten minutes, the Narkose's new course had been set. Waltraud hung up.

The exterminator coughed, gave Nester an apologetic look, as if he
hated to spoil the good mood.

"May I lie down please?"

Waltraud showed him the way to her bedroom. As soon as he had gone, she said, "I've always had a soft spot for this *Mensch,* you know. He's Ichabod Crane. Always chased by the pumpkin."

Nester kissed her on the lips and ran a finger down the bumpy ridge of her nose. She settled into his arms to listen.

3.

"THAT'S ABOUT IT," he said.

An hour had elapsed. Her shot glass was half empty. She had re-filled it twice with vodka and was working on her third.

"I've decided to take him to Major Coogan." Nester stood in the door of the kitchen with a steaming teakettle in one hand.

"Why?" She downed the last of the vodka in her glass.

"I've gone over and over it in my mind, and it seems to me the best bet is just to turn him over to Coogan, and let the army evaluate his testimony." He gestured with the teakettle. "In the end, it's a simple enough case. Unless I am very much mistaken, everyone will agree that Stuart lied to his brother, that he is simply a mole who got caught. I will be vindicated, quietly of course, and the army will owe me one."

She pointed at him with the empty shot glass. "*Um Gotteswillen,* I'm surprised at you!"

He waved her words away in irritation. But she only talked louder. "You are not facing the reality, my love. Major Coogan must produce something to save his own ass. He doesn't have Stuart, so that something is you. No civilian bug killer will placate him. Coogan hates you already, and this will give him an excuse to exercise the hate. You didn't recognize the traitor, he will say. You, the great wise man of East Germany. You, who were supposed to be the smartest man on the damned Teufelsberg."

She's right, Nester thought. He might not have betrayed his country, but he *had* failed to detect an act of probable treason when it lay right beneath his nose. His own reputation, his pride, had blinded him and made him a fool; and it had allowed a man with God knew how many state secrets to flee across a heavily watched border, compromising the United States government and damaging the credibility of the United States Army. All of it happened, he told himself with mounting rage, on my watch.

He poured hot water onto a chamomile tea bag, placed the teakettle back on the burner, and switched off the heat. Waltraud was a tough woman. Her husband had beaten her. She had almost gone bankrupt a couple of times. People like her might not be decorous, but they knew how to survive. All their hope and glory hung on survival. Besides that, he had often wondered about Waltraud's institutional contacts. Stuart's girlfriend Uta had accused her to her face of being West German intelligence, and once or twice the thought had crossed Nester's mind too, though he had never uttered it.

In a chastened voice, he said, "What would you have me do, Waltraud?"

She pointed at the door to her bedroom. "Keep him as a bargaining chip. Keep him till you know Coogan's intentions."

Nester winced. "Coogan's an ambitious officer with a ticket to Leavenworth in his pocket. He has a reputation to protect. I know his intentions. He'll do everything in his power to vindicate me, because it's in his best interest."

This time, she waved the dismissive hand. "People are full of surprises. You, for instance . . . "

"It was not my fault, Waltraud."

"*Nein, nein, gar nicht . . .*"

A lump formed in his throat. His career was finished. That's what he feared. All his adult life he had dreamed of serving as a high-ranking officer in the United States Army, just as his father had. He might not fit the job, peg to hole, but he had made his way, earned his keep and well beyond. The military had been his home, and now he was accused of betraying it. Tomorrow morning, if he didn't produce Stuart Glemnik—and he couldn't— he would be charged with espionage. Douglas Gleaming, a civilian with a fishy story and a vanished brother, would not help him. Only Coogan could do that. Only Coogan, who hated his guts, could defend his honor.

In a much lowered voice, leaning forward on the couch, he tried to apologize. "You have no idea how hard this is for me, Waltraud. No idea."

She whistled. "Nester, my love, I think you are a fine man with fine feelings, but it's time to face facts. Use your head. Without Stuart Glemnik, it's either you or Coogan or Styles. Do you think I am telling you to make you mad, my darling? It's all true. Glemnik has embarrassed all three of you, and those other two, believe me, are going to wipe their asses with you." She paused a moment. "You have to fight back."

The very idea scared him. It entailed active disobedience. It meant revolt.

"I'm sorry." He was afraid to look her in the eyes.

She rubbed his shoulders. He was trembling now. She kissed his lips. "I'm sorry too."

They edged to the couch. He kissed her—to stop her—but she insisted, and his willpower gave way. History had begun to curl up like a wave. It curled above them, about to crash, but as they stood together in her apartment, Nester thought of an old shibboleth about unidentified flying objects. In most of the case histories he'd read—and there had been thousands of them—people who had witnessed a bogey from the ground—civilians, that is—invariably pointed to their watches and said that during the time of the visitation, time had stopped; literally stopped. Seven minutes would get lost, or an hour, sometimes more. Nester had once shaken his head at this. People allowed their own fear to alter physical reality, he had once supposed. But now he apprehended the truth. Time—the thing itself—did not stop. People just stepped out of it. They climbed out, in fact, in order to see better. Time was movement, and it blurred the low-tech photographic lens of the human brain, which had trouble grasping anything traveling too fast. And so, lacking any means to stop the thing in front of them, be it a UFO or history, people stopped themselves. When they had absorbed as much as possible, they pushed some inner button, switched their watches back on, and arrived back in time again, which they celebrated by checking the hour and the minute. And afterwards, when they gave their statements to the police, it only seemed as if time had stopped. In reality, *they* had.

Time stopped for Nester now. Waltraud would make love to him, and he would behold history in the darkness. To his mind's eye, the things he had witnessed at the bridge had a crystalline shape, like snowflakes, and he slid along their volutes and spandrels as she ran her fingers down his ribs. A ritual began. Between them, there was never foreplay, at least not of the spontaneous kind. She had a well-planned route, and Nester traveled it like a man on a bus tour of an extravagant city. She produced a lime-green air mattress, a bottle of olive oil, a candle, and a Bic lighter. He tried to imagine Hegel's history, a great, blazing god, distilling itself in the bridge over Bornholmerstrasse. He sank in light and flesh.

4.

WALTRAUD CAME DOWN from her ecstasy. She rose from the air mattress, and in all her tough, flushed nudity, poured another glass of vodka. The cow skull had dropped from the wall during their lovemaking, and she regarded it with disdain.

"That's enough theology for now, *Maus*. Yes?"

He nodded, not really hearing. The orgasm retreated down his spine.

"So I have an idea."

He turned his eyes to her.

"The Wall. Let's go. Now."

She pulled the plug on the air mattress.

"What about *him?*" Nester nodded in the direction of her bedroom, where Douglas slept.

"We leave him. He's not going anywhere. I locked the door."

"What if someone is watching your place? What if they see us leave?"

Waltraud shook her head. "No one but you and Trude know about this place, and Trude will never tell a soul."

Nester could see no harm in it. These might be his last hours as a free man. He left one more kiss on her chin and got dressed. The sex becalmed him. Waltraud always made Nester feel good, but on this night, she had lifted him from despair, saved him, in fact, and he felt a new, unwarranted optimism. "All right. We'll go. But only for a couple of hours. Then I take Douglas in."

She didn't argue this time. She dressed and had another vodka. He drank one too, for the first time in years. It made him a little woozy, but did his spirits good. Waltraud locked the door behind them, and they hurried to the bus stop.

5.

MIDNIGHT CAME. The bus was packed. The driver laughed. He told them it was a holiday and returned their coins. Other people got on the bus, and the driver showed the same magnanimity. Waltraud gazed out the window into the darkness, head full of orgasmic unities. Half asleep, still abuzz from sex and vision, Nester thought of Stuart.

They had met nine months ago in a class on critical thinking. Nester had been working on his master's degree in English, Stuart on a bachelor's in the humanities, and the critical-thinking course at the military annex campus of the University of Maryland in West Berlin was required for each. The rest of the students had an unmistakable whiff of infantry about them, dumber than moss, and like two artists forced to sit among dilettantes, the intelligence men gravitated to one another. The teacher, an idealistic young woman, saw their aloofness and gave them a hard time. She especially liked to challenge Nester when he quoted Malcolm X, tossed the usual defensive white line on that great man, but generally did a good job of motivating the two field station boys to participate. Nester had never had much respect for the other military people in West Berlin. Most of them, including the officers, were not thinkers. They took the prerogatives of the structured life for granted. Stuart was different.

When he first arrived at field station, Nester had heard rumors of ge-

nius, which proved false. Stuart, so the scuttlebutt went, was a man for all
seasons. You name it, he knew it—interferometrics, splatter encryption,
Wullenweber systems, phased-array radar, and even Project Moon Dust.
That stint on the Turkish-Syrian border had steeped him in the most arcane
lore of the business.

At first, when their eyes met across the classroom, they hardly acknowledged one another. Stuart had no doubt heard of Nester's reputation as the
outstanding expert on the German Democratic Republic, but he kept his
distance. An incident in critical-thinking class, simple and stupid, finally
brought them together.

Against procedure, they were both using their downtime at field station
to finish essays for class, when a general inspection was announced. All loose
paper had to be shredded, and somehow, in the confusion, both essays were
destroyed.

The teacher gave them F's. Nester pleaded with her, but she scoffed. In
protest, the two men fumed out of the room. Stuart suggested they file a
complaint, and this effort took them to a bar, where Stuart drank beer and
Nester coffee. In a furious five-hour session, they ate boats of *pommes frites*
with mayonnaise and discussed Nietzsche, Robert Musil, and a warrior
church built by Roger I in northern Sicily, which they had both coinciden-
tally dreamed of visiting one day. It was not possible, he told himself, was
absolutely impossible, that Glemnik had concocted this relationship in order
to get closer to him, in order to cast an obscurity before the eyes of the man
most likely to see through him. On top of everything else, Glemnik did not
seem mentally capable of it, or was that merely an act?

Nester was deep inside this mystery when the bus pulled into the Zoo
station.

6.

MULTITUDES ROILED IN THE DARKNESS. East cascaded West.
Nester and Waltraud jumped off the bus and were immediately swept
back against it by humanity. With his hands, Nester shoveled people away, as
if they were drifts of snow. He headed in the direction of the zoo, which lay
dead east of its namesake, the Zoo train station. Above them, the night's last
locomotive roared in, from Frankfurt or Hamburg or Paris, he didn't know.
Its wheels screeched in the trestles.

Nester hunted for a footpath to take them around the back of the station
to the Street of June 17 and from there to the Wall. They had a couple of

kilometers to go, he reckoned. More people blocked their progress. Champagne fizzed in his face. A woman lifted the bottle to his mouth, and he took a swig before handing it to someone else. It was East German stuff, Rotkäppchen, with an aftertaste of natural gas. Beer bottles crashed. Klaxon horns whooed in his right ear. A man in a tuxedo blew on a cornet while his partner, stuffed inside a parka, slapped bongos.

Nester checked his watch. It was one in the morning, almost four hours or so since the Wall had opened, and the central part of the city distended like a water balloon attached to a tap. Half a dozen languages chittered around them—in addition to German and English, he made out Turkish, Italian, French, something Arabic. A man in a seven-foot bear suit bounded past. Paper tongues darted.

"Hey!" Waltraud cried. "I'm suffocating."

Nester dragged her down the footpath. In the darkness beneath the chestnut trees, he overheard an unbelievable story. According to a woman with a thick Swabian accent, people had climbed up onto the Wall itself. They danced with umbrellas. The East German police had tried to spray them off the top with fire hoses, but no go. More champagne flowed, this time of the Western variety. On the two of them went. Like explorers with machetes, they hacked their way through. Even with this effort, it took thirty minutes before they were out in the open again, a few hundred yards from the Street of June 17.

There, before his eyes, like a rare, drab species of bird, was an East German Trabant, navigating between merrymakers who coursed down the street. They pounded on its hood, doused its windows with champagne, and handed plastic flowers to its driver. The Trabi had a simple shape—a square placed upon a rectangle placed upon two spheres, like a child's diagram of a car—and a massive exhaust problem. Violet smoke poofed from its rear. Nester had seen photographs and film footage before, countless times in fact, but never the real thing on a West Berlin street. Other Trabis trailed behind. Dim yellowish headlights stretched back down the boulevard toward the gate, too far away to be seen. There were camera crews everywhere, bearing down from the sky in helicopters, blocking traffic with their vans.

Not too far ahead, on a single column, a Prussian angel took flight in gold. Hordes undulated below her. She was alive, Nester thought, and watching for Lucifer.

Nester hammered once on the roof of the Trabi. The driver rolled down his window and asked for directions to Steglitz. His sister lived there, he said. Nester screamed at the top of his lungs; the man didn't understand. They were parted by whirling blue light before the matter could be settled.

"Aren't you proud of them?" Waltraud gasped. "I'm so proud of them. This is what Germans ought to be. Look at them. They're like children at an amusement park. I'm going to feed every single person who makes it to my bar as much goulash and beer as they can eat. No charge!"

She began spreading the news to people around her. They joined the flow along the southern side of June 17. In the Tiergarten, stretching away to their left, movement could be seen, but indistinctly. Flashlight beams struck the boles of trees. Bushes shook. Sparklers erupted between cupped hands. One ignited beneath Nester's chin, as if the night itself had short-circuited.

They passed beneath the angel. Chopper blades shuddered. It was possible to climb up to the top of the angel and see a panorama of the city, but Waltraud vetoed the idea. Let the choppers have the air. More and more Trabis were coming from the north, from the Invalidenstrasse checkpoint, maybe.

Far off, Nester glimpsed more crowds, layer upon layer, schools of human beings, wiggling, flashing, dipping into the darkness. They must be coming from all over East Germany, he thought, gushing across the borders in a massive irresistible flood. And no one had fired a shot.

Soon, they were at the Brandenburg Gate. Beyond the Wall, it reared—solemn, totemic, brownish dark, like a sacred object that had, from the depths of its mysterious heart, created the night's madness. How many times had Nester seen it on the other side of the barrier, the national mastodon rotting in the death strip? Now it had moved to the heart of things. It coaxed events forward. Atop the Wall, right in front of the central pillars of the gate, just as the woman had said, a few people gyrated. They reminded Nester of acolytes in a religion. They reeled and gestured, called to the people below to join them. Water spurted out of the East. One woman jumped in panic, but someone else opened an umbrella, squatted, and took the force of the spray.

Nearby, a man in a kilt struck up a bagpipe version of the "Lorelei." The notes of the bagpipe in the midst of the furor moved Nester deeply. He put a hand over his eyes. It was real. This was happening.

He turned to speak to Waltraud and discovered she was gone. A moment ago, she had been there, waving a half-eaten *Wienerwürstchen* in her fist, peeling her eyes for Dagmar. Suddenly, he was alone. She had been sucked into the morass. Nester called out for her, but the reveling around him absorbed his words. He whipped around. His voice choked in his throat. Had someone taken her? Was she being dragged away through the mob?

Nester froze where he stood. Oh Christ, he could feel panic rising. He thought of war, and it seemed to him to mass above the Brandenburg Gate like a storm front. Annihilation was coming. The more Nester saw, the more he feared and the less innocent it all became. He did a quick math of horrors in his head. The Western Group of the Soviet Armed Forces had 365,000 men stationed in East Germany, the majority of them in the immediate vicinity; they were crack troops, the best Moscow had, and they could strike against Berlin within minutes of an order.

Same went for the East German army, which had half that number, a force that could be combat-ready in forty-two minutes, according to his sources. Add to that the East German police force, Mielke's private army of Stasi, and the troops of the Interior Ministry, not to mention every official, high or low, in the East German government who owned a registered firearm and the *Kampfgruppen* in the factories, and you had damn near a million people poised for the slaughter. All the haystack needed was a spark.

The Central Committee dinosaurs would never let the borders open, not this way. It would mean the end for them. Nester looked the thing in the eye, and forced down his emotion like a man pushing back a plate of sweets. You don't fool me for a second, he said to invisible bureaucrats, you will shoot your own just as you did in 1953. But this time, the people will rise up, and you will slaughter them by the thousands before you allow even a fraction of your grip to weaken. This whole city will be razed.

He ran to a phone booth, called Waltraud's apartment. Twenty rings went by. No one answered.

7.

HE FOUGHT HIS WAY BACK to the zoo and managed against all odds to get a taxi to Waltraud's place. Even in Spandau, the word was out. In the Dalmatian restaurant, folks were braying to Dubrovnik mandolins. He ran up the two flights of stairs and found the door to her apartment open. He crept inside. The coffee table had been placed on top of the lime-green air mattress, and someone had finished off the decanter of Waltraud's favorite Madeira wine. Next to it was a half-empty bottle of olive oil. On the far side of the den, the door to the bedroom hung wide open. Nester tiptoed into the kitchen and slipped a knife out of a drawer. He peered through the doorway into the bedroom.

It was empty. The lock was not smashed. Someone had opened it from the outside and had taken Douglas away. Like a fool, Nester had left him alone, and someone had come.

He sniffed around the apartment, returned to the den. Without exoneration in the form of Douglas Gleaming, he was completely vulnerable. No one could defend him but himself—and his people. No other choice, he thought, time to dial up the old network, his collection of Warsaw Pact abductees and Ufologists. The Green Men, as he called them, were rusty from disuse, but still intact. In the past, despite certain idiosyncrasies, they had been his eyes and ears in Eastern Europe, and one more time, they must perform for him. They must locate Stuart. He would call his old friend Bruderlein. There would be no more mistakes.

Fists knocked at the door.

"Military police," a voice announced. "Open up."

Nester stiffened.

"Captain Cates, you in there, sir?"

The door to the apartment swung open. A detail of MPs entered the room.

"You might want to pack a bag, sir."

An irrelevant objection died in Nester's throat. He was under arrest.

CHAPTER NINE

1.

DOUGLAS AIMED THE LAMP on Waltraud's nightstand at his genitals and methodically sifted the jungle for *Nosopsyllus fasciatus*. He was naked. The shades were down. The rest of the room crouched in darkness. Beyond the locked door, little could be heard.

Several times, he thought he saw one scurrying away from his fingers, but when he grabbed at it, wires of hair came up in his pinch. After the genitalia, he went down his legs to the feet, to the crawl spaces between the toes, then back up his near-hairless belly to the point where he could no longer see himself. He found no fleas. There were no bites.

And yet he felt the compelling urge to scour his body with chemicals. He wanted to be cleansed, and not just because of the fleas.

He shivered. Waltraud had locked the door behind her. He had heard the clear click of a turning latch.

In spite of everything he knew about insects, he imagined the pests to pursue a guerrilla strategy. For the moment, they must have bivouacked on his head, where he could not see them. When the lights went out, they would descend again to suck and nest.

To his right, within reach of the bed, wind bumped against the window. He pulled his underwear back on, turned out the lamp, and whipped up the American-style shade. Light from the apartment across the courtyard drizzled down on him. In its window, a woman hung laundry on a line: bra, panties, T-shirts. Her movements evoked an eternity of quiet, kind domesticity.

Fuck the fleas, he told himself. For once, get up and do something. They'll be coming for you.

He plucked up the phone and dialed information. A recorded message told him all information lines were busy, he should call back later. He tried three more times and got the same response. News was beginning to travel. Lines would be busy all night. He hung up the phone and tried to recall phone numbers. He knew Stuart's by heart; that wouldn't help. Linda's popped into his head. Without considering the various consequences, he snapped up the receiver and dialed his ex-wife.

He hung up. It was a bad idea. He had thought about asking her to contact the State Department and tell them his story, but that would have been foolish. For one, she might have been dragged into the mess too.

Even worse, he realized, his part in Stuart's defection could be seen in a variety of lights. He might be seen as an accomplice rather than a victim. He had slept with Uta, who was also involved. And there was Grams to consider, who must still be lying in the fifth level of the air raid shelter, overrun by rats, ticks, and other little monsters.

He popped the shade back up. Across the courtyard, the woman had stopped hanging laundry. Abandoned, a pair of insane, yellow panties grinned at him. Had their owner rushed off to the Wall? Did she know?

He got out of the bed and opened the window. Every move he made echoed down into the courtyard. Baltic air chilled his fingers. He stuck his head out. Waltraud's building was like many in West Berlin. Once, it had had a nice facade decorated with all sorts of pomp and circumstance, protuberances down which Douglas could have climbed. But a bomb had destroyed the original, and its replacement was a sheer, straight mass of poured concrete interspersed with windows. If he tried to descend, he would fall to his death or break a limb.

He closed the window. Vodka would be nice. Waltraud had offered. He tried the door handle. It was still locked. He knocked several times. No one answered.

"Hey out there!"

Surely they had not left the apartment.

"Open the door!"

With a heel, he kicked at the knob, a narrow finger of steel common to all West Berlin apartments he had seen. Nothing happened. No one came. His thirst increased. He must have something to drink.

"Waltraud!"

Long minutes went by. Douglas got back into bed, snatched the phone again, tried information one more time. The same message told him to call back later, this time, he thought, with a tinge of resentment. Then, suddenly free of flea fear, exhausted, he fell asleep. When he woke, the latch was turning in the bedroom door.

2.

CARLTON STYLES SAT ON THE COUCH across from him, one leg thrown over the other, a pistol in his right hand, a decanter of ruby-brown liquid in the left. He had found Waltraud's liquor cabinet and was pouring himself Madeira wine over ice. He did not offer any to Douglas. The room was a mess. The den table had been pushed against one wall. A deflated lime-green air mattress lay on the floor in exactly the spot where the table had been.

Styles looked different. He had shucked the diplomatic business suit and now wore a wine-red sweater over a black turtleneck. A black woolen over-coat with glandulous silver buttons lay across his shoulders like a cape. His gaze passed over Waltraud's John Wayne poster, her fallen cow skull, the photo of some old cabin, to the things on the floor.

"I'm prepared to go to the authorities," Douglas said.

Styles grunted. Douglas noticed with admiration how he managed to work around his deformity. He had no lisp. There was no inflection trace-able to the broken barrier of teeth. His voice emerged as confident as that of any dignitary Douglas had ever heard on television. It had a calmness and a moral certainty which, despite the gun, reassured Douglas. Of course, this was something of an illusion. The man meant harm, and the look in his eyes did not convey an abundance of reason. Since their last meeting, the diplomat had grown shaggy. His chin and cheeks showed a four-to-five-day growth. His hair spiked out from his ears. This element, more than anything else, gave the jagged clutch of teeth a less than hospitable quality. Other-wise, Styles's demeanor conveyed a subtle and pleasing urbanity.

He poured himself another Madeira.

"Do you know what I've been thinking for the last few minutes? I've been thinking about how people love to drape satin on a mystery. My God, I tell myself, he's either lost his looks or the rumors were deeply exagger-ated. Your reputation is unbelievably flattering, what with the seduction of the wife of a French ambassador, the bedding of God knows how many German aid workers, and one or two high-profile American journalists. Not a day has gone by when I haven't tried to remember exactly what you look like, to remember if you were handsome or not, and I can say with great relief, you are plain. What do you think of that?"

Douglas managed a head-shaking grimace.

Styles gestured at him with the glass. "I saw you once, as you may re-member, but I was bleeding and delirious. I didn't exactly have time to study your features. I recalled this, of course."

He put a finger to his cheek to indicate Douglas's housefly.

"So I asked people," he continued, "what does he look like, and my sources told me you were the handsomest man in the Levant! Oh, that gorgeous Dalmatian, my sources in Istanbul would say—oh me, oh my, he's got such beautiful Adriatic skin tone, so dark, so mysterious. If he weren't a terrorist, he'd be a movie star or the president of a country. But they would be heartbroken, wouldn't they?"

He took another sip of the Madeira. Douglas saw he was going to empty the entire bottle, and wondered how long it would take. He grasped now that Stuart had been telling the truth, that Styles did indeed believe that Douglas was Jiri Klek, and might even be planning to kill him. Douglas owed an apology. He tried to plead his case with Styles.

"I know this isn't going to sit well with you, but my name is Douglas Gleaming, and I've never—" He stopped in midsentence.

"Save it."

The gun slammed onto the coffee table.

"You've been drinking too much, sir. It's clouded your reason."

Styles lifted the gun from the coffee table and aimed it at Douglas's head. The accusation of drunkenness had riled him. His eyes lost a fraction of their urbanity. His teeth dripped dark Madeira. Douglas realized he was closer to death now than he had ever been in his life, even closer, if possible, than he had been at the East German border. The man intended to kill him. Douglas's nausea resumed, as if it had never ceased, and he imagined a chalk line on the floor at his feet.

"One," Styles counted. "Why are you in West Berlin? Planning a new job, are you?"

Douglas thought it better not to answer.

"Two. Did you have any contact with the Libyans in East Berlin? We know Tripoli planned the La Belle Disco job, but you planted the actual explosive. Those were American boys, Klek. Ever raise a son yourself?"

Douglas kept silent, though the crack about the child hurt. No, he had not. Linda had not been able.

"Three." Styles lowered the pistol to his side but cocked the hammer. "Lockerbie?"

Douglas gaped at the suggestion.

"Four. Is Cates involved in the new deal? Silk? How did Glemnik find you? Was it through that old Kraut in Turkey? Talibor. Is Silk RAF? Is she your liaison for explosives, as I suspect? East Germans supplying you? Soviets? Don't let my disability fool you. If you don't start talking, I'm going to splatter what's left of your Adriatic charm all over that record collection."

Douglas spoke without hesitation. He refused to die without a fight.

"No. My brother and Uta work alone—"

Styles's mouth moaned an objection. "You don't have a brother."

Keeping his gun trained on Douglas, he put one of his arms through the coat, as if preparing to leave.

"Want me to recite your cover story for you? The story of little Jiri, who was playing in a vineyard one day on the Adriatic in 1942 when a scouting party of Italians hung his father with chicken wire, then raped and shot his beautiful young mother, a Czech partisan from Daruvar, and threw his two siblings into the sea? I'll give you this, Jiri—if a word of it were true, it would make a fair justification."

Menace tightened the man's voice.

"But it's idolatrous nonsense, of course. Like everything else about you. You're just another spoiled child of the revolution, a postwar kid like me, and I wouldn't give a damn for you, or for anyone you killed, if you hadn't planted that bomb beneath my safe house—"

Douglas leapt in. "I swear to God, I didn't plant that bomb! I wouldn't know a bomb if I saw one."

Styles seemed to sniff something new, a notion that might or might not have been what Douglas intended. He clasped his legs together, slumped back into the couch, and rested the gun on his lap.

"My brother told me about the similarity in backgrounds," Douglas went on, "how Klek's ancestors and our ancestors came from the same place, from Dalmatia. That's why there's a resemblance. My name, Gleaming, is a corruption of Glemnik. Old Vink Glemnik, my great-great-grand-father, immigrated from Dalmatia. It's that plus my housefly, which is just pure coincidence."

Styles mulled this over. His face grew sad, so sad Douglas thought he might cry.

"Show me an American driver's license then."

Douglas dug into his pocket where the wallet should have been. The East Germans had taken it.

"That's what I thought. You had me going, though. You may not be as handsome, you may not entirely fit the profile, but that's what makes a good cover, doesn't it? Nothing too definite. You could afford a little cosmetic surgery, I should think. You should have gotten rid of the powder burn too. My health plan doesn't stretch like it should, and even if it did, my doctors hardly know where to begin. They *did* offer to take out my jaw and give me a new one, but somehow, somehow . . ."

Douglas shook his head in resignation. Every event of the night, not to mention his genetic background and personal history, had conspired to ruin him.

"I want you to know something, Klek. I don't hate you. I'm just tired of you. Like I'm tired of my own reflection."

Douglas's heart beat more quickly.

"Close your eyes," Styles said.

Douglas did so.

"I am going to count to ten, and in those ten seconds, I don't want you to think of all the people you have slaughtered. Or of the destroyed families and marriages and childhoods. I want you to think of me. Of my mouth."

The hammer cocked. Douglas wrapped his arms around himself. On his own internal count, at the number ten, he heard a thud, and his last thought, had he died at that moment, would have been of his housefly, growing larger and larger, engulfing him in its blackness.

But he didn't die. His eyes fluttered open. Styles lay unconscious across the couch, his teeth hidden from view.

Uta leaned over him with a black rubber truncheon. She gasped when she saw him.

"Did he hurt you?"

"He was fixing to."

She took something from a coat pocket. The wig had vanished, he saw, and she was blond again.

"From now on, you are vice president of the Parasitological Society of the German Democratic Republic," she informed him. "If anyone asks, you have just won the C. A. Rudolphi Medal for contributions to parasitology and are on a lecture tour."

She laid a passport in his hands.

"Your name is Ralf Rahnsdorf."

3.

ONCE IN THE CAR, Douglas flipped through the document. Inside were his picture and the fake name, Rahnsdorf. He could not remember ever sitting for the photo and wondered if it had been taken in his sleep. Or was it the photo of someone who bore a resemblance to him? In the space of an hour, he had acquired two new identities. All things considered, he preferred being a parasitologist.

"What did I win the medal for?"

Uta shrugged. "You discovered a new bug, I suppose."

The car's tires hit cobblestones, and Douglas felt another surge of nausea. The car, a model he'd never seen before, was cramped and smelled faintly of body odor and tacos. A disinfectant Christmas tree jiggled from the rearview mirror. The word *Wunderbaum,* inscribed on the flimsy piece of green cardboard, danced before his eyes.

Uta checked a map.

"Where's Stuart?"

She drew a circle on the map and folded it.

"You'll find out."

He marveled at the tightness in her voice. She spoke as if her words might shatter.

"You like honky-tonkers?" she asked then, in an absurd conversational voice, rummaging through the glove compartment until she produced a cassette tape. He regarded her with astonishment. She popped the tape into the deck. "My first concert was Johnny Cash. When I was six years old, my father took me to see Cash at the American military base in Frankfurt, and Cash told a story about Johnny Horton, who was one of his best friends. He said Johnny Horton hypnotized him once, and he went back to the time when he was six years old. *Wunderbar, nicht?* Can you imagine what effect that had on a six-year-old German girl?"

Douglas did not share her enthusiasm, and he felt entitled to say so.

"I hate country music."

The car climbed a ramp and struck the highway, headed south through the western reaches of West Berlin. Country fiddles sawed from the speakers, and a hillbilly voice began to howl.

"Johnny Horton," Uta went on, as if she might summon him out of the ether.

Douglas switched off the music. "You two picked some night to defect."

Uta tapped a cigarette into her mouth. She looked like another woman; older, he thought, and more cynical, like a waitress in an all-night truck stop, like a woman in a Johnny Cash song, come to think of it. Cars honked, and she made gestures of anger with two fingers. By the light of the radio, Douglas could see a sag of unconditional surrender in her mouth. She ignored his remark, switched the music back on. A song he had learned in history class came on: "The Battle of New Orleans."

"Johnny Horton saw the coming of his own death, did you know that?" she inquired loudly above the din of military drums and guitars. "After Hank Williams died, Johnny Horton married his widow, Billie Jean Williams, and this widow, I believe, she was the angel of death for both of them. *Verhängnis,* you know. Right before Johnny Horton died, on the very last day of his life, he kissed this Billie Jean Williams goodbye too, just as Hank Williams had done the night he died. He kissed this already one-time-before angel of death, and then he drove down to Austin, Texas, where he played his very last gig. And all the time, he knew his moment had come, and he was satisfied with his life, *nicht wahr,* because he had made peace with God and said goodbye to his loved ones. He had told them all he was going to die, and late that night, at two in the morning in Milano, Texas, on his way home, he was struck down by a car coming the other way on a bridge." She paused, in strange awe. "I have always known that I will see my own death too, like him, just like him."

Douglas found the remarks so demented that he lost some of his anger and began to wonder about her sanity. She stubbed the cigarette out in an ashtray beneath the tape deck. Her Johnny Horton reverie appeared, thank God, to have exhausted itself.

She changed the subject. "Stuart's still in East Berlin."

Blood rushed to his head. He couldn't even open his mouth to form a question. She had been talking crap this whole time to avoid the only subject that mattered.

"They kept him. I don't know why."

He slammed a fist into the knob of the tape deck. The music spluttered. "Then why are we leaving Berlin?"

"Because it's not safe here."

They came to a West Berlin border crossing, a checkpoint for cars on the western edge of the city. Hundreds of tiny automobiles passed them, all headed in the opposite direction, all headed north and east into the city. Headlights receded into a hazy dark distance. As if in mockery, the border guards let Uta and Douglas through with hardly a glance. They couldn't have been friendlier.

"Believe me," Uta said, once they were clear of the checkpoint, "nothing you can think of me will be worse than what I have already thought about myself. No hatred you feel for me can be worse than the hatred I feel for myself."

She talked without anger or enthusiasm, and he knew she meant every word. He stole a peek at her and realized she was far away. The line had spilled from her mouth, directed not at him but at an interior partner, who spoke to her as the road slid beneath them.

For the first time, he recognized the depth of her shame. In all its easy happiness, the country music betrayed a presence, heightened a contour which stood out sharp and unmistakable as a church tower in the night. Shame surrounded her, coiled at her heart. Shame was the primordial condition of her life, unconnected to any act; it was arrogance and self-hatred in one. It was not guilt. Compared to Uta's shame, guilt was the most trivial of conditions.

Douglas recalled shame at moments in his life, as when he had accidentally poisoned the puppy, but those moments had never lasted—unhappiness might be permanent, but never shame. His soul was clean. He was innocent. He had not created the world. He had not eaten the apple, killed Abel, or crucified Christ. He had not invented spite or want or greed or jealousy. He had not made the locusts multiply or the rats plunder. These things stalked the earth long before his entrance, and he disowned responsibility for them, even as he did his little part to set them back. But Uta didn't believe in her own innocence, he could see. In her eyes, the world and its evils were her fault, and she must put them right, once and for all, or die a failure.

No apology would ever come. What she had done to him was small compared to the general crimes of the race, and the particular crime of her own, the worship of blood, the extermination of the Jews, the destruction of Europe. Against all reason, she drew a line between the worst atrocities ever committed and her own tiny life, and that mental feat erased the need to apologize for less stupendous moral failures.

With the pallid slowness of the undead, a convoy of Soviet trucks overtook them. The moon passed through a glaze of vapor. The song began to fade. Its drums grew faint, the chorus dwindled to silence. The entire world seemed to go still. The Christmas tree swung from the rearview. The spectral convoy passed on. Uta rewound the tape.

CHAPTER TEN

1.

SHE COULD NOT FORCE the German shepherd from her mind. The animal tumbled and cracked before her in the darkness—a small creature with pink gums, flattened ears, and the gentlest of eyes for a guard dog. Through corridors of beech and poplar she drove. Twigs and branches locked above her head. Trabis broke wind as they trundled by. They honked their feeble horns and flashed their pale yellow headlights. People rolled down their windows, gurgled out cheers. *"Idioten!"* Uta wanted to cry back at them. "Bananas! Stereos! Potato chips!" But they were gone before she could speak, gone to West Berlin to find their destiny in the glow of a coin.

The animal must have been young, less than two years old, puppy down still on its muzzle. As she carried Douglas south, away from Berlin, she reconstructed it in her mind. She was on the Bornholmer Bridge again. She was putting the gear into reverse, lifting her foot off the clutch; the car was screeching backwards. She had expected the East Germans to shoot out her tires, but they didn't even fire into the air. She swung around, desperate to go back west, to whatever judgment awaited them. But Stuart would not let her. His nails dug into her knee.

"Turn us round."

She whirled the car back east and floored it. The dog materialized out of darkness. It thumped beneath the wheels. For an instant, she lost control of the vehicle, but Stuart jerked the wheel back to the right and screamed, "Drive, Uta! Just fucking drive!"

Hours later, she still drove. Whenever she hit a pothole, she imagined the dog, and there were more potholes than streets in East Germany.

"Drive, Uta! Just fucking drive!"

An hour after they crossed into East Berlin, after losing two shocked squad cars of police that had tried to follow them from the border, Stuart made her stop the car in Mulackstrasse, a narrow street of forgotten, bullet-ridden tenements and lightless windows. He climbed out. She waited in the car. He crossed the street and pressed the buzzer on the door of a building that looked abandoned. Two floors up, a light came on. A minute passed. Someone opened the door, and Stuart stepped back. Mundung appeared, and to her shock, the old man began to shout.

Stuart shouted back. She rolled down the window. Earlier that evening, before they picked up Douglas, Stuart had told her that his mission at field station had been compromised. She must drop everything and come with him to East Berlin. Otherwise, her life would be in danger. Herr Mundung awaited them and would explain everything. Those had been Stuart's words.

Above the street, a window rattled open.

"Hey down there!" a woman's voice called. "Want to fuck?"

Mundung ignored the question, crossed the street, and opened the car door. His chest heaved, as if he'd been exercising. Stuart remained by the door.

"Listen to me," he rasped. "I don't know what the devil you're doing here, but your friend over there is demanding that I get him out of East Berlin at once, and I'm going to try and do that before my section chief gets wind of this. You must go back—"

The words took her breath away.

"You've let me down, Uta!" he spluttered. "I am extremely disappointed. You should have stopped him. I will be ruined!"

His voice rose to a near shriek on these last words. Uta struggled to form a question.

"But weren't your superiors expecting us? Didn't they know?"

"Of course not, you stupid cow!" he screeched. "No one knows!"

She fell forward against the steering wheel. "You have to ditch this car. Take mine and get out of here now. Go to Checkpoint Charlie. Go home. No, wait here a moment! This is a disaster, a disaster!"

He rushed back into his building. The voice from the window above cried out again.

"A quick, hard fuck for hard, quick currency!"

Stuart said nothing. He did not confess that he had lied. He came to her, caressed her hair through the window, and told her he would call. Mundung returned with car keys.

She left the Volvo and took the East German's vehicle, a Wartburg with a Japanese stereo system, and made for Checkpoint Charlie, which she cleared with a mere flash of the high-priority East German document procured for her by Stuart.

That had been around seven o'clock. Three hours later, a blind man had knocked on her door, given her an envelope, and asked her if she knew what was going on at the Wall. She told him she didn't, tipped him in case he was really blind, shut the door, and tore open the envelope. Inside were two notes, one from Stuart, one from Mundung, and an East German identity pass like the one she possessed.

In the confusion at Bornholmerstrasse, Douglas had escaped, Stuart's note informed her. She should check the apartment, Nester's place, and Waltraud's too, just to be on the safe side, and if she found him, she should make her way to Mundung's safe house in a farming village near Leipzig. This was imperative; Douglas's life was in danger. Attached to the note, she found a map with directions. Mundung's note was bitter. It said he would reestablish contact when possible. It said his entire career had been wiped out because of her lover's blunder, but did not say why. It said there would be a reckoning. Then it reiterated the urgency of getting Douglas out of West Berlin and the importance of giving him the identity pass. He included a few lines about Douglas's new persona.

The note did not specify what she should do after delivering Douglas, and this fact filled her with a suspicion colder than the night. She had been duped. Herr Mundung had lied to her about the entire operation. He had always implied that he was acting with the sanction of a higher authority, namely his government. But that was an illusion. His superiors didn't know. No one knew. The old man had admitted so himself. What did it mean?

Stuart she forgave. She loved him and knew he would never have betrayed her without reason. Perhaps he had been trying to protect her. But she was finished with Mundung. Once she delivered Douglas—she did this out of devotion to Stuart and for no other reason—she would go straight to the headquarters of the Main Directorate for Intelligence in East Berlin and demand an explanation. Her life might be in danger. She didn't care. She wanted answers.

2.

THE FARMHOUSE WAS GRIM, East Germany at its most backward. It belonged to Herr Mundung's invalid brother, whose legs moldered beneath a dark red blanket, whose head rested on a potato sack stuffed inside a grimy pink pillowcase. The room smelled of chamber pots and goulash. Its warmth had an intestinal quality, and Uta unwillingly entered behind Herr Mundung's niece, who led Douglas to a cot. The old man bolted upright. He trembled with an alertness bordering on hysteria, and she realized he must not have been asleep at all, but had waited through the long hours of the night for Douglas and her to arrive. Perhaps he never slept. Whatever the case, Uta was sickened by him.

Douglas was so exhausted he fell asleep immediately. After leaving him on a cot next to the old man's bed, the two women went to the kitchen, a coal-smoked space cobbled together out of detritus. Shelves of railroad ties and crumbling bricks climbed up one wall. The stove in the opposite corner had once served as the body of a tractor. Four Trabi tires rose beside the stove, one on top of the other, and the hole in the middle made a container for brown coal, which heated the place. Herr Mundung's niece, Marthe, reached into the tires, pulled up a few round lumps of lignite, opened a hatch on the front of the stove, and tossed them in. Orange light flickered out of the tractor innards, and Uta saw that the walls of the kitchen were papered in dingy sheaves of old East German magazines. She was surprised at the poverty of the room, but somehow comforted by it. The cold air of the early morning knocked at the roof, whistled through cracks in the plaster. It even managed to touch her arms, but the stove kept it from penetrating any deeper.

"Where is your uncle?" she asked.

Without answering, Marthe guided her to a bench, dragged a four-legged card table out of a closet, extended its four metal legs, and placed it in front of the bench. Uta said she had to go back to Berlin, but Marthe ignored her. She went into a pantry at the back of the kitchen, rummaged around, and returned with a plate of cold boiled eggs and sausage. She brewed hot water on the stove, took a jar of instant coffee, and placed it on the card table. Uta whispered her thanks. The woman went on working. The shelves contained cans of food from every decade of the last five, Uta saw, including what she thought must be tins of bully beef from the British army in the last World War. There were bowls made of helmets, cups made of bullet casings, and one long apron that bore an odd resemblance to a uniform. The woman took two shell-casing cups from the shelf and wiped them clean. Her clothes, Uta saw, were plain and brown, the same hue as the kitchen walls, and did not look as if they could be warm. There was nothing in the least remarkable about her. Her hips were wide and slow, with no sex in their movements. Her hair was thin. It fell across a face which was as kind and thoughtless as a potato. Uta cracked open a boiled egg and ate it in one gulp. She was starved.

Finally, Marthe spoke.

"My uncle was supposed to be here hours ago. I don't know what happened. Normally, he doesn't bring people here, but I agreed, because he sounded so upset."

She spooned instant coffee into the cups. "I'm sorry that your friend has to sleep with my father, but we don't have much room here. He's old, and his brain is gone. He fought on the Russian front as a political officer for the Fascists, unfortunately, and after he was captured, our Russian brothers kept him in prison for ten years. Normally, they would have shot him, but he'd saved the life of a few of their comrades, so they spared him, so to speak. He never quite recovered. Ten years . . . can you imagine?"

"A long time."

"It was a good thing, I suppose. The Soviets reeducated him until he was as well-read in Marx and Lenin as any scholar in Leipzig. But when he came back, there was no work for him because he had been a Nazi Party member. The state gave him a tiny pension. And my uncle was terribly ashamed. Most of his colleagues don't even know he has a brother. Or a niece, for that matter."

At this, she gave a quaint smile, as if it were a little joke between the two of them. Uta felt a sudden rush of shame at having played Mundung's niece on the night the old man had met Douglas. Marthe shrugged. "I take care of him, and he doesn't see many other people, except for my uncle, who comes every so often."

Marthe poured scalding water onto the crystals and apologized for having no milk.

"Please eat. I slaughtered this pig myself, and believe me, we have more than enough sausage."

Uta tried to explain that she was a vegetarian, but Marthe interrupted.

"Is that an American in there?"

She gestured toward her father's room. Uta nodded.

"America. *Imperialismus pur.*" She smiled at this recollected term of her youth. "What part of America?"

"Texas."

This made a happy impression. "The cowboys. The wild horses on the plain. The savages."

Uta let it be. Marthe went on. "And you've come from Berlin just now?"

"That's right."

"Is something happening there?"

Uta didn't answer at first. But an idea pressed at her mouth and slowly opened it: "Your people are free to travel. They are crosssing into West Berlin by the hundreds of thousands. It looks to me like a revolution."

Marthe squinted.

"A revolution?"

Uta broke into tears. "The people have risen up. They have truly risen up."

Marthe contemplated these words, unconvinced, as she chewed on a slice of sausage. Uta sipped on her coffee, the worst she had ever tasted. Grains of it stuck to her tongue. Marthe handed over a piece of gray toilet paper as tissue for her nose.

"Do you know I've never even been to Berlin?"

Uta wiped, rubbed her eyes, ashamed at the outburst. "But that's only a few hours from here."

Herr Mundung's niece sighed and pointed in the direction of her father's bedroom.

"Uncle always told me if I'd had a husband, it would have been different, but I never had. I've lived my entire life in this village, which is a very interesting place really. Have you seen the grave of our famous philosopher down the road? The mayor says he's a Fascist, and I wouldn't know, because we're not allowed to read his books, but a lot of interesting people come here because of him, people from other countries. They come here to see his grave and the house where he was born. I've met a man from Japan, and lots of Italians. Only one American, but Uncle wouldn't let me talk to him."

Suddenly, Marthe sniffed. "What is that?"

Uta didn't understand.

"That smell?"

She had a thick, pinched Saxon accent, like her uncle. It chewed vowels as if they were gum. Uta wondered if she had misunderstood. But Marthe pointed at her neck.

"There's a smell on you."

An irrational horror came over Uta.

"A smell? There's no smell."

"Yes there is." Marthe came close, truffling like a pig, her eyes lighting up in delight. "It's fruit!"

She raised her arms, soft as dumplings, and let the fingers of one arm rest on Uta's left shoulder. There was a smell now, Uta thought, of manure, mud, tractor grease, and coarse femininity. No, Uta thought, I forbid you to touch me—get your hands off me, you oaf, you dumb wheezing mammal, you *German*. But she didn't speak. Marthe's nose reached her chin.

"Aha!" She pulled back. "Soap!"

Uta knew her mouth hung open, but she couldn't do anything about it, and Marthe didn't seem to care.

"Yes. Soap."

"Strawberry soap."

Uta had thought herself incapable of more shame. But now a new stream rushed in, as it seemed to her, across the surface of her skin.

She said a quick thank-you for the coffee and food, pushed away from the table, and hurried out of the farmhouse to the car. As she did, she had an image of herself as a piece of pink soap shot through wet fingers. The woman hurried behind her. She waved from the courtyard as Uta drove away, and called out, "What about the Texan?"

3.

BACK IN BERLIN, dawn broke. Champagne bottles, banana peels, subway stubs, and cake littered the sidewalks. There were flyers everywhere—for political actions, department store sales, beer parties. An old woman screamed at the top of her lungs from a third-story window, shook a fist at the pedestrians on the street, as if the entire city had kept her up and she was threatening to sic the police on it. Uta saw an imperial German flag in a shop window.

It was cold, but Trabants were on the move. On the radio, she heard that the chancellor had interrupted his trip to Poland and was on his way to Berlin. The radio also said that record numbers of people were expected in the city in coming hours.

Uta parked the car and made her way to Checkpoint Charlie. Its gates had swung wide open, and people crossed back and forth in front of the indifferent eyes of the East German *Volkspolizei*. She had never used this crossing before, but had passed it many times and had come to think of it more as a propaganda tool than anything else; like every West Berliner, she had seen the pictures of American and Soviet troops watching each other through binoculars as the Wall went up, but it had all smacked of lies, and she'd ignored it. The real enemy had been at home.

Now, the act of walking through without showing a passport, without meeting the stare of a soldier or casting a glance at the sign which read, "You are now leaving the American sector," infuriated her. What had been going on all those years? How was it possible for the gates simply to have opened without a fight? She could not fathom it. People around her hugged and laughed, danced and chanted, but she could not grasp the meaning of the event, could find no reason to rejoice. She had been told a vast lie, it seemed to her, a lie as enormous and intricate as a government. It included the armed struggle, the crisis of bourgeois capitalism, brotherhood, proletariat, and planned economies, all of it capped by the globular head of that misanthropic old German rabbi, Karl Marx; yes, a lie had been told her about the "whole goddamn deal," as Stuart would have said, and she would get to the bottom of it.

She came to Herr Mundung's offices, a fortress of coppered glass and gray concrete. At the main entrance, in the Normannenstrasse, she entered a small building and was told by a woman behind a window to wait. Eventually, a man in pink-tinted glasses appeared. With a frown of insolence, he snapped, "What do you want here?"

"Until yesterday, I worked with a man named Mundung in West Berlin, and he works for you. I am here to find out about him. To find out what he has really been up to."

The man took off his glasses.

"What on earth are you talking about?"

She repeated herself. He scoffed, said he knew no one by the name of Mundung, and even if he did, it was no business of hers. She mentioned Stuart's name. He said she should leave. He replaced the glasses. The eyes beyond the pinkish lenses blinked.

"I've risked quite a bit for your government. The least you can do is tell someone I'm here."

There was a glass door behind her. He swung it open and gave a gesture of dismissal with his hand. Uta felt her cheeks go ice cold.

She was being ejected? She didn't understand. It made no sense. She had risked her life for them.

"Out!" the man cried.

4.

THE NEXT EVENING, on her way to an emergency leadership meeting of the Communist Party of West Berlin, she bicycled into a demonstration of revolutionary Kurds. Night had fallen on a street lined with Turkish grocery stores and kiosks. Men stood in the doors of bars and gambling halls, drinking tea and beer, as they might have done on an evening in Istanbul, as if nothing had happened. She could hear voices cheering at a soccer game on television. Off in the distance, feet stomped in unison. Women with covered heads and downcast eyes walked together on the sidewalks. They pushed baby carriages or held the hands of small children as ancient eyes watched from windowsills above.

A bullhorn sounded. A green-and-white police van pulled into the street, and behind it marched a column of young men with faces wound in woolen scarves. They waved scarlet banners and chanted in a wild loud language; Kurdish, she realized. Uta leaned her bike against a wall. The police van and two ambling cops came even with her. One of the cops gave her a sideways glance, as if to make sure she was not a provocateur. She knew the routine well. For the last two years, she had worked as one of the principal organizers of the May Day demonstration, and both years, she had watched as these arrogant shits taunted her people into fistfights.

The banners went taut in a cold November wind. They were lurid against the darkness, and their flapping recalled the beat of drums. Booted feet stomped beneath them. A man's voice screamed an indecipherable but impassioned phrase through a loudspeaker, and the voices of the marchers repeated it. The strollers and the men drinking tea and beer gathered along the sidewalks to enjoy the show. Some of the Turks yelled insults, and she wondered where they got the nerve. Their government had been oppressing the Kurdish people for decades, ever since the days of Kemal Ataturk. Lately, the Turkish army had become murderous. Its security people tortured dissidents. Its soldiers executed women and children. The lights from the grocery shops threw the banners into high relief. The writing on them was round and violent, as if the designer had intentionally made each letter into a scimitar meant to cut a Turkish throat. Uta recognized the initials PKK, the Kurdish Workers Party, and an intense joy rose within her.

This was the answer. This was why she had become involved in the struggle of the people against the vested might of the ages. Kurds had lived for centuries upon one of the richest corners of the earth, as if God had shoveled them like dirt into a hole filled with oil, water, and gold. The hands of the nations had torn at them ever since, hurling them aside in their blind greed to claim what had never belonged to them. But the Kurds had survived and become almost holy in the effort, like the Jews. They wanted a state based upon genuine egalitarianism, where their children could grow to adulthood, without fear of hunger or repression, where the poor could learn to read and write in their own language, where women might become whatever they wanted, seeking their own truth! Her goals were coeval with the goals of these wild boys from the Tigris and Euphrates. At the top of her lungs, she was about to shout "Solidarity! Solidarity!" when the smell of her own strawberry-scented Western body clouded her senses, and the knowledge of her father's deeds returned with a new force.

Joy turned to bitterness, bitterness to fear. She did not want to go to jail. What if someone took notice of her? Everyone knew West German counterterrorism kept an eye on organizations like the PKK. A couple of the demonstrators urged her to join the parade, but she grabbed her bicycle and hurried into the darkness.

The restaurant chosen for the leadership meeting lay a couple of blocks to the west of the demonstration. She entered in haste, and a man washing glasses behind a counter gestured toward the room at the back.

Her mentor, Renate, reclined against a wood-paneled wall, dipping sesame-pocked bread into a plate of cacik and listening to a speech from a podium at the front of the room. Uta dropped into a chair beside her.

"Have I missed anything?"

Renate kissed her on the cheek. "Very little. We've drafted a resolution to oppose the opening of the border as a cynical maneuver on the part of reactionary elements in the East German government to get a restructured debt from the International Monetary Fund. We are going ahead with a demonstration tomorrow. I'll need you to make some phone calls."

Uta let Renate finish chewing on a last piece of bread, then broke the news. "I'm quitting," she said.

Her friend and mentor did not seem as shocked as Uta had expected.

"Ach ja?"

For the first time, Uta looked around the party room and realized it was half empty. Most of the people in attendance were non-Germans: the Peruvian who wore Ayacucho peasant pants, a ragged, smelly T-shirt, and a red bandanna and always brought his enormous black mastiff with a studded leather collar; the fastidiously dressed Greek who made objections to every speech, took notes in the most elegant handwriting Uta had ever seen, and smoked Turkish cigarettes with an affected decadence that, to her mind, suggested a bureaucrat of the Ottoman Empire rather than a revolutionary; Struwwelpeter, as she liked to call him, after a character from a German children's story, a man of indistinct nationality and expansive hair who never spoke and never smiled, but owned a telex machine that supplied the movement with information from the most obscure regions of the world; the gangly, Hindi-speaking American academic who used every meeting to urge them all to watch as many Bobcat Goldthwaite movies as possible; and most remarkable of all, the Turkish terrorist, an avowed member of Dev Sol, who only emerged for these meetings to make an appeal for funds, then submerged again into the underworld of Kreuzberg. He was good-looking, thought Uta, but had a sour disposition. She could easily imagine him breaking someone's neck. The few Germans in the room looked either bored or distressed. The woman at the podium appealed to them for engagement. A good third of the leadership were missing.

"I find it shocking that so many of us have shunned their responsibilities at the precise moment when the world struggle is entering a new phase!" cried the speechmaker.

From the floor, a bespectacled man who ran an alternative bookstore around the corner replied in a fit of pique, "Scandal! I came tonight to hear what you would say about the opening of the border, and I think it's a bloody scandal! Do you people never change?! Do you grasp nothing?! Ask the people coming across the border what they think of Karl Marx and Mao!"

The Peruvian spat on the floor at the man's feet.

"He's Sendero Luminoso," Renate whispered in Uta's ear. "I'm quite sure of it. What do you think of him?"

"Nothing."

Renate sighed. She was forty years old, with short-cropped gray hair and thin silver-rimmed glasses, not outstandingly attractive, but no ugly duckling. In her younger days, she had fallen in love with a succession of Latin revolutionaries and had even gone to live in Cuba for a time. Aging had been a difficult process for her, Uta knew, and she was especially self-conscious about her looks around young men.

"He's a bit too close to the cradle for me, don't you think?"

"I can't talk about this now, Renate."

"Anyway, I bet he's better in bed than your American."

It took a moment for Uta to register the implication of this comment. "Which American?"

"*Yours.*"

When had she told Renate about Stuart? To her knowledge, never.

The conversation in the room ceased. The woman at the podium glared at Renate. "A little respect, please, Comrade Klipstein and Comrade Silk."

The Greek looked at them with interest, as if this development must be reported immediately to the Grande Porte in Constantinople, and scribbled more intensely on his notepad.

"Fuck off, I'm quitting," Uta hurled back, rage rising in her, at herself, at everything she had been forced to learn. Right then, she knew she could have nothing more to do with these people.

The Peruvian and his dog regarded her with contempt. The terrorist winced in suspicion, as if the announcement signaled to armed men outside the room, as if he expected an assassination attempt. Struwwelpeter did not react. He kept his face straight ahead, and dreamed, perhaps, of telexes from Neptune.

"How very *au courant,* Comrade Silk."

Uta was growing angrier by the second. She stood.

"I am quitting because I no longer believe in either the goals or the principles of International *Marxism-Leninism.*"

"Bravo!" cried the alternative bookseller. He stood too.

Renate whirled on the man, scarves like helicopter blades flying from her throat. "Stay right there!"

Suddenly, without knowing exactly why, Uta found herself disgusted with all of them. She compared this gathering of conspirators with the people who were crossing the old frontiers by the hundreds of thousands, who had risked their lives by walking in the streets of East Germany with candles in their hands, knowing they might be beaten or shot by the soldiers of their own government. She could no longer bear to look at them. Even worse was another conviction, a feeling at the root of all other feelings, that she was an impostor, a fraud, unworthy even of these pathetic souls. If they knew what her father had done to six train-car-loads of Serbian women and children in July 1943, if they had even an inkling, they would shun her, and be right to do so.

"I'm done with the armed struggle!" she cried, ripping her party card in two. "It's a fraud!"

The speaker's mouth widened in outrage. Uta charged out of the room with Renate on her heels. They rushed past the man washing glasses behind the counter and out the front door of the restaurant into the night air. Far off, the stomping of Kurdish boots could still be heard.

"Reconsider," her former comrade said.

"Never."

Uta unlocked the padlock on her bike, trembling but resolved within to set things right, once and for all. Renate threw her arms around her. "I need your passion, Uta," she said, emotion welling in her voice. "Please reconsider."

Fear and rage blossomed in Uta's chest.

"I meant what I said, Renate. I'm done with all of you."

She heard the woman moan as she cycled away, and this evidence of pain seemed to her just one more subterfuge.

CHAPTER ELEVEN

1.

NESTER WAITED AT FIELD STATION; for what, he did not know. No one spoke to him. He was not allowed a phone call. Waltraud would be asking after him, he was sure, and they would give her some excuse. Sorry, Fräulein, gone to Wiesbaden, back in a week, back in a year.

Hours seemed to crawl by, or were they days? He had no idea. They had taken the hammer-and-sickle watch away from him, along with his other belongings—wallet, military identification, dog tag, all paper signifying Nester Cates.

In an exquisite act of torture, someone sent that official lickspittle, Tunt, to keep watch over him. The corporal brought food from the mess and served it with a disingenuous smile on his face. The phone conversation in the Box hung between them like a personal insult.

For the moment, Nester concentrated on his food.

"The men are all very concerned, sir," Tunt remarked, putting hands behind his back and standing at ease. "But I tell them it will be cleared up soon and you'll be back among us."

"Is that what you tell them?"

"Yessir."

Nester picked at the hamburger on his plate. His prison was an empty, gleaming space once envisioned as a telemetry center, then as a storage depot for electronic tracking equipment. A pen in Washington had scratched through the funding, and the space, already built, fell into disuse. A cot and a Dopp kit had been improvised for him. Nester sat down on the former. Tunt spoke up again.

"Mind if I ask you a question, Captain?"

Nester ignored him. Tunt cleared his throat. His colleagues were probably eavesdropping. The entire room would have been wired top to bottom, standard procedure but particularly useful under the present dispensation.

"How does it feel to be wrong?"

Nester put the hamburger down. It was cold anyway.

"Wrong?"

"Yessir."

Nester didn't bother accusing Tunt of insubordination. The corporal obviously had a superior's blessing.

"You predicted a civil war. Remember?"

Nester laid the plate on the cot and dabbed a napkin against his lips. Tunt continued, as if with a purpose. "With all due respect, Captain, you have been disgraced."

"Have I been?"

The corporal's eyes flashed with resentment.

"Yessir. You have been disgraced by poor judgment and poor choice of company."

Major Coogan would never allow one of the lower ranks such levity with a superior officer. He was too much a soldier for that. Styles lay behind this abuse, Nester was sure of it. He decided the time for civility had passed. "Tell me something, Jerome, is it your dutiful Jamaican upbringing that makes you a zealous altar boy for the Company, or do you just enjoy lifting your robes?"

Nester readied himself for a physical attack. He wished for one. If the man attacked him, he would have to be expelled. But Tunt knew better. He sneered at Nester's reference to the Central Intelligence Agency and went on with the sanctioned insults.

"The great Cates, who befriended a traitor—"

Now he'd come to the point. Styles wanted a confession. Circumstantial evidence already made Nester an accomplice, but that wasn't quite enough. So the owl had sent Tunt down to rub him the wrong way, to goad him into spilling the beans. Waltraud had been right. Without Glemnik, Styles needed a scapegoat, and Nester was his man.

Sweat broke out on Jerome's face. Styles had put the corporal in an unenviable position. He was meant to apply psychological pressure, but it didn't come easy. Nester used a moment of discomfort to change the subject.

"Who you named after, Jerome? Your father or your grandfather?"

Tunt eyed him, wondering where this question would lead.

"My uncle. What's it to you?"

"They say you can tell a lot about a family by knowing what they call their children. Saint Jerome was a nasty old priest who asked nuns to whip him but he couldn't muster up the potency to get them with child. Sad, in a way—"

Jerome scowled at the insult, but kept his cool. "So what about you, Captain? Who you named after?"

"After a character in a book."

"Naturally."

"My father wanted to name me after Nestor in the *Iliad*. But my mother made him compromise. She reminded him the Greeks had been away from home, fighting the Trojans, for twenty years, and she didn't want her boy's name giving him any ideas. So she named me Nester with two *e*'s, as in a bird that nests. A divided legacy. What do you suppose my name says about me, Jerome?"

Jerome swallowed and shook his head. "That's just like you, Captain, pulling erudition to intimidate me. I know you're well educated."

Nester's diversion had planted a seed of uncertainty, but Jerome's ambition led him on.

"See, I have a theory about why you think you're so special, now that you mention my name and my Jamaican heritage, which, just so you know, gives me a sense of genuine pride that I'm sure *you* have never known!"

"Jerome, Jerome. Pride goeth before a fall, and the fall will be long, and at the bottom, nails."

"You believe you're German. That's my theory. When you speak German, you don't even know you're speaking another language. You don't put it on like a uniform you have to wear, all pressed and nice. It's your skin."

Nester felt himself getting warm, and Tunt saw it.

"Shit, all this time I wondered what makes you tick, and at some point, I realized the man grew up in Germany, speaks German, he thinks like a German, sleeps with a German, and so he thinks he is one! The Jet Kraut! And do you know, Captain, that makes you a traitor in more ways than one."

Nester took up his plate, rose from the cot, and walked to the other end of the room. He munched on a fry. Nerves, rage, and lack of sleep had brought him as close to a breakdown as he'd ever been in his life. Jerome was edging him toward that brink. An assault on the corporal would discredit him badly. It could be construed as an escape attempt.

"And how it must hurt, Captain, for you to realize they don't like us Negroes any more than they like Jews. Hell, that goes double for a man like yourself, who doesn't know his proper place, who thinks just because he's read all of Brecht in the original and can tell his masculine from his feminine articles that he's a native son. You offend them more than all the rest of us combined."

Violence awoke in Nester.

"And the weird thing is," the corporal continued, "somewhere in your heart, you know it. Back in college, you hooked up with the Nation of Islam. Isn't that so? You occupied a bell tower and staged a hunger strike, didn't you? Oh yes, I heard all about it. So you must know that your ancestors didn't fight at the battle of the Teutoburg Forest, and at some point, you must have been proud. It stands to reason."

Among his acquaintances in the service, only Glemnik knew about Nester's college involvement in the Nation. Styles had obviously shown the corporal his dossier. Nester was not ashamed of it, never had been, never would be. But it puzzled him why someone would use this information to get at him. As Tunt went on, Nester came up with an explanation. Maybe someone figured the connection could help make a case against him. The affiliation alone would not be enough. But if it was attached to an unsavory espionage case, the army might go along with it. Disgruntled ex-Muslim possibly in league with known spy poses threat to security. It might wash.

"What do they want, Jerome?"

"Excuse me?"

"Why don't you just spit it out, man? Why waste your time baiting me?"

Jerome cracked a smile. "You think I'm a lapdog, don't you?"

"I *know* it. Just as I know you lured me up into the Box with that phony conversation. I've had my doubts about you for some time, but now I'm sure. Your presence here, this little talk we're having, confirms it. So who are you working for? Styles? You're not a soldier at all, are you, Tunt?"

Jerome gave a brittle chuckle.

"I got to hand it to you, Captain, you are one dense motherfucker."

Nester prayed for the man to leave.

"You call yourself an intelligence analyst, but you don't know shit. You were tossed out of the Pentagon—yes, I know about that too. When you got here, word among the brothers made you a hero. We heard you took on the system on behalf of your people. But that's bullshit. You fucked up there, just like you fucked up here. You're a dead loss." Tunt dropped his words, one by one. "As a man. As a soldier."

Nester lunged. French fries flew. MPs had to tear him away from Tunt's leering face.

2.

AFTER TUNT, Nester was left alone. A guard with a rifle took post. The two men exchanged few words.

The next day, as he reckoned it, a new order came through. He was to be removed from field station. Dawn had not yet arrived as he left the building. Faint stars shone above the rose edge of the world. Coogan appeared. He was dressed in civilian clothes, a V-neck sweater and khakis, as if about to go somewhere on vacation. He caught Nester on the tarmac before the gates.

"Give us a moment," he told Nester's guard.

"Major, am I glad to see you—"

Coogan kept him at arm's length. "I'm sorry, Nester, I can do nothing for you. You've been officially discharged from the United States Army."

Nester felt a quake in his chest. "Discharged? But that's insane."

"This whole matter comes under an extraordinary clause in the national security charter. It's no longer a military matter. You're being placed under other jurisdiction."

"Other jurisdiction?"

Coogan glanced over at the dark blue sedan waiting for Nester. "That's right."

"We're both soldiers. If I've violated the national security, then tell me how. Allow me to defend myself. Give me at least that courtesy . . ."

Coogan gave a nod to the guard. He turned away, and just as his mouth came close to Nester's ear, Nester heard a whisper, inaudible to the guard, but clear just the same. "Working on it."

With that, the major disappeared into field station. He was working on it. As Nester stood in the bracing wind of a November morning and smelled the richness of firs, he experienced a vague relief. It wasn't much, but at least he knew his people were looking out for him. Nester felt his old antipathy for Coogan giving way to a new sense of kinship. A grand blunder had occurred, but it was not his, and he would be vindicated, just as he'd told Waltraud. The army would see to that, thank God. He climbed into the sedan. Field station vanished behind him.

3.

THE SEDAN came to the frontier of West Berlin at Checkpoint Bravo, the Glienecke Bridge. Castles turreted up on both sides of the checkpoint. Schloss Babelsberg loomed across the water to the left, eastern sector; Schloss Glienecke strutted on a bluff to the right, still in the West.

Or was that just antiquated thinking? Nester didn't know anymore. Outside the sedan's back window, a shard of bright sun glittered. Clouds thick as dough bore down on it. Beneath the bridge flowed the Havel, grim iron. A few days ago, the bridge had been a geographical stratagem. Agents had been swapped on it. Now strollers moved. Boys kicked around a soccer ball. It was a public park.

The sedan crossed the bridge, and without a search, without an interrogation, without anything to mark the occasion, Nester was behind the Iron Curtain. He had imagined the moment for years, and now it had passed. He looked back. There, on the other side, was West Berlin. They had all been fools.

The sedan left the main road, pushed down a lane of exposed brick, and stopped at a villa not too far from the bridge. Helmeted, bare-breasted women clutched at linden branches above the portal. Snakes writhed, birdcrap-crusted.

Nester was shown to a windowless room containing a samovar on a buffet table and several bookshelves. In a corner of the room, hanging beyond the samovar like an upside-down parody of it, was a desiccated blowfish hung from a hook in the ceiling. The door locked behind him.

He took a seat at one end of the divan, suddenly exhausted. The things Tunt had said lingered in his mind. He tried to make them vanish, as he had made Tunt vanish, but they would not. He was no traitor, neither to his country nor to his race, but what then, he thought, what the hell am I?

4.

NESTER RECALLED A BIKE RIDE early in his friendship with Stuart. On a pair of borrowed Schwinns, they had taken a twenty-mile spin around one of West Berlin's ensconced forests, the Grunewald, and had ended up at a beer garden beside a beach for spoiled German dogs. It was the first time Nester had gone on a friendly outing with another soldier in

West Berlin, and the whole thing felt tense to him, like the beginning of a romance.

At first, they had chatted about work, about the people they liked and despised, the long hours, the merits of their superior officers, a typical run of shop talk. Then Stuart grew pensive, and with a stutter of insecurity in his voice, as if unsure of his audience, he started to speak German. Something wistful came into the afternoon—the blaze of sun off the water, the sound of dachshunds splashing on the beach, the distant gaze of an old woman seated at a far table.

It was the first time Nester heard the words *"Es gibt sowas wie eine zweite Heimat, wo alles was wir sagen und tun, unschuldig bleibt,"* which Stuart later gave in his own translation: "We all have a second home, where everything we say and do is innocent."

It was an odd thing to say, but vintage Stuart—a mixture of silly portentousness, sentimentality, and whimsy, a defiance of military conformity. The words opened a door, created an intimacy between the two men.

A cat leapt on the fence surrounding the beer garden and watched the dog beach in paw-licking boredom. From that moment on, when Stuart and he spoke German together, they were like two refugees from a vanished country, acolytes in a mystery religion. Without saying so, both acknowledged a feeling of deep knowledge whenever their tongues uttered sentences in that language. German was an ancient church, and Nester had wondered at the time if Stuart meant their second home lay there, amid the masculine, feminine, and neutral articles, beneath the umlaut tree, in the steady, secure light of words as long as candles.

In German, safely hidden, they began to talk about themselves, first one, then the other; Nester remembered vividly what he had said of himself and what Stuart had given in return.

Who he had always wanted to be, he knew, began with junior-high classes in Heidelberg, those sessions of German literature in which he'd come to love the language and philosophy of the civilization which had then surrounded him. Herr Blomquist had been his teacher, and it was he who first told Nester about W. E. B. Du Bois, and how he had loved German culture and taught it to black folks back in Tennessee and used it in his own works, a few of which, in German translation, the teacher gave to Nester as gifts. Du Bois had been a student in Berlin in the 1880s, Herr Blomquist informed him, and *he* knew the value of the language. The teacher, whose stern face had always cried out for a pince-nez, also gave him Gotthold Ephraim von Lessing, Bertolt Brecht, and Friederich Schiller, taught him that German literature, despite the Holocaust, was the most moral in the world, and that's what had attracted Du Bois. Look at *Nathan the Wise*. What a subtle and enduring portrait of Jewish wisdom! Or take *Galileo Galilei—Jawohl,* Herr Brecht was a Communist, but his play about the great astronomer went to the very heart of the immorality of science, the immorality responsible for the atomic bomb. And of course, Schiller's *Aesthetic Letters,* Nester's Bible, his solace in times of worry, his rock. In those letters, he had eventually learned how to re-create himself as a moral human being, had defined how he felt about race and politics and genocide and everything else in the world.

Stuart credited the army with most of that. From the minute he walked into the recruiting office on Commerce Street in downtown Dallas, he felt it. He could smell potential in the burning asphalt of the street. Consequently, he was signed up and shipped out. Boot camp ground him down, but he excelled. While there, he was encouraged by a sergeant from West Texas to get himself educated and to set his sights on intelligence. That had worked out, and after two years of shuttling around, picking up this or that expertise in satellites, signals, infrared imaging, and whatnot, he'd found himself at the Pirinclik base, one of two army liaisons allowed onto the grounds of the air force facility, responsible for watching the Soviet Bloc but, increasingly over the years, devoting more time to the Arab states south. And that was where he discovered German, which, even more than the army, changed his life. German, not intelligence, was the potential he had sensed on the day of his recruitment in Dallas, and an old German air-force guy who lived in the souk in Mardin helped him realize it. The guy, named Günter, Nester recalled, taught Stuart to read and write the language. He loaned him books. "It may sound strange"—Nester remembered Stuart's words—"but I was introduced to myself through another tongue."

Nester had been too, he saw in hindsight, but then he had been ripped away from that tongue and dropped like an airborne parcel into the United States of America and the English language. It was a confused time in his life. He wanted to stay in Germany, but his parents wanted him to have an American experience. They longed for him to feel comfortable in his real home, which he hardly remembered at that point.

Things went wrong from the start. Almost immediately, Nester realized that his peers thought him odd. Perhaps it was his accent, an idiot mixture of submerged German and countrified Oklahoman, picked up from his mother, so that he would sometimes find himself using "y'all" while at the same time pronouncing consonants like *v* as *f* and *w* as *v,* as if he were still speaking German. From time to time, this resulted in awful linguistic embarrassments like, "Y'all don't forget to safe me a seat in the Folksvagen." Or maybe it had been his *Weltanschauung,* his mixture of black pride and Teutonic romanticism, which no one could really understand.

At Morwenstowe, the small, mostly white liberal-arts college which had given him a scholarship, he experienced a frantic first year. With a few freshmen, a couple of self-proclaimed anarchists who were white, and a radical black poetess named Albertine Jax, he started a newspaper called the *Communiqué,* which had a brief moment of notoriety when Albertine's poem about her clitoris appeared in its second edition. The *Communiqué* died out after its third issue, but Nester fell in love with Albertine, who spoke French as well as he spoke German and considered herself a disciple of the Marquis de Sade. "If you're not careful, *chéri,*" she told him once, "you'll end up a Fascist"—words he had much later taken to heart. After a lyrical winter together, she dumped him, and he transferred to Morton University in Atlanta, a historic black institution where he hoped to settle down and become a real student.

Instead, his Nation of Islam phase commenced, and he got into so much trouble he was ultimately thrown out of school.

"Religion," Stuart had said with a knowing smile. "I knew it. There was something about you. I went through a fundamentalist Christian phase myself, but that was in junior high, before I discovered pot. I read a lot of Nietzsche in those days," he had said, "and listened to heavy metal, but I was never one for joining organizations, never went in for church."

Nester tried to orient himself at Morton, but his love of German civilization was not very fashionable, even when he showed how perfectly it could be applied to black causes and concerns, even when he pointed out how influenced Du Bois had been by it. German philosophy, except for Marx, was destroyed by the Final Solution, one aggrieved sophomore had told him, and that about summed it up. There were others like Nester, exiles from Afrocentrism, but they made him feel worse, not better about himself.

So, after reading and loving, with a great burning love, *The Autobiography of Malcolm X,* he embraced Islam. The autobiography was the first book he had ever read to compare with Schiller's *Aesthetic Letters,* a work filled with all the longing and passion for justice and all the delight in learning of the German idealists. Nester respected Dr. King, loved Du Bois, but he revered Malcolm.

To his parents' stunned horror, he got into the movement, gave up pork, drink, and smoke. He changed his name—for all of a year—to Amin, studied the Koran and the teachings of Elijah Muhammad, met a woman named Surya, who wouldn't allow him to touch her. Then, as usual, he got restless. With a couple of other Muslims, he formed a breakaway group called the Sorrowers, inspired by Du Bois, which called for a stress on moral absolutes, a renunciation of religious law, the emancipation of women in

Islam, the recognition of the importance of German culture, and the necessity of the mingling of the black, white, and Asian races. As a result, all three of them were thrown out of the Nation, and in reaction, they wrote and distributed a manifesto titled "Souls in Revolt," forced their way into the Morton bell tower, locked themselves in, and began a three-day hunger strike that culminated in their suspension from the university.

God, what a terrible moment that had been. Nester's father caught a plane from Frankfurt to Atlanta, took Nester to Uncle Bud's for a meal of fried catfish, and told him he had two choices. The terms were succinct and final. As of that moment, neither he nor Nester's mother would spend another dime on schooling. Nester could either go his own way, earn a living, and God bless him in the effort, or he could join the military, and eventually finish his bachelor's degree there. He had an hour to decide.

So that's how you ended up in the army, Glemnik had said, the fucking minimum-wage army? They both laughed out loud. In Nester's memory, the startled cat plunged into the growing dusk. Stuart had another beer and told Nester he had loved the army for five of his eight years in the desert. Out there, housed mostly with civilians contracted to run the radar, he was happy and exceptional. When on leave, he walked the black basalt walls of the crusader city of Diyarbakir, now the capital of the Turkish Kurds. He went swimming in Lake Van and climbed the shoulders of Mount Ararat. And always, always, he gathered news about the war in Lebanon, about the Russians in Afghanistan, about Syria and Jiri Klek, the terrorist, who waxed into a legend in those years, the mid 1980s. Yes, for five years he'd loved it, and then life had gone sour. He didn't say exactly why. The old German had died. The army had reneged on a promise or two. There was something to do with Jiri Klek. The desert began to get to him. That's when he'd begun to think about betrayal, Nester thought in retrospect, out there, with no friends, nothing to do but scheme and hate and gnaw at himself.

Nester hadn't reached disappointment till much later and had never truly fallen out of love with the military. In his book, it had saved him, and he owed it everything. In the beginning, of course, he had hated it, the lack of freedom, the hierarchy. But that soon passed, and he rose through the ranks quickly. With lots of hard work, he completed his bachelor's degree in a year and a half and graduated with honors.

At the Defense Intelligence College, where he eventually landed, he impressed people, and by the time he was twenty-four, he was on his way back to Germany for his first assignment in the covert world, as a reconnaissance officer attached to the 66th Military Intelligence Group in Munich. And from that, indirectly, came his posting to the Pentagon and the UFO Working Group and the life-changing dispute with the brigadier general who ran the group. The man had put white-supremacist, UFO nuts on the government payroll, and when Nester objected, the general kicked him out. Next thing he knew, he was on his way to West Berlin, Stuart, and the defection, to this blowfish-haunted room . . .

Man, he must have liked it. On November 1, after all, he had turned thirty-five years old. That meant he had spent over a decade in the service of the unseen world, delving into the secrets of others, hoarding his own and those of his country. With the 66th, he had debriefed Czech and Romanian émigrés about their time under Communism and made reports to his superiors, including recommendations regarding the potential usefulness of each interviewee. Usefulness! He didn't know if the word really applied. In terms of information about the system, his most effective contact over the years had been Klaus Brüderlein, a Romanian minister of armaments who had been expelled from his own government, the Communist Party, and ultimately the country after revealing to Ceausecu that he had been abducted by gray-blue men who had conducted experiments on his backside. Nester had never told his superiors the whole story, for fear they would scorn his source.

Somehow, crazy as he was, Brüderlein had been useful back then. Communism had shown its true face to Nester through him, and together the two men had built up a network of Eastern European extraterrestrialists who had done their little part to fight the system, to fight against the darkness of totalitarianism. That was the context of everything Nester had ever achieved in the United States Army, the crucible for exerting his sense of justice—

At that moment, in midsentence, Stuart had cut him off. Back then, his words had struck Nester as dangerous; now they were prophetic.

"Justice?" Stuart said. "Each piece of intelligence, each fragment of knowledge is like a snowflake, pure and cold and original. Each spandrel of the snowflake burns with the light of creation, Nester, no matter where it comes from, whether from Syria or Mongolia or the Ivory Coast, whether the coordinates of a missile or the preference of a prime minister for young boys or the name of a honeypot in Amsterdam, it's all the same, wherever you go, and it's all beautiful, but none of it is just—"

At first, Nester thought Stuart must be drunk or kidding. The idea made no sense.

Stuart's voice rose in conviction, as if he were uttering the pledge of allegiance. "I am convinced of the beauty and infinite malleability of all information, Nester. I live in a gorgeous blizzard. I do not serve the United States of America, I serve intelligence, because in the context of intelligence, my country doesn't exist. It's just another pattern placed upon the blizzard, a meaningless configuration . . ."

The spell cast by German dissipated. Nester switched back into English, suddenly angered by the arrogance and naïveté in Stuart's voice. His objection resounded loudly across the evening, so loudly that the old woman cocked her head in their direction. Dachshunds on the beach pricked up their ears.

"Listen up, brother, and I'm going to tell you something," Nester broke in. "You serve the United States of America, and if I ever hear you say otherwise, I'll report it. You understand? What we do, what we think, what we live and breathe, these things are all in the service of our country. Your second home is a sweet illusion, but that's all it is, and I suggest you never forget it."

In retrospect, Nester should have reported Stuart's state of mind to the field station psychiatrist, who was used to personnel snapping under the strains of cabin fever. He could have—and should have—filed a report to Major Coogan. The entire conversation should have gone into Stuart's dossier. There were so many sensible things he could have done, but didn't, because in that instant, as Stuart's face grew red with shame, Nester was moved to emotion. This man reminded him of himself. He had no friends, no real principles except a hash of notions that would disintegrate under any close inspection. He was quietly going out of his mind, and somehow, in the blink of an eye, in an almost metaphysical sense, Nester had adopted him, because—despite his treasonous bent—Stuart was a good man at heart. He had a fine soul and a complicated mind. If possible, Nester had told himself, as the last masters of the last dogs turned homeward, as the sun set over the lake—or did it set now only in his mind?—he would try to bring Glemnik out of the darkness, help him to the light of reason and duty. He would be a role model for this stumbling white man.

The door opened. Nester snapped out of his reverie.

5.

STYLES SHAMBLED INTO THE ROOM. He pressed an ice pack to the left side of his face. With the other hand, he snapped the lid off an amber container and popped pills. His head flew back. He swallowed, dropped the container back into a pocket, and pulled out a gun.

"Move," he said to Nester.

Nester hesitated a second. Styles noticed the blowfish and scowled.

"I told Mundung to be here at noon," he said. He kept the ice pack against his face with his left hand. "That's now."

He went back to the door and peered out. Nester wondered who Mundung might be.

"If he's not here, then I'm right about everything, and someone is going to be very sorry."

He jabbed the gun at Nester. "Come on."

They entered the hallway. There were no guards. In fact, the villa seemed empty. Their footsteps sent echoes vaulting up. Hours seemed to have passed since Nester's arrival. He had not known the reason for his transport to the eastern sector, but he had expected a high-level conference with the Soviets to take place. He had expected American State Department types and even a few owls to emerge. With the right inducements, the KGB might be talked into handing over Stuart, and Nester, as a possible accomplice of the defector, would convince them that their mission had collapsed, their agent's cover was blown, something like that. Now he saw there was no such plan, no KGB, no diplomats, and only the one owl.

Styles reached the villa entrance, cracked open an oak door with windows of beveled glass, and looked out. He put the ice pack into a pocket of his coat and waved his gun at Nester, beckoning him to follow. Outside, it was gloomy. Across the street, on the packed dirt in front of a kindergarten, two boys jousted with dead linden branches. Nester's sedan had disappeared.

"Left," Styles said, peering back every few seconds. His gun now nestled against Nester's rib cage. "I'm parked on the next block."

They came to a bent-fendered Citroën. "Wait," Styles said. Nester stopped on the pavement a few yards behind the car.

The owl went to the rear of the Citroën, inserted his key, and popped the lid. He glanced around, then lifted and crooked a couple of fingers. Nester's legs felt suddenly hollow. He didn't want to go in the trunk. Styles gestured again. Nester inched forward, prodded by an invisible hand. He stepped into the street. Styles grew impatient. He took Nester by the collar and pulled him.

There was a dead man inside, his V-neck sweater and khakis soaked in blood, his body cradled in shimmering plastic. Nester's heart sank. Major Coogan's face held a vestige of officious surprise, as if he had not received orders about his execution and therefore refused to believe it. The eyes had not fully shut. Nester clutched the edge of the trunk lid and tried to stay erect. He had spoken with the major. When was it? That very morning? And the major had promised to look out for him. He could not be here. He could not be dead. Styles shoved him away. The lid slammed down.

"You're mine now. Understand? Far as anyone else knows, you are part of my operation, and if I go down in flames, so do you."

Styles trained the gun on him. Nester moved around to the passenger side of the Citroën, barely able to keep himself standing, fighting back nausea. What in the name of God had Styles done?

The owl returned to the driver's side of the Citroën. "Get in."

Nester did. Without a clear destination, Styles drove. He narrowly missed a streetcar.

"Glemnik never told you what he was up to?"

Nester shook his head in disgust. "I have nothing to say to you."

"Spare me, Cates. If you'd done your job and caught on to Glemnik like you should have, none of this would have happened. That man in the trunk would be alive. So answer the question. You knew nothing?"

"You know damn well I didn't."

They drove awhile in silence. The owl checked the rearview.

"So you honestly believe Douglas Gleaming is Stuart Glemnik's brother? Is that why you didn't turn him over to me as soon as you had him?"

Nester shook his head at his own mistake. Stuart had been telling the truth to Douglas. Styles *had* snapped. He *did* believe Douglas was Klek. During that first interrogation the night of the fire, Styles claimed to Nester that he'd actually spoken with the terrorist. But he hadn't. He'd spoken with Douglas Gleaming.

"In all his years of service, did Glemnik ever receive a visit from members of his family? No, he did not, as you well know, and suddenly a brother turns up in West Berlin, a brother who just *happens* to bear an exact resemblance to the most famous terrorist in the world . . . ?"

Nester exploded. "How do you know he looks like Jiri Klek? Are you the one man in the world who's actually seen Klek's face?!"

Styles took his right hand off the wheel and snatched Nester by the shirtsleeve.

"As a matter of fact, I am."

Nester jerked his sleeve away.

"After Klek blew the safe house in Beirut, he made the mistake of enjoying his handiwork. He stood over me, believing that he had killed me. He studied my face, and through the blood in my eyes, through the smoke, through the darkness of my fading consciousness, I studied his, and made out one unmistakable feature."

He pointed to a place on his cheek.

Nester tapped his wrist. The Citroën wound into a parking lot beneath a buttressed hill. The lot was packed with cars, half of them clapped with West Berlin license plates. Styles peered at the plates, one by one, but if he discerned anything, he kept it to himself. An approaching storm deepened the grayness of the day. Wind made the trees toss. No one seemed to be following. They got out of the car and walked up a long drive to a baroque palace.

They could not have been more conspicuous—a tall, striding white man with a face as hideous as a gargoyle and a black man in American military fatigues. But with so many strangers pouring in from the West, gazes did not linger.

They walked beneath a colonnade past the entrance to the palace, and Nester stared off into the distance at a folly of classical ruins. Coogan was dead, and with him, Nester's last hope of rescue. After serving the better part of his life in Western Europe, waiting for a Soviet attack that never came, the war to end all wars, the major had been murdered by one of his own. Nester counted well over fifty people streaming toward the palace, which he now realized was Frederick the Great's old home, Sans Souci; "without care," he translated from the French, and the phrase took on a new meaning. It described a dead man.

They rounded the far end of the palace and came to the edge of a wintry garden, a series of terraces descending to a fountain. At the center of the garden, connecting the terraces, ran a steep length of stairs, and Styles made for them. Once there, he looked back at the other visitors, scanning them for any sign of pursuit. No one stood out. With a prod, he goaded Nester down. After a while, they reached the fountain. Styles ordered him to stop. He retrieved the ice pack from his pocket. In the distance, thunder rumbled.

"My enemies are here."

Nester spun around. He saw golden light within the palace perched atop the slope they had just descended. Silhouettes moved in the windows. When he looked back at Styles, the man was cupping his jaw in his hands. All of a sudden, Nester did not fear him.

"You and Stuart were working together on something. That's what his brother told me."

Styles swallowed another pill, then lowered himself to the rim of the fountain. He pressed the ice pack against his face and became so still Nester thought he might have fallen asleep. Beyond a circle of statuary—Muses, Fates, and heroes in a bacchanal—stretched Frederick the Great's old estate grounds. Lindens like masts drifted upon blackish grass, broken here and there by hunting lodges and the bright parkas of stray tourists.

Styles ran a trembling hand through his hair and stared at leaves in the fountain's basin. "I made a mistake. I freely admit it."

Nester contemplated taking the gun. Styles seemed to read the thought. The barrel stiffened up in his hand. Nester backed off. He crossed his arms.

"So you made a mistake?"

Styles's head leaned forward in acknowledgment. He began to speak low. "Everyone does."

Nester could not bear to look at the murderer. He fixed his eyes on the silhouettes in the palace. As he recalled, Major Coogan had admired Frederick the Great. Once, when Stuart suggested the old Prussian was homosexual, Coogan had bridled. Just because he cared more for his soldiers than for women? *That* makes him homosexual? For most of their acquaintance, Nester had not liked the major, but he had never once wished this on him.

Styles went on. "One year ago, by coincidence, I ran into a member of East German counterintelligence in a restaurant. We were both dining alone at Mirnik's, at separate and quite distant tables."

The man's eyes closed to slits. He swallowed again.

"The restaurant was full that night, lots of rich old West Berlin widows using their husbands' Nazi ministry pensions to dine on caviar and champagne. Lots of dubious émigrés. The usual crowd. Because of my mouth, I can only eat very soft food, so I had ordered the salmon mousse—"

He noticed Nester's angry impatience.

"It's relevant! I had ordered the salmon mousse and pureed potatoes, but the waiter brought me eel. I am not one to eat eel, so I yelled at him, and before I knew it, a fat man with an overdone Bavarian accent approached my table, carrying a plate of salmon mousse and potatoes. The orders had been switched by mistake, he said. I had his eel. The waiter apologized, and being a gentleman, and being alone, I asked this eel eater if he would like to sit. For a few minutes, we chatted about nothing at all. Then suddenly, he began to ask me polite but pointed questions about my jaw. I suspected him immediately, of course."

Intelligence attracted the saddest animals on the earth, Nester thought, no doubt about it. The owl paused for breath. For the first time, Nester noticed a bruise along the left side of his face, a semicircle of purple.

Styles went on. "I confronted him. Right there. Instead of denying it, he merely raised his glass in a toast and said, 'A votre santé,' very softly, just like that."

A first drop of rain plopped onto the leaves in the fountain.

"As a patriot and a professional, I'm always happy to meet a potential friend," Styles continued. "So I laid off the bad mood, and since we were both more or less finished with our meal, I invited him to share a bottle of *Sekt* with me. We had a few glasses together—it was late, and the place was mostly empty. I got a little tight, I will admit, and by the time Mirnik's closed down, we had cooked up an idea."

Nester grasped now that if he had believed Douglas's account of Stuart, he would never have left the exterminator alone. He would have taken Waltraud's advice and hidden the man away until the truth came out, until Styles had been neutralized. But it was far too late for such regrets.

"Now, understand something. It was completely in tune with the Gorbachev mandate, our idea. It was *perestroika* squared. Together, this fellow Mundung and I would run an espionage operation. It would be like a war game, except for spooks. A man of ours, an American, agreed upon by both sides, would be tasked with stealing secrets—fake ones, of course—from field station, with only the knowledge of the chief operations officer, in this case, Coogan, and after a year of this, the operation would be shut down and studied."

"Oh nonsense!" Nester interrupted. "What *possible* advantage could there be?"

"Plenty, if you ask me. Our side would get a security test, see how long it took for an infiltration to be spotted—to see *if* the infiltration would be spotted, Captain, which it wasn't, I might remind you—and their side would get to practice setting up a faux organization in West Berlin, pick a few West German civilians, like this bimbo revolutionary Uta Silk, who would know nothing about our real motives, and simulate a spy ring. I felt we could both learn something by it, have a little fun, smoke the peace pipe and all that, and it would be so innocuous that no one higher up could possibly object. Ergo, no one really needed to know. You follow me?"

Styles glanced back at the gates to the palace grounds, which looked to be closing. Tourists were exiting. Nester put his head in his hands. He saw now.

"Why Stuart?"

"That is a very good question. After my meeting with Mundung, I thought about it awhile. I didn't want to rush into anything, of course, and the more I thought about it, the more I realized the success of the operation depended on finding exactly the right man for the job. So I contacted one of my talent spotters in West Berlin, and we batted around a few ideas. Your name came up and was dropped, as a matter of fact—"

"Tunt."

"Never mind who. We chose Glemnik because he had intelligence connections outside the army, and because he was anxious to make a lateral move into my branch. And because he was just loopy enough to love the idea of a purely abstract mission. He never once complained about it being a waste of time or a masturbatory exercise, as so many others would have.

No sir, once he heard, he was an eager beaver, even came up with a name for the operation, called it Operation Second Home."

Nester closed his eyes and saw Stuart's face again. He heard the pop of a cap. Styles dropped another pill onto his tongue. Nester quoted aloud: "We all have a second home, where everything we say and do is innocent."

"That's right. That was our mantra—our password and operating philosophy all rolled up into one. It exactly states the true nature of our little venture. We were all innocently playing a game, relying on the new openness advocated by our liver-spotted lover boy in the Kremlin. Goddamn him. If it weren't for Gorbachev, this never would have gone so far. He's like some B-movie zombie, like Trotsky returned from the dead, spouting *glasnost, glasnost, glasnost*. Goddamn him right to hell, I say."

Nester wondered if Stuart had ever fully grasped the meaning of his mantra. In the second home now before his eyes, Nester saw legions of the dead, throats cut, limbs scorched, ashes flushed up into the sky. In that wonderful place where all people were innocent, all crimes were innocent too.

"But what in the world did you stand to gain, Styles? Did you never ask yourself that?"

Styles sighed, shook his head.

"I thought maybe Glemnik would help me find Klek. I knew Klek was in East Berlin, and I thought, if I can just get Glemnik over there, get him to keep his ears open, there's no telling what I might find."

Nester was perplexed.

"But you yourself wanted Glemnik to go to East Berlin. You just said so. And now you're upset because he's gone? I don't understand."

Styles lifted his head from the basin and stared, for the first time, deep into Nester's eyes. "The whole thing was a fake-out, Cates. Mundung was acting in bad faith. The minute I saw the man you call Douglas Gleaming, the minute I saw Klek in West Berlin, I knew it. It was too obvious. Mundung had been running a terrorist operation with my help, but I didn't see it, because I was too busy overseeing Second Home. Glemnik made that possible. Glemnik reassured me time and again about the intentions of these people. He kept telling me he was onto something about Klek too, that Klek was in East Berlin, but he needed to find out more before he could give me anything definitive. Now I know what was happening. He was buying time. He knew Klek and Mundung from before, from southeast Turkey. Mundung suggested this operation to me knowing full well I would choose Glemnik to run it, knowing that my desire to find Klek would blind me to everything else."

Nester felt sick thinking of the body in the trunk, and of something else. Operation Second Home must have been compromised by information in the hard drive of the computer at Terminal Sixteen, and Styles could not afford to be compromised. The operation had been a rogue effort—completely below the radar of legitimate authority—and he would hang for it if anyone found out. So his man Tunt had fabricated the conversation between the two East Germans to get Nester into the Box, and when the moment was right, when the scapegoat had taken his seat, the computer had been destroyed.

He steadied himself on the rim of the fountain. In the name of a ridiculous game, played falsely, two men were dead.

"You destroyed the computer in order to hide this, didn't you? Once you knew the whole thing had gone south, you torched the PC and its contents. And you killed a man in the process."

Styles lowered the ice pack from his face.

"That was an accident. A colleague of mine planted a far greater charge than was needed. He used Semtex—"

"Tunt again—"

"No names, no names—"

Storm gusts rushed through the trees of the park, flattened the grasses. Cold drops smacked Nester's head.

"Go on."

Styles cleared his throat.

"Klek had a job working as an exterminator in a cafe one block from the Amerika Haus. Need I remind you of the La Belle Disco bombing a few years ago? Need I remind you of the cost of complacency? Well, it wasn't going to happen again, not on my watch and certainly not with my help. And I wasn't going to take another fall for the Company. No indeed!"

Styles perceived the coming of rain. He raised the gun. "Let's move under the trees."

They moved from the fountain to a bridge running over a stream. Styles veered right along the bank. Linden trees stretched before them. Here and there, dark pines broke the ranks.

Nester tried to fit it all together. Glemnik had been chosen by Styles to play the rabbit in what was supposed to be a laboratory mission, an experiment in *perestroika*. But the mission had been a sham, because the East Germans had less than noble intentions, according to Styles. They were not interested in the pure research afforded by Second Home. Instead, despite every indication that East German intelligence chiefs wanted change, that they were reformers willing to work with the West, Styles believed that they had used Second Home against him.

Beyond the lindens rose a wall of stone, an ancient thing draped in dead ivy. A stone faun crouched in the shadows. Nester half expected to see the gaunt, dead mastiffs of Frederick the Great, buried somewhere on the grounds, come bounding toward them out of the dimness. Styles urged him toward the wall.

"You have to help me, Cates. If you do not, as I said, best-case scenario, I make you an accomplice in this whole affair. Worst case, I kill you."

Nester stopped dead in his tracks. "You'd better kill me then."

Styles halted too.

"I'm going straight to the military authorities. I'm going to tell them everything."

Styles arched an eyebrow. His teeth climbed up his face as he grinned. "No you won't, Cates, because they won't believe a word. You know that."

Nester didn't reply.

"Don't you see? Your politics in college, your insubordination at the Pentagon, your friendship with Glemnik—all of it points to this mess. You think for a minute people will believe that you *weren't* involved in Second Home? Hell, you're a disaster waiting to happen, as far as the military is concerned. Just the same, I've taken the precaution of inserting your name into our log of operations, which, by the way, was in Terminal Sixteen. I am the sole owner of its hard drive."

Styles headed for the wall, which lay just a few dozen yards ahead.

Nester called after him. "What do you want?"

"Get Klek." Styles turned and pocketed the gun. "Apparently, he trusts you."

"Not if he's who you say he is, not anymore—"

Styles didn't want to hear it. "Get Klek and bring him to me in Vienna. If I have Klek, then I don't care about the rest. I get Klek, you get exonerated. I give you the hard drive from Sixteen. That will be your insurance policy. Agreed?"

Nester shook his head. He would not be part of this.

"But he's vanished. He could be in Moscow for all I know."

Styles grimaced. "The Kremlin is in the middle of the greatest public relations coup in its history, and they're going to shelter these criminals? Please, Cates. As soon as you have Klek, leave a message for Herr Radetzky at the Carinthia Haus in Vienna. He'll arrange a meeting."

Styles reached into his coat pocket and plucked out the near-empty pill bottle. He downed the last of the medicine.

With a sudden burst of energy, he reached into the dead ivy on the wall and hauled himself up. From the top, he peered down at Nester, his eyes bloodshot and weary. Then he flung himself into the undergrowth on the other side. A howl of pain ripped from his throat. Nester grasped the ivy, thinking to leap over and grab the man while he was down. But the moment passed. Styles was up again, and the forest beyond the wall crackled with his movement.

Suddenly, from a thicket to Nester's left, shot a young stag. Its antlers tossed white on its gray head. Never looking back, the animal glided away from him, over the dead grasses, between the pale lindens, until it vanished into darkness. On the other side of the wall, Styles too had gone. Nester was utterly alone.

CHAPTER TWELVE

1.

DOUGLAS PEELED THE COVERS from his body. For an instant, sleep clutched at him. He had been unconscious for a long time.

His clothes smelled foul. Vomit crusted his shirt. He sat up and looked around. A basin of water rested on the floor near the cot's rusted legs. A change of clothes lay beside the basin. He spotted a towel and a washcloth. For the first time in days, someone had shown genuine concern for him.

"Thank you," he whispered to whoever it was. First, he took off his shirt, knelt on the floor, and dipped his head into the basin, gasping with pleasure at the sensation of coldness. His mind livened. Goose pimples tickled up his arms. He dipped his hand into the basin and tried as best he could to get the vomit off the shirt. After minimal success, he laid the shirt aside, dried himself, took a new shirt from the pile of clothes, and pulled it over his head—an orange turtleneck, not very warm, but clean. He changed pants.

The room looked familiar, as if he'd seen its contours in a dream. The walls consisted of thick old stone and gave off an aroma of earth. Greenish rubber carapaced the floor.

He was not alone. A fly buzzed in the warmth of a chamber pot. A foot wiggled within a blue sock. The sock belonged to an old man, lying in a bed to his left.

Rain skittered across the roof. A tree branch tapped against a wall; he realized now that he had heard the sound all night and had not been able to place it.

Grease hissed. A smell of hot pork wafted in, and Douglas was diverted. The smell tugged him out of the room, down a corridor. He came to a door brimming with breakfast light. His mouth watered. A plump, ample-breasted woman greeted him as he entered the kitchen. Silver curlers shaped like cigars bounced in her hair. A plain brown dress strained against her bust and hips. She smiled, and again he experienced déjà vu. He had seen this woman before.

She gestured at a bench beside a table. He sat. She poked with a wooden spoon at the contents of a skillet, passed the skillet over the surface of a burner, lifted it away. Hunger gripped Douglas, as if he, newly created, had never tasted food. The wood-burning stove was nice, but it struck him as an odd appliance for a ring of villainous East German spies. His great-grandmother had owned a wood-burning stove. The woman brought the skillet close to his face, showed him sausage slices, scrambled eggs, and fried potato chunks mixed with onions. She dropped the mixture onto a metal plate and set the plate in front of him. He gobbled the meal with his hands, stopped himself suddenly, when he became aware of her stare, and thanked her. *"Herzlichen Dank, gnädige Frau."*

He went back to gobbling. She didn't seem to mind his bad manners. He received a cup of fresh hot milk and coffee tasting of lignite. She asked him if he needed anything else, and he signaled no.

She mentioned a name; not Stuart, not Uta, somebody else. Her father?

Without caring to understand, Douglas nodded. Whoever was coming would have to wait. Douglas planned to eat and drink till he was sick. The food made him deliciously drowsy. The woman sat at the table for a moment.

"Schmeckt's?" she asked.

"Ja, sehr gut," he complimented.

"Du kommst also aus Texas und sprichst deutsch?"

Ja, he told her, he was a Texan who spoke German.

He asked how long he had been in bed. She lifted two fingers.

"Two days?"

She nodded. He was astounded. Never in his life had he been out for two days, but then he realized he must have been coming in and out of consciousness the whole time. That's why he remembered her.

She got up, served him another portion, and left the room. Five minutes later, she returned in a coat of mauve, a scarf of the same material around her head. Douglas turned his body to face her. She lifted a metal pail on her forearm.

"Uta?" Douglas called out. The woman made a flying gesture with her unpailed hand. *Weg.* Gone. Douglas shrugged. She shrugged back.

"Danke," Douglas said again.

He used the solitude to investigate the kitchen. It pleased him well enough. Its quaintness seemed real—not manufactured, as so often in American suburbia—with genuine old things in the cupboards, ancient cans in weird shapes, and preserves in dust-blanketed jars. The store-bought food was straightforward: no bright packaging, no clever catch phrase, no cheerful name. Just the words "snapping beans" above a picture of out-of-focus green beans on a dull orange can, or "goulash with kraut" on a glass jar filled with reddish glop. It struck him as rather honest.

He could detect no creatures. A pesticide had been sprayed long ago, probably last spring, and it had done the job; the same family of stuff they used on the death strip in Berlin, by the smell of it. The warmth of the stove licked his bones. The gentle ashes tumbled down. He wanted to curl up on the floor, catlike, and sleep forever. Someone should rub his sore temples and sing him lullabies. Beside the stove, in a container made of stacked tires, the woman stored coal, the same stuff he had seen and smelled in Uta's apartment on those warm summer afternoons when they'd made love.

He put down his fork and reached for a piece. The feel of the dusty carbon reminded him of her somehow. Despite everything, she had been an event in his life, a truly incredible woman. A tender part of her did exist, he was sure. He wondered, as he rolled the coal over in his hand, if she had ever read his love letter. She had never mentioned it, of course; but that didn't mean anything, not with Uta. Quietly, without much effort, he forgave her.

He put the piece of coal back onto the pile. From the bed in the back room came a feeble creaking.

Douglas's pulse quickened. He had made up his mind to flee, to make his way back to the West and turn himself in, and he figured he should get out while the getting was good. If the past week was any indication, in a matter of seconds, his life could be in danger again.

In a closet in the corridor, Douglas found several old coats. He reached for the mustiest of them, a long gray thing with black buttons and a high black collar. It looked military, and Douglas knew it must belong to the man in the blue sock. No harm in taking it, he told himself. The owner wouldn't miss it.

He stepped into galoshes, grabbed an umbrella, and tried the knob of the front door. It gave with a shudder. Within seconds, he stood under the befumed sky of the German Democratic Republic.

The weather was bad. A sky the hue of the military coat had been thrown over the earth. Rain misted down, too light to be a nuisance, but heavy enough to give the air a tendriled quality. A narrow courtyard led away from the door. In its far right corner sprawled a German shepherd. Pig viscera surrounded the animal: small, glistening studs. In the house, he had seen no evidence of fleas.

"There, there," he whispered, as much to himself as to the dog.

Beyond the dog, the courtyard opened onto a road. Douglas looked out and realized he had been optimistic on the matter of escape. Uta had brought him to the end of the world, to a village no bigger than a shopping mall in what must be one of the most obscure corners of the country. As a consequence, he understood, there would be little or no help for him. The entire village probably belonged to Stuart's cabal. To escape, he would have to run through fields extending for kilometers on all four sides of the village. Everything was visible to the naked eye.

He ventured into the street and glanced around, as if his step might have set off alarms. Mashed birch leaves melted like gold into the mud of the street. It had never been paved. Pipe guts reared from the ooze. Membranous earth sucked at his galoshes.

To his left, as he headed roughly south, piles of brown coal glistened on doorsteps. The doorsteps themselves seemed well swept and clean, but the houses beyond the doors had an abandoned quality. They resembled old barns. Thick wooden beams and soot-grimed brick showed through gaps in plaster that had been applied decades ago. Where it existed, paint bubbled and peeled. Douglas checked up and down the street for signs of modern convenience, but there were no cars, no telephone lines, not a single telephone booth. There were no people either. His hostess should have been somewhere in the vicinity, but he saw nothing of her.

He looked down the street at a decrepit two-story manor. Crows flapped on its cupola. Shingles had been torn away, revealing skeletal beams. No one had been home for many years. Uta had talked about the landowning Junkers with contempt. This must be one of their old houses, a German version of a southern plantation.

He headed away from the manor, in the direction of an old church which reared its head above the walls of the northern half of the village. He rounded the front right corner of the church and came into a cemetery, or the ghost of one. Six tombstones backed up against the church. If there had been others, they had long since been removed. Grass grew high. He strolled past the first two graves, read the names, drifted on. But the next four made him curious. Two of the stones lay oblong in the ground. They were black granite, and on one of them—to his cautious delight—he found a candle burning. Flame flickered on a pool of wax within a blood-red glass. Above the candle flame, obscuring the name on the grave, someone had laid a wreath. Douglas lifted the ornament.

FRIEDRICH WILHELM NIETZSCHE. The letters of the name

marched across the granite. Each consonant and vowel had spent a year of training in a Prussian military academy. Was it *the* Nietzsche? Stuart's Nietzsche?

Grass was trimmed at the foot of the grave. Wind-stripped roses had been planted at its head. Next to Friedrich lay Elizabeth, some relation, and next to her were older stones of a slightly neglected quality.

Douglas had always hated "Naaay-chah," as his brother, in a Texas drawl, used to pronounce the name. "Naaay-chah!" Like "gotcha!" The two syllables conjured up Stuart smoking pot with his buddies behind the school gym while ceremoniously reading from *Thus Spake Zarathustra* and cranking Aerosmith on someone's new car stereo. Nietzsche had been Stuart's justification for skipping school, blowing off homework, doing drugs, and being an asshole to his family. On the other hand, Douglas reflected, Nietzsche had also been his barricade against the banalities of a Texas high school, against football, Bible thumpers, and all the rest of the enforced mediocrity.

He wanted to talk to his brother. He wanted to hear the whole story again, how Stuart got involved in some bizarre operation because of his connections in Turkey, how the operation could be confused with treason if you looked at it the wrong way, how he was an innocent man, betrayed by that lunatic Styles.

Stuart had tried to warn him. Douglas looked back with sorrow at the conversation during Oktoberfest. His brother had grabbed his hands and implored him to go. Why hadn't he left the very next morning?

At the very least, had Douglas listened more closely, he might even have been able to prevent the defection. Now Stuart had thrown away everything. The rest of his life would be spent either in hiding or in prison. He was lost for good.

Douglas looked down at the grave again. Nietzsche's visage had glowered on a wall of Stuart's high-school bedroom—that ridiculously big mustache, the dome of black hair, the deep-set eyes settled inside a skull big enough to be an insectarium. He was like a long-lost member of Douglas's family, a relative he had avoided while growing up and now remembered with a generic affection.

Silence lay across the churchyard. It folded up the tombstones and extended like a gray blanket to fields of turned earth just visible beyond the church. To the west, a smokestack touched the sky's murk, the lone high thing in that country. Fresh rain fell.

Douglas popped open the umbrella, forgotten till now. Time to go find a road, he told himself, time to leave this godforsaken place.

"*Guten Tag,*" a voice uttered low behind him.

He pitched around. The umbrella threw him off balance.

"*Beruhige dich,*" the voice commanded in German, then in English. "Calm, please. Is no danger here."

It was Uta's fat, forgotten cousin, Herr Dampfer, shaking rain beads off a worn black coat. His face shone with wetness. A cigarette burned between his lips. Douglas put a hand to his chest. Dampfer was no longer decked out in a Tyrolean hat and suspenders. Instead, he wore a dark beret too small for his bloated head. Beneath the beret lay a scrap of silver hair, and his eyes were a somber blue, not warm exactly, but not without compassion. Douglas knew before the man spoke that his presence in the graveyard could not be a coincidence.

"*Ach ja,*" the man then said. "That coat. It belongs to my brother. *Nicht?*"

Douglas's heart beat a little faster.

"Or not?"

"*Ja,*" Douglas said, "it does."

"Do you know what sort of a coat it is?"

Douglas shook his head.

"It is the coat of an officer of the SS. *Schutzstaffel.* Better not let anyone here see you."

The rain had stopped. Douglas pulled down his umbrella.

"Where is everybody?"

Dampfer plucked the cigarette from his mouth.

"A third go west, mostly young people, a third go to work, either on the farm or at the chemical works to the south, and a third die behind these walls, like my brother." He pointed at the graves before him. "*They're* always at home, of course."

Rain rivulets ran from his eyes.

"Your brother stood right there once," he said, "where you are standing."

Douglas gave Dampfer a closer look. His belly hung between the buttons of his coat, which dangled to a pair of mud-clotted boots similar to those Douglas wore. A gray and black checkered scarf wound about his throat. In his left hand, gloved in black, he clutched a walking stick, which had gone unnoticed in the folds of the coat. He was much older than he had seemed that night in Uta's apartment.

"Herr Dampfer, please tell me what has happened. Where is my brother?"

Herr Dampfer tossed his cigarette to the earth at the foot of the grave.

"My name is Mundung. Department Twelve. *Hauptverwaltung Aufklärung.*"

Douglas wiped his nose. Here was another man with two names. He began to wonder if everyone in the world didn't have at least one other identity tucked away in case of emergency.

"I keep vigil here," Mundung said.

Douglas followed the man's gaze to the graves.

"If the Antichrist rises again, I will be there with my cross. I will stake him to this Saxon earth."

With that, Mundung gestured toward the alley. Resignedly, Douglas obeyed.

2.

THEY HURRIED PAST the shattered windows of the Junker estate and out of the village. They walked on a cement footpath delving between walls topped by broken glass. Before long, it meandered out into open fields. Directly ahead, half a kilometer away, lay another village.

As Mundung bobbled along, he talked about himself.

"You know the Spanish Civil War?"

"Yessir."

"And the name Albacete?"

Douglas didn't.

"I was recruited for the cause in Belgrade. By Tito. Don't ask what I was doing there. Chasing women. It was 1937, before the fall of Bilbao. I was seventeen years old, without attachments. They sent me to Albacete and taught me how to roast a pig."

In the midst of his speech, Mundung almost slipped off the footpath. He reached back for Douglas's arm, balanced himself, and continued with his story. "I make *Spanferkel*. You know *Spanferkel?*"

"*Spanferkel?*"

The old man halted. "Little pigs," he replied. "Succulent little pigs."

Douglas gave him a confused smile. "With the apple in the mouth?"

"Correct." Mundung moved on. "I was a cook in Albacete, and I saw terrible things. There are a few of us who survived. Not many. A few. It was a time of greatness and terror. Tell me something. Do you believe your brother could be working for Nester Cates?"

Here, Douglas stopped. It was an astonishing question. He had still been thinking about the suckling pig.

"Nester Cates?"

"Yes. Would you think it possible that your brother is a Western agent, working for Nester Cates? Is it possible, do you suppose, that Nester Cates sent him to Turkey, to my friend Günter Talibor?"

"Um—"

Mundung had stopped too, and was looking back at him quizzically.

"I'm a little confused here, sir," Douglas admitted. "I thought my brother was working for you."

Mundung gave a terse little smile. "Oh he is, he is. But one might work for any number of people these days, mightn't one? It's not like the old days, when everyone respected the terms."

Douglas experienced a shiver that had nothing to do with the cold. He didn't know what this man wanted, but the more he heard, the more distressed he became. Mundung's curiosity gave way suddenly.

"Come, come, it's not as serious as all that." He gave Douglas a squeeze on the arm, a quite painful one. "Your brother is like a son to me, and parents become concerned. That's all. Never mind the question. Let's move on."

Douglas helped the old man over the remains of a stone wall. A little farther on, Mundung stopped in front of a square house, a concrete block with flower boxes in the windows. It was the newest, cleanest, brightest thing Douglas had seen. A fence surrounded the front yard, a square so perfect it might have been another room in the house. An elf in a red stocking cap hoisted a beer beside its gate. The old man led Douglas to the door, bade him take off the wet coat before entering. Douglas obeyed.

"We have a coffee, and I send you on your way," said the old man, removing his beret and placing his cane in a stand beside the door.

Douglas hesitated at the threshold to the family room. They were not alone. A boy stretched out on a brown sofa lining the far wall. He'd shaved his head.

"This is Knut, my niece's son. My great-nephew," Mundung explained. Douglas took a few steps closer to the sofa and noticed with faint surprise a Dixie flag sewn into the shoulder of the jacket. "He'll be your driver."

3.

KNUT AND DOUGLAS SET OFF at three p.m. The day had already begun to wane. Before their departure, Mundung had made his nephew hand over the SS coat Douglas had been wearing, saying it would be waiting for him when he returned, a reward for a completed mission. The deal did not please Knut. He scowled until his great-uncle slapped him across the chin. The boy kept quiet after that.

Mundung had taken Douglas aside. "The train leaves Dresden tonight at eleven p.m. Do not let him go astray. He's a young *Dachs*, like I was, and he'll make trouble if you let him."

Douglas didn't know what to make of this comment, so he gave his word and shook Mundung's meaty fingers. The car, a brownish-yellow Wartburg with a toy soldier dangling from its rearview, tilted in a rut beside a toppled wall. It was impossible to enter on the passenger side.

Douglas waited until Knut backed up. The teenager had brought a black duffel bag of cassette tapes: Jimi Hendrix, German punk bands, marching music.

Mundung stared at them from his front porch. The walking stick propped him up. No emotion appeared on his face. He did not wave. Douglas did not believe that this man loved Stuart as a son. Maybe once he had, but no more. Like everyone else who had tried, the old man had seen his love somehow violated.

That reminded him. Along with a new coat, Mundung had also given him an envelope. Douglas tore it open. Inside, he found a letter from Stuart.

Dear Doug,

Last night, I watched you sleep for a whole hour. I sat beside your bed and watched, and you know what I thought of? I thought of that time Grandpa Lou Gleaming, you, and I blew up the anthill behind his house in Nacogdoches. Maybe you don't remember. You stuck a thunderbomb into the hole and blew it up. I went after it with a hose. Grandpa took up a shovel. One of us got stung by the biggest red ant I've ever seen, I don't recall who anymore. Maybe me, probably you. Afterwards, we all went for hot links. There's a lot I can't remember, but that day stays with me like it happened yesterday. But it didn't, of course. It happened in another lifetime, when we were all different people. Grandpa Lou's been dead more than ten years. Do you realize that? Anyway, I wanted to wake you up, but I thought to myself, after everything he's been through, he needs his rest, and soon enough, in Bucharest, we'll be together.

Which is the point of this letter. I cannot tell you everything, but suffice it to say, I have spent the last 48 hours dodging around East Germany. I am in terrible trouble, but that's my beer, as the Germans say, and I have to drink it. The important thing is to get you out of harm's way. As I told you, Carlton Styles, my colleague, has become obsessed with you. As unlikely as it sounds, he believes you are the man who planted the bomb in his safe house, and means, I'm pretty sure, to kill you. (Bet you never thought anything like this would ever happen to you. Chalk another one up to your fucked-up brother!)

You must get out of East Germany as quickly as possible. Herr Mundung, whom you know as Herr Dampfer—sorry about that, by the way, I guess it would have been better if I'd been honest right from the start. Anyway, he is my friend. He will give you a first-class train ticket from Dresden to Bucharest, the capital of Romania, as well as 1,000 West German marks, which will buy whatever comforts you need. Without going into too much detail, I can firmly predict that I won't be in Bucharest for a while. I have to keep moving, as I may have several different people on my trail. So take your time and get to me on or around December 15. That should do it. I will be booked at the Hotel Intercontinental, under the name Sven Karst. Bucharest should be safe. There will be no revolution there. The government is real strong. Herr Mundung has a friend named Olestru who will get us safely to Australia, where we will spend a few months until this thing blows over.

I can't tell you how sorry I am about everything. I didn't mean to leave you at the border. Not a day, not an hour of the rest of my life, will pass without my seeing you behind me, at that checkpoint. I lost my nerve. I was scared to death, I am a bad person. But I told myself I would come back for you, and I have. Perhaps you won't hate me so much. I love you.

Stuart

The letter ended, but there was a last page. Douglas counted ten one-hundred-mark bills and checked the time on the train ticket. Knut's eyes widened at the sight of the money. Douglas read on.

P.S. I am writing this in the kitchen beside the old wooden stove. I should have left an hour ago, but I have been debating whether or not to tell you something, the hardest thing I will ever have to tell you, and I have decided to do so, at the risk of losing you for good. Should you be caught, you will have this confession, but honestly, it probably won't be worth much. I doubt anyone will accept it as evidence of your innocence. Still, at least you will know the whole truth. For lack of a better term, I have betrayed my country.

Douglas shuddered. Though he'd never completely believed Stuart's story, the news came as a terrible shock. His brother had lied, after all. He was a *traitor.* That word horrified Douglas more than he'd ever expected it could. But this went beyond the act of treason. For months now, ever since he had come to West Berlin, Douglas had been struggling to believe in Stuart—just as he once fought to believe that his dad would come home, that the family would be made whole again, just exactly like that. And now, at one blow, it was as if the entire campaign, with every one of its illusions, had been decimated. He turned toward the passenger window, away from Knut's glances, wiped his eyes, and read on.

And in the process, I have now cast a shadow across you. But I'm going to set this all right. That's why it's imperative that you come to Bucharest, no matter what you may think of me. I'm the only one who can exonerate you. I wish I could take you with me now, but until I'm in a safe, secure place, you're better off without me. Until then, you will have to trust my comrades, whom you should see as your own flesh and blood, because that's what they have been to me.

Douglas folded the letter, put it back inside his coat with the train ticket and the money, and stared off into the ashen distance.

4.

MEANWHILE, Knut disobeyed his uncle's orders to go straight to Dresden. In one village, he picked up a friend, Kai, a fat boy squeezed into military green. Pimples dotted Kai's lower forehead. A German flag strained on his shoulder, and an iron cross dangled from his throat. His voice had not yet cracked.

Kai kicked Douglas out of the front seat. He ejected a Jimi Hendrix tape from a stereo purchased with hard currency by Herr Mundung and popped in marching tunes. The two boys spoke in hushed tones about someone named Frank. Knut seemed delighted. Frank, according to Kai, had just been amnestied out of a juvenile penitentiary; he wanted to be picked up near the cathedral in Naumburg. He had beer glasses to sell. Douglas objected.

Knut yodeled. Douglas realized he was among louts.

"Your uncle won't like this!" he cried out in German.

Knut waved a finger at him. "Yes, yes, we go to Dresden!"

Farther south, in the large city of Weissenfels, they picked up Arne, who had once been a boxer, or so they said. He was big enough, God knew.

Kai and Arne clapped to the marching music. The Wartburg sailed past a police car, which stayed immobile, a pathetic gray Trabi with a sad blue light on its top. Arne had large biceps, a bad case of beer breath, and a pained rage in his eyes, as if someone had swatted him across the nose once a day every day of his life. He took up half of the back seat and talked to

Douglas in an accent too swift and thick to be understood, but Douglas nodded, laughed, and asked him to repeat everything he said, anything to get through the ordeal.

After an hour or so, they arrived on the outskirts of a city called Naumburg, took a wild spin around its medieval walls, and came to rest beside a trash dump. Kai lit a cigarette. They rolled down the windows and jeered at a few schoolgirls. One of them, a blonde with a poodle cut and sparkling green eyes, yelled out at them.

"Nazi Schwein!"

Frank appeared. He wore a black leather jacket with epaulets. Under one arm, he held a gray paper bag. All of the boys got out of the car and went to him. Kai gave up his place in the front seat and took the bag out of Frank's hands. Frank peered through the Wartburg's windows at Douglas and asked who he was.

"Ein Amerikaner?!" he called out after Knut explained. *"Gibt's ja nicht!"*

He came to the car. Douglas heard the soft, ticking sound of bootheels against pebbles.

"American?" Frank asked, leaning into the window. "Jew?"

Douglas shook his head. Frank gave him the thumbs-up.

He'd slicked his dark hair down with oil. His ears stuck out. Despite the air of masculine dominance about him, his face possessed a feminine quality, something thin, delicate, and pale, as if he'd been coddled as a child. The eyes conveyed intelligence, but had narrowed in suspicion. His leather jacket was clean, free of insignia.

Douglas insisted on the importance of going to Dresden. Frank ordered everyone back into the car and settled into the front seat. The boys wanted to know about prison. Kai hung on every word. Arne picked through the beer glasses. Frank had bought them in prison from a man who sold them to tourists for hard currency and to Soviet soldiers for weapons. For thirty beer glasses, Frank had heard, you could get three hand grenades and a Kalashnikov rifle. The boys cackled in disbelief.

"A Kalashnikov!" exclaimed Kai. "Vowvee!"

They hit the highway for Dresden as Frank detailed the routine at the penitentiary—card playing, three bad meals a day, physical exercise, occasional interrogation by men who never stated their business, fistfights with other inmates, masturbation, and old movies about great German generals who surrendered to the Soviets in order to save the lives of their people.

Frank was God. He had been thrown into prison for *"Rowdytum"* and *"Fascistische Schmiererei."* At the time, he had been sixteen years old, an aspiring rock-and-roll singer. With a few of his friends, he had gone to the Buchenwald concentration camp memorial and sung a Nazi song, the

Horst Wessel Lied. Only as a joke, he explained in a sly, resentful tone. For that, they had taken two years out of his young life.

"I was a political prisoner!" he shouted.

Now the government had let him go, because it was panicking, and he intended to take his revenge on the enemy that very night. He had been thinking some more about Dresden, he said, and decided it was a good idea. They could perform a great feat for the German people, a feat to compare with Hitler's march into the Rhineland. The boys giggled. Frank smiled and let it be known that he was exaggerating for effect. He was a boy who had read one history book in his life, Douglas thought, and been deeply impressed by it.

From the front seat, Frank eyed Douglas. "You think we're all Communists over here, don't you? But I'm living proof that we are not. I am a hero, a dissident."

Douglas had been trying to vanish into his cramped corner of the car. He wanted to avoid conversation.

"We are not Communists. We love our people, and we're going to show that in Dresden." Frank cleared his throat, spat out the car window, and turned back to Douglas, the toy soldier swinging behind his head. "We're Johnny Rebs."

They arrived in Dresden after dark.

"Please take me to the train station," Douglas begged.

They stopped at a restaurant in a suburb. While still in the car, Knut told his friends that Douglas was carrying one thousand West German marks on his person; squeals of disbelief and delight exploded from Kai and Arne. In the parking lot of the restaurant, Frank made Douglas hand over the money. Douglas hated to do it, but had no choice. Just before that, Frank had sold twelve glasses to a Soviet soldier skulking around an empty vegetable market. In exchange, he had received an antiquated Polish pistol with a thick, flat barrel. Now, the money in his hands, he gazed at Douglas with a terrible intensity. Frank had never been close to that much money in his entire life, Douglas was sure, and the presence of it clawed his brain. Standing in the parking lot, Frank counted the bills. He looked around at his cronies, broke into a grin, then let out a howl. The others joined in. They went into the restaurant, and Frank ordered schnitzel and beer for everyone.

During the meal, Frank told them where they were going. South of Dresden lay a small city called Freiberg, a place where the German Reichsbahn built sleeping wagons for trains. In prison, a cellmate had told him about the Vietnamese workers who lived in quarters near the factory. They ate and slept better than the Germans and looked down on anyone who wasn't Vietnamese. His friend, the beer glass seller, had gone on and on

about it. He had lived in a permanent rage against these Vietnamese, because he had been thrown in jail on a false accusation made by one of the
filthy yellow bastards. "Tonight, we're going to get them back," Frank swore.

The other boys grinned at one another, toyed with the dregs of their
beers, flicked cigarette ash on the floor, and gazed at Frank with a pleading
in their eyes. They looked afraid.

When the check came, Frank handed Douglas one hundred marks and
told him to pay for dinner. If Frank paid in hard currency, the proprietors
would think he'd stolen it. The other boys were pleased at his cleverness.
They watched Douglas with curiosity, to see what he would do. Somewhere in Frank's jacket waited the Polish pistol. Douglas excused himself,
crossed the restaurant to the waiter—the boys' eyes on his back—and pulled
out the one-hundred-mark bill. The waiter's eyes widened.

Douglas had to go into the back and negotiate a deal with the restaurant
manager, who pulled a small metal box from a safe behind a picture of Gorbachev. Douglas was relieved to see that Frank hadn't followed them. The
manager gave Douglas seventy West German marks in change and told him
to go out the back.

"Those are Fascists, aren't they?"

Douglas nodded.

"I'm calling the police."

Thanking him, Douglas dashed out the back.

5.

THE DRESDEN TRAIN STATION was enormous, a vast, dark hall
with a ceiling of beams crisscrossed like spiderwebs. He hurried up
slick steps and checked the destination board. As it turned out, the train for
Bucharest was departing in a matter of minutes from the very last rail. Men
in uniform watched him run, but no one stopped him. He heard an announcement for Prague, Budapest, Bucharest, and Sofia, and picked up his
speed. A long gasp came out of the locomotive as it stopped in a half-lit
back corridor of the station. The train had come from Berlin. *Deutsche
Reichsbahn,* Douglas read on its side, a very old machine. Customs officials
climbed aboard. Women wrapped in several layers of scarf trundled off.
Steam erupted. Douglas reached into his coat for the train ticket. It was
gone. He found the East German identification document, but the ticket
was definitely gone.

He ripped off the coat and dumped it upside down. A box of East German matches spilled out. He slammed a fist against the metal skin of a train car.

The ticket had been in the envelope along with the fucking money. He must have handed it to Frank by mistake. A numbness came over Douglas. He wanted to fall right there, fall to the ground and never get up again. His options had run out. The train moved forward an inch, shaking Douglas from his despair. One thing was sure. He couldn't remain in Dresden. He must use the priority stamps in the fake identity pass. With them, at the very least, he could get the hell out of East Germany.

The train had paused, as if for him. He leapt aboard. A woman's voice called a last time for passengers to the south. From one end of the car, he gazed out a window, his chin pressed against the cold pane of glass. The train moved again, and this time it was on its way. It lumbered out of the station, and Dresden slipped into darkness.

The notion that his East German document would work as an all-purpose ticket within the boundaries of the country now struck Douglas as foolish. Even under Communism, people had to buy train tickets. He began to look for a place to hide. He crept down the dark cars, trying to behave with the aplomb of a recent winner of the C. A. Rudolphi Medal for contributions to parasitology. Every compartment was full. He beheld hallucinations. In one car, clothed in civilian dress, sat a dragonfly reading a newspaper. In another, mangled teeth glinted from the shadows. He ducked past these apparitions, pushed them out of his mind. Here and there he stopped to rest, leaning over the sink in a bathroom, rubbing cold water onto his face.

Finally, he came to the first-class cars. The windows were lightless, the curtains drawn. His best hope lay here. If someone was sleeping in one of the compartments, he would sneak in quietly, try not to wake them. He cracked the door of the first compartment and interrupted the boozing of a drunken Soviet officer. The man snarled. Douglas backed out, crept down to the end of the car, and opened the doors to the last compartment. Someone lay inside—as best Douglas could tell, one person, a woman breathing in slumber. He took a step forward, closed the door behind him. He lowered a hand and found a leg.

A flashlight beam seared his eyes.

"Who are you?" an alarmed American voice inquired.

It was a woman, but he couldn't see her features in the darkness behind the light. Instinctively, as if she held a gun, Douglas raised his hands.

"Get out now, or I'll scream."

She pressed the flashlight right up to his face and became suddenly silent, as if she was having second thoughts. He took two steps back. Light from the corridor fell on her dark, shoulder-length hair and her unforgettable eyebrows, and an irrational joy came over Douglas. She wasn't wearing her cobalt-blue turtleneck, she wasn't scribbling on postcards, but Douglas knew her. The face had stayed with him. It was the woman from the cafe.

"Oh my God," she said. "You're Douglas Gleaming."

CHAPTER THIRTEEN

1.

A T FIRST, Jodie hadn't recognized him. Which wasn't surprising, because she had been distracted; not asleep, but drifting amid intense sensations. Her head buzzed, her arms tingled, her heart hammered in every corner of her body. She did not want sleep, did not even want to be stuck on the train, because she knew that outside its windows, everything was still alive. In every little village and collective, in apartment buildings and bars, people were suddenly grasping what had occurred, and that thing—that event, which she had witnessed with her own eyes, the fall of the Wall—was as immense as the sky. It meant everything and nothing. She wanted to be omniscient, to see into all windows, hear all conversations, know every contradictory emotion running through the hearts of every person in East Germany. She wished to be a foreman in a factory, a stooge for the Central Committee, a punk with a nose ring, a soldier on alert.

The feeling of magnitude was so overwhelming it even managed to dim the elation of gainful employment. After her first story on Berlin, *Probe* magazine had given her a retainer to cover Eastern Europe—not just a few hundred dollars a month to keep her quiet and hungry, but a small fortune, more money than she'd ever made in her life.

So when they ordered her to go to Prague, she went, even though she wanted to stay in East Germany, even though she was afraid she would miss the great story churning there. She was ecstatic, nervous, proud, all at once. She hoped Pansy Buckner thumbed through *Probe* now and again.

"May I sit?" Douglas Gleaming asked.

She had almost brained him with the flashlight.

"God, you startled me."

"I'm really, really sorry."

She shut the door to the compartment, gave him one of her blankets, and threw on her robe. He wrapped himself in the blanket and took a seat opposite her slumber unit. The train squealed to a stop. Another train passed north. Jodie drew the curtains and propped the flashlight against the wall.

He stared at his knees.

"So what are you doing here?"

He didn't answer. She became impatient.

"Please say something!" she finally insisted. "What the hell are you doing here? How did you find me?"

The oncoming train screamed past them. Their locomotive wrenched back into motion. "Okay. Let's do it another way. My name is Jodie Blum, and I'm a reporter. Your brother must have told you about me."

"My brother?"

"I met him at the barbecue. He didn't tell you?"

Douglas shook his head. "He kept everything from me. To protect me, he said."

"Oh my God. Something must have happened."

"Yes."

"There *was* something going on."

Jodie reassembled journal entries in her mind: Gleaming, Glemnik, Klek, Styles. Those had been the names.

"Yes."

"Jesus. You know I actually *spoke* to Styles."

Here, Douglas stopped. He became guarded.

Jodie reassured him. "I was *investigating* him. Because of what he said to you."

"He is trying to kill me. He thinks I'm a terrorist named Klek."

"No shit!"

She snatched up her purse, which lay on the floor, and pulled a new piece of gum from it. Gum was no substitute for a cigarette—she had been craving one for weeks—but it would have to do. Come to think of it, she *had* a carton of Marlboros in her computer bag, but she forced herself to resist. Those had to be saved for bribes and gifts. She chewed.

"Where is your brother now?"

"Now? God knows. In December, he will be in Bucharest."

"And that's where you're going?"

He nodded. The train creaked and jumped. She closed the robe around her throat. She recalled her interview with Styles. He was a dangerous man for sure. She had sensed it.

"I want to hear everything."

He took a few deep breaths and was about to speak again when a commotion down the corridor broke his concentration. Five or six compartments away from them, a door opened with a brutal slam.

"Don't panic. It's just customs."

She unzipped her overnight bag, rummaged for her passport, visa, and train ticket. They lay beneath everything—beneath equipment, yellow legal pads, toiletries, socks, bras, panties, even beneath her terribly wrinkled black dress, crushed silk stockings, and rose-red shoes. She arranged the travel documents at the top of the bag. "Better have yours ready too."

Douglas did not move. His eyes fixed on the compartment door, as if his name had been called from beyond the glass. She couldn't believe it.

"No ticket."

He shook his head.

"And no visa."

Again, he confirmed. Doors down the corridor slammed again. They were getting closer. "I will jump off this train before I let them catch me."

Jodie acted without thinking. She grabbed one of his hands.

"Get in here with me."

"What?"

"Do it or you're dead! They'll *arrest* you!"

She jerked him across the aisle between her cot and his seat. The entrance to the compartment next door slammed open, and the loud command of the border police pressed through the walls. *"Ausweise! Fahrkarten!"*

"Take off your shirt."

Douglas acquiesced. He shucked off the coat and turtleneck. She wiggled out of the robe and lifted the blanket. He was hairy, cold, ribby; pale as meringue.

"No! Switch places!"

He hopped over her, wriggled against the wall of the compartment. There was no room for him to hide, not if they turned on the lights, which they would. She batted away all her midwestern reserve and good Jewish upbringing and made a snap decision that would have horrified her parents and scandalized Aunt Rachel.

She slid around on top of him. "Maybe they'll leave us alone if they think we're doing it . . ." He nodded without quite understanding. "Put your arms around my back. Give me your passport! Hurry!"

He fumbled the gray document from his pocket and placed it in her hand. "This won't work," he stammered.

"Fuck that! Arms around my back!"

He obeyed. The doors of the adjacent compartment slammed shut. The customs team flagged for a moment, which gave her a split second to slip out of her long-john shirt. She adjusted herself in the bunk so that her covered back and derriere would stand out suggestively when the customs officials walked in, pressed her cheek against Douglas's rib, and flipped her hair over the hem of the blanket.

The door slid open. Douglas opened his mouth in terror, about to scream. She kissed it, put her palms on his shoulders, and lifted herself up to simulate sex. The blanket dropped down from her shoulders to her lower back. Douglas struggled for a moment, brushed her exposed nipples, then grabbed hold of her rib cage to steady himself.

She had an extraordinary sensation, as if he were using his hands to pull himself inside her body, to hide there.

"*Hoppla!*" one of the intruders cried in surprise.

"*Fahrkarten! Ausweise! Visum!*"

Lights flicked on. As the men waited, she pulled away from Douglas, shot a hand into the bag beneath the cot. She plucked out tickets, visa, passport, vouchers for five nights in a floating hotel—a botel, as it was called—handed them over; all, she noted happily, without revealing an ounce of raw, uncensored self to the authorities. She pretended to receive something from Douglas and gave them his document as well. Then, she turned on her side to face the guards, her bare shoulder blades against Douglas's chest.

Something about his passport excited the customs agents. The foremost leaned over Jodie and examined Douglas's face. He brought the identification close to the bed. He crouched and checked the photo against the original in front of him.

"*Ach, Herr Vizepräsident Rahnsdorf!*" he exclaimed apologetically. "*Ich bitte um Entschuldigung.*"

Horrified, the customs agent returned all the documents and tried to explain the extreme need for security. The Czechs had insisted on it. No one else would bother them that evening, he assured the man whom he clearly took to be his superior. Douglas didn't respond. Jodie felt his heart fibrillating through her shoulder blades.

The two men retreated. A finger flicked into the room and switched out the light. The door slammed shut. Jodie could feel her face going red with embarrassment and iritation. Had she known about this document, she wouldn't have ripped her clothes off so quickly.

"Vice president?"

Douglas's hands fell from her rib cage. His voice buzzed around the compartment like a trapped fly. "Yes, yes, I'm the vice president of the Society for Parasitology, and I've just won a medal, and I'm on a lecture tour—I must be important. They looked scared. My hands are shaking."

"Quiet."

"They're coming back. I know it!"

"*Shhhhhh.* They're leaving. Hopefully, thanks to your very interesting passport, they'll tell the Czechs to leave us alone too."

A few long minutes passed as the customs teams left the car. The train slowed again, then screeched to a stop. Jodie hated the sound. She bit the back of her hand in agony. After a few seconds, the screeching eased up. She found her long-john top in the darkness. The exterminator did not move.

"Out," she said.

He might have died, so rigid and cold was his body.

"I'm sorry. I should have told you about my passport. There wasn't time."

"Right. Now get out of my bed please."

Shadows lingered outside their door for a few seconds. She felt herself perspiring. His touch on her ribs, the fleeting brush of his fingers against her nipples, would stay with her, she feared, like an irritating song.

"I'm asking nicely for the last time."

He crawled out of the space beside her, crepitated back into the ugly russet turtleneck. She gave him two of her sweaters, and he made a pillow of his coat. Two men, Soviet officers, she thought, smoked a last cigarette in the corridor outside their compartment. The butts of their smokes glowed through the curtains. For the moment, they were in the clear. For Douglas's sake, they had to stay that way.

Douglas coughed into his hand. He looked as if he was praying. "God get me out of this country," he said.

2.

THE TRAIN ARRIVED IN PRAGUE a good hour before dawn. Jodie pressed her nose to the cold glass of the corridor window. Mist clotted the sky. Bats flittered against the platform lamps. Douglas had a cold. After talking most of the night, he had gone silent. Jodie could see why. If a quarter of his story was true, he was in real trouble. She couldn't decide whether she should believe him when he protested his innocence. The passport, in particular, bothered her.

Men in gray uniforms were watching as they stepped off the train. She passed a scowler in a leather jacket whose attention seemed more than casual. He kept a rigid eye on Douglas. Jodie scowled back at him. Already, she had a bad feeling about Prague. The most beautiful city in northern Europe, her editor, Chubbs, had said, but she couldn't imagine beauty in such a place. The reek of train exhaust caught in her throat; the people around her smelled of grease, decay, and dirt. They descended stairs into a blackness. Water pooled at the bottom, its surface reflecting the same dim ochre light that had radiated from Dresden.

Douglas reached for her arm. After passing a one-legged janitor with a shovel over his shoulder, a begging child, and a line of seated, unconscious Soviet soldiers, they came to the money-changing booth. A woman with pinkeye and a mask of lavender pancake took Jodie's three hundred German marks, did some mathematical figuring on an abacus, and shoved a few thousand korunas back through the slot. She seemed angry. Jodie stuffed the money into her computer bag. They came to the entrance of the station. Wind whistled between buses huddled against the cold. Red and yellow lights flashed in the iciness. Czechs climbed aboard. More exhaust filled her lungs, the thickest, vilest stuff she had ever inhaled.

Her ride, a woman whom Chubbs knew from his own coverage of Eastern Europe years before, was nowhere in sight. Ten minutes later, a kid with a blond Mohawk showed up with an apology. The car was a Soviet Lada borrowed from a friend at the British embassy. They careened down a defile between walls and onto a wide avenue. Headlights followed at a safe distance.

The kid, Zdenek, asked them a thousand questions. What was going on in Berlin? Had the Wall really opened? Were people dancing on it? He laughed out loud when Jodie told him they had been dancing. Then, a second later, at a stoplight, he put his head down on the steering wheel. He murmured something in Czech.

"Are you okay?" she asked.

He lifted his head, gave an enormous smile, the most brilliant and truly happy she had seen in weeks, and said, "I am."

The light turned green. He explained arrangements. They would be staying with his mother, who typed out samizdat literature for the dissident community and who had known most of the famous Western journalists who had passed through Prague, including Jodie's editor, Mr. Chubbs.

During the day, his mother served strawberry milk shakes at the Koruna Automat on Wenceslaus Square. By night, she acted as a conduit between Radio Free Europe and the movement. Her apartment in the suburb of Bohnice was watched by the police, especially these days, but the security wouldn't dare make trouble with Western journalists, not with the eyes of the West focused on Czechoslovakia. Just the same, he recommended they register at the district Department of Passports and Visas in Olsanska Street, a precaution against interference. After a pause, he asked Jodie if she wanted an interview with Vaclav Havel.

"Definitely."

Chubbs believed the Prague government teetered on the brink, and if it fell, he believed, the tide would be irreversible. Revolution would sweep the entire region. A demonstration was scheduled for the following day, a Friday, the fiftieth anniversary of the murder of a Czech student by the Nazis, and he—Chubbs—wanted her to go, file as early as possible, and predict, if she could, the approximate timing of the regime's demise. He would hold the issue through Saturday night, if necessary. Her piece would be the lead in a cover package on the transformation of Eastern Europe.

Fine, she'd told Chubbs in a cool voice, as if her heart had not been about to burst through her chest, but she had never been so scared. She, Jodie Blum, was competing against the greatest journalists in the world for one of the stories of the century.

"The *New York Times* is here," Zdenek said. "I helped Mrs. Buckner get an interview with Havel for Mr. Hammond Stamps, who is very famous, and Mrs. Buckner paid me a hundred dollars for my time."

Jodie broke out of her worry spell.

"Who did you say?"

"Mrs. Buckner. She belongs to Mr. Stamps, I believe."

Jodie collapsed back into the seat, hands over her eyes. It could not be. Could *not*. Pansy had no business here. She was not a journalist. She was an assistant.

The demonstration the next morning wasn't expected to be a big deal, Zdenek told her. The Charles University Students Council had voted to stage it at a poet's grave on the old fortress of Vyserad, and Vyserad lay a good distance from the seat of government, so the demonstrators must not want a confrontation with the police. The real upheaval would probably happen in December on Human Rights Day. That's what everyone was saying. If she wanted, Zdenek told her, she could cover the demonstration, but with events still moving quickly in Berlin, her magazine probably wouldn't be that interested.

"I've got to talk to Havel." She gave him a hundred-dollar bill. "You *have* to arrange it."

Bundled souls made their way against the wind. Lines congealed in front of bread shops. Within the brown-gloomed businesses, piles of rolls clumped like quarry stone in metal cages. A streetcar shunted to Jodie's left, just outside the car window. Blue sparks shot from wires overhanging the street. An ancient woman stared from within the glass. *She* must have seen it all, Jodie thought. She must have experienced the betrayal of Czechoslovakia in 1938—her dead Uncle Mordecai had been in Prague back then too—Hitler's invasion of the Sudetenland, the murder of the Jews, the expulsion of the Germans, and all the years of Communism since. And now this! Another convulsion, Jodie thought. What in the world must she be thinking? That was a story for sure.

"Prague is beautiful," Zdenek asserted, noticing her attention to the woman, perhaps. "Prague is extraordinary."

"Yes," she suddenly found herself agreeing. "It is."

3.

IN THE APARTMENT, Zdenek made coffee and directed Douglas to a room at the back, where he immediately collapsed.

She looked around the kitchen, a tightly packed place with lots of homemade shelves, an electric stove, a state-of-the-art German refrigerator, and a heating cylinder as round and high as a classical pillar. From time to time, the cylinder burbled. Not much heat came from it. Every few seconds wind whistled through a chink in the window at her back, and outside the door to her left, up and down the six flights of stairs, moaned a deeper draft.

Zdenek gave her coffee and a piece of Moravian sugar wafer, and she went into the den. Shelves of books on folklore and folk music in English, French, Czech, and German lined one wall. On the bottom shelf, she saw stacks of loose paper—the typist's samizdat material, no doubt. At right angles to the shelf, at one end, sat a heavy oak table, crowned in the middle by an ancient Olympia typewriter, oiled to a shiny black and cherished, she could tell, like a family diadem. On the desk beside the typewriter were pictures of family, empty coffee cups, an ashtray crammed with butts. Jodie would leave a few packs of Marlboros.

A sofa stretched beside the desk, a long, lumpy thing piled high with pillows and afghans. To her right, on the wall opposite the bookshelves, was a panorama of the Tatra mountain range, a single sheet of paper stretching from the floor to the ceiling and detailing a glade between peaks, a sunny place beneath a blue sky. She crawled into the couch and closed her eyes.

Around noon, Zdenek's mother, Ewa, rushed into the apartment. She was buried inside a brown cowl-neck sweater and a winding wool scarf, which hid most of her face. Before 1968, according to Zdenek, Ewa had been an ethnomusicologist specializing in medieval Bohemian folk songs, particularly those about the legendary figure of Rübezahl, a mountain wizard and proto-hippy, according to her theory. She had also been the happily married wife of a prominent Slovak poet and a reformist member of the Communist Party. Twenty-one years later, she had lost her job; her books were banned, her party membership had been taken, and her husband had emigrated to Canada. She lived alone with her sixteen-year-old son, who was actually the product, he diffidently revealed, of an affair with a visiting French journalist. The samizdat work, a continued interest in folk music, and the beloved Olympia sustained her. Jodie took one look at the woman and believed herself to be an unwanted intruder in an intensely private world. Within seconds, the woman dispelled that impression.

"Tell me everything!" Ewa unwound the scarf so fast she looked like she might choke herself in the effort. "It's really happening in Berlin, isn't it? You want tea?"

Ewa led her to a seat at the kitchen table, then disappeared back into the den. Jodie heard a cassette being dropped into a tape player. The opening strains of *The Marriage of Figaro* burst so loudly out of the den that Jodie jumped from her chair. She peeked into the room and saw Ewa adjusting the volume. Then Ewa came back into the kitchen, dragging one of the speakers behind her.

"Last month, a colleague of mine from the ethnomusicology department called me." She aimed the speaker, more or less, at the refrigerator. She was yelling. "I have not seen him in almost twenty years, but he claimed to have thought fondly of me all this time, and as a show of affection, he wanted to give me a new refrigerator. So last week, two men installed this beautiful thing, and it keeps the ice cream frozen, but guess what?"

Jodie shook her head, straining to hear over the music.

"It's *bugged*. I found a microphone in the cooling unit on the back. Zdenek tried to get it out with a screwdriver, but it won't come."

Ewa seated herself and lit a cigarette. "I don't suppose you've seen Zdenek, have you?"

Jodie shouted that she hadn't seen him since the morning. Ewa flicked wafer crumbs away and watched their tumbling with tired but excited eyes. "Tell me what you saw in Berlin. Was there any violence?"

Voices boomed from the stereo. Jodie laughed. "None!" she cried.

Ewa shook her head in disbelief. "You cannot understand how that sounds to me. No violence. After all these years. And Germans too! They aren't exactly known for their pacifist ways."

The boiler shrieked. At first, Jodie thought it was the opera. Ewa rose from the table, opened a cupboard beneath the sink, pulled out a broom handle, and used one end of it to swat the cylinder three times. The shriek choked off. Within the cylinder, steam tinkled. Ewa returned to the table.

"You must write this week?"

"Tomorrow."

Jodie repeated her request for an interview with Havel, thinking it could do no harm, and Ewa grimaced. "He's hard. Everyone wants him. The *New York Times* has asked for my help too. You've spoken with Zdenek?"

Jodie nodded.

Ewa shrugged. "If there's a way, he'll find it. In the meantime, you speak Czech?"

Jodie responded with embarrassment. "No."

"German?"

"Ein bisschen."

"The elder people speak some German, the younger ones a bit of English. I would translate for you, but my hands are full, and besides, for me it's quite dangerous. I do not particularly want Zdenek at this demonstration, but he is his own person. You may ask him and perhaps he will help. But I have a very bad feeling, you see. A friend of mine from Brno heard that thousands of riot police are being sent here. I don't think our government plans to follow the German example."

Douglas entered the room, hands over his ears. Jodie made introductions. Ewa excused herself to return to work. "We'll dine here tonight. I bought some spaghetti. I will ask you many questions about Berlin, so be prepared."

"How do you feel?" Jodie asked Douglas when they were alone. He took Ewa's seat beside her.

"Does it have to be so *loud?*"

"The refrigerator's bugged. Have some tea."

Jodie poured him a cup and offered a wafer.

"I can't sleep with this racket," he complained.

Jodie had made a decision.

"Listen, Vice President, I've decided to go to Bucharest with you."

Douglas's head sank. She couldn't tell if he was upset or relieved. His emotion possessed the entire room. Even the boiler and the Moravian wafers seemed to be waiting for his reaction.

"In my old job," he finally said, "I never liked reporters. They always got it wrong. One guy I remember referred to a cockroach as a cricket, if you can believe it, but"—here he paused and shifted his gaze away from her to the window—"I don't see any other way out of this jam. And besides, after last night, I owe you one."

Jodie took his hand. It would work out just right. Douglas's brother expected him in Bucharest in December, which meant he was in no rush. She could take her time and finish the Czechoslovakia story. Meanwhile, she'd have to come up with a story for Chubbs to hide her real reasons for going to Romania. She'd have to promise a story on Ceausescu. If her editor got wind of the spy story before she could prove it was true, he'd think she was a sap.

"Promise me something," Douglas said.

"What?"

"That you're going to exonerate me. Promise me, this isn't just going to be some sensationalistic piece of crap."

Jodie smiled. Rule of thumb, never make promises to a source. She wanted to exonerate him, and she would, if the facts bore out his story. If, on the other hand, he was guilty of treason, she would have to nail him.

"It won't be sensationalistic crap."

He looked deep into her eyes. "Let's go then. Right this very minute. I'll wait for my brother in Bucharest. He says it'll be safe there."

Jodie squeezed his hand. "Day after tomorrow."

They shook on it.

5.

HE WAS SEXIER than he had been in West Berlin. She could not deny it.

That afternoon, as they took the subway into the middle of town, he described the mating ritual of the dragonfly, how he had seen two of the insects doing it beneath an apple tree in West Berlin, and it actually sounded romantic. She took stock of his olive skin and deep-set eyes. He was almost Slavic in appearance. That thing he called his "housefly" intrigued her. It could easily have been a powder burn, she reflected, though she said nothing about her impression to Douglas.

They wandered up and down the narrow streets. In the neighborhood of Josefov, the old Jewish quarter, they bought a cheap lunch of potato pancakes and apple sauce and listened to an old woman complain loudly from the next table about the authorities. "It's coming!" she cried in Habsburg German. "The moment of truth is coming!"

Jodie glanced over at Douglas from time to time and recalled that she had not been with a man since leaving home. Back in Minnesota, she had taken up briefly with a high school flame who now played in a local garage band, but it was a fling, nothing more. Her only serious boyfriend had been Ozzie Yakes, a lacrosse-playing photojournalist whom she met her freshman year at the University of Wisconsin. She had fallen in love with Ozzie, despite his self-absorption. Three years later, not long after his graduation,

Ozzie moved to Los Angeles and broke her heart. She had never quite recovered, though she didn't like to dwell on it. Sooner or later, everyone
took a fall. That was hers, and she did not intend to take another.

After lunch, she and Douglas made their way to the ancient Jewish
graveyard, headstones attached to the earth like Stone Age mussels clasped
to the side of a boulder. While there, a small, interesting thing happened, a
thing that Jodie could not push from her mind as she tried to get to sleep
that night.

She had never been what you might call deep about her Judaism, thanks,
for the most part, to her parents. They talked like Minnesotans, got misty-
eyed when they listened to "Tales from Lake Wobegon" and generally held
themselves to be St. Paul natives first, suburbanite Americans second, Jews
last. They were Reform Jews, but it didn't mean much: Chinese food on
Sunday nights, matzoh ball soup at Passover, dreidels for Hanukkah. Trips to
the synagogue were rare and almost always guilt-inducing. At Christmas,
the Blum family actually exchanged presents, because as far as her parents
were concerned, their daughter shouldn't be left out on account of religion.

Home had been pretty much de-Semitized. But once a year, a Jewish
hurricane blew in from the East Coast, and its name was Aunt Rachel. Jodie
thought of her aunt with affection and a new respect as she meandered
among the crazily tilted headstones. She could almost believe that Aunt
Rachel had encouraged her move to Germany for the express purpose of
getting her to this graveyard, where some piece of her identity had been
squatting, like a patient relative, ever since her birth.

"Your father is a disgrace!" she had told Jodie on one of Jodie's visits to
New York. "Can you imagine? After what Hitler did, after half of our family in Europe went to the gas chambers, your father is still ashamed to be a
Jew! Well, Jo, as long as I'm alive and have anything to say about it, *you*
won't be!"

As she walked among the headstones, a forgotten memory of Aunt
Rachel popped into her head. Douglas, of all people, made her think of it.
Out of the blue, as if consciously trying to jar her recollection, he picked a
rock off the ground and put it on top of a headstone.

"My cofounder of the Hemiptera Club in high school, David Green-
berg, showed me this once," he said, searching for another stone. "We were
tracking grubs in a Jewish cemetery."

Jodie stopped in front of a grave, a stone with lions on it.

Aunt Rachel lived on the East Side of Manhattan, where Jodie's father's
family came from, and every so often, in high school and college, Jodie paid
a visit. Aunt Rachel was a real New Yorker. She took Jodie to plays, poetry
readings, and art history lectures. They ate dinner in French bistros, strolled

in Central Park, attended chamber music recitals, and had a fine old time. But on one trip, something sad had happened. Rachel had taken her to the family graveyard in Brooklyn, to see where her husband, Mordecai, was buried. Mordecai had committed suicide when Jodie was twelve years old. As a young Jew during the war—that huge old war appearing every week on PBS in black-and-white footage—he had lived in hiding in Kosice in Slovakia and seen terrible things. Jodie's parents never liked him, and the feeling was mutual. He considered them foolish, empty people who were fulfilling Hitler's mission without even a pistol at their backs. They thought him a depressive character, always putting people down and talking negatively about Americans. They grew quiet and resentful whenever he was around and blamed Rachel for their feelings of repugnance. After he died, not much more was said about him in Jodie's house.

On that day in Brooklyn, Aunt Rachel had searched the ground for rocks to place on Mordecai's grave, and Jodie had watched with fascination and even horror at what seemed both a strange, prehistoric custom and an act as familiar as eating or sleeping. To her everlasting shame, she had withdrawn a few feet from her uncle's grave, afraid someone would see her aunt and think badly of them both. Tears formed in her eyes now. Aunt Rachel had seen and understood. You hardly know you're a Jew, her eyes had said.

That's true, Jodie thought.

In the Prague graveyard, she made a small amends, the beginning of atonement. One day, she would have to apologize to her aunt, but for the moment, she contented herself by putting rocks on four or five headstones. Not for Rachel or Mordecai, but for herself; because she knew that she had acted badly, and that the act had stayed with her. It was a small enough thing, that memory, but it seemed to have an echo which she heard after they left the graveyard, as they wandered. Had Mordecai ever been to Prague? As a child?

It seemed to her he had, and the thought of it, that a relative of hers had been there, had been on familiar terms with this ghostly city, gave her great comfort, as if an arm had been thrown over her shoulder.

The day waned on them. The streets of Josefov flooded with shadows. Douglas suggested they find a place to have coffee and discuss his case, so they wandered through coils of stone, past Bohemian-glass shops, bookstores, baroque angels, and Gothic portals, past the apartment where Kafka had been born—as a young street urchin had informed them in exchange for korunas—making their way toward the Charles Bridge in a haze of nostalgia for vanished things that brushed against them like curtains in a dark room. Stone lizards scampered up cornices. Great carven caryatids humped pilasters. Douglas reminisced about reading Kafka's "The Metamorphosis" in high school. The other kids had made fun of him, especially the jocks, because they knew he was captain of the Bug Club, as the popular kids derisively called his organization. One girl had called him Gregor until the day he graduated, after Gregor Samsa, the man who turns into a giant bug in the story. For all these reasons, Douglas spoke of Kafka as if he were a relentless bully who got whatever he deserved. But he laughed at the memory too, and Jodie liked that.

They passed beneath the Gothic tower at one end of the Charles Bridge and found themselves in a mist rising off the water. Statues of saints and heroes fenced them on either side. Fists bore crosses. Martyrs reared out of the dusk. Somehow, her hand found its way into Douglas's palm. It had not been a romantic gesture, merely gratitude. They stared down into the water. Kestrels swooped, bats nattered. Some unknown bird cawed in the twilight. Far down the water, on the right bank, lights fizzed among the shadows of trees.

Here, Douglas had wanted to talk, but Jodie stopped him. They walked a little farther in silence. Beneath the statue of Saint Vitus, they stood together, her head pressed against his shoulder, gazing up. Neither of them spoke. They passed under the Mala Strana bridge tower and found an inviting *kavarna*. Jodie switched on her microcassette recorder. He retold his story. She asked questions, and by the time he had finished, the waiters were holding the door open for them. And she felt she knew him better than he knew himself.

"So what's the deal between you and Uta now?" she asked, carelessly, blushing.

"Nothing," he replied, looking at her with curiosity, "nothing at all. She's my brother's concern."

CHAPTER FOURTEEN

1.

UTA WAS SOAKING in the tub. The radio crackled about crowds in Dresden who had chanted "Germany United Fatherland" to a stunned West German chancellor. The chancellor, she thought with contempt, was a fat man who had always resented the way his own people, particularly the young people, were always calling him "the pear" and making fun of his eating habits, his yearly trips to the spa, his clunky way of speaking. And now, after so many years of humiliation, the chancellor would go down in history. She saw what would happen. The East Germans would give up their souls, their firstborn, their livelihoods—certainly, they would sacrifice their shabby little country!—to get their hands on the German mark. They would bow before it, and a new country would be birthed, a nation more frightening and terrible than any she had ever imagined, a new Germany that would erase memory and swallow the world. That's why the crowds in Dresden were cheering at the first appearance of Helmut Kohl, a man who had been their sworn enemy a few months before. How her father would have wept for joy.

The door buzzer sounded again. Tante Greta reappeared with word of the old man's death, determined to fetch her home for the funeral. This time, Uta went.

They tried to catch a train for Marburg at Wannsee station, but the cars strained with East Germans. Men, women, and children thrust their limbs out windows. They waved and whistled like soccer fans.

Tante Greta rented a Volkswagen. By nightfall, the two women were under way, past the defunct checkpoint at Dreilinden, past the lines of East

German cars entering West Berlin, into a country of thickets and lakes that girdled the western half of the city. Uta had been this route with Douglas just a few days before, but she had not really noticed the landscape then; that's how it had always been. In her three years as a student in West Berlin, she had *never* noticed the landscape of East Germany. It had been dead, she thought, buried beneath another terrain, beneath geopolitical facts as real in their own way as plains, hills, and forests.

Now she saw the truth in those facts: There had never been a Cold War. Later generations would understand this clearly, she was sure. The Cold War had been an illusion, a pretense of peace to calm the blood-drenched masses. There had been only the one war, the terrible three-way war between Germany, Russia, and America, her father's war, which had not ended in 1945, as the history books said, but now, in 1989, without a shot, without a declaration. The people had ended it. The Wall, the division between East and West, real existing Socialism, the American and Soviet troops—these were all World War II, a conflict so terrible that it had frozen things in place for half a century, as if people had been afraid to move for fear of starting it up again; what men had called the Cold War was merely the long, bitter end of the cataclysm, everything locked in place until the time came, finally, for forgetfulness.

Overnight, Berlin had ceased to be West. Germany had lost its East. The spell of the war, in which, she realized, she and her father had fought on opposite sides, had been broken. Everything had become *land* again, and the land passing outside her window was alive. The ideas, it turned out, were dead. That's what Uta had felt in the farmhouse with Herr Mundung's niece. That's why she had run. But in the safety of the car, she could begin to grasp the beauty of the thing, the sense of sad clarity that signals the true end of massacre.

"When was the last time you saw him?" Tante Greta wondered aloud. She looked older than she had in the summer, less formidable.

Uta's fingers slid along the seat belt.

"Do you remember?"

"Who?"

"Your father, *Liebling.*"

She let go of the belt. "It was in Metz."

"Did you never think of going home after he became ill? Sitting beside his bed, holding his hand?"

Uta shook her head. It had never occurred to her. She simply couldn't muster the courage to face him again, not even in that state.

Tante Greta's concern continued to flow. "He suffered greatly after you left home. He let that beautiful fruit tree of his go to ruin. Two years in a row, he didn't pick the cherries. Last summer, they attracted so many flies that neighbors alerted the police."

"And all my fault, isn't that what you mean to say?"

By eleven, they were in Marburg. Uta's mother met them at the door. She threw her arms around Uta's shoulders and whispered into her ear: "Thank God, you're home."

2.

THE DAY OF THE FUNERAL, the local paper carried an obituary. "Hans Silk, professor of theology at the Philipps University in Marburg, who died last week at the age of 86, will be remembered for his engaging work on the letters of Saint Augustine and for keeping alive the spirit of medieval Catholicism in an age of lapsed faith." Her mother read the obituary aloud.

Tante Greta hid like a sphinx behind a cup of Darjeeling tea. That morning, a chill wind blew through the Lahn Valley. The trees on the hills groaned. The skies turned white.

The funeral would take place in the Elizabeth Church on the north side of town, and the burial would follow in a graveyard across from it. Arm in arm, mother and daughter climbed up into the old town, Tante Greta a few steps behind. They passed a seldom used park where a synagogue had once stood, skirted the university lecture hall where Uta's father had listened to Heidegger's lectures, walked past the market square where he had marched in his brown uniform for the first time and where his organization "The Crusade of German Christians" had called for a cleansing of Jewish elements from the Bible.

Tante Greta suggested the three of them stop for coffee at Cafe Vetter, one of Uta's favorite old haunts. The wind drove them inside. They sat at bay windows overlooking the Lahn River, brown as bread between the bare branches of trees.

"Now you know, of course, that your father's first family, the family of his youth, you might say, lived near the train station and were killed in an air raid in February 1945 . . ." her aunt began to relate.

In the depths of her soul, Uta wanted to forgive her father. An orphan of the First World War, he had grown up under the tutelage of a Protestant history teacher, his mother's brother, in the Catholic hill town of Amöneburg, a few miles from Marburg. In the valley below Amöneburg, the folk had been Protestant, but in the town itself, a lump of rock a few hundred meters above sea level and still surrounded by its ancient walls, the citizenry professed the faith of Rome. Uta had been to the town. She had seen it with her own eyes, a Catholic abbey and graveyard, floating like a ship upon a sea of *Evangelium*. Amöneburg was one of the first fortresses built by Saint Bonifacius when he set about converting the German tribes, her father had told her.

According to him, the children were zealots. Ten-year-olds had established inquisitions to torment him, the orphan who lived with the Lutheran history teacher. Bullies had beaten his face. They'd stepped on his glasses and called him the blind pope of Amöneburg. So when he graduated and came of age to attend university in the next valley, he abandoned religion, to the horror of his guardian, and became a philosopher. He rebelled against everything he had ever known, and the Nazis, who believed in nothing but their own power and some mystical nonsense about the German race—his very words!—must have been happy to have him, she thought, a lapsed theologian who could tell them they were right in their efforts to cleanse Christianity of its Jewish element, who could make his dead religion a tool for their future state. He had joined the party almost as soon as he got to university. From that moment until the end of the war, he had been a National Socialist.

Tante Greta offered a slice of *Baumkuchen*. Uta declined.

What had her father seen in those men? Because of them, he had sent women and children to their deaths, so it must have been something. There must have been an appeal. On the other hand, maybe it had been those petty little demons of his *Unterhimmel,* devouring him as he stumbled about in confusion. Yes, she thought, maybe that's where her father first discovered the idea that would make him famous, the *Unterhimmel,* or the "lower air," as Stuart had translated it. In the *Unterhimmel,* as opposed to the *Oberhimmel,* where angels dwell, or heaven itself, demons mix with the human race, and nonbelievers are their prey. In their cleverness, the demons appear not with horns and forks, but as abstractions and distractions. They are sex, power, money, politics—National Socialism, she thought. Back in 1931, her father had fallen prey to them. Heidegger had been seduced too, and if the greatest thinker of the age could forswear every intellectual principle for the demons of the lower air, then who was her father to play the saint?

In the end, in the final days of the war, a destroyed man, as he had so often told her, he had returned to the faith of his tormentors, to Catholicism, and since that time, he had seen with clear eyes. The demons had not confused him anymore.

Uta's mother began to cry. They had not even touched the coffee. Tante Greta paid the bill.

3.

AT THE CHURCH DOORS, a problem arose. A Lutheran pastor pushing long brown strands of hair back from his face blocked their way. He could have been one of Uta's Berlin friends in his dark green scarf, torn jeans, and cowboy boots. Herr Silk could not be given a burial in this church, which had a record of commitment to social issues, until the matter of his past had been settled, the pastor informed them. The charges were serious. Didn't they know? He had authorized the murder of women and children in Yugoslavia.

Uta's mother refused to listen. The pastor spluttered that she must. Uta stood back from the argument and scrutinized the doorway she had seen so many hundreds of times during her childhood.

As a young girl in Catholic school, she had fallen in love with the brave life and beautiful death of Saint Elizabeth, whose figure and face adorned the tympanum of the church door, just a few feet above her head. Agreeing with her father's interpretation, Uta had seen the saint as a political revolutionary who mixed faith in God with an aggressive love for the less fortunate. Now she feared Saint Elizabeth. She feared the saint's wrath for what her father had done during the war, and for what she had done to Douglas Gleaming and to herself. Her nightmares about the church had never ceased, and as she stood there, in the clear light of day, she resisted an urge to flee.

With the help of the priest who would do the funeral service, a personal friend of the deceased who had come all the way from Cologne to perform the ceremony, Tante Greta settled the matter with the pastor. He would have his day to discuss these matters, the priest informed the indignant man, but not now, not here, so close to the shadow of death. In the end, the pastor took pity on them, Uta could see, and departed. She drew a deep breath, accepted her mother's hand, and walked through the door into ecclesiastical gloom. Tante Greta led them across the grave of Baron von Hindenburg, around the rood screen to the pew, to the second row from the altar. An organ thundered, and the service commenced.

A few old people from university circles had gathered, along with a pair of mysterious young men in loden coats, who sat with vacant stares at the back of the sanctuary. At the request of Uta's mother, the altar was awash in chrysanthemums. Upon them, buried in the blooms, was the casket, an oaken juggernaut stained dark brown. Mercifully, at her mother's request, it was closed. Incense tickled Uta's nose. For the length of the service, her father would sleep among hallowed Aryans. In a chapel visible to her right rested the dead of the royal house of Hesse. Uta remembered one tombstone in particular, the corpse of a knight in decomposition, frogs, lizards, and snakes roiling out of his flesh, as being particularly apt. Behind her, near the door into the sanctuary, lay Hindenburg, the general who had handed Germany over to the Nazis; and in a room behind the altar was the reliquary of the saint herself, a Bratislava girl who died at twenty-four, far from home. Its relics had vanished long ago.

"This man was a friend of mine," the priest announced, "but he was also a holy child of God, a crusader in the modern era."

Uta looked up at the casket embedded in chrysanthemums, and a schoolgirl chill went through her body. As she smelled the blooms and listened to a strain of organ music, she was eight years old again and subject to the whims of ecclesiastical fantasy. Miracles had accompanied Saint Elizabeth's death. Her corpse did not stink; it had emitted perfume, like that of chrysanthemums. Birds had gathered on the eaves of the church—of that very church—and chirped a symphony. Oil had poured from the limbs of the saint's body. In the weeks that followed, pilgrims came from far and wide—to be cured of blindness, of aging, of frozen limbs. If such things had accompanied the death of a good woman, what prodigies might appear to honor the demise of an evil man?

The priest intoned the last phrases of the holy liturgy. Uta pondered the mysterious young men at the back of the sanctuary. When the benediction was over and the river of Latin petered out, she looked back over her shoulder for them, but they had slipped away. Organ music sounded again. Uta helped her mother out of the pew and forward to the coffin. Neither of them chose to linger.

Six elderly men lifted the casket, and a funeral procession formed from the small chaos of mingling bodies. The priest moved at its head, a censer swinging from his fingers. The procession exited the front of the Elizabeth Church, waited for the traffic light on Hubertusstrasse to change, bobbed across the street and up a flight of cracked stone steps to the pilgrims' graveyard, where no human being had been interred since the Second World War. It had been her father's request, a special dispensation granted in his last few months by the archbishop of Cologne.

The cemetery was neglected. Dark firs, beeches, and bare oaks surrounded it. In the midst of the graves stood Saint Michael's chapel, locked and mute. Its windows had been shattered by the rocks of vandals. The eyes of stone skulls, memento mori blunted by centuries of rain and wind, stared from the heads of propped tombstones. More words were said over the grave. As pallbearers lowered the coffin to the ground, holy water was produced. Uta counted twelve people standing on the uphill slope of the cemetery, the bones of near a thousand years of dead believers beneath their feet. She waited for a putrid stench to burst suddenly from the casket, for a legion of crows to settle on the twisted fingers of the oak trees and begin a sacrilegious cawing, for blood instead of holy oil to leak from the casket. It was obscene for him to be buried here, among the poor and suffering of Europe who had crossed river and plain and mountain to get to this spot, to be healed and die in the arms of God in the days before medicine. Her father belonged among the outcasts, like a suicide or a vampire. Here at the end, she could see with horror and sorrow that a last spark of love for him remained in her heart. But that love made it all the more necessary for her to disapprove of his final resting place. In a just world, his corpse should be burned, its ashes scattered in the gorge where infants had been hurled. He should become one with his victims.

Her mother gasped. The priest looked up from his *De Profundis*. Uta turned her head to gaze back down the slope. The mysterious young men from the church had reappeared, and now she saw what they wanted.

Arms rose in salute. They had stripped off their loden coats to reveal a pair of neatly starched brown uniforms. On their sleeves they bore red armbands, and on the armbands were swastikas, black and staring. With precision, heels clicked. No one at the graveside moved.

"Heil Hitler!"

The name dropped from the sky, like a crow stricken dead in midflight. It landed on the coffin, crisp and clear and absurd. Uta could almost see the letters, lying there in the grave. The young men pulled their jackets back over their shoulders, marched down the steps of the pilgrims' graveyard and out of the sight of the mourners.

4.

A FEW DAYS LATER, back in Berlin, Uta woke in a sweat. The phone was ringing. She picked it up.

"Uta?"

She didn't recognize the voice.

"Who is this?"

The presence on the other end of the line waited.

"Is it really you, Uta?"

The voice was American, but clipped. It wasn't Stuart. She hung up.

A few minutes later, the phone rang again. She let it. A tourmaline day blazed cold outside her windows. She placed a teapot on the oven, wrapped herself in a tattered blue robe, and went to the telephone, which had not shut up. She waited a moment before snatching it. As if it were a normal day, as if nothing at all were wrong, she answered in typical German fashion with her last name: "Silk."

This time, the voice identified itself.

"It's Nester."

Yes, of course, she thought, it would be him.

"We need to talk."

"I have nothing to say."

She had never liked Nester Cates; and that bartending crypto-Fascist concubine of his made her physically ill.

"Your life is in danger."

This was redundant, as far as she was concerned.

"I'm coming over."

She hung up and lay back on the futon. Here she had made love to Stuart and Douglas both. The latter's letter lay on the floor beside her. She had never opened it and never would. The shame would be too great. Her father had always ranted about the thoughtlessness of youth. From the time she was fifteen, he had raised her to make adult decisions, to think with her head rather than her heart (or loins), to weigh every contact and decision as if lives depended on them. She stared down at the envelope.

Helped along by brown coal, her apartment warmed up. She would have to do something now, would have to act. But how?

She went into the sitting room. There, unshaken by events, the collected works of Karl Marx in an East German edition ruled the disheveled literary universe of her apartment; they were twenty kilos of cold, dark *Geist,* overshadowing poetry, intimidating history, crowding out science, obliterating politics.

Though her friends had gone in for Adorno, Bloch, and Marcuse, the intellectual descendants of Marx, she had remained a purist, unable to free herself from the original source of her conversion to the cause. She pulled the works, volume by volume, off the shelf—*Das Kapital, The Manifesto, The Eighteenth Brumaire of Louis Bonaparte.* They had been such a comfort to her and such a great weapon against her father. The Salvadoran priest, Father Ernesto, had loaned her that first Marx, *The Eighteenth Brumaire,* in a tiny yellow Reklam edition, telling her the work had great religious significance, if one considered religion the establishment of the kingdom of God on earth. That had been three years ago, not long before she left Marburg for West Berlin. At first, she had read the book in secret. But the more she read, the more clearly she saw where her father had erred, and where she herself had been led away from the truth. Revolution, not the church, was the answer. God's justice would never arrive without human intervention. On Christmas Eve 1986, seated at the dinner table, Uta delivered a prayer to this effect, and her break with her father officially began. Strangely, the revelations about his Nazi past had not strengthened her convictions. On the contrary, in a matter of weeks—it had only been a month and a half since she made the discovery—she had seen her certainties erode one after the other, as if his transgressions banned her too from the Promised Land.

The pages of her volumes were worn from days and nights of use. They smelled of cigarettes, tea, and ink. She took *Kapital,* volume one, into the toilet with her. When she came back out, a fist pounded on her door.

"Uta!" Nester's voice cried. "Open up!"

"Hau ab!"

"Mach doch auf!"

He continued to pound. She dressed, made another tea, and went to the door.

"Thank you," he said.

Uta was surprised at herself. The sight of Nester's face reminded her of Stuart, and she was gladdened. She could even feel a smile pulling at her lips.

"Come in." She waved her hand.

Nester glanced at the pile of books. She offered tea, and he accepted. After a moment of uncertainty, they sat. She expected an interrogation.

"It's crazy, all of this, isn't it?" he began.

A tight flip of the hand indicated her volumes of Marx, the windows giving onto Berlin, everything.

"Yes," she acknowledged, and then she blurted out, she didn't know why, "My father has died."

Nester said he was sorry to hear it. He reached for a volume which lay near his boot.

"I was intoxicated by this in college. Malcolm X was my hero, you know, and he knew the value of German idealism."

Uta was surprised. This black man, whom she had called an Uncle Tom to his face, expressed sympathy with her. It did not seem possible. Were it not for the expression of genuine sadness on his face, she would have taken his comments as gloating. On the other hand, she told herself, he probably wanted something.

He said, in a voice near a whisper: "Let me tell you what I know."

A pigeon settled on the windowsill. Its fluttering cast dim shadows across the floor. When he was finished, he reached with a hand for her shoulder and held her steady.

Tears welled in her eyes.

"It's all true, so help me God."

She nodded. Nester's words provided explanations to so many unanswered questions. They explained why the East Germans had turned her away, why she had received no further instructions, why Herr Mundung had never made contact in all the days since the defection. They explained Stuart's silence.

Yes, she thought, these men had *both* betrayed her. Her decision to work for the East German government, to risk life and freedom in the service of her cause, had been window decoration for something else, for some banal game of espionage. Two years ago, after their meeting at the Rilke symposium in Göttingen, Herr Mundung must have done his research. He had learned everything about her, from her father's past to such seeming marginalia as her love of country-western music. When the time was right, he had sent his old friend Stuart to learn how to do the Texas two-step in her honky-tonk dance class. Mundung had wanted Stuart to seduce her, knowing what would happen, knowing that Uta would think she had stumbled across an opportunity to act on her convictions. She put her head in her hands. Mundung had given her the illusion that *she* had discovered this wayward American spy; that *she* alone had the power to persuade him to steal secrets from his country; that *she* was at the center of things. And Stuart had made her believe that he was in love.

Nester went to the window.

"I have to know where Douglas is. Can you help me?"

Uta deliberated the question.

"What will you do to him, if you find him?"

Nester shrugged.

"He couldn't possibly be Klek, could he?"

"No chance."

She joined him at the window. A chimney sweep in black top hat and breeches rode his bike down the middle of the street. East German cars were parked up and down the curbs, odd as Martians.

"You want to help Douglas? Not hurt him?"

Nester nodded.

"Then I will tell you where he is. But you must promise me something."

Nester scratched his wrist. "That depends."

"When you find out where Stuart is, alive or dead, you must tell me. That is what I want from you."

He looked into her eyes. She could see that he had his doubts. But he agreed. They shook hands.

"The last I saw Douglas, he was in a village southwest of Leipzig, staying with Herr Mundung's niece. It's the place where Nietzsche is buried. Röcken. Stuart used to talk about it. But I'm afraid, if what you're saying is true, that Douglas may already be gone. Is that possible?"

Nester wrote down the name of the place. She invited him to stay for breakfast, but he declined. There was too much to do. With another expression of sympathy for her father's death, he hurried out the door.

When he was gone, she dressed and went to work. Action was required, an initial expiation. She wrenched open the window above the street. She had been betrayed by others, that was true, but she had also betrayed herself, and that required penance. Now that liberation had come for East Berlin, she must set things right within. Saint Elizabeth would guide her. She saw that she had followed her father's example in renouncing her faith for an ideology, but she would not compound that mistake, as he had done, by embracing the old religion again. No, she would seek her own path through the demons besetting her on all sides. Marx too was of the lower air. This she now comprehended. She stacked the pile of books on a chair next to the sill and began to drop the tomes, starting with *The Eighteenth Brumaire of Louis Bonaparte,* onto the sidewalk three floors down.

CHAPTER FIFTEEN

1.

BY FIVE O'CLOCK on Friday evening, November 17, in Prague, more than fifteen thousand people had gathered at the Institute for Pathology on Albertov Street, five times as many as expected. Jodie sniffed woodsmoke on the wind. The failing sun touched her fingers as she scratched notes on a legal pad. She could feel the crowd growing around her, and it made her nervous. She didn't want to flub the head count.

Banners whipped like torches. In the far west, Gothic spires burned a reddish gold, their peaks just visible beyond the crowns of ragged oaks. She could make out the Powder Tower, the Old Town Hall, the tip of the Hradcany church across the river. Czech voices rose in animated conversation. Familiar words sprang from the unintelligible mass, and Jodie tried to write them all down, guilty for not speaking Czech, as she had been ashamed at her poor German the night the Wall fell. But she was hungry for whatever could be hers—*prestavba,* the Czech word for *perestroika;* names of dissidents, Havel and Dienstbier; names of tyrants, Jakes, Husak, Adamec; and once, fleetingly, the name of a folk hero, the great Masaryk, father of Czech democracy.

There were more sinister words too. They slithered like snakes through conversations between ponytailed girls and peach-fuzzed boys wearing the Czech tricolor—red, white, and blue. Ewa had written them down for her on a piece of paper so she would know them if she heard them: *bile prilby* and *cerveni berety,* the white helmets and red berets of the riot police.

But Ewa had used another word nonstop for the last forty-eight hours, and this was the one sticking in Jodie's head now. *Fizl,* or as Jodie transliterated it, "fizzle." *Fizl* was slang for a security agent, a spy, and fizzles were everywhere. They slid in and out of her sight, men and women staring at her, whispering, making notes. Zdenek stalked interview subjects somewhere in the crowd. Trying to ignore the fizzles, real and imagined, Jodie wrote and wrote, her mind on fire. She could think of a thousand leads already, but she couldn't decide whether to start with an image—the faces, the carnations, the candles—or go right into the piece with a newsy line, like, "Reeling with the news from West Berlin, angry at their leaders for blocking reform, thousands of Czechs gathered, etc. etc."

Albertov was a narrow piece of road bound by parkland, studded here and there with university buildings. Between the oaks and plane trees in the park, an incandescence moved. Candles glowed in cupped hands. Their mellow, avid light flickered onto carnations, and the carnations glowed like lightbulbs.

The crowd had looked young at first, which made sense. The demonstration was sponsored by the League of Young Socialists. But as Jodie studied the people around her, she saw they were a cross section. She made mini-portraits in her notebook—women in old woolen schmattes, one of them with a pale blue number tattooed into her forearm, and men in their best brown prewar suits bent down on canes; goateed artist types, bandannaed waifs, workers in overalls with faces red, hard, and wrinkled as old apples. There were professorial types too, and men in leather jackets, who brought to mind the watcher at the train station and Ewa's conspiracy theory—that the Interior Ministry planned to use the students to topple the government for its own ends.

Speeches began. The effulgence of the candles became a sound, a slight rasping, as people tried to listen to the voice from the podium. In the dusk, Jodie glimpsed hundreds of the tiny tricolor ribbons, a bed of national color submerged in darkness. Here and there, flags snapped in the wind. Douglas appeared at her side.

"Have you seen Zdenek?" She was losing her patience with Ewa's son. "He's supposed to be translating for me."

"Over there somewhere." Douglas gestured at a clutch of people to their left. "His girlfriend showed up. Last I saw, they were making out."

"Stay close to me," Jodie whispered. But he didn't.

In one short day, their relationship had changed. They had gone from near strangers to business partners to close friends, maybe even something more, and she was not able to resist the flow. It felt like unseen currents might be at work. For the hundredth time since it had happened, she summoned up his touch on the train, the involuntary brush of his fingertips against her breasts. She felt herself blushing, banished the thought, and, feeling someone watching, jerked her head around. No one was there.

She scribbled a note on the legal pad. She glimpsed again the blue numbers tattooed on the old woman's arm.

2.

ZDENEK RESURFACED, hands raw and ungloved. He was a cheerful punk with eyes of bright blue and that ragged gold-brown Mohawk. "The atmosphere is changing."

"You think it's going to move onto Wenceslaus Square?"

"Quite possibly. Later. First Vyserad."

Another speech ended. Dusk deepened. Jodie had a spooky thought. She imagined fizzles stalking them in the crowd, fizzles closing in with silencer pistols. And the thousands of stone creatures clinging to the facades and cornices of the city's ancient buildings joined the fizzles; come to life, they slid down parapets and slouched between students on their way to apprehend Douglas. Candles hissed. Carnations trembled. The crowd raised its communal voice in the national anthem.

People began to move. In a mass, the candles and carnations flowed down Albertov in the direction of Vyserad Fortress, to the grave of Jan Opletal, the poet murdered by Nazis. She took notes by the available light, wondered if she would be able to read a word later. Douglas bobbed around, smiling as she had never seen him. Something like hysteria had gripped them both. Now and then, he whispered what he heard into her ear. She wrote down some of it, mostly to please him. She did a few interviews with Zdenek's help, but they broke her concentration, so she gave up and succumbed to the mood of solemn dissent.

The parade wound its way up to Slavin, the hill of Czech national heroes. Around them, Prague floated, a sea of expectant edges. The poet's grave lay in a garden of crosses and statues. The crowd had grown enormous—well over twenty thousand people. It swept up into the national cemetery.

More speeches resounded. Zdenek brought news.

"They're going to Vaclavske Namesti! Someone told me so. Mother would want me to leave now."

"Then you'd better go!"

"But my girlfriend is staying!"

Zdenek was right. His mother would be cross. She would lay the blame on Jodie if anything happened to Zdenek. But Jodie needed him. He would be her interpreter if something bad happened.

"Get your girlfriend and stay close to me. If anything happens, I'll tell the police I'm an American reporter, and we'll be fine."

A smile lit up Zdenek's face. "Really?"

"They won't touch me." She knew it was a lie, but nothing less would do; any show of fear, and the boy would leave her.

Arguments burst out. Some of the people in the crowd had begun to criticize Gorbachev and *perestroika*. Other voices shouted them down. This time, when the crowd began to move, it did so with tension. A new kind of energy rippled through the people. The sentimental effect of the candles and carnations held, but an uneasinesss lurked beneath. Jodie felt it inside her body. Douglas took her hand.

"I'm a little nervous," he said.

"Me too."

Whistles blew as a train passed the crowd.

3.

AHEAD, Jodie saw a line of white helmets.
Nothing happened for a while. Helmets and red berets milled on the other side of a police cordon. The light from thousands of candles reflected off Plexiglas shields and the sides of paddy wagons. Chants rose and fell. No one seemed to know the plan. They had been walking for hours, past Charles Square, down the banks of the Vltava, up Narodny Street. Coldness had stolen off the river and slipped into Jodie's bones. Some of the demonstrators tried to reason with the police. Jodie asked Zdenek to eavesdrop on a conversation or two. He came back and said the police weren't saying much. They just wanted the demonstrators to turn back, but as it turned out, retreat was impossible. A second police unit had come up behind.

As a mass, the students inched closer and closer to the police cordon in front. They jangled keys, taunted. One by one, they began to sit, and a funny memory came into Jodie's head. In her entire life, she'd participated in one demo, a protest against nuclear weapons. In front of the student union at the University of Wisconsin, she and fifty undergrads had thrown themselves on the grass in various positions of horrible atomic death. After an hour, the chiggers had begun to bite.

Jodie wormed her way through the crowd to the cordon and tried to talk to one of the police, a young man. He shrugged. Didn't speak English or German. A girl reached over Jodie's shoulder and handed the man a carnation. He did not accept the flower. A truncheon of rubber hung at an angle inside his belt. They wouldn't make it to Wenceslaus Square, Jodie thought. As it was, only four or five thousand of them had reached this point. A police line behind them had cut off the rest. If she left now, she'd have time to file to *Probe* before midnight. Chubbs wouldn't get the whole story, but he'd have something at least.

Whistles burst from the demonstrators. A man near Jodie jangled his keys at an annoying pitch. Candles hissed. Through a bullhorn, a voice called for the crowd to disperse. Jodie could not be sure, but she thought she saw a truncheon rise from a belt.

Their small group hung together now—Zdenek, his girlfriend Milena, Douglas, and she. They could not leave if they wanted to; there was no obvious path out. She saw words on a sign, Mikulandska Street. Milena stared down into her candle. She could not have been more than fifteen years old. Her mother had forbidden her to go to the demonstration, but she was a defiant girl. Zdenek chanted as he held on to her jacket, and the two of them stuck close to Jodie and Douglas.

"If anything happens, where will we meet?" Zdenek suddenly asked.

The question hadn't occurred to Jodie.

"In Stepanska Street," Milena suggested. "There's an indoor promenade. It's usually open at night. The drunks sleep there. We'll meet in the middle. My uncle's apartment is in that building."

Jodie reached out for her. "It's going to be okay."

Milena gave her a look of disbelief. Keys jangle-jangled in Jodie's brain. She wanted them to stop. A camera whirred on a platform on the other side of the cordon. The bullhorn bellowed. The corner of Mikulandska and Narodny felt tight as a shoe box. Too much flesh, Jodie thought, too much sweat. She stood up and leaned back against the wall of the apartment building at the corner of Mikulandska.

A feeling rippled through the street, something Jodie could not quite catch. Two masses of people—riot police and students—tensed. All night, violence had been suspended above them. Now it dropped. For one second, every man and woman in that square had a chance to glance up to the heavens and see it plummet.

Truncheons began to fall. Blood blurted across a helmet.

What had provoked it? She had seen nothing but a drunk screaming at one of the cops. Jodie tried to write, but her hands shook too badly. She called to Zdenek and Milena. They glanced up at her, but didn't seem to understand. Maybe they couldn't see over the heads of the people around them.

"Get out of here!" Jodie screamed.

Douglas jumped up, Zdenek and Milena too, but not fast enough. They were caught in a tide of fleeing bodies. Jodie tried to keep sight of them, but they vanished.

Jodie found herself alone. She watched as bodies collapsed before an army of hammers that dipped and reared in a professional, almost desultory rhythm. It was as if the street were a field of ripe grapes and the police were stomping on them, pressing them out, till the juice ran in rivers. It was mesmerizing.

She became aware of her own danger. A man in a red beret crossed the asphalt with deliberation. His uniform was green and heavy. Jodie began to see human shadows in a wild dance. Truncheons swung. Terror rooted her to the ground. She had never felt such terror. It bordered on unconsciousness. She had a sense of intimate balance. The ground buckled everywhere else, but remained firm at her feet, so firm she couldn't move. The face beneath the beret had crimson lips and a single, thick eyebrow; its blazing eyes met hers. Her feet would not move. A martial beat sounded. Beautiful, she thought, as if she stood at a great distance, a new world dawning. A West German press card bounced in her fingers. The man in the red beret screamed at her. His truncheon lifted. Let it be soft as down, she thought, soft as a cloud, so it won't hurt. He barked something at her again, and the words tumbled with everything else into a blizzard of carnations, candles, and keys. Her body might have been floating. She might have been flying up and away from this place. The press card and notepad dropped from her hands. She made a steeple with her palms.

The truncheon came down. She saw its shadow, felt the wind of its descent. Esperanza "Pansy" Buckner appeared in an auburn-haired, green-eyed haze. There came a crack.

CHAPTER SIXTEEN

1.

DOUGLAS TACKLED HIM. He didn't have time to feel anger or make a decision. The cop hit Jodie, and Douglas sprang at him, punching with awkward fists, gouging at his eyes. Not that it helped much. The truncheon struck her three times before he could attack.

At first, the element of surprise was on his side. Despite inequity in their respective hefts, Douglas knocked the cop off his feet and pinned him by the neck to the ground. The advantage couldn't last long. The guy weighed at least 250 pounds, 60 pounds more than he.

His adversary called out to others. Douglas kept the point of an elbow against the man's throat and tried to think up a plan. Any minute, another of the police would come to the rescue, would swat Douglas down. He didn't have much time. The cop kicked out with his legs. Douglas squinted at the pavement. Ten yards away, Jodie lay still.

He was losing control. His maneuver, a variation on a forward block he had learned during an otherwise useless semester of physical education in high school, had tumbled his adversary into an awkward position. The boot buckle of the cop's left leg had snagged in the pants hem of his right. Also, Douglas had knocked away the truncheon. But already, the feet were kicking themselves free.

Douglas seized a final moment of opportunity. With his fist, he pounded on the cop's groin, one, two, three, and ran for it. The man moaned and doubled up.

Douglas lifted Jodie in his arms. His legs staggered under her weight, but as he started to run, fear gave force to his legs, and he bore up. Demonstrators hurtled into him, trying to get out of the street.

He managed to stay erect, but he'd lost his sense of direction, lost any idea of how to get beyond the pincers of the attack. On the edges of his vision, he saw Black Marias waiting to take prisoners away. He felt a powerful undertow in their direction, but fought against it, like a swimmer against a violent tide. There was one right in front of him. He turned away from the hungry vehicle, bolted forward, and slammed headfirst into the side of a building. Reeling, he made his way along the wall to a door. White helmets burst out, like a magician's doves.

He fled in the opposite direction, headed more or less back the way he had come, down Narodny Street toward Wenceslaus Square, back, goddammit, into the intersection of Mikulandska and Narodny, where Jodie had been attacked and he had tackled the cop, the worst possible place he could be. As he loped-lurched-limped along, clearing prostrate bodies as if they were track hurdles, a truncheon caught his knee. Of course, he thought as he collapsed with a groan to the ground, I have run into him again.

Miraculously, he didn't drop Jodie on her head. He sank to his knees and let her rear end hit the asphalt. A banner gentled down on top of him, and for the briefest moment, he was alone in an enclosed space, the sound of his own breathing loud in his ears. He looked down at her, and an emotion of terrible force swept through him. She was precious. That was all he could think. She had used her own body to save him on the train. She had placed her naked torso between him and the East German government, and now she was bleeding. Douglas wept. It seemed to him a great hand had taken the pieces of her precious face and moved them all around, so that he would never again behold the woman who had been his protector. Her eyes, her mouth, her nose, were lost in dark blood and flesh. She is precious, he thought, and I must now place my body between her and the slamming darkness of the street.

The banner was ripped away and he blinked into the face of a vespoid woman in a silk scarf. She wore a chic leather jacket with narrow lapels and kid gloves.

"Oh-my-*God,* I know her!" the woman cried in loud American English. Then she tilted her head back over her shoulder and spoke to someone Douglas couldn't see. "I know this girl, Vasek! It's Jodie Blum!"

The moaning of human beings and the thwack of truncheons sounded in Douglas's ears. He tore a Kleenex from his pocket and swabbed blood from Jodie's lips. He lifted her body off the pavement. In that position, head hanging down, she might swallow her tongue. Slowly, with great care, he lifted her head.

"Jodie." He cradled her head. "Can you hear me?"

The woman in the scarf knelt beside him. Perfume surrounded her like a hotel room. With her gaunt cheeks, thin waist, and even thinner fore-limbs, as brittle, truly, as the tarsi of a wasp, she reminded Douglas of the Languedocian Sphex in Fabre's *Entomological Dictionary.* He took it as an omen of good fortune.

"Can you help me get her out of here?"

The red berets ignored them for the moment, concentrating their efforts farther down Mikulandska, a one-block lane buried between two six-story buildings. Truncheons thwack-thwacked against human skulls, against limbs.

"Vasek says he knows the way out—"

Douglas took a deep breath and rose again to his feet. His chin ached, his knee throbbed. He gritted his teeth. A tear of perspiration rolled down his cheek.

"I'm Esperanza Buckner of the *New York Times*—"

Pansy Buckner, he thought, remembering Jodie's words about her, but he didn't care. As far as he was concerned, she was the Wasp of Heaven, come to lead him out of hell, and he didn't need to know anything else.

"Follow me," spat her friend Vasek through the mass of saliva, gravel, and blood clotting his mouth.

Everything occurred in a flash. Pansy Buckner dashed beside him, one hand on Jodie's dangling leg, a gesture of propriety. Vasek came to a sudden halt. Douglas kicked aside flags, flowers, broken candles. One minute they were in the street, the next beneath a stone canopy fronting a department store. They were in complete darkness, stepping on hands, dodging walls. They broke out of the darkness and collided with two police in white helmets, who let out snarls. Vasek barreled through them. One cop snatched at Pansy's neck, caught hold of the scarf. Douglas threw himself into the man's chest. The scarf twirled up and away. Pansy spun. She was free.

They rushed on. For a time, he heard himself breathing, heard Jodie's heart at his chest, or thought he did, but saw nothing except Vasek's back, which led him on. His imagination came to life in the heat of his labor, and he fancied a subtle pursuit. Once or twice, it turned out to be Pansy, but other times, he heard, just at the edge of audibility, a solitary pair of heels coming behind them on the street, a slight thud in time with his own movement, and whenever he heard it, he asked a little more of his knee, begged that much more of his legs, faster, faster.

They seemed to burrow into the old city, as if down into an abandoned wasp nest—

Or no, he thought, with an eerie sense of familiarity, as if down into an ancient, endless warehouse like the one where he had once worked, the warehouse with its two dozen bays, its legions of trucks, class warfare be-

tween forklift drivers and management, piles of Turkish apricots, frozen
beef sides, fertilizers, cheeses, peanuts, and everything else consumed by a
nation. Prague had become a nightmare stone version of his vanished warehouse, and he was lost in it, unable to get back to his office or find his car
or even call security to come and get him . . .

Wide streets gave onto narrower ones, onto alleys, onto darkened porti-
coes. There were church doors, more department stores. And the silence
grew around them, grew into a noise.

Douglas was nearing the end of his strength, and behind him, never flag-
ging, came the heels of their invisible pursuer, who stopped when they did,
panted in time, marched when they marched. At some point, Vasek's back
disappeared. He had fallen in a doorway behind a row of trash cans where
rats rustled. Douglas smelled schnitzel grease.

Pansy touched Douglas's elbow, and he jumped.

"We can't stay here. It's not safe."

Douglas gave her a nod; he understood, but what could he do? He lowered Jodie to the ground, removed his coat and wrapped her in it. Vasek
blacked out. After a minute of unconsciousness, as if a force outside his
body had lifted him, he was up again, kicking against the trash cans, scatter-
ing the rats. He was dizzy but walking. "This way," he said.

"Vasek, wait—"

Pansy held him still. "Where exactly are we going?"

He licked his lips and gave no answer.

"I have to get back to the Intercontinental, Vasek. Ham will be wondering about me."

Vasek had lost most of his strength. What remained would get him into
hiding somewhere, and no more.

"How far are we from Stepanska Street?" Douglas hoisted Jodie again.

"Not far." Vasek pointed indistinctly away from the trash cans.

"My friends are there. In a department store." Douglas directed his
words to Pansy, who rubbed her neck where the scarf had been torn away.
"They will get you to the hotel."

She didn't have time to argue. They set off across a square and down a
street called Spalena. Here and there, they glimpsed police, but no red
berets, no white helmets. At least one red beret will be hunting for me in
particular, Douglas thought. The police watched but made no move to prevent their passage. Their movement slowed as they lost strength. Douglas
wondered when the dawn would come. It had been night forever. But the
sky above, far above, was black as pitch, unlit by stars. The windows above
the streets had gone out, as if in fright at the tumult below. Neither cars nor

trams moved. A few lamps continued to function on street corners. Their light shimmered on a triangle here and there, ephemeral as a gnat swarm, an aid to obscurity rather than illumination.

Douglas prayed for Stepanska Street. His arms could just barely hold Jodie. If he stopped for a second to think about his situation, he would fall in his tracks and never get up again. Behind them came the heels in lone pursuit. When he asked Pansy if she heard, she shook her head.

At last, after what seemed like hours, they came to Stepanska. They caught their breath in another doorway. Douglas spat upon a hand and washed the blood off Jodie's face.

"Come on." Pansy poked him in the back. Vasek pushed off again. Douglas lifted his burden, the last time, absolutely the last.

"So." Moving beside him, Pansy tried to embark on something like a normal conversation with Douglas, distracting him from the noise of pursuit, which had evolved into the character of a musical performance, now loud, now soft, picking up themes from the street, plucking along in pizzicato. "So has Jodie told you anything about me?"

She snapped a rubber band over the auburn hair falling to her shoulders and made a ponytail.

"No."

"We were at Columbia together, then I got a job as a clerk at the *New York Times* and she had to go off to some small-town newspaper, which is absolutely the best thing to do . . ."

Her thin, high voice made a pleading echo in the street, a thrumming not so distant from that of Fabre's wasp.

"I mean, we weren't exactly close in J-school, but we stuck together. She gave this really controversial report on Mexicans in Harlem, on how their conversation was reminiscent of the rattling of machine guns, and the class just ripped her apart, I mean, totally crucified her, and I stood up, and I said, give me a break, people, it's a *great* image—"

The entrance to an arcade yawned before them.

"This must be it." She lowered her voice in relief.

Vasek rattled the doors. The bust of a woman's head rose up from the peak of the arch above the doors, rose out of the lines of the arch into the faint glow of a nearby streetlamp. The glow of the lamp filled the bust's eyes with a live darkness, emboldened the tendrils of the hair, which became pilasters framing the doorway.

Vasek twisted a knob. The hinges fought, then creaked open. A charge of human presence touched them. It came first in the form of body heat, followed by a twitch and shiver of movement. Douglas could not make out details in the dark, but felt a tangible human relief, as the inhabitants of the

arcade discerned Vasek's face, saw that he had been beaten too. A somnolence came over the corridor, which, as his eyes adjusted to the darkness,
stretched ahead in a brownish haze, lit here and there by matches. Douglas
felt his limbs returning to life. Outside, he had been freezing. His fingers
had gone numb.

Dozens of refugees from the demonstration huddled in the arcade. Some
wept, others snored. Cigarette butts burned, their red tips reflected in the
glass of shopwindows. A line of crumpled bodies dwindled ahead into
smoke and darkness.

Vasek stumbled. Douglas smelled beer and vomit. Behind him, he noticed, the heels had stopped. Whoever their pursuer was, he had stopped at
the doors.

Finally, they reached an empty stretch of the arcade. Vasek collapsed on
the bottom step of a stairwell. Pansy leaned against a marbly column. They
were in a square space, a kind of indoor piazza.

"Okay." She coughed. "We're here. So where are your friends?"

A sharp tone entered her voice. She seemed to hold Douglas responsible
for something.

"Hurt?" Douglas tried to be nice.

"Not like those two."

Vasek lay on the bottom step of a stairwell leading up to a chain-locked
movie theater. Gilt masks of comedy and tragedy gaped in the ceiling. Six
steps above Vasek, in a nook at the first landing, a distinguished head sat on
a rectangular pedestal. Dead eyes stared from bronze folds. Douglas didn't
know what to tell her. He had expected to find Zdenek and his girlfriend
waiting.

"Just let me think for a moment."

He climbed the first flight of stairs and laid Jodie at the foot of the
pedestal. He glanced at the name beneath the head: Julius Fucik. Douglas
knew Fucik. Jodie and he had passed the Julius Fucik Park of Culture and
Rest in their wanderings. Fucik had died in 1943, murdered by the Nazis
probably, like everyone else who had died in 1943 in central Europe. His
ghost would be an offended one.

Up the next flight of stairs, someone moved. Douglas threw himself
over Jodie. Pansy tripped backwards down the steps. Ewa Craissova's hooded
head rose to stare at Fucik's in the darkness.

2.

THE POLICE HAD RANSACKED her apartment and had taken her typewriter. Then Zdenek had phoned from his girlfriend's uncle's apartment and told her what had happened at the demonstration. She had picked him up and left him to wait in the car. She had been waiting in the stairwell for about ten minutes.

"We're leaving Prague," she said.

Douglas hoisted Jodie again. Pansy and Ewa dragged the unconscious Vasek back to the other demonstrators and left him in the care of an impromptu nurse who knew him from school. Ewa agreed to drop Pansy off at the Intercontinental, then led them out of the arcade to her car, the Lada. In the front seat, Zdenek scrutinized a map.

Getting out of Prague wasn't easy. Zdenek gave directions and helped his mother to identify streets. Pansy and Douglas sat together in the back seat, Jodie across their laps. Wenceslaus Square kept sucking them back to its edges.

They must reach Nuselsky Most, Zdenek explained, the bridge that would take them to the Brno highway, Route 1. Every time they came close, it seemed, the appearance of a policeman forced a detour, or the way was blocked by construction, or they had erred in their memories. Back into the suck of Prague they went.

Meanwhile, Jodie would fly into fits of pain. Douglas detected a growing fever.

Most of the time, she lay unconscious. Her head rested in Douglas's arms, her feet on Pansy's knees. Douglas caressed her hair. Pansy watched. She didn't say much, but her body spoke of indignation. She had lost her scarf. Her boss didn't know where she was. She did not want to be in this car, among misfits, in a country she didn't know. Ewa had promised to take her to the Intercontinental Hotel before leaving Prague, but they kept circling farther and farther away from the riverbank, and every time they did, Pansy heaved a deeper sigh of protest.

Then, out of the murk, came police. They raised flashlights. Ewa braked the car. Men leaned into the car window and shone their beams into the vehicle, asking short, rude questions.

Ewa made short answers. The beams lingered on Jodie. Douglas suppressed his rage. These men were pigeons. They descended everywhere, upon everything, pecking, scavenging, defecating. How he would have enjoyed breaking their necks one by one, watching their eyes go dead and their beaks fill with blood. The beams rounded his face.

He considered flashing his vice presidential document, but didn't dare. What if it backfired and he lost the document? He'd have nothing.

Just for an instant, he thought of Stuart. In all of Stuart's peregrinations, his quest for justification, had he ever imagined this scene? This smashing of heads in the darkness? Did he understand the people with whom he had allied himself? The police checked a list of some kind. They asked Ewa to step out of the car. From the back seat, Pansy intervened. She handed over her *Times* credentials.

"Give them this."

Ewa did. The men conferenced. The ID came back through the window. A hand waved them on. Ewa drove out of their sight, put the car into park, and exhaled over the steering wheel.

"Thank you." She handed the credentials back.

Pansy wanted something in return.

"The Intercontinental, please."

Ewa put the Lada back into motion. They reached a quiet street corner beside a white church. Saints and bishops lunged off its sides. Ewa turned off the car's ignition.

"You are a journalist?"

"I work for the *New York Times.*"

Pansy pushed against the door, which wouldn't give. Ewa slapped a hand down on the front seatback. "*No!* Your press card is invaluable. We may need it between here and Bratislava."

Pansy pounded on the Lada's door. "*Bratislava?* That's five hours from here!"

"My ex-husband's dacha is near Bratislava."

"Tough shit. I'm not going."

"We need you, miss."

"But I don't need you."

Ewa reached out for her. Pansy shrank back, but listened. "I personally know your boss Mr. Stamps from many years of association with your newspaper, and if it's any comfort, I will vouch for you. I will explain everything, and Mr. Stamps, who has a rather exaggerated love for anyone from this part of the world, will make it his business to understand."

That was the end of the discussion. Ewa had spoken. Pansy seemed pacified by the mention of her boss's name. And she was clearly exhausted. Her hands dropped from the door onto Jodie's calves. The car arrived at Nuselsky Most. Within an hour, they were racing southeast, clear of Prague, clear, for the moment, of police.

3.

"SOMEONE'S BEHIND US," Ewa said.

Douglas eased his head around as best he could. Pine forest ranged the hills on either side of the highway. Moon-blue cloud smeared the sky, and by its light, a blue and empty road could be seen. Far back, though, just where the road became indistinguishable from the forest and the sky and everything else, the soft twin points of another car's headlights glimmered. In the rearview, Douglas could not even see them.

It was bad news. They had half a tank of gas, not enough to get them to Bratislava. Somewhere along that highway, they would have to stop, and the thought filled Douglas with dread. The memory of pursuit returned, of the relentless heels. This time, death would get him. He would never get to Bucharest, never see his brother again, never get to tell Jodie how much she meant to him. He would be as dead as all the ants he had ever expunged.

He became conscious of Ewa's stare in the rearview. What chance would they have, the five of them, against even a single man with a gun?

He squinted over the back seat again, trying to get a better look at the phantom car. "They're following us or just behind us?"

"One of the two headlights is dimmer than the other, so I noticed the car when we left Prague. At Nuselsky Most. Trust me. We're being followed."

"It's an old East German Wartburg, I'd say." Zdenek was peering back at the road now. He wore the headphones of a Walkman, which beat with rock and roll. "Who drives old Wartburgs?"

Ewa shrugged. "East Germans?"

Douglas thought of Herr Mundung and his Wartburg. It was near two in the morning. After a night of demonstrations, of yelling and screaming and violence, after fleeing through the streets of Prague, the quiet within the car both soothed and terrified him. He could hear Pansy's pen scratching against paper. She wrote despite the complete absence of light in the car.

The night wore on. With the help of the moonlight, he glimpsed towns in the folds of land between hills, and within them, he imagined soft beds with clean sheets. He wanted to fall asleep on Pansy's shoulder, but didn't want to disturb the work of writing.

"Yep, it's definitely a Wartburg," Zdenek said. "I'm sure. See how low it's riding. I think it's gaining."

Douglas could feel Jodie beneath his hands. Her body was warm, despite its sufferings, and that was a good sign. But he had a distressing thought. She would never be able to write her story on the demonstrations, due tomorrow morning in New York. Even if she regained consciousness this very minute, the story would be too great a challenge, and her editor, Chubbs, the man she had told him about, would not be happy. She might lose her job.

"How is she?" Pansy had stopped writing and was rubbing her throat again.

"I can't really tell. She's breathing steadily. How's your neck?"

"Fine. Hurts a little, I guess."

"I bet."

"Not as much as the loss of that Hermès scarf, though."

Douglas took a long look at Pansy, and in the darkness, thanks to the chitinous glitter of her eyes and lips, the Sphex-like aspect was reinforced. What had Fabre written? Douglas had only read it a thousand times since his mother gave him the *Dictionary of Entomology* on his sixteenth birthday. "She always lives apart, not caring what others do, a genuine misanthrope among the Sphegidae." Pansy was a small woman, younger than he by five years, at least, and extremely waspish, in the biological sense of the term. Her features stood out in relief against the backdrop of the drab car—a fine aquiline nose, a pair of intimidating dimples, and straight reddish-brown hair, now undone from the ponytail and hanging to her shoulders. Douglas could almost imagine a pair of gossamer wings descending down her back. The mouth had a diagonal tilt, as if drawn back in skepticism most of the time, and the eyes were merciless in the shadows. They lacked any trace of sentimentality or self-doubt or empathy, could see through this car, this night, this bleeding woman, these fleeing people, to a spot in the future where prestigious employment lay, as certain and undying as the North Star.

"I must ask you a favor."

Pansy's mouth tilted up.

"On Jodie's behalf."

She crossed her arms.

"She has to write a piece for her magazine tomorrow. It has to be in New York. It's a cover story. If she doesn't, she'll probably get fired . . ."

Pansy was listening. She hadn't cut him off.

"She obviously can't write this piece. She's in no shape—"

She raised an eyebrow. "You want me to write the story?"

Douglas nodded.

"Under her byline, I presume?"

His hands were trembling. He knew so little about journalism and nothing about this woman. He didn't even know whether Jodie would want him to make the request, or whether she would be fired if she failed to deliver the story. But it didn't matter. He had already asked. If she refused, he would write it himself.

Pansy smiled; it was not an entirely benevolent expression, but it contained a measure of compromise.

"I'll do it on two conditions."

"Name 'em."

"She never knows until the day, if and when it comes, I decide to tell her."

Douglas agreed.

"Second, you never speak of this, never tell a soul, till the day you die."

They shook hands. He wondered about her motives, but decided they didn't matter. The story had to get written. Thinking of Jodie's American Express card, praying it was still in one of her pockets, Douglas promised to book Pansy a room in a hotel of her choice in Bratislava, to pay all her dining bills, and to rent her a car to return to Prague as soon as she was done with the story.

"He's still there," Zdenek warned.

Their pursuer kept a distance, but had not strayed. They passed through the sleeping city of Brno on a quarter-tank of gas. Ewa switched lanes, pretended to move for the highway exit. The car behind them did the same.

"Damn." Ewa switched lanes again, sweeping across to the other side of the highway. The car followed suit.

Douglas lifted his hand away from Jodie's cheek. She opened one swollen eye.

"Mom?"

Douglas took one of her hands. "It's me."

The eye closed again. Pansy watched, inscrutable as the night.

4.

AN HOUR BEFORE BRATISLAVA, Jodie woke again, whimpering and complaining in a distant voice. Douglas caressed her hands. Big tears rolled down her cheeks.

They were out of gas. For the last half hour, Ewa had been searching for a station. The Wartburg kept pace behind them. The sky lost its deep blackness. Gray patches showed between the clouds. The land fell, as hills gave way to the Danubian plain.

Suddenly, Zdenek pulled the headphones off his ears and pointed through the windshield.

"Petrol."

Sure enough, there below them, at the point where the last of the hills flattened itself out, was a station. They slid into a hutch of orange and ochre light, a lovely vision, suggestive of fireplaces in hunting lodges on cold winter nights. The attendant sat on a chair in front of the office, a blanket wrapped around him to his chin, his chest pulsing in a gentle sleep. Behind them, their pursuer pulled onto the shoulder of the road and dimmed his lights. In the gray dawn, the car stood out against the land. A line of diesel trucks whistled past the station. The road awoke from its sleep.

Ewa filled the car. She put a finger to her mouth to urge quiet. The attendant slumbered on, heedless of visitors. After slipping several bills beneath his blanket, Ewa came back to the car. She tapped on the window. Pansy rolled it down.

"I have an idea," Ewa said.

Douglas waited. Pansy put a hand over a yawn.

"This guy." A thumb jerked in the direction of the Wartburg, which was moving now, inching toward the station with a distinct purpose. "He's not interested in you. He wants me."

"How do you know?"

"Because he's been tailing me ever since I left my apartment this evening. I didn't want to say anything until I was absolutely sure, but now that I see him, I know. It's a security detail. I think it's better if I leave you here."

"*Oh no you don't!*" Pansy was wagging her head back and forth in adamant refusal. "You said we were all going to Bratislava together."

Ewa took the nozzle out of the tank. "We will be arrested before we ever get to Bratislava. Trust me."

Douglas was too numb and tired to argue. He didn't know what Ewa was up to, but he didn't want to get arrested. She seemed adamant. With Pansy's reluctant help, Douglas got Jodie out of the Lada.

Ewa gave them a couple of chocolate bars and a trowel, to be used as a weapon, she told them, just in case. Zdenek took Jodie's things from the trunk, a computer bag and rucksack. He knelt and kissed Jodie on the forehead, which moved Douglas. Ewa ordered him to get back into the car, and he waved as they hit the highway again, headed east, red taillights dwindling out of sight. For a moment, it seemed the Wartburg would follow her. Headlights came on, and a turn signal pulsed. But the car turned into the station.

"Shit," he heard himself murmur. Ewa had thrown them to the dogs. The driver cut the engine and sat for a minute. The attendant woke with a splutter, wiping his eyes. Douglas hoisted Jodie in his arms and prepared to run. Pansy brandished the trowel. Nester Cates stepped out of the car.

BOOK III

KILOMETER ZERO

CHAPTER SEVENTEEN

1.

FIND KLEK, Styles had said. Well, after a fashion, Nester had.

He took Jodie to a hospital off the Ringstrasse in central Vienna and waited until the doctor had ruled on her condition. She'd sustained a mild concussion, a broken nose, and a deep cut on her cheek. She had a fever as well, picked up in the cold. The doctor gave her painkillers, set the nose, and stitched the cut. Orderlies forced Douglas from the room.

From a hotel nearby, Nester phoned Herr Radetzky at the Carinthia Haus, as Styles had ordered. He left a short message on an answering machine, location and time of meeting the morning after next. He wanted a day to fill in the gaps in his own knowledge. He had found Mundung's niece in the village, but the man himself had fled, and she could tell him only so much. A few days before, her younger brother had driven Douglas to Dresden, where he had caught a train heading south.

Nester dialed again, to make sure no one was there. Once more, the answering machine picked up—no voice, just a beep. He made another phone call, this time to an impromptu relay service set up by one of his technicians. After a series of clicks, Waltraud answered in West Berlin. He told her he had found Douglas, and she could call off the search. She expressed surprise. His loose but comprehensive band of Eastern European UFO devotees, his Green Men—abductees like Brüderlein, Polish crash-site mavens, Serb ham radio nuts, and Romanian cultists, among others—had never impressed her.

To his mind, they had more than paid off. It had taken years to develop the Green Men into a sound intelligence organization; Nester's entire military career, in fact. The work had been mostly thankless, training human oddities persecuted by various regimes for their belief in extraterrestrials into a crack team of listeners who could supply him with useful information about the Eastern Bloc. Most, when he discovered them, were outcasts of one kind or another: ex-scientists, ex-politicians, ex-journalists, ex-engineers. In exchange for their help, he built a UFO support group, supplying foie gras and the latest bizarro news from the West, Roswell and the rest of it. Some Green Men had been helped to escape their countries, others received U.S. hard currency to stay—American tax dollars at work. Over the years, a few had made their way into the lower echelons of government, though none had come as close to the very levers of power as his first acquisition, the man who had started it all, Klaus Brüderlein, a Saxon from Transylvania who had been tossed to him in a kind of freshman hazing ritual when he first arrived at the 66th in Munich.

In twenty-four hours, acting on the information that Douglas was bound south through Eastern Europe on a train originating in East Berlin, the Green Men had rallied, watching stations from Decin to Bucharest. Waltraud had manned the impromptu phone bank. Nester set up shop in Dresden. Sure enough, on the morning of November 16 Douglas had been spotted in Prague, getting off a train with a woman believed to be an American. They had been met by a young man in a Mohawk, and this had jarred the memory of another member of the team, a folklorist denounced by the Ministry of Culture for a satirical essay theorizing that Rübezahl, the Czech national elf, was the offspring of a milkmaid from Pilsen and a crash-landed Zeta Reticulan. According to the ministry, the essay mocked Slavic folk tradition and therefore the Slavic peoples and therefore the People as a whole, and that made it a crime. A dashing man in his late forties, the folklorist knew everyone. He had partied with some of the hipper nomenklatura back during the Prague Spring, and one of them, a disgraced ethnomusicologist named Ewa, had come back into his life recently as a server in the Koruna Automat at Wenceslaus Square. She served him strawberry milk shakes and bitched about the sorry state of Czechoslovak ethnomusicology. More important, she had a son with a Mohawk, and, as the folklorist recalled, lots of contacts among American journalists.

The rest was easy. The folklorist approached Ewa. Nester rushed down to Prague. As soon as Ewa discovered the identity of her guest, she wanted him out. By virtue of her associations, she was already in danger, and Douglas made things worse. Events overtook them. They had been devising a plan to get Douglas to Nester when Ewa's son called in the wake of the demonstration. There had been an attack. People were badly hurt. If they escaped the police, the Americans would meet him in the arcade in Stepanska Street. Nester had simply followed Ewa.

Waltraud asked him what he would do next. Nester didn't know just yet and didn't want to say over the phone anyway. He hung up, took a beer from the minibar, and downed it in a gulp. With the fall of the Wall, his personal ban on alcohol had lapsed.

He noticed with curiosity that Douglas checked the *Times* reporter into a suite and settled some journalistic business with her. He would have to ask about it later. When Douglas was done, Nester insisted they share the room, for safety's sake, and the two men fell asleep. At noon the next day, Nester woke in dread. The other bed was empty. He dashed to the hospital and found Douglas tending Jodie. In the wee hours, he had returned to her bedside and, after convincing the doctors she had no family in Vienna, stayed awake in a chair.

In the meantime, the other reporter had taken off, which was fine with Nester, who hated journalists with a passion. Douglas assured him the *Times* woman knew nothing of his identity. She had her own fish to fry.

In Jodie's hospital bathroom, Nester took a bath and shaved. His appearance embarrassed him. Never, in his decade and a half of adulthood, had he looked so shabby. The fringe of hair around his bald pate had grown out, and he'd gained a potbelly, which insulted his entire frame. His language had deteriorated, and in the wake of that first glass of vodka in Waltraud's apartment, he had begun to drink—beer, wine, spirits. So much personal decay in so short a time, as if demons had been waiting for the smallest slip to devour him.

"For that makes man human," Schiller had written, and Nester took it as a religious creed, "that he does not rest satisfied with nature's raw version of himself, but possesses the capability, which nature has anticipated within him, to transform flesh into moral necessity—"

He'd get back on top of this, one way or another. Scrubbed, well shaven, he returned to Jodie's bedside. That evening, she opened her eyes and recognized Douglas. She expressed curiosity about Nester. Then she asked about some article she was supposed to write. Douglas took her hand and told her she had done it. Her editor had been pleased. She went back to sleep.

Nester left them for an appointment. A few blocks from the hospital, in a fast-food joint where roast chicken dripped from rotisserie spikes, he ordered a beer and waited. Before long, Brüderlein limped into view.

Of all the contacts Nester had made over the years, of all the violets in his secret hothouse, Klaus Brüderlein was easily the most valuable. He was also the least stable, having never recovered from his dual trauma of close encounter and earthly exile. Used to running things, still in his soul a Communist bureaucrat, Brüderlein had nevertheless cooperated with the West for near a decade now, passing Nester news about dissident movements, suspect émigrés, technology improvements, and so on; more out of spite than anything else, he admitted. In the meantime, at the age of eighty-five, he was an adjunct professor of German literature at the University of Salzburg, specializing in the works of his native region. He was, as well, a blunt subscriber to what the Visitors had conveyed to him that fateful night in the mountains: Ceausescu was alien vegetation.

Forty-eight hours ago, before driving to Prague, Nester had told Waltraud to call Brüderlein and ask him to find out whatever he could on the subject of Mundung.

Evidently, Brüderlein had news. When he came to the table, Nester rose, and the old man dipped into a partial bow. To Nester's dismay, he looked rather windswept, as if the elements had roughed him up since their last meeting. He wore a familiar wool coat with a faded needlework of birds and flowers, the favorite motif of some forgotten Saxon village. His boots were cracked and ice-rimmed, his Greek fisherman's cap a blot of black. One of his hands grasped a scuffed oak cane, its grip the head of a Transylvanian dragon. On the lapel of his jacket hung a scarlet button that read: "Marx, Mars, Martyr." Nester offered schnapps and chicken.

"Nee," Brüderlein replied with a wince. He sat. When he leaned forward, his chin nearly bumped the tabletop. The waitress hovered. *"Tee, Fräulein."*

He had a faint silver mustache, Nester saw, those same sad eyes that could break into amusement or tears at an instant, a believer's thrust-out jaw. The right ear didn't work, so he often tilted his head to one side, which gave his conversation a conspiratorial quality. He released the cane into a crook of wall, clasped his hands together on the table, and gave Nester a grimace of general displeasure.

"What does that mean?" Nester gestured at the button.

Brüderlein's eyes shot a defensive spark, and he broke into English. "The title of my autobiography. Very succinct. Do you think Americans will buy it? I'll die before it's finished, of course."

The old man took a sip of tea, sneezed, then proceeded immediately to business.

"This chap Mundung used to be called Karlheinz Schlapp. Back in Spain. Isn't that what you wanted to know?"

Brüderlein had fought with the International Brigades in the Spanish Civil War and knew most of the survivors who had fought on the Republican side against Franco.

"Karlheinz Schlapp?"

Brüderlein sneezed again, and grappled for a handkerchief in the pocket of his coat. "An unlucky fellow, really, one of those stumbling souls who cares immensely but never truly understands the cause. In Spain, he was betrayed by Stalin's man Andre Marty, so he had to run. That was 1938. The Nazis nabbed him in '39. He spent the war in a camp. Later, after the war, he ran into black market trouble with the occupiers, went to prison again, had ideological problems under Stalin, prison again, this time in Bautzen. When Stalin died, the comrades let him out, and he joined the Main Directorate, East German intelligence under Wolf. He never excelled, and in the end, I take it, they had all but forced him into retirement."

Nester endured some scorching remarks about the ruthlessness of youth before Brüderlein returned to the point.

"A few years ago, after I defected, this fellow Schlapp came to see me in Salzburg. He tells me about an organization called the Verein Albacete. You understand? The Albacete Association."

"What is it?"

Brüderlein squeezed lemon into his tea.

"I don't know all the details, you know, because I kicked the fellow out of my apartment pretty fast, but this Schlapp, or as he calls himself now, Mundung, tells me, some of the old fighters from Spain have formed a secret organization to revive the true spirit of the party, to make another revolution, from inside, very dangerous, of course—starting a fraction like that."

"When was this?"

Brüderlein shrugged, closed his eyes, tapped his forehead above his left eye. "Five years ago. Maybe."

"Who did he say he had recruited?"

"Old guard who fought in Spain. That's all. Most are marginal nomenklatura. One I know personally, a terrible fellow, Anton Olestru, a Romanian. He skinned a mother superior, as I remember. That was in Valencia. He works now at the Information Ministry in Bucharest but is attached to Directorate Five, which means he belongs to Ceauçescu. Anyway, a terrible fellow, and the most senior of the Verein Albacete. I believe Bucharest is their unofficial headquarters, or so Schlapp led me to believe."

"And Klek?"

Brüderlein nodded. "I think so, yes. I did not know him, but he was in Spain at the time, they say. I am certain he knows Schlapp, but they keep their distance, you know, because Klek is such a notorious figure."

Nester wondered if Stuart knew of this association. He had been friends with that old German in Turkey—what was his name? The one who fought in the Condor Legion for the Germans, then changed sides? Nester told Brüderlein about him, and the incident rang a bell with the old man, but he could not think of the name either. Nester sensed there must be a connection. Anything that brought Klek and Mundung into the same subset had to be relevant.

"So tell me a few things, young Nester. Where is your friend, this defector, now? Has his brother said?"

Nester shook his head.

"Bucharest, perhaps?"

Again, Nester could tell him nothing.

"Because if he has gone to Bucharest, then he is already dead."

Nester was startled. "Why do you say that?"

"Quite simple. I know these men."

Nester didn't follow. Brüderlein grew testy.

"If I were one of these Albacete associates," he said, leaning close, "I would be terrified. Like me, they see what happens in Berlin and in Prague. They know the revolution from inside, *their* revolution, will never come. On the contrary, on the contrary. They have *no* friends, *no* allies. They have formed a group condemning both Communism and Capitalism, and they are men of action. If Klek was skulking around East Berlin, which I have heard, they had probably identified a target for their grievance, had planned some assault, and now your friend, by defecting, has exposed them before they could carry out their assault. And I tell you, they may even suspect that he did this thing on purpose. They may suspect, Nester, that he was working for someone else the whole time, and that he is still spying on them. Remember, they are surrounded by foes. Their paranoia knows no bounds. So I ask you, what in the world is left to them? Can you think? There is nothing. All they really have left is vengeance. And if this man has failed them, still worse, if he has *betrayed* them, well, they will kill him, as I would, be assured."

Nester could see enraged sympathy in his old contact; for a moment, he was alarmed, but let it pass. Had Brüderlein maintained relations with such men, he would never have spoken so candidly of his feelings. "How many are still alive, do you think?"

Brüderlein lifted four fingers. Nester thought it over.

"I don't know, Professor. I haven't heard anything about these people. I don't really know what to make of it."

The old man shrugged.

"I say only this. If they have not killed your man, then they are using him as bait. You say you have his brother? Then his brother is being lured south to Bucharest, and with his brother, you are being lured. And when all the fish are in one basket, one of two things will happen. The Albacete men will gut you one and all or they will make you a bargaining chip to get themselves out of hot water. That is *my* prediction. Ignore it at your peril."

He wiped tea off the rim of his saucer, reached for his cane, and fiddled with the dragon's head. Nester had dozens more questions, but the hour was late. The old man was tired. Nester read his button again: "Marx, Mars, Martyr." Very succinct, he thought. The last word would be "Market," no doubt, if he ever managed to sell the book. After a moment of silence, Brüderlein raised a frayed smile. He brushed the stitchwork on his coat.

"I've lived too long." He glanced out the window in the direction of the sky. "I shouldn't have to be here to see this, this capitulation."

"Surely there is reason to celebrate, Professor?"

The old man didn't answer the question. He continued to stare out the window. "One last thing, my boy. I would not be surprised if these old men have become quite obsessed with *you*. You are this defector's best friend, are you not? And, if these men have access to any decent information, they will know as well that you have quite a résumé, that you have worked at high levels in the Pentagon. And here you are, after all, chasing this fox through all the lengths of central Europe, coming ever closer to Bucharest. Truthfully, I would not be at all surprised if they thought you had masterminded the whole affair."

With that, Brüderlein lifted himself from the chair. Nester tried to lend a hand, but it was brushed away. The professor made a deep bow, till his head sank to the level of the table. Mother-of-pearl eyes glittered in the dragon's head of his cane. Brüderlein touched Nester on the shoulder. *"Sei höchst vorsichtig,"* he whispered. Be most careful.

Then he waved at the waitress and limped out of the restaurant into the Viennese night. Just before disappearing, he stopped, turned, and pointed, for Nester's benefit, at a star visible beside a bell tower in the eastern sky. People were just insane enough to buy Brüderlein's autobiography in droves, Nester thought. The old Red would probably end his days a millionaire in Palm Springs. And I, he thought, I will probably die out here.

2.

THE NEXT MORNING, before the meeting with Styles, Nester talked Douglas into breakfast. With a brisk wind behind them, they walked into the old city.

Nester disdained Vienna. To him, it had the embarrassed glow of a

Christmas tree in a funeral parlor. Yes, the city had its charms. Viennese women were a shade more sophisticated in their beauty than other Germanic females. The cuisine—particularly tafelspitz with horse radish—tasted better than most Germanic food. Vienna's architecture enchanted him. But Nester always felt that if he kept his eyes fixed on these glories, and not on the ground at his feet, he would inevitably trip across a corpse.

Euphoria burbled through the streets. Everyone knew of the collapse of the Berlin Wall and of the fall of Bulgaria's dictator and of the demonstration in Prague, which had ended in such ugly violence—the *massakr,* they were calling it on Czech radio, to which Nester had listened the night before, gleaning what he could from a language he didn't know well. The old town rippled with a profusion of a patriotic red, white, and blue, the national colors of Czechoslovakia. Dyed towels flew from windowsills. Ribbons unfurled from taxicab antennas. The hopes of thousands of émigrés from the country had been sparked; they were waiting for the dictators to stumble, just as they had in East Germany and Bulgaria, waiting to go back and help to tear the bastards down.

Nester led Douglas to a cafe in the Marcus Aurelius Street. A woman in midyawn unlocked the doors. Nester opened one of them for Douglas. They entered a cozy room of small tables and wooden chairs. The smell of coffee beans steamed from bright silver machines. Fresh strudel baked. The waitress lit a Turkish cigarette and tracked their progress to seats in a far corner of the cafe.

Nester ordered coffees with lots of schlag, orange juice, and strudel. He told the waitress to keep the food and drink coming. She rattled coffee cups. He excused himself to the men's room.

The English-language bookstore was five minutes away, and Nester didn't want to be late. He slipped out a back door into a courtyard, returned to Marcus Aurelius Street, hit the Judengasse, and from the Judengasse found the Sterngasse, where the bookstore appeared just as he remembered it from a previous visit. He had given Styles an exact hour. He checked his watch. To the second, Nester was there. Styles was not. The bookstore would not open for another five minutes, so Nester took a nervous stroll. At a synagogue nearby, soldiers with AK-47's patroled. A few hundred yards beyond the synagogue rose a parapet. From there, Nester could see a dirty stretch of the Danube Canal. Junkies dragged themselves along its banks. He felt someone watching him, turned, and saw no one.

"Carinthia Haus," Styles had said before leaping the wall at San Souci. That was the name of the establishment, no question about it. Nester had found it in a phone book. But maybe Styles had grown impatient. Or maybe he was dead, murdered by Brüderlein's Spanish association. Or maybe he was watching from a window above the street.

Nester hurried back to the cafe. Douglas was on his second piece of strudel. Nester seated himself.

The exterminator looked thin, paler than he had ever been, but his cheeks were red. His hair had gone uncombed and, by the look of it, unwashed for days. It fell around his face in a black rag. His hands trembled as he cut into the strudel. His nose ran.

"Where is Stuart?"

Douglas put down the fork, swallowed.

"Bucharest. I'm to meet him there on December fifteenth, and then we're supposed to go to Australia. But I'm not going to Australia. I've told this reporter my story, and she is going to clear me of espionage charges. She met Stuart, you know, at a barbecue . . ."

Douglas hesitated, as if he had something else to say, but he seemed to think better of it and was silent again.

Nester knew he'd seen her before. She was the girl who had come to Colonel Redding's house. Stuart had said she was some American tourist he'd picked up in a bar, screwed, and dumped. But that was a lie, of course. She had somehow sniffed out the story and tracked him to the barbecue.

Nester wondered what Douglas could be thinking about all this. Did he blame Stuart? Did he intend to clear his brother's name too, or did he believe his brother was guilty? And if guilty, of what crime? For the moment, these were secondary concerns. Right now, Nester needed very specific information.

"Is there a contact in Bucharest? Besides Stuart, I mean?"

"Some friend of Mundung's."

"Mundung has a friend in Bucharest? Do you remember his name?"

"Seems like it begins with an O."

Olestru, Nester thought. Had to be.

"Tell me something, Douglas. Have you actually spoken with your brother?"

"No."

"And this letter you saw? It looked like his writing?"

Douglas thought about it. "Close enough."

"But you have not actually heard his voice, telling you to come to Bucharest?"

Douglas shook his head.

"Then how do you know it's not a trap?"

The exterminator started to answer, but Nester interrupted.

"How do you know your brother hasn't been coerced by Mundung's people to Bucharest?"

Douglas stared down into his plate. Nester could see that he was withholding information. He could see that Douglas did not trust him, which was understandable. Nester did not really trust Douglas. He knew that Douglas had nothing to do with his brother's activities before the defection. But now? Both were being hunted. Neither had many friends. And they were family, after all.

In any case, Douglas had to be sequestered. As long as he was safely hidden, Styles couldn't make a move, and that would give Nester a breather to consider his options. Douglas, he decided, should go to Budapest, capital of Hungary, a country free of turbulence. The man needed a rest. His companion, the reporter, would need time to recover. Hungary was close. It was stable. It lay between Austria and Romania like a buffer zone. When the moment came, if they should have to go to Bucharest, the Romanian capital could be easily reached from Hungary by train, plane, or car.

Douglas finished off the strudel. His eyes turned red. "I have to get back to Jodie."

"Wait." Nester grabbed a napkin and wrote a number on it. "Do you trust me?"

Douglas gazed at him a long time.

"Not much. Why?"

Nester gave him the napkin. "I am in trouble too, just like you. If you will let me, I'll try to get us both out of this jam. What I need is a little time."

Douglas looked at the number on the napkin. "What's this?"

"I want you to go to Budapest. There's a hotel on an island in the Danube. The Mohacs. Very secluded. Check in there, and call Waltraud the minute you arrive. Let her know that you are safe. Give me two weeks. That's all I ask. No later than mid-December, I will be in touch, and if nothing else, we will go to Bucharest together."

Douglas folded the napkin.

"You don't seem to be scratching your wrists anymore. Should I be worried about that?"

Nester touched his left wrist with the index finger of his right hand. Douglas was right. The flesh had not been scored in days, but Nester hadn't noticed.

"What do you know about that? It's actually a good sign, I think. First I've had in a while."

Douglas got up from the table. "I'll see you in Budapest in two weeks."

Nester steered him out the back way, through the courtyard, and returned to his seat. The cafe had filled up. Old men ruminated over chess moves. Newspapers rustled. Beautiful Viennese girls read Elfriede Jellinek. Nester paid the bill. It was time to go.

3.

HE HURRIED TO THE BOOKSTORE. Something had definitely gone wrong. There was no sign of Styles.

In a square at the end of Marcus Aurelius Street, he decided to take a drastic step, one he had been contemplating for days without seriously considering it. He was in an impossible situation, and he must get some advice. He made a phone call.

"Daddy?"

It would be late afternoon in Checotah, Oklahoma.

"Nester?"

"Yessir."

By the sound of it, his father had just raided the refrigerator. He was eating, and the insistent munching gave Nester an odd comfort.

"Can you get to a pay phone?"

The munching stopped.

"Take me ten minutes to walk to that pay phone near the Red Cardinal. What's your number?"

Nester read him the one on the booth.

"Stay put."

In the meantime, a woman tried to bang her way into the phone booth. She glared at Nester with personal antipathy.

Nester tried to imagine his father standing at the closet, debating whether to put on the old Borsalino or go bareheaded. He would grumble a little, search the house for a few quarters, give up and go to the Red Cardinal grocery store across from the AME Zion church. His parents had moved to Checotah after his father's retirement from the army and seemed at home there. Nester's mother came from a rural county not too far from the town, where her Creole forefathers had settled decades ago. Her childhood home was now buried beneath Lake Eufaula. So they lived in Checotah, where she still taught school.

The phone rang. Nester snapped it up.

"How many quarters am I liable to need?"

"A handful, I guess."

"I brought eight. Can you hear me all right?"

"Yessir."

His father paused, perhaps taking off the hat. "Kind of surprised to hear from you, boy. Are you okay?"

"No sir." He could think of no diplomatic way to put it. "I'm in big trouble."

His father's distress could be perceived in the vacuum.

"What kind of trouble?"

Nester should not have called. He should have left his parents in the dark. After a distinguished service to his country, a career of jobs well done, why should his father have to worry about such a mess? After all these years of good behavior, it felt like a horrible repeat of the disaster at Morton College.

"Nester?"

"I'm here."

He had resisted calling home for days. His father had never wanted him to get involved in intelligence work. He had preferred Nester stay out of the military altogether rather than get involved with a profession he viewed as dishonest and, more often than not, obstructive to real soldiering. He was a sixty-five-year-old man with a small house and a big lawn that he'd bought with his military pension.

"A friend of mine has defected."

"Oh Lord in heaven—"

Douglas had never heard his father take God's name in vain, not in all the years, not even that night in Uncle Bud's. A groan followed the sacrilege. A quarter clicked through the pay phone. Their time was running out.

"The Company is looking for a scapegoat."

His father didn't make a sound.

"And that's me."

Nester drew a breath. "I just needed to talk to someone."

Another sigh came down the connection. His father dropped a few more quarters into the slot. The response did not come easy to his father, Nester knew, because he had been clean all his life.

"Is there something you want me to do? Some of my old cronies from Heidelberg ended up in the State Department. Should I call them?"

He didn't want that. "No. Thank you. Thank you so much, but it wouldn't help."

A clicking hit the connection. His father was running out of quarters. "You just remember something," his father called out over the clicking. "You there, Nester?"

"Yessir?"

"You're a Cates, and Cates is as strong a line as they come. We don't

go down easy. If someone is trying to do something to you, you just remember that. I'm going on the assumption you had nothing to do with
this."

"That's the right assumption, sir."

His father went silent. Any second now, he would be gone.

"How's Mama?"

"Fine. Teaching still."

"And May?"

"Your sister's—"

The connection went dead. Nester headed for the car.

4.

FOR FIVE DAYS AND NIGHTS, he had traveled undercover, an
American agent behind the Iron Curtain. He had driven hundreds of
kilometers through enemy territory, bought laughably cheap gas with
enemy currency, and seen with his own eyes the subject of an entire career's
speculation: roads, bridges, cities, future theaters of war. One morning,
fresh across the Green Border between East Germany and Czechoslovakia,
he had stopped at a Czech beer garden shaped like a barrel. The beer garden
was closed, but Nester parked in front, sat on the hood of the car, a Wartburg borrowed from the CIA's miniature fleet, courtesy of Styles, and gazed
across the hilltops. Here and there, church spires had poked through the
dense thickets of fir. Beyond them spread a morning sky as fluid as slivovitz.

And he'd thought, I am safe here.

For five days and nights, he had moved with the freedom of a ghost
among villages of the Warsaw Pact. He had been posed as an Angolan, a
graduate of Patrice Lumumba University in Moscow. No one had accosted
him. The police looked through him, as if he were invisible. Old women
sold him coffee and soda without raising an eyebrow. He was as free as he
had ever been in his life, as free as he ever would be. For all intents and purposes, he had been Rübezahl, an extraterrestrial elf passing lightly through
the affairs of men.

Now, back in Vienna, back in the West, where he should have been safe,
he feared for his life.

Nester squeezed into the car, jammed the key into the ignition. He sat
for a moment, once again feeling watched. He closed his eyes and took a
deep breath. Out to his left, beyond the hospital parking lot, eyes were
watching. He was sure of it.

He counted three, opened his eyes, glanced around fast, and there, across the Ringstrasse, bundled like a Viennese burgher in fur, stood black-assed Jerome Tunt.

Nester leapt out of the car and, with a glance back over his shoulder, made a dash for it. Caught off guard, a look of true distress on his face, the owl came after him, hands flinging out of the pockets of his coat. Nester led him back into the heart of the old city. He lagged just enough to allow Tunt to follow. He passed the Anker clock, reentered the old Jewish quarter via Marcus Aurelius, returned to the Sterngasse. There, he stuck his head back into the bookstore, just in case Styles might be waiting. When he came back outside, Tunt had halted and was glaring from a distance.

Nester moved on, slower now. He walked through a series of squares as the sun climbed to noon, never taking a direct line between two places when a circuitous route would do. He rounded the Cathedral of St. Stephen, climbed up a sluice of medieval stairs, tunneled down cobblestoned alleys. The day grew colder as the sun moved west. People vanished into cafes and restaurants for lunch. The two men were increasingly alone.

Finally, they stood on either side of a fountain in the Freyung, a square bound by churches, palaces, and other odds and ends of Viennese history. A single bell rang from a tower of the Schottenkirche, a noise deep and thunderous, containing a dirge for the dead. A troop of boy scouts filed into the square, gazing up at the church. Tunt peered at him from the other side of the fountain, a deep contempt in his eyes.

Nester said nothing. He stared at the man and smiled.

"Where is he?" the Jamaican finally asked.

Nester shrugged. Tunt indicated a bulge in his right coat pocket.

"Don't play games with us. We're long past that."

Nester shrugged again.

Tunt spat. "I saw Douglas Gleaming sitting with you in the cafe. Where is he now?"

So Tunt hadn't seen Douglas leave the cafe. That was good. Nester kept smiling.

Tunt grimaced. "I could kill you right now."

The owl squinted as the sun caught his eyes. Styles is watching, Nester thought. The scouts fanned out around them, leaping upon the rim of the fountain, slapping the allegorical heads of the four great rivers of central Europe.

"You think I won't kill you, just because he tells me not to?"

Nester drifted into the middle of the boy scout pack. Tunt followed with his eyes. His threats were empty. Styles needed Nester alive, because Nester was his only chance of getting to Douglas, and Tunt didn't have the nerve to buck Styles. That would have been his death sentence.

In the meantime, Nester grasped that he had gained a sudden tactical advantage over the owls. Tunt had seen Douglas in the cafe. He knew beyond a shadow of a doubt that Nester was in possession of the man. Styles might be able to pin a murder rap on Nester—he might even be able to implicate Nester in Stuart's spy ring—but he wouldn't do it, Nester believed, except as a last resort. He wanted the man whom he considered to be Jiri Klek too badly. That meant Nester could play for time. To an extent, he could even dictate terms.

Surrounded on all sides by the scouts, Nester pretended to admire the cornice of a palace. Jerome stayed at the edge of the mob of boys. "You set yourself up, Captain," he said in a trembling voice. "Haven't you figured that out yet? No one but you decided to befriend that sorry ass Glemnik. No one but you. Of all the allies you might have made at field station, you chose the one despised and feared by everyone else, and he's destroyed you, sure as I'm standing here. He made you the target, and Styles was just smart enough to see it. That's why you ended up in the Box that night. No matter how this all comes out, your career in the military is over."

This time, the threats didn't bother Nester. He knew they were made out of hysteria. Nester flashed an even warmer smile.

"All we want is Klek," Tunt continued. "For what he did to Styles, for all his crimes. The rest is a matter of indifference. If Klek goes to Bucharest to meet Stuart Glemnik, then we will follow him there, and if you try to stop us from reckoning with him, then we will kill you. So just tell me where Klek is, and you're off the hook."

"You'll hear from me," Nester called.

Tunt made no effort to follow the scout troop. Like a flock of geese, it bore Nester away.

5.

HE HAD ONE LAST OBLIGATION. Pulling a tiny notepad from his pocket, he found a number. He dialed and prayed. Uta was home. He had given his word.

"I'm doing as promised."

"Who is this?"

"Stuart's in Bucharest."

He did not like what he heard—the electricity of interest.

"Uta?"

She was smoking, deliberating. He could hear thoughts in the static of the line, the puff of air from her lips as she exhaled.

"And Douglas?"

Nester hesitated.

"Where *is* he?! You tell me that, and I'll never ask anything else of you!"

Nester swallowed. "You will receive the address. The phone's not safe."

He could hear the heavy pulse of her breath.

"But listen to me, Uta. Are you listening?"

"I am."

"You must not go to Bucharest. You hear? Whatever you do, do not go there. It's going to be too dangerous. I'm not even sure Stuart is alive."

To his horror, she had already hung up the phone.

CHAPTER EIGHTEEN

1.

ONE WEEK AFTER Nester called, Uta received the information she had requested from him, a scrap of paper slipped under the door and bearing a scrawled address: Hotel Mohacs, Budapest, Hungary. That very day, December 1, the parliament of the German Democratic Republic apologized to the Czechoslovakian people for the invasion of 1968. In a bar in Prenzlauer Berg in East Berlin, Uta wrote a postcard to Douglas and watched the speech on television. She had been born during the era of the Prague Spring, in 1967, a year before the Soviet Union led its allies in the Warsaw Pact across the borders of Czechoslovakia, crushing the country's reform movement.

By the time she became interested in politics, she recalled, no one had talked much about that invasion anymore. Her friends and fellow activists, like Renate, had been far more obsessed with the crimes of the United States of America, with Vietnam, El Salvador, and Libya. And even if the events had been more recent, Uta admitted to herself, neither she nor her friends would have given a damn. Truth to tell, she still didn't. Czechoslovakia was nothing, a small, pragmatic country that would always follow the lead of other, greater powers: America, Russia, Germany.

On the television set, a member of the East German Volkskammer made another speech about the Warsaw Pact and injustice, then Alexander Dubcek, the leader of the Prague Spring who had been in political exile for twenty years, gave his reaction to the speech. There were demonstrations in Bratislava. People rose everywhere; now it was the Slovaks, who had caught the fever from the Czechs, who had picked it up from the East Germans. It was like watching kernels of corn burst in a skillet, first one, then another.

Uta could not imagine the great powers of the earth *wanting* so much popcorn. She finished her beer and left the bar.

Dusk crept up. The sun gilded a bank of clouds to the west, framed by tenements hung with banners and freshly washed sheets. On the side of a six-story building, she saw the faded logo of a business that had perished before or during World War II, a textile business run by a family named Schmidt; Jews, most probably. A blond woman in a muffler handed out flyers on a street corner in front of a magic shop. The shop was closed, but a homemade wooden puppet, a Saracen in a helmet, hung in the window.

Uta took a flyer. It called for the formation of a people's committee to address the problems of hunting lodges and tropical fruit. The leadership of the German Democratic Republic had enjoyed both over the years, the people had not, and now the former must answer for it.

In East Germany, the time of demonstrations had passed, Uta reflected, and the day of committees had dawned. They sprang up everywhere: in parliament, on the streets, in cafes. If you weren't on a committee, you did not count. She checked her watch. It was almost time for the meeting of the staff of a publication run by the Third Way, a group of dissidents who had already shifted focus away from the old regime to fight the onslaught of West German money. The Third Way wanted to find a path between Socialism and Capitalism, a middle ground, and Uta had an idea or two about that.

She could be an adviser. She could help these East German neophytes deal with the Western media and with the Americans. If the Third Way was to succeed, they must understand the virtues as well as the vices of capitalism. They must grasp the felicities of strawberry-scented soap, among other things. And by teaching them, she would flow forward herself, a positive charge. What had happened at her father's funeral must be dealt with in this way, by helping others.

At the door to the apartment building where the meeting of the Third Way would take place, a man smoked a cigarette. His cheeks dissolved into purls of a beard that cascaded to his belly. His head was bald and glittery, and though disguised as a hippy, he reminded Uta of a Greek priest.

"Who are you?" he wanted to know.

"Uta Silk. I'm here for the meeting."

"I don't know you."

His rudeness annoyed Uta, but she persisted.

"I'm here as a volunteer," she explained. "I want to help."

The sun sank from sight. Dull beams came from a streetlamp nearby. The man tossed the butt of his cigarette at the ground. He gave her a quizzical look.

"You're from West Berlin?"

"Kreuzberg."

"Well then. Have you seen what your chancellor said today? He wants the two Germanies to be part of a confederative structure. The ass. He thinks he can gobble us up like a plate of pork bellies."

Without asking another question, he led her down the steps into a basement where a few people had already gathered. The bearded smoker told her to stay at the door. He went over to a man well over six feet tall whose eyes scanned the same flyer Uta had been handed that evening. His friend pointed at Uta, and the tall man gestured to her to come over. At his feet, she saw, beneath a table, sat a box of pineapples stamped with an official party seal. No one in East Germany had eaten pineapples—Americans ate pineapples, West Germans ate pineapples, but not the citizens of the German Democratic Republic—and yet here they were, as guileless as naked children. The scent of a West German beach vacation emanated from the cardboard box. The tall man himself reeked of fruit.

"You like them?" he asked.

"No—"

"But you've eaten them?"

Uta nodded.

"That's more than I can say. Take at least one."

To be agreeable, Uta did.

"What can we do for you?" the tall man asked. She could tell that he resented the fact that she had eaten a pineapple before, but she refused to be deterred from her purpose. She wanted to be honest. No more lies, she told herself, no more secrets. Just service. "I want to help out here. Any little work you have for me will be fine. I believe the Third Way can work."

The two men, tall and bearded, exchanged glances. All of a sudden, they looked defensive.

"Do you now?" The tall man scratched his chin. "Then it must be true. What can you do for us, anyway?"

Uta was losing her patience.

"I can hand out flyers. Anything."

The men returned hostile stares, as if she had insulted them. The smell of the pineapples was beginning to make her sick.

"You see," the tall man explained, "the problem is that your chancellor is trying to tell us what we should do with our country—"

"He's not *my* chancellor!" Uta retorted.

"But we don't want to be West Germans! All you do is shop and go on vacations and eat pineapples, and you make us sick. Your chancellor is trying to eat us alive!"

Uta couldn't believe her ears. She was being blamed for Chancellor Helmut Kohl, a man she had demonstrated against repeatedly over the last two years. She told them so. They dismissed West Berlin protests as insignificant.

"Our demonstrations have toppled a government. What have yours ever accomplished, hmmm? They're just games. If you really want to help us, go stage a *real* one."

Uta bowed her head in frustration. "That's it then? You don't want my help?"

"It's not that we don't want it. It's that we don't need it."

The bearded man lit another cigarette.

"But you're welcome to stay," he said, "as long as you promise to take that pineapple when you go."

Clasping the fruit to her chest, mortified, Uta staggered out.

2.

IT WAS THE SAME EVERYWHERE. She attended a dozen meetings over the next week, and each time, her help was either refused or dismissed or ignored.

Once, she almost got a break. At a church in Prenzlauer Berg, she ran into other West Germans and an American, all of them musicians. They were friends with some of the dissidents who had formed a political party, the New Forum, and were helping to pass out pamphlets. One of the musicians introduced Uta to an East German actress, a leader of the Citizens' Movement, and the woman took an immediate liking to Uta, as if she sensed a fellow penitent.

But over the course of the evening, as plans were made for new demonstrations, new general strikes, and for the formation of new committees, as more and more people entered the church, Uta felt herself pushed to the side. The musicians got drunk and left. The actress drifted farther and farther away, until she disappeared completely. Uta was alone in a sanctuary with hundreds of people who had been hurt by a system she had tried to serve. The whole thing made her dizzy.

By midnight, the church cleared out. She walked home alone.

3.

THAT WAS THE END of her service. The warm, quiet water of the bath lured her into its arms. As before, she lay for hours in the water. Her skin wrinkled. She didn't eat, barely drank. She listened to Johnny Horton, and when he wasn't playing, she sang songs she'd learned as a girl in Catholic school and concentrated on dying. The water would accept her blood as gladly as it did her flesh. Why not take the blade out of the razor and apply it to her wrists? There would be little pain. She had done half the work already by consigning herself to the liquid element. Her mind had already been sucked down the bathtub drain. Only the technicality of her heartbeat remained behind.

She lifted herself out of the water to look for the razor, last used in the month of August; on her legs, she recalled. Stuart had shaved her legs while sitting on the lip of the tub. He had cut her, but in the wrong place.

At last, beneath a washrag, she found the implement. With a hammer, she smashed the handle and lifted the razor out. The bathwater had grown cold. She let it out and filled the tub anew. While the water ran, she hunted down Douglas's letter and ripped it open. It was long. She returned to the tub, sat in the exact spot where Stuart had cradled her ankles, and read the words. She turned on the radio. The Czech government had fallen. People were dancing on Wenceslaus Square. Voices sobbed into a microphone held by an overwhelmed German radio reporter.

Hours passed. She waited for something to happen, a thought or an impulse that would lead the steel down to her flesh. Anything would do. Now and then, the door buzzed. She never answered it. She pondered her nakedness. It was pleasing. For once, she lived up to the rigorous rule of Saint Elizabeth, by denying her flesh everything it required: clothing, activity, food, companionship. Elizabeth had died at the age of twenty-four in the year of Our Lord 1231, seven hundred years before her father had gone to university and become a Nazi. The numbers mattered. They gave Uta courage to submit to a higher fate.

She did it. She placed the razor against each wrist and drew it down, vertically. The first time, it didn't work. She tried again, harder, and succeeded. She sank into the water. The liquid flushed pink, deepened red. The radio talked to her, talked to her, the voice of a monk chanting her into the next existence. There was trouble in the Romanian city of Timisoara. Government forces were massing. Unbelievably, a single Hungarian pastor had caused this vast reaction, a man whom the government had tried to silence before, a man named Laszlo Toekes.

Romania, Uta thought, as the water touched her lips, as she bled. Stuart was in Romania. She drew Douglas's letter to her eyes and read it again with subsiding consciousness, letting its ink fade away in the pool of blood.

"The reason I am writing this letter, dear Uta, in case you haven't figured it out yet," Douglas wrote, "is that I am a lost man, a man seeking some particle of the greater light, and I have found it in you—"

She wrenched herself out of the tub, scarlet streaming down her forearms, and called an emergency line. She wrapped herself in towels and screamed at the top of her lungs. God had spoken. Through Douglas, she had understood. She must go to Stuart. She must forgive him. *He* was the lost man seeking some particle of the greater light. He was all she had, even if he had betrayed her.

Two days later, she bribed a dullard for a Romanian visa and borrowed a few hundred marks from her mother. In a blizzard of activity, she wound up her affairs in West Berlin. She paid utilities, took care of the rent, closed her bank account, gave her deregistration form to the police, who couldn't have cared less. She scribbled a postcard to Douglas, an incoherent but sincere apology, which he might or might not understand. Finally, her life in order, wrists wrapped in bandages, she flew to Bucharest.

CHAPTER NINETEEN

1.

DOUGLAS TURNED THE POSTCARD OVER in his hands. Uta had chosen an arbitrary image, a black-and-white picture of James Dean purchased, no doubt, at one of the kitschy tourist shops on Breitscheidplatz. It had been addressed to him care of the Hotel Mohacs, Budapest, Hungary, without zip code or further address. How, he wondered, had she discovered his whereabouts? The message had been written in extreme speed, by the looks of the script, and was cryptic beyond belief. "Douglas," she had written, "Johnny Horton was right. We know our fate, and we are free. Everything's my fault. Yours, Uta."

Jodie had a terrible fever. It had been increasing every night since their arrival, and no matter how he tried to cool her with ice packs, it persisted. A week ago, when he took her out of the hospital in Vienna, the thermometer had read 98.6. She had looked terrible, but the doctors said all she needed was rest, and Douglas figured she'd be safer with him in Budapest than anywhere else in the vicinity.

But as soon as they reached Budapest, she got sick again and hadn't been able to cover the Hungarian presidential referendum, which had taken place the day before. An old Communist who now called himself a Socialist—the Communist Party had ceased to exist in October—had just barely won the vote, and all the Hotel Mohacs bellhops were calling it a victory for democracy. Douglas asked why, taking notes for Jodie, and they told him that the election proved the old days were over, because that old Communist who'd tried to disguise himself behind the word "Socialist" should have won by a landslide, but the people saw through his charade. Douglas borrowed a hotel typewriter, turned to the one German station on Hungarian television, uncapped a bottle of Hungarian Tokay, and wrote a note to Jodie's boss about everything that was going on. In Czechoslovakia, the government had collapsed. The same day as the Hungarian presidential election, almost a million people had massed in Prague, and this time, no police tried to break them up. In Berlin, the East German government had agreed to meet with the dissidents. He typed these things up, threw in a quote from one of the bellhops about Communism, signed it Jodie Blum, then had the office fax it to the number for *Probe* magazine that he'd found in Jodie's computer bag.

Later on, when the fax had been sent, he sipped at the Tokay and pondered Uta's postcard again.

His eyelids grew heavy. He felt the Tokay bottle slide out of his fingers, heard it thump on the carpet. Jodie lay beside him, her face a mass of green and blue bruises behind her bandages, her dark brown hair splayed out across the sheets. Moisture from the ice pack beaded on her forehead. He took his hand and wiped the moisture away. She was beautiful, he thought, and she would be all right.

Then he dreamed. There was an island in the middle of a great river, and the island moved, like a cork in the current. Douglas stared at the stars and tasted Hungarian Tokay on his lips. The island floated westward past dark hills rising on either side of the river, and on those hills glowed a West Berlin skyline: destroyed churches, discos, cinemas, and gambling parlors, with here and there a Jewish grave from the old cemetery in Prague. They were snaggly teeth jutting from an open mouth. Douglas heard the baying of dogs and the throbbing beat of synthesized music. Jodie slept behind him on the sand. She was warm and well and naked. Every now and then, Douglas would drop his head to her lap and kiss it. After a very long time, the hills vanished, and the island floated into the sea. They were safe. The long journey was over. Then the moon appeared, and something fantastic happened to the mainland receding behind them. There were people on it. Hammers beat against nails. People worked. They built a gallows, which mounted in the moonlight. High and square, made of balsa wood and fiberglass, it resembled his insectarium, but wasn't. He saw the hangman's noose. Rivers of blood poured. Entrails twisted up like vines. Life erupted from the guts of the mainland, a mass of buzzing creatures. Douglas tried to make them out—ticks, wasps, hornets, dragonflies. Their flight took them high against the sides of the structure. Wings obscured the stars. He gazed upon the greatest extermination job in history. The moon cleared a cloud, and he saw it was no moon at all, but the face of his brother Stuart, pale and bloated, cinched up in the noose.

He awoke. Jodie was beside him, roasting alive, it seemed to him. He prepared more ice packs. What else could he do? If he took Jodie to a doctor, he might prescribe some godawful medicine or report them to the police or something even worse, and it would be Douglas's fault. She whimpered, and he smoothed the wet hair away from her eyes. This couldn't go on much longer.

Her breath rattled through a hurt nose. Outside, the Danube flowed past the Mohacs in peace. The continent was still.

2.

THE NEXT MORNING, journalists descended. The lobby banged and clattered with tripods, reflectors, and a snapping swarm of black Nikon cameras. They were everywhere. The bar rattled with glasses and sizzled with frying grease as two dozen people ordered Coca-Cola and hamburgers at the same moment. The gift shop could not stock enough newspapers.

From Hong Kong, Sri Lanka, and Nicaragua, they came; from Liberia, Singapore, El Salvador, and Lebanon, where stories had dried up instantly as word disseminated of events in Berlin and Prague. These journalists bore no resemblance to Jodie Blum and Esperanza Buckner, the only reporters Douglas knew well. Older, more cynical, far more exotic, they reminded Douglas, in a fanciful way, of pirates. The light of destroyed and burning countries gleamed in their eyes.

Some of them looked as if they'd been on safari in the veldt. Khaki and sunglasses wrapped around blazing flesh. Others wore red bandannas and camouflage vests, as if they'd hacked their way through jungle to reach Europe. They called to each other across the crimson plush of the lobby, clasped hands, slapped backs, asked about the availability of work and sex. There were photographers sprawled on the floor sorting out lenses; television anchors with perfect tans practicing lines before a live camera, and one man in a vest and Afro shaking the sand from the chamber of a pistol. From what Douglas gathered, everyone wanted to get to Bucharest, where a Hungarian pastor was evidently causing problems, and where, despite Stuart's thoughts on the subject, the next convulsion was expected. But first, the Hungarian capital offered a little R and R. A sudden unprecedented change in the climate, a hike in the temperature by some twenty degrees, had transformed a cold winter into a momentary steam bath, and the media community took full advantage. Some of the less inhibited stripped off their clothes and went swimming in the Danube, which flowed a few hundred yards from the hotel entrance.

Into this hedonistic chaos, almost kneecapping Douglas with her valise, walked Pansy Buckner. She was dressed for battle, it seemed to him, with spectacular oyster products—pricey spawn of *Meleagrina margaritifera,* if he was not mistaken—in her earlobes. A black wool skirt hugged her hips, a pearlaceous silk scarf trailed like a soldier's bandage from her throat, and a blue silk blouse opened just enough to reveal the pink of her chest.

Behind her trudged a valet with the rest of her luggage. Douglas hid behind a potted plant.

At first, the reservations girl refused her accommodation. As of noon, the hotel had no more vacancies. All of Budapest was booked, she explained, because of the revolutions. Too many journalists, she opined, and Douglas gathered that the hotel staff had been whining to one another so profusely on the subject that they could no longer withhold their scorn in front of guests. Pansy was undaunted. She tossed a credit card onto the marble-topped counter, plucked several American bills from her purse, and mentioned her affiliation. A room was found.

Douglas crept upon her. He cleared his throat. "Jodie's got a high fever," he said.

She turned toward him. "Then get her to a doctor, for God's sake. Not that it concerns you, but I'm headed for Romania. I'm supposed to set up a temporary bureau there for Hammond Stamps. I have no time for any more nonsense."

Douglas helped her get the luggage to the elevators. She relented slightly.

"You really should get Jodie to a doctor. Maybe the United States embassy here could recommend one. I would stay away from the hospitals."

The elevator dinged open. Douglas swallowed. He didn't know why Pansy held him in such contempt. She didn't even know him. But he comforted himself with the knowledge that her attitude toward him was part of a generalized disdain for the world as a whole, a sufferance of the billions of souls who made up the population of the earth and did not work for her paper. She had come to Eastern Europe no more than three weeks ago, he reflected, and yet she acted as if that part of the world, about which she seemed to know very little, was no more than the foyer of an expensive restaurant where everyone knew her boss's name; and in that restaurant her table waited, her champagne was already chilled, and her favorite dish had been prepared from a secret menu. Needless to say, those she loathed would not be seated near her table. She was irreproachable.

"I haven't said a thing, by the way. Nor will I. You can count on it. I'm very grateful for everything you did."

Pansy arched an eyebrow. The elevator bumped against her valise. His words seemed to have an effect. She pressed a button, and the elevator door stayed open. "Look, after I've tended to a few things, I'll stop by and see how she's doing. Okay?"

"Okay."

The elevator doors closed.

Douglas found the hotel casino and proceeded to drown himself in ginger ale and whiskey. The day crept toward dusk. He noticed a trail of ants at the foot of the bar. He must take Jodie to a doctor. Maybe Pansy was right. Maybe he should just go to the embassy. He might not even have to give his identification. If he could get his hands on some American dollars, some cash, he could do a deal, no questions asked. But all he had was Jodie's credit card.

A few businessmen mixed with the journalists in the part of the establishment known as the Mathias Casino, which consisted of a long wooden counter overhung by stag antlers, a despondent croupier named Laszlo chain-smoking over a roulette wheel, and a drag queen named Ginger Bathory who, in a bright red and green cape, sang show tunes on a barstool. All of this occurred under the glare of spotlights refracted through a mirror ball hanging from the ceiling. Here German, American, and Italian hacks gathered with the heads of state-owned factories and their potential investors to whisper about joint ventures, privatizations, and hard currency.

A man watched him from the other side of the room, a beetle-browed fellow in his sixties or seventies who wore a silver cross around his neck and an expensive suit.

The flintlike eyes watched as Douglas drank. They watched as he waved Laszlo the croupier over to his table and pointed out the ants. Laszlo said the ants were nothing, he should see the meal moth problem in the kitchen. Call girls in togas and hot pants skimmed his table. The man wearing the cross watched and waited. Douglas grew more nervous by the minute.

Laszlo asked him what he did for a living, and when Douglas, sick of lying, answered truthfully, that he used to be an economic entomologist, the croupier repeated the tale of the meal moths and asked Douglas if he would have a look at the kitchen.

"Not my line of work anymore, Laszlo."

More call girls skimmed him. For every guest of the casino, a girl had been provided, like a complimentary drink. And these girls suggested Texas high-school cheerleaders dressed up for a play about courtesans in ancient Vindobona. They were sheathed in lavender makeup, draped in crepe-thin fabrics, and helmeted heavily in peroxide curls. Douglas paid his bar tab.

Laszlo followed him out, pleaded with him to check out the kitchen's problem. He said the flower, nuts, and sugar were all tainted by moth webs.

They had found larvae in the cinnamon. Douglas gave in and offered advice. He told the man to buy a fogger, and if that didn't work, to let him know. The man wearing the cross appeared in the doorway of the casino. Douglas hurried away.

An hour later, after he'd won another temporary victory against Jodie's fever, the manager of the Mohacs showed up and explained that he did not know where to acquire a fogger at short notice. He offered to pay Douglas three hundred marks to get rid of the meal moths.

In his gut, he felt the desire to work again; not the craziness of trying to eradicate pigeon ticks, but the simple labor of clearing out a normal infestation. After all, in the absence of a family, of a home, of a job, what was left of his identity but a trade? Furthermore, the three hundred marks would allow him to help Jodie. He could pay a doctor in cash.

Douglas shook hands on it, and that very night, after eating a hearty meal of chicken paprikas in the room, he launched a radical assault on *Plodia interpunctella,* which had laid eggs in most of the flour and sugar supply in the kitchen. The eggs had hatched, the larvae had fed on the food, then migrated to the ceiling corners, where their pupal cases could be seen, thin as cobwebs. The cinnamon did indeed contain larvae, and he reflected on the breakfast of French toast he'd wolfed down the morning of their arrival. Most of the powdered goods had to be thrown out. In the meantime, he sprayed bleach and lye into the nooks and crannies where the larvae might crawl in the future, scraped away the pupal cases on the walls, and ordered a dehumidification of the entire kitchen space. Bins were sealed, all suspicious grains were removed, and within forty-eight hours, he estimated, the moths would begin to wane. He felt like a million dollars and received three hundred marks.

3.

AT THE END of the night's work, Douglas went downstairs to the bar, which was empty. The first gray hint of morning came through the windows of the Mohacs. He found a thick, warm chair beside a cold fireplace. Laszlo brought him Irish whiskey from the manager's stash, winked, and walked away. All of a sudden, Douglas began to shake. He put the whiskey down.

An extraordinary thought had occurred to him. Who would miss him if he died right then? In all the world, only one person, and that was Jodie. He was attached to the human race by her alone, the human being tossing in a fever two floors above. Stuart had disappeared. Nester had vanished. Uta had lost her mind. He didn't know if he would ever see any of them again.

Not one of those who had known him in his old life, not a one from those Christmases of years past, would recall him with fondness. Linda would think of him as the man who married her under false pretenses, the man who seemed to be an idealistic young insect sociologist but had, over the course of five years, turned out to be an insecticidal whore, a mere exterminator.

If the insects of Dallas, Texas, had memories buried in their collective unconscious, he would be a scourge, a fountain of poison—at best, a half-assed god of death.

There was Fleischmann's, of course. A community of sorts had developed there, but in that community, if he was honest with himself, he had not been much loved. He had been ambitious and unkind, in thrall to power. The forklift drivers would remember him as the man who had accidentally murdered a collie puppy with strychnine and old man Fleischmann would think of him as the employee offered a second chance who had flung that second chance back in his face. Two weeks ago, at ten a.m. on the morning of November 16, the day of his arrival in Prague, Douglas had missed an appointment with Fleischmann in his office in Dallas, Texas. At that exact moment, his professional life had ceased to exist.

That appointment had flowed past him, like a point on the Danube never to be revisited. His mother's death lay back there too, as did his brother's betrayal, and somewhere very distant, at the source, his father's disappearance, which had set the card fall of his life in motion.

Douglas was a child of the revolution now, a ward of the new world. And the revolution had brought him this woman. That was how he saw it. The rise of peoples, the fall of governments, the collapse of ideologies, led inexorably to her.

"To you," he whispered, taking a long drink of the whiskey. Then he hurled the glass into the fireplace and went upstairs to bed.

CHAPTER TWENTY

OVER TRANSYLVANIA, Uta's jet began to lose altitude. A Communist stewardess dropped into the adjacent seat and began to cross herself, left to right, in Orthodox fashion. They were at least an hour from their destination.

Uta looked out the window of the old Russian Tupolev and saw clouds punctured by the summits of a few, hubristic, snow-blanched Carpathians. Luggage rattled in the compartments, which seemed as loosely attached to the structure of the plane as saddlebags to a horse. Moisture dripped onto Uta's head.

The Tupolev continued to descend. It skipped along the surface of the clouds. Uta peered down gulfs of silver. The plane flared into them. Everything became a wet, white blur. Condensation streamed down the windowpane. Fissures of darkness broke open. She waited for an explanation from the cockpit. The Tupolev descended beneath the clouds. A blue range of mountains walled off the south. Below them lay farmland.

They were not exactly plummeting, but Uta could feel the machine lurching too fast down great gulps of space. A blue uniform bounded past. Bells rang. There was no airstrip visible on the ground. In her hands reposed a duty-free item, a piece of Wallachian cheese, given to her, she guessed, on the assumption that once touched, it would be irresistible.

Next to her, the stewardess wiped her eyes with the backs of her hands, smeared mascara down both cheeks, and by doing so, regained a bit of lost composure. Lufthansa employees would never have shown such fear to passengers, Uta thought with a burst of involuntary pride. They would have been censured on the spot.

A semblance of a human voice blipped and crackled in Romanian over

a poorly circuited PA system. Uta heard words that sounded vaguely Latinate, and tried to apply her vacationer's knowledge of Spanish, but she
failed to grasp a thing. The other passengers buckled themselves in. To Uta's
dismay, the eyes of her two immediate neighbors across the aisle glittered
with sheer, unabated terror.

Until that moment, she had been feeling pretty good; better than she
had in months.

She buckled too, not sure what good it would do. A Russian-made plane
smacking Transylvania at thousands of miles per hour would leave behind,
at best, a smear. Her wrists started to ache. She had worn one of Stuart's
button-down oxfords for the journey, and the cuffs of the shirt ran all the
way down to her palms, hiding the bandaged wrists.

Random worries flapped through her brain. What about her visa?

She had her doubts. The Romanian official at the travel agency in West
Berlin had accepted a one-hundred-mark bribe. He had retreated into a
back room and returned with a piece of blotted paper. This would do, he
assured Uta. The Romanian government had a special fondness for West
Germans, he said, because West Germany had been so good about buying
back its countrymen, who had lived for eight hundred years in Transylvania
and now wanted to live among their own people again; which was nonsense, Uta recalled. The Saxons of Romania, who had moved to the region
as settlers before the idea of a Romanian nation even existed, were leaving
because they no longer felt welcome in the country. Ceausescu the dictator
had used their desire to escape, and the West German obligation to repatri-
ate them as people of German origin, to extort hard currency from the
Bonn government. Everything came wrapped in a lie, Uta reflected, and she
seemed to be the only one who hadn't understood that principle. Just show
them the mark on the paper, the official insisted, which was a circle containing several words in Romanian.

The plane gouged through bricks of turbulence. It twisted up, thrashed
down. Uta refused to look out the window anymore. Wrapped in cheap
plastic, the Wallachian cheese began to crumble in her hands.

She closed her eyes and saw herself with unaccustomed tenderness, as
she might see her own child. A delicious thought emerged, Stuart shaving
her legs in the beloved bathtub of her apartment.

Across the aisle, sobs erupted. She tried to block them out, forced her
gaze deep inside. Herr Mundung quizzing her at the zoo. The car hitting
the dog. A luggage compartment came open, spilling its contents into the
aisle with a crash.

Stuart made love to her in his apartment. Music videos played in the
background, splashing colors across their limbs. Douglas buried a May bee-

tle. Her mother wept. The boys in the graveyard Sieg Heiled. Her father gave her a book as she sat cross-legged on the floor of his study. Her heart soared. She put her hands together and tried to lose herself in early memories, which had been unfairly neglected and begged to be touched a last time. She picked cherries amid bees during a forgotten summer, back before ideology and the past intruded, way back when the silhouette of her father above her hovered in the tree like the protective canopy of the sky.

She said it, her own voice stating the most profound feeling in her chest: "I remember."

The plane jolted. Her eyes flew open. It was no good. She glanced out the window. The plane rattled within a few thousand feet of the ground. Uta felt the sharpest of disappointments. If she had wanted to die, she would have done so in the bathtub in West Berlin. It would have cost less and been far more comfortable. She could have sunk into her memories without having to fear the impact of machinery against earth. The sobs continued.

She wanted to sob too. As a dying human animal, surely she deserved to. Even jackals and hyenas had that right. But she couldn't, because in her heart, the conviction ached, she believed she ought to die in an inferno, as her father had not.

She could hear landing gear trundle out of the belly of the plane. More luggage compartments dropped open. Coats and belts and underwear streamed from cracked suitcases. Reams of computer paper, stockings, and hundred-dollar pairs of blue jeans festooned the aisle. Silence, and within it, the longing for life, filled the plane. Men and women consigned to flames waited to be repatriated back into existence. Uta could feel it coming from the cockpit, she could feel it in the sudden absence of the sobs, in the rhythm of communal breath pulsing at the edge of her perception. Wheels touched ground. The structure groaned, as if a vast body had leaned upon it. Metal wrenched and screamed.

Uta clutched the seat in front of her, turned her gaze to the world. Out the window, she saw farmers seated on wagons, women with pitchforks and scythes. A goose nestled in a girl's arms.

They taxied on a country road. A lone passenger clapped. Most of the rest of the people within Uta's view sank into a bliss that defied articulation. It was time for prayer and then, maybe, dinner.

Uta began to sob now. The stewardess sat down beside her.

"Danke," Uta gibbered out. "Danke."

The plane came to rest. Farmers gathered in the fields. Uta pulled away from the stewardess, thanked her again, paid her ten marks for the destroyed cheese, and they both laughed.

Military jeeps rumbled past her window. She was in Romania.

CHAPTER TWENTY-ONE

1.

WITH THREE HUNDRED MARKS in his pocket and a lunch sack in his hands, Douglas set out for the United States embassy to find Jodie a doctor. He would have to walk the first stretch. The Hotel Mohacs sat in the middle of Margaret Island, a mile-and-a-half-long wisp of land floating like a handkerchief in the middle of the Danube River. At either end of the island was a bridge where Douglas could catch a taxicab, but it was an hour's walk in either direction.

He took a path running south down the eastern length of the handkerchief. He was aware of being followed by the man wearing the cross, the one from the casino, but didn't let that deter him. The presence might be mere coincidence.

Across the river, to his left, Douglas saw the Hungarian Parliament, a reddish edifice with spires as exquisitely thin as hummingbird beaks. Inside that building, Hungarian Communism had suffered a heart attack and died. God, how Stuart had misjudged things. Douglas passed the remains of a cloister, the busts of several Hungarian notables, ragged goats in a petting zoo.

The man wearing the cross continued to follow, so Douglas veered off to the right, into a dense thicket of firs, dogwoods, and dwarf plums. Paths crisscrossed the island. Sooner or later, he would hit one of them again, and his tail would be left behind. Dead thorns tore at his blue jeans. The ground beneath his feet became soggy. He pushed on, hoping he was not about to strike the Danube, but growing worried. He began to smell sulfur. He stopped, inhaled. Thermal water was in the air. He pulled aside the prickle-fingers of a fir and saw, with disbelieving eyes, a natural spa. In a small clearing surrounded by deciduous trees and overhung by a calming palm of rock steamed a pool of water about six feet across.

He pushed through needles, which poked him in the cheek. Careful not to get his lunch wet, he skirted the edge of the pool, a natural depression in the ground that had only recently, it seemed, filled with water. He took off a shoe and stuck in a toe. It was warm as bathwater.

Once a nunnery, a prison for a royal princess, and a sultan's harem, Margaret Island was now known for its thermal waters, which percolated unseen but odiferous in the guts of the Hotel Mohacs. In a very few days, Douglas had grown to love the spa smell. The sulfurous, eggy reek held a mysterious power—on Margaret Island, the reek suggested, he was safe from harm.

He made a mental note and moved on. His pursuer, by the looks of things, had vanished.

2.

THE GUARD LOWERED his thumb onto the tabletop and with a deft index finger pried open Douglas's document. He read its first page and let the cover drop.

"I need a doctor," Douglas announced. "I'm here to ask about a recommendation for a doctor."

The guard tapped twice on the cover of the passport.

"Is someone sick?"

Douglas rolled his eyes and nodded. He was told to wait in the foyer outside the metal detector, a bare, uncertain space without a place to sit. A marine perused him from behind dark glass. The embassy was a soaring villa of three to four stories, with a heavy oak banister accompanying marble stairs down to the first floor. The stair steps gleamed before him on the far side of a pane of bulletproof glass. For all its grandeur, the villa had succumbed to decay. Cracks ran up the walls. Putti had lost nostrils and wing tips. The tiles of the floor were of a much more recent vintage; linoleum, he thought.

The guard returned to his desk, and Douglas was allowed to walk through the metal detector. The guard kept his passport and gave him a plastic pass. Before long, a young man in coat and tie descended the great stairs and padded over to him on tennis shoes.

"May I help you?"

Douglas sprang up.

"A friend of mine is ill and needs a reliable doctor. I was told you might be able to help me."

Douglas was surprised to see an intense curiosity grow on the man's face. "And where is this friend?"

He felt his plans go clammy. "At home."

"I see. Is she an American citizen?"

Douglas nodded.

"I see. But you're an East German? That's what I was told."

Douglas nodded, getting nervous. It was going badly already. He had made a mistake.

"You don't sound East German. May I see your passport?"

Douglas pointed at the guard, who handed it over. He didn't know what else to do.

"Vice president of the Parasitological Society? Can that be right? You are a science official of some kind? What are you doing in Budapest?"

Douglas considered running. Instead, on a breath of inspiration, he demanded a doctor in an irritated but fluent German, the best he had ever uttered.

"Ich habe gesagt, dass ich einen Arzt dringend nötig habe! Also?"

The young man was startled. Fingering the three hundred marks from the extermination job in his pocket, Douglas resumed English. "I can pay, if that's what you want."

Apologetically, the young man returned the passport.

"Please don't be offended. We're as shell-shocked as everyone else by what's happened. We never know who will show up next. And you need what kind of a doctor?"

He pulled a notepad from his coat pocket, clicked the butt of a pen.

"She's sick with a fever, and she was beaten badly too. In Prague. She's a journalist."

The man took notes. At the mention of Prague, his eyes shifted away from the page and to Douglas.

"You were in Prague together? My God, I can hardly believe what's happening there. Did you see that Alexander Dubcek is addressing demonstrations? It wasn't so long ago that he was under house arrest, if you remember!"

"Please. I'm in a great hurry."

"Of course. We have a list of doctors. I'll see what I can do."

Douglas watched him mount the marble stairs of the villa. His steps were loud as hand claps. The echo crashed up and up, diminishing into the depths of the building. And at that instant, as the man's departure completed itself, Douglas experienced a rush of raw terror. Could he have been so stupid? It was a trap. He had set it himself. The marine spoke on a phone and watched him. Must keep calm, Douglas thought, hold firm to my resolve. He had made a grave error. Suppose there were people in this building who knew about the Glemnik affair but, like Styles, operated in a rogue fashion? Suppose they had seen him coming down the street and had already prepared a van to take him away, to trundle him off to West Berlin, where he would be summarily—what?—executed by Styles? The bureaucrat had raised his eyebrows at Prague. It was more than possible that he knew something.

Douglas jammed the passport into his pants pocket, glided past the guard, who was reading a tabloid, shimmied through the metal detector, and hit the embassy entrance at a dead run. On his way out, he heard the garbled voice of the marine through the telecom in the darkened glass. He stumbled off the curb, tripped across asphalt. He got up again and raced for the end of the block, for a taxi stand there. The embassy official burst from the front doors, pointed at Douglas, and cried out for help. Behind him was the marine.

Douglas jumped into a cab. The driver punched it.

3.

A S SOON AS he reached the Mohacs, he was presented with a firm offer. The hotel manager tapped a cigarette from a gold-plated case. Laszlo the croupier lit it for him. They were standing in the lobby.

The Mohacs was old and infested, the manager explained. Laszlo winced and nodded with empathy. Rats seethed in the cellar. Bats teemed in the cupolas. Ants invaded bathtubs every spring, and termites supped on the master suite, which had been occupied in 1910 by no less a personage than the Archduke Franz Ferdinand. If Douglas expressed interest, the Mohacs would pay him a regular salary of two hundred thousand forints a month in addition to free room and board. All he had to do was rid the premises of vermin. Their agreement would be made between gentlemen, a handshake deal, so to speak, since the Hungarian government would frown upon an American taking work away from a native. As a show of good faith, the manager offered Douglas a bottle of Transylvanian muscadet from his own cellar and a down payment of forints for the first month's work.

Douglas pleaded for time and shocked the hotel manager, who thought he'd made an offer no sane man could refuse. Douglas apologized. Everyone wanted a piece of him.

He pried himself away from the man with a promise to think about it. He forsook the elevator, afraid to be trapped in there with yet another supplicant, and galloped up the steps to the third floor.

Jodie nabbed him by the crook of his elbow as he hurried out of the stairwell.

"Whoa."

"Oh thank God!" He threw his arms around her without thinking. She didn't resist. He pulled away in embarrassment.

"People are after me."

"Are you sure?"

Without waiting to hear an answer, Jodie coaxed Douglas down the hall and into the room. He turned both locks and put his ear to the door, listening for pursuit.

"People followed you here? To the hotel?"

"I don't know!" Douglas blurted out. He retreated from the door, watching it. "Christ, I'm sorry."

She put a hand on his arm and led him to the love seat.

"Ginger ale?"

He shook his head, looked up sheepishly. "I'm just nervous. The guy at the American embassy may have been onto me—"

"The embassy?"

"I went to see if I could get you a doctor—"

Now he began to focus on her, and what he saw astonished him. She was up, she was dressed, she was gorgeous. He felt a smile ripple up his face, felt his entire body metamorphose out of a state of fear and into a condition of unexpected delight, as when he had stumbled across the thermal spring. Her dark brown hair had grown long, and she'd tied it back in a ponytail that bounced as she moved her head; she'd tied it with a thin black ribbon that curled at the base of her neck. She had taken the bandages off her face. Though blue-and-brown marks darkened the left side of her face, where the worst blow had fallen, though the traces of stitches could still be seen on the same cheek, her eyes glowed with a warm alertness beneath their sharp, smart eyebrows. Her smile no longer seemed an effort.

On top of all this, she had slipped on a flouncy black dress and a pair of red shoes, their color accentuated by silk stockings running dark up her legs, disappearing like smoke beneath the hem of her dress.

"Wow," he said.

"Yeah. I'm up."

"You look . . . I can't even think of the word. Beautiful. Meeting some-one for dinner tonight?"

"You."

"Me?"

She plucked a letter off a table next to the love seat. "This came under the door. An invitation from Pansy Buckner. She's in the hotel. You re-member, I told you about her."

Douglas shook his head in feigned disbelief.

"I always thought she hated me, but we've been invited to a dinner party being thrown by Hammond Stamps, her boss. It starts downstairs in an hour. It's going to be amazing, Douglas. Anna Strogar, the *Times* correspon-dent from Warsaw, will be there. And Oliphant Smeaton, the senior Euro-pean correspondent for British Occidental Radio. You have to get dressed up, though. At least comb your hair."

An hour later, on the way to the party, he wanted to tell her everything that had happened since the beating. But he couldn't speak. Her recovery struck him dumb. The last time she had been awake for more than an hour at a time was in Prague. Since then, she had passed through Vienna and landed in Budapest, more like a parcel than a human being. Douglas looked into her eyes and saw an unconcealed wonder.

"How long have I been out?"

"Three and a half weeks. More or less. But you haven't really been out. In and out, I'd say."

Her brows knit together. "*Shit*. Chubbs must have been wondering about me. Have you talked to him? Have I been fired?"

Douglas told her where things stood, leaving out the origins of her Eastern European cover story. He blushed with the memory of that night, ashamed to know what she could not. They stopped at the doors to the casino, which had been closed for the private party. Douglas could hear the murmur of people within. He could hear ice clicking in glasses, loud bursts of laughter, the thump of a finger testing a microphone. Jodie checked her ponytail and straightened the dress at her shoulders. She looked at him.

"Well?"

Douglas didn't know what to say that could possibly express the feelings welling up inside of him, but he couldn't contain himself any longer.

"Have you ever baited a spring trap?" he blurted.

The doors to the casino swung wide open. Pansy Buckner crossed her arms.

CHAPTER TWENTY-TWO

1.

AFTER A MOMENT'S HESITATION, Jodie and Pansy hugged, and as they did, Jodie experienced a sudden vivid recollection. She had seen Pansy in Prague in the second before the riot cop attacked her.

"Congratulations on your string with *Probe,*" Pansy said.

"Thanks, Panse. How's the *Times?*"

"Maddening." She lowered her voice and jokingly added, "But you're really not allowed to ask."

For a long moment, as they exchanged these pleasantries, Jodie was plunged into memory.

Pansy had been there when the cop's truncheon fell. She had appeared, then vanished. In that instant, Jodie heard a crack, and pain stabbed her face. She tumbled to the ground, still conscious. Her own blood seeped into her mouth, her nose, and her eyes. It rose like a tide from within, engulfing her. She thought she was dying.

Later, flashes of awareness had come, but these were islands in a sea of delirium. Eventually, the pain receded. It never went away—neither did the image of the cop who had beaten her—but she found the worst agonies could be kept at bay while she concentrated on a fierce internal struggle that now, as she trafficked among people again, became part of an untranslatable existence in the shadows. She would never find adequate words to describe it. Somewhere in those shadows, for instance, Jodie could not recall exactly when, she discerned what she now figured must have been God. The experience had not felt like a conversion. It was not momentous or grand. There had been no moment when Jodie stood before her Creator and said, "Yes I believe." But it was real enough. One moment, a darkness enveloped her. She could feel earth thudding on her coffin in the Jewish cemetery in Prague. She could hear Aunt Rachel wailing. The next, a light incandesced beside her bed, and that light, quite simply, was Him—not necessarily a Hebrew Him, though why not?

"Hey? You okay?"

Jodie nodded to Douglas, who had spoken, and hooked her arm through his elbow. She did not want to think about these things anymore. They exhausted her. Pansy looked smashing as usual, in a blue silk dress and pearls. Jodie didn't care. It was enough to be alive.

"I was just coming to get you," explained Pansy, leading them through a darkened bar to a table at the far end of the casino. As they walked, Pansy whispered into Jodie's ear, "Ham is still at the Foreign Ministry, but I just talked to him, and he wants everyone to wait. That's what I told Anna Strogar. But she ordered the waiters to bring out the soup anyway. She treats me like I'm Ham's chauffeur, for God's sake. She doesn't even call me by my name."

They approached the table, which, isolated from the rest of the empty room, seemed to cast its own glow and appeared to Jodie like an image from one of her fever dreams. Candles flickered in mounts on the walls, casting light up into the antlers and tusks of stuffed game heads. Beneath the heads, wine stewards uncorked dripping black bottles of Freixenet, a waiter ladled cold cherry soup from a folkloric tureen into bowls, and a wizened violinist in a tuxedo struck up a waltz.

Pansy didn't bother with introductions. As they sat, a few people looked up from their conversations. One, a bespectacled Brit in a Savile Row suit, asked Jodie what had happened to her face, and when Jodie told him she had been beaten at the Prague *massakr*, he said, "You were there too, eh? Well done. Most of these lot came late."

Jodie blushed with pride. As they sat, Pansy gave a rundown of the guests, most of whom were either friends or friends of friends of the great Hammond Stamps. At one end of the table, beneath a boar's gnarled head, sat the imperious, Pulitzer Prize–winning Anna Strogar, listening to a deeply tanned man, an American television correspondent, make dire warnings about Romania. Strogar was one of Jodie's heroes, and she looked formidably pretty in her close-cropped blond hair and maroon cashmere sweater. On her other side sat Oliphant Smeaton of British Occidental Radio, the man who had complimented Jodie. He examined a cherry in the curve of his spoon and corrected the American journalist on a point of Romanian history. Next to him, across from Jodie, were a pair of Germans: a West German millionaire, who had made his fortune off a tiny semiconductor firm, and his East German guest, an official from the embassy. The two were locked in an argument about the health of the East German economy. Completing that side of the table were a few more Americans: a Marxist legal scholar, a cigar-puffing, ponytailed photographer on assignment from *Time* magazine, and, alarmingly, a young American diplomat who, Douglas whispered, was staring. On their side of the table, almost out of view, were the Serb daughter of a famous Yugoslav painter, on her way to Belgrade from Paris, where she worked as a model, and an obscure Croat poet in town for the release of her first work in Hungarian translation. Finally, in all his leonine glory, on the other side of Douglas, was the Hungarian Jewish writer and intellectual Sandor Kis, who had sent back the cherry soup and asked the waiters to bring him instead a gin and tonic and a cheeseburger.

Anna Strogar's severe gaze fell upon Pansy.

"Where's Ham?" she asked.

Pansy started to explain, but Strogar cut her off. "He'll take an hour to file his story. Why don't we start the toasts?"

"Because he said not to!" Pansy shot back.

Strogar took up a knife and tapped the blade against the side of her water glass.

"I propose a toast!"

"Here, here!" voices called. "Let her toast!"

Before Strogar could speak, Oliphant Smeaton raised his glass and declared: "The year 1917 is hereby eradicated from history."

"Like hell!"

All eyes turned to a hairy man in an Armani jacket who seemed on the verge of hurling his champagne flute down the length of the table. He put out a cigarette. "Just because a few totalitarian regimes collapse of their own internal rot doesn't mean the Russian Revolution is overturned. On the contrary, my friend, I would argue that for the first time enlightened Marxists have a chance of seeing their political dreams realized. Who do you think is going to be running these countries once the smoke clears? They're all going to be reform Socialists, and they're not going to throw the baby out with the bathwater. They're too smart for that—"

"Aren't you the fucking dinosaur!" cried the *Time* photographer, slamming his fist down hard and laughing.

"And it's not lost on me," the Marxist scholar continued, thrusting his flute at Oliphant Smeaton as if it were a blackboard eraser, "that you were paraphrasing Goebbels!"

"My dear chap," the Brit sighed, clearly in contempt of his accuser, "you're quite right about the Socialists. They may remain in power on one condition. Do you know what that is? They may remain in power if they jettison from their program anything that remotely smacks of Karl Marx."

Once more, Anna Strogar tapped her knife against her glass. "You sabotaged me, Ollie. I want to make a toast to the Soviet premier. To Mikhail Gorbachev, a great man. On that, we can all surely agree."

"To Gorbachev!" almost everyone cried in enthusiastic agreement.

"Nein!" objected the East German diplomat.

"He's unreconstructed and *stinkblau!"* roared the West German millionaire, a boisterous man in a loud yellow sweater. "He tells me that Gorbachev stabbed his country in the back, and I tell him, good! Good that he stabbed that *Schwein* Honecker in the back, and then he tells me, this is all the work of the CIA, and Gorbachev works for them, and I say, good again! Good that he works for the CIA, *Mensch!* Don't you see! Democracy has triumphed! The people have risen like in 1789, when they tore down the Bastille in France—two hundred years ago exactly!—"

"Democracy!" shouted someone. The glasses went up again. Waiters removed soup bowls and introduced plates of Hungarian goose liver on toast. The American diplomat watched in curious silence.

"You're all fucking crazy!" The photographer reared up, extremely drunk. He poked at the millionaire with a smoldering cigar. "You think the people are rising for democracy? Bullshit! You should know better. They are rising for *this!"*

He reached beneath the table with his free hand, lifted his camera, and began wildly snapping pictures. Flashes burst in Jodie's eyes and made her dizzy.

"They want the *goods,* man!" The diplomat snatched the camera away from him and tried to get him to sit down. "They're no dumbasses! They want Michael Jackson! They want Cuisinart! They want Hershey bars and Mercedes-Benzes and frozen yogurt! They want hundred-dollar Cuban cigars! That's what this shit is about! Where's Ham? He'll tell it like it is!"

With a curse, the photographer staggered back, nearly tumbling over his chair.

"I completely disagree with *everything* you just said!" Jodie cried.

She felt herself getting hot in the face. She was angry and exhilarated. Everyone was looking at her, including a horrified Pansy.

Jodie swallowed. "I'm younger than most of you, and my first real political memory is of Watergate. The hearings, I mean. I watched the hearings on television, because they preempted the cartoons. And that was my first exposure to politics. To me, Watergate has always *meant* politics: corruption, testimony, failure. But this? *This?* It's none of those things."

She struggled to find the words. "I am filled with awe by what I've seen.

All my life I've read about revolution. The French Revolution, the Russian Revolution, the American Revolution. But it was all dead to me. It was talk. It was code. That's what I thought until the night the Wall fell, and now . . . I'm not even sure I understand now. Maybe it's what democracy is all about. Maybe it's the truest form of politics. Maybe it's not political at all. Maybe it's divine. I don't know. But to say that it's all for the sake of a Cuban cigar? Well, to me, that's just a failure of the imagination, and God help us if that's how we see it."

Next to her, Douglas seemed caught in his own deep paranoia about the American diplomat. He had neither listened nor heard. Pansy's thoughts could not be read. Jodie could feel another wave of dizziness coming, but at the same time, her pulse was racing, and she felt supernaturally prescient, as if she grasped what no one else at the table could possibly see. Just as she thought she might tumble out of her chair, Sandor Kis, the old Jewish intellectual, cleared his throat. The violinist took a break, and a silence overcame the table.

"Unlike this young lady, who has spoken very eloquently, I am not young at all," Kis's baritone boomed. Beneath his great white eyebrows, his dark eyes burned. "I am now seventy-six years old, and I have seen enough revolution to know how dangerously *boring* it can be. But I will say this. As a native"—he shot a withering glance at the drunken photographer—"I may tell you that Cuban cigars have less to do with these marvelous events than meets the eye. In fact, in my opinion, these regimes murdered themselves many years ago, and the people are just now discovering that their governments are corpses. Here, in Hungary, the murder took place long ago, in 1956, when the Russian tanks suppressed a popular revolt. At that moment, and no later, these Communists died to their people. In Czechoslovakia, it was 1968. And on and on. So here's to political murder." He lifted his gin and tonic. "After much ineffective slaughter, it's finally paid off."

For a moment, people were stunned, as if the candles on the walls had suddenly blown out. Then the Croat spoke up.

"Very funny, my friend," she said, pointing at Kis with a goose-livered piece of toast. She had sensuous lips and dark circles under her eyes. She looked as if she had suffered a lifetime of nightmares. "In my country, we are on the verge of disintegration, and you make jokes about political murder. Let me say with all due respect to everyone here, freedom is not an unalloyed good. Freedom unleashes demons. In June, the leader of the state of Serbia, a Serb nationalist and a thug, celebrated the six-hundredth anniversary of the battle of Kosovo Polje, and this event had a very specific message. In this time of freedom, he is preparing the annihilation of the

Albanian people. *Genocide.* I'm telling you, such a thing would never have happened under Tito, and Tito was a Communist!"

"Amen!" cheered the Marxist scholar.

"Croat propaganda!" shrieked their neighbor, the Serbian model from Paris, flinging her long blond tresses over her shoulder and pounding her fist into her hand. "You side with Communism when everyone else is throwing it out! Typical Croat! We Serbs have been under the yoke of the oppressor for six hundred years, and we're fed up! We watch the fall of the Berlin Wall on television, and we think, that wall stood for less than three decades. It is nothing! Is it wrong for my people to want justice at last, when everywhere else in Europe the day of justice has arrived? Freedom is an unalloyed good. Freedom is everything!"

With that, everyone started to shout. The waiters came running with more alcohol. The violinist launched into a Gypsy folk dance. The American diplomat stood up. Jodie could feel Douglas prepare to run.

"Romania's going to explode!" cried the tanned TV reporter. "Mark my words!"

"One people, one fatherland!" shouted the West German millionaire.

"Nationalist!"

Anna Strogar tried to restore the peace. "Everybody please—!"

"Collaborator!"

"Fuck you!"

"Oh God," Jodie heard herself moan. And she hit the floor.

2.

A MINUTE or five minutes or twenty minutes later, she didn't know, Jodie awoke in the parking lot of the Hotel Mohacs.

"Can you hear me?"

She blinked. "What happened?"

"You collapsed."

Douglas sat beside her on a bench. The fresh air was delicious, a warmth touched by cool river breezes. The weather was odd. A wayward sirocco had blown up from the south, as if Africa had burped. Suddenly, where snow had danced, condensation formed. Fog rose off the river. Winter withdrew like a shell-shocked army beyond the horizon.

"No, no," she replied. "I'm fine. I just needed to get away from those people. Let's go for a walk."

Douglas shook his head. "I don't think that's wise."

She insisted. She was sick of the smell of her bed, of convalescence.

He supported her with an arm, and they strolled into the meadow behind the hotel. The Danube misted around them. She could hear the river through the soil and the trees and the rocks, a constant, libidinous presence. Lamps glowed within fists of cotton. Budapest devolved to a shadow.

Douglas stopped near one of the lamps.

"Want to see something?"

A tone of conspiracy had entered his voice.

"Sure. But what about that diplomat?"

Douglas looked back at the hotel, visible through the trees. "I thought maybe he was the guy from the embassy, but he wasn't. Guess I'm just on edge."

They moved along a gravel path, disturbing a pair of men intertwined on a bench. A bringohinto carriage whirred down a lane intersecting their path.

"Which way now?" she asked.

"Straight," he said. "I think."

They encountered busts of famous Hungarians, made their way around the last standing walls of a medieval cloister, saw the forms of goats in a petting zoo.

"Now," Douglas said. "It must be . . . just to the right."

He took her hand and drew her away from the path into the woods. Dead leaves crackled underfoot. A gorse bush ripped her stockings. She heard the squish of shoes in water.

"Hey!" she cried. "The Danube!"

"Nope."

Laughing and angry at the same time, she slipped off the rose-reds. A black dot floated in her mind. Douglas gave her a hand. To her surprise, the water beneath her feet was extremely warm, as if someone's bathtub had spilled over.

Douglas made a quick move. Suddenly, she was a bundle in his arms. He tottered, achieved his balance, and she could not believe her eyes. He had carried her into the midst of a dark, steaming pool, a rough oval, bound on one side by a shelf of rock and on the other by a dense thicket of pine. Steam curled up. Pine needles floated. The rest of the island was muted beyond layers of fog and silence.

"It's a thermal spring," he told her.

To their left, Jodie saw the shelf of rock rising into darkness, an overhanging wall that cupped the evaporation from the water like an enormous hand and drove it back downward, making a natural steam bath.

A shiver of delight ran up her spine.

"Is it deep?"

"About six feet right there in the middle."

He moved farther into the water. Now she felt its wetness against her back.

"Drop me," she said.

"What about your clothes?"

"Hell with 'em."

He let go. She plunged. Water came howling in upon her, and the sensation was tremendous. For an instant, all boundaries vanished. What she perceived, her feelings, her thoughts, her desire, became inseparable from the element around her. She was dispersed into a livid unconsciousness. Scars and bruises effervesced. Her flesh became elastic, her senses exploded.

She began to remove everything—dress, bra, what was left of the stockings, even her underwear. All were gone, and she wondered whether she had actually removed them or whether the water itself had dissolved the fabric, as her skin had dissolved the stitches in her cheek. Everything smacked of dream. Her mouth emerged from the water to take a breath, and she went down again into dark heat.

She touched the bruises on her face, caressed her own breasts, ran fingers down her thighs to her toes. My God, the feel of one's own flesh at one's own fingertips! Who knew how good that could be!

Once again, she broke the surface. Her clothes were floating on the water, and there was Douglas gathering them, along with his own things.

"Are we allowed to go skinny-dipping here?" Jodie asked.

Douglas climbed out of the water onto the shelf of rock, where he dumped their clothes in a neat pile. She studied his bare body for the first time. It looked different, far different, than it had that night on the train. The skin was almost translucent, and it flowed so smoothly down his throat across his rib cage to his loins, where his penis dangled between dripping, mossy thighs. Steam curled around him, and he was, in that instant, the most beautiful man she had ever seen.

Even during the worst hours of her recuperation, when the pain jagged through her and made the blood boil behind her eyes, her desire had been speaking from a great distance. Even when she was semiconscious, staring up from bruise and stitch and scar, she remembered wanting to touch his lips.

Douglas was not the world's most handsome man. He was skinny, unkempt, deficient in dimples. When she first laid eyes on him, way back in West Berlin at the cafe near Bahnhof Zoo, she had pitied his disorientation.

But now, she saw him transformed. He was her nurse, her support, her one true friend in the maelstrom.

Of course, lack of sex played a role in her feelings. She had not been with a man in ages. On the train, when Douglas accidentally brushed her breasts, she had been deeply turned on. No real way to deny it. It was like a sexual fantasy come to life: strangers on a train, border guards, forced nudity, terrified embrace. She had involuntarily wanted to be intimate with him. But since Prague, it had become much more than lust. In her dreams, she had embraced him. Douglas had spoon-fed her pudding, wiped her chin when she couldn't get the tea down, wiped her ass when she was finished shitting, while she glittered in and out of the world.

She could feel exactly the place on her breast where he had touched her that night on the train, and all through her ordeal, the spot had itched and tingled and burned, as steady as if his fingers had never once left it.

Again, she dove under, this time to hide her embarrassment. She touched the bottom of the pool, which seemed to be mud and grass, here and there a tree root. At one point, she thought she'd found the place where the water welled up, a rift in the ground maybe a foot long.

When her lungs were about to burst, she shot up for air. Douglas had descended into the water and waited nearby, grinning. "Well?"

"Well what?"

"Pretty cool, hunh?"

She splashed water in his direction.

"Yup."

He splashed back.

"This is kind of like that dragonfly pool you told me about, isn't it? That place in Berlin where you saw the bugs doing it."

Douglas seemed abashed. "A little. No apple tree."

"And no East German motorboats or nasty women with spades."

He backed into the shallow end of the pool and sank into the waters up to his neck. She followed him, rising out of the water and lifting her arms in a stretch. The water dripped off them. It wasn't cold at all, not in their little corner. She stood over him, staring down. She could sense her body filling his senses.

"Just us dragonflies," she said.

She reached down, clasped him on either side of the rib cage, lowered herself, kissed his forehead.

"Thank you, Douglas."

For a time, she did nothing but touch, her fingers bouncing up and down his body, astonished at the sensation of being naked with him in the open air in the merry month of December. It was as if her near death had been rewarded by an excess of life. She drew him back out into the deeper water, and they went under. Their mouths locked, their tongues mingled.

The bandages on her soul tore away. That's how she felt. Her brain hung out over a ledge. She was reeling, drugged, and a thought came into her head, a repugnant and totally thrilling one. Margaret Island held her in its lips. She was being cradled like a cherry on the tongue of an enormous mouth, swished around, sucked, almost swallowed. The mouth kissed her everywhere, inside and out, millions of kisses in one big, incomprehensible wallow.

She was upside down. The mouth held her gently.

She came to her senses. Douglas was there. She floated on her back, and he was taking her thighs in his hands, opening them, and the sensation of that night on the train, when he had touched her breasts for the first time, came back in a tremendous reverberation. They dragonflied.

3.

MUCH LATER, she awoke in a bed in the Hotel Mohacs, hair wet, body drying. The spot next to her was empty.

"Douglas?"

He stood at the window, which was open. The night had grown cold again. The heat had retreated. But he didn't seem to mind. Wrapped in a quilt, he stared out. Something outside emitted loud music and strobe lights.

"What is that?"

"Come see."

She gathered the top sheet around her body and hurried to the window. Shutters banged in the wind. Douglas gave her a kiss and nodded at the source of the noise. Out on the Danube, a boat was moving, and on its upper decks, music thundered, strobes flashed. Lightning bolts of color hit the river, the island, their hotel room: hot tamale red, banana yellow, lollipop green. The colors reached into the room, beat against its walls, rendered Douglas chameleonic. It was past midnight, and there was no other sign of life in the world.

"Do you know," Douglas said, "I have the oddest feeling that my brother is aboard that boat."

"What?"

"Yes." He pointed. "In the midst of all that."

Jodie put her arm around his waist.

"I don't think he is, honey. Why would he be?"

Douglas shook his head. "I don't know. It doesn't make much sense, does it? And yet it's as if I could walk through these lights like I'd walk through the gate of our backyard in Dallas, and there he would be, right in front of me, if only I could do it."

Jodie didn't understand and thought he might be talking in his sleep.

"The weird thing is, I don't see any people dancing. Do you?"

Jodie peered at the boat, which moved away from them now. The current took it fast, and the lights grew smaller as they passed beyond the tip of the island. What had once covered half of the river now danced in an ever tinier pool around the edges of the vessel. The noise of synthetic drums receded. She did not see anyone dancing.

"Maybe the party's over," she said.

"Must be."

He turned and looked into her eyes. "We can't stay on this island, can we?"

"No."

"We have to go to Bucharest, don't we?"

"We do." She felt a great new resolve in herself. "We must finish our business."

He kissed her mouth. She took a last look at the boat and experienced something like panic, as if aboard it were all the crutches she had ever relied upon in her life.

CHAPTER TWENTY-THREE

UTA HAD BEEN SITTING in an office at the back of an indoor sports facility for the better part of a day and a night. First, the soldiers had transported the passengers of the downed plane to a barracks where everyone received stuffed cabbage rolls and black bread. Afterwards, some people were allowed to phone Bucharest. Arrangements were made for them. Slowly, passengers disappeared. Uta heard unintelligible conversations, the ignition of trucks, the movement of jeeps. Very soon, she was alone.

She tried to find a German speaker. No one spoke adequately, it seemed. She tried in English, implored a series of men as mute as the cabbage rolls to let her go. She must attend a meeting in Bucharest, she told them. She must meet with a colleague named Stuart Glemnik who was staying at the Hotel Intercontinental. He had friends in the government, she said, friends among the elite. One officer tried to communicate his dilemma. He did not mean to be unkind, he explained in a pidgin French-English-German. Under such circumstances, he simply could not let a foreigner go without an official sanction. But he would contact the Interior Ministry and see what he could do. With her help, he wrote down Stuart's first and last name. She also provided Herr Mundung's name, in case someone might recognize it.

Unfortunately, he could not allow her to stay in barracks. They were on high alert and off limits to civilians. The officer mulled over the predicament. So much had happened on his watch that day. A jeep and driver were found. Phone calls were made. Around midnight, by her estimate, Uta was taken from the barracks, down a mountain road, through a small city utterly without electricity. The jeep surprised a wagon in the middle of the road.

The vehicle's lights picked out a coffin riding in its bed, a pink oblong on a pile of hay. The driver of the jeep cursed the hearse, made his way around it. Uta peered into the gloom behind to get one last glimpse of the horse and driver, but the darkness gulleted them. *"Domnula, Domnula . . ."* she heard trailing away.

They came to a vast structure that resembled, at first glance, an airplane hangar. But Uta saw no planes. The building looked neglected. There were no lights, but another jeep waited. Soldiers shook hands, swapped cigarettes for plum brandy, shivered. Uta was led through a door padlocked with a piece of iron as big as a heart. She entered a wide, echoing space. One of the soldiers had a flashlight. Its beam glanced off bleachers, exercise equipment, straps drooping from metal bars. Uta was shown down a corridor behind the bleachers. How many years had passed since the building was constructed, since it was lit at night, heated during the winter? When had the last competition been held? Yesterday or a decade ago?

The soldier with the flashlight unlocked an office and gestured at a chair crammed back into a wall of papers, wooden tennis rackets, and dead plants. He gave her the flashlight and closed the door behind him. Miraculously, she slept. When she awoke, her wrists ached, and morning light shot through the stacks of paper.

A stranger extended his hand to Uta in a shake. He called himself Olestru and spoke in an English as smooth and comforting as red wine. She took the hand, which felt powdered. He told her the borders of Romania were closed. The government had closed them that very morning for security reasons.

"Why?"

Olestru poured out the warmest of smiles, laughed long and lugubriously. "We live in such shallow times. The international media is calling an act of terrorism an uprising."

"How did you find out about me?"

Olestru had received the information transmitted by the nice officer. He knew Stuart Glemnik.

"But what will you do now?" he asked.

A woman who could have been a nurse brought a bowl of mamaliga, more stuffed cabbage and smoked pork bits, and a bottle of mineral water, and left the two of them alone.

"I must get to Bucharest," she replied to Olestru's question. He was a slight man with graying hair, cropped short at the tops of his ears, but mussed here and there, longer in some places than others. The overall effect suggested grass cut in haste. He wore glasses and smiled with bad teeth, but his manner was cosmopolitan. He could have been sixty or eighty or even older; sometimes youth seeped into his smile, other times age. A constant wink lay at the corners of his eyes, ready to spring at any moment, and she received an impression of bizarre solidarity from him, as if the two of them alone were in on a joke too subtle and filthy for the rest of humanity.

"I am returning to Bucharest this very day. And, if I may presume on this remarkable catastrophe that you have survived, if I may presume to offer a few words of advice, it will be healing, I think, for you to drive through the countryside of our beloved Transylvania, which is so very beautiful, even in winter."

"Thank you, Mr. Olestru."

"Call me Tony."

"Thank you." She placed the bowl of mamaliga to the side and tried to be informal, as he wished. "Tony."

"May I ask if you have made formal plans to meet with Mr. Glemnik?"

He knocked a cigarette from his pack and inserted it between graying teeth. He was as desiccated as a shoestring.

"Not exactly. We set an approximate time, but our schedule was changed after everything happened in Berlin . . ."

He gave an awful grin. "Ah yes. And what is the nature of your business, if I may ask?"

"*Germanistik.* We are both students of the German language." She had to think fast. "And wanted to explore some of the dialects of the German population in Transylvania."

"But," Olestru objected, without removing the cigarette from his mouth, "Bucharest is hundreds of kilometers south of Transylvania."

"That's true, but to get there from Berlin, you have to fly first to Bucharest."

Wind banked against the wall of paper. Sheaves of it burst like wings. Cracks in the mortar whistled.

"You are right, of course."

She would answer all his questions, but first, he must get her out of that haunted building. "I'm freezing, Tony."

Olestru jumped up, a winking pain on his face. "Why, of course, my dear! How rude of me. We shall leave for Bucharest this very minute! *Auf geht's!* Is that correct?"

"*Sprechen Sie denn deutsch?*"

Olestru made an absurd bow, then plucked the cigarette from his mouth. "To tell you the absolute truth, I was born in the Saxon city of Schässburg, where I had many Saxon friends. I do speak a little of that dialect which interests you, but please"—his submerged wink came to the surface—"do not quiz me, Fräulein!"

They left the sports facility. The jeeps and the soldiers had gone. The only car remaining was an old blue Dacia belonging to Olestru. He opened the door on the passenger side with an Old World flourish, as if Uta were stepping into a gilded troika. The sun blazed cold between two jagged peaks, and Uta thought she'd better clarify some things.

"Tony," she ventured as he started the car.

"Yes?"

"Are you with the army?"

Olestru bent over his steering wheel and chuckled. The laughter made him thump his chest.

"Oh dear, oh dear, I'm afraid not. My military service was completed years ago, and these"—he displayed the cigarette—"have made me an unsuitable candidate for high rank."

His laughter turned into a cancerous cough.

"I am with the Information Ministry," he said, "and I would like for you to think of me as a good friend."

"How do you know Stuart?"

Olestru gave her a wink. The Dacia bumped down a stretch of road through dark pines. Uta had been warned many times in her life about the men and women who worked for the information ministries of the Eastern Bloc countries. They were KGB, her father had said, Renate had said, Stuart had said. Olestru was probably an agent of some kind, but he was the only friend she had. After a while, he asked his own question.

"Do you know, by some chance, a fellow named Nester Cates?"

Uta stared at him. How could he possibly know Nester, unless, of course, Stuart had talked about him? She couldn't know for sure what Olestru knew, but she figured the truth would be the safest policy. After all, Stuart had defected to the Communists, and this man was a bureaucrat in the machinery of a Communist state. He must think she was on his side.

"I know him. He's a friend of Stuart's."

And she added without thinking, "He's the one who told me Stuart was here."

What could it hurt, telling Olestru that? But she was sorry she'd done it just the same.

Olestru braked the car, pulled the cigarette from his mouth, and allowed himself a long, insinuating, businesslike grin. Another wink came to the surface.

"He's coming, isn't he?"

Uta heard a soughing of wind through trees. Olestru waited for an answer.

CHAPTER TWENTY-FOUR

WITH A PAIR of World War II binoculars bought in the Budapest flea market, Nester staked out the Hotel Mohacs. Each day, as he secured a place in the thickets on the far edges of the meadow surrounding the hotel, Nester thought to himself, today is the day Stuart appears. And each evening, his head sank disappointed—but also relieved—into the pine needles. Douglas had not lied to him.

His surveillance held risks. Once, the local police caught him and demanded an explanation. In the old days, he would have been hauled to the state security apparatus and locked away for questioning, if not a beating. Now he was treated merely as an inexplicable character. He pantomimed being an Angolan naturalist on the trail of a rare form of migratory vireo. He showed them his fake Angolan passport. A substantial bribe finished the matter.

Another time, he was accosted by a couple of correspondents who swore they'd met him while covering the Angolan war. One of them, a Brit with a pipe and a bad habit of calling Zimbabwe Rhodesia, said he did not buy all this "rubbish about bird-watching."

Finally, of course, he was almost seen by Douglas, who once purposefully turned and squinted in his direction.

Nester studied Douglas as if he were a beetle. It was not the most thrilling of stakeouts, but the weather was decent. For days now, a temperate climate had prevailed, a damp warmth cut by breezes. The last of the crisped deciduous leaves kited down onto him. Dead pine needles made a natural bed, and when he got tired during the day, he put down the binoculars and fell asleep. At night, he climbed into a military-issue sleeping bag, ate chocolate bars and oranges brought from Vienna, and recited lines from Brecht's *Galileo Galilei* to amuse himself.

He studied Douglas eating French toast for breakfast, getting toasted on whiskey for dinner, reading a book about Romanian history, chatting with that *New York Times* reporter, fumigating the kitchen. He picked the lock on Jodie Blum's door, searched the room while she was taking a bath, found nothing, not one damn thing that would tell him how much she knew. Occasionally, he squatted on the stone bank beside the Danube and cast his binoculars up. Now and then, Douglas's paramour came to the window and stared down into the water, but as far as Nester could tell, she rarely left the room.

Clearly, Douglas was waiting for his woman to mend. And he waited for Nester's call too, as Nester had told him to do. That made Nester feel guilty, but what else could he do? The Green Men had been put back to work, trying to find Stuart, but had come up cold.

Waltraud tried the Intercontinental in the Romanian capital, where Stuart might be expected to stay; nothing. She tried other hotels in Bucharest, other hotels in other cities. She kept in hourly touch with his man on the ground in Bucharest, a UFO cultist named Ion Voicu. But Stuart Glemnik was nowhere to be found. Nester didn't want anything to happen until he could be reliably located. If he was dead, there was no need for anyone to go to Bucharest. If he was alive, then perhaps he could be contacted and drawn out of Romania. The more Nester thought about going to that country, the more he feared it.

There were other concerns. A chubby man wearing a silver cross was staking out Douglas. One morning, his body covered in dew, Nester caught the interloper blatantly staring at the exterminator across several plates of scrambled eggs, and from that moment on, his pursuit became a regular fixture. Could he be one of Mundung's emissaries? A member of the Verein Albacete? Or did he belong to Styles?

Then Douglas went to the American embassy, and for an instant, Nester believed he had been betrayed. But a few minutes later, the man burst out of the doors and almost ran smack into him. Whatever he had wanted, he had given up quickly. Nester saw that time was running out. With or without Stuart, he was going to have to act. Given more time, Douglas Gleaming would probably crack, and Nester couldn't afford that. Still he hesitated to show himself.

And then there was his terror. Every day, it became more difficult to suppress. In the woods at his back, each creak of timber contained a spook—a Mundung, an Olestru, a Styles. Nester had been cast out upon the waters, cast out and compromised to his very core, so that he no longer knew himself what he believed in, to whom he could turn. The army had been the frame of his existence for thirty-five years, and now the army had washed its hands. God too had abandoned him. Nester had believed in God up until November 9, 1989, when the first knocks of the Devil hit his door. Now he believed only in Satan on earth, walking with cloven hoof across the mountains, valleys, and graveyards of Eastern Europe. God was dead. Nietzsche and Glemnik and all the rest of those doomy white men were right.

One day, a week into his surveillance, he laid his binoculars in the grass, and for the first time in a very long time, out of the blue, he was overcome by the urge to laugh. His depression had hit rock bottom, but he snorted with laughter. A memory provoked it. Back in the old days, a few short months ago, Glemnik and he had played a stupid Cold War game. Where would you go and what would you do if the Iron Curtain fell tomorrow? At first, the answers were sober-minded and serious. Go see *Don Giovanni* at the Czech National Theater in Prague. Check out the Bruno Schulz house in Drogobych. Cross the Turkish bridge at Mostar. But as time wore on, the list got progressively less edifying. They would drop bon mots as they passed each other in the halls of field station. Dress as Uncle Sam and take a fruit basket to the admiral of the Soviet fleet in Kaliningrad. Run naked through the Hermitage in Leningrad while holding a Fabergé egg over your nuts. Moon Lenin in his tomb. Make noisy love to Miss Teenage Texas on the front lawn of the Romanian Palace of the People. Take a dump in a paper bag, set it on the doorstep of the premier of Albania, set the bag on fire, ring the doorbell, run.

His laughter died. Stuart knew everything about him. Nester lowered his forehead to the pine needles. He would never trust another human soul.

CHAPTER TWENTY-FIVE

Douglas was perusing a map of Romania. Jodie flossed her teeth. The BBC interrupted a broadcast of the Bartok opera *Duke Bluebeard's Castle* to announce a massacre in the Romanian city of Timisoara. Jodie rushed from the bathroom, fingers attached to her mouth by a triangle of pale string.

For days now, the tension had been building in Timisoara, a city of some size on the Bega River in the southwestern part of Romania. Douglas found it on the map. Tens of thousands were believed dead, slaughtered by government troops.

He remembered what Stuart had said about Romania in his letter. It would be safe, he'd written, stable.

"Pack your things," Jodie said. "We're heading out tonight."

It was no use arguing. Jodie dialed Chubbs. Douglas crammed the few clothes he'd bought in Budapest into a plastic sack. Jodie cupped her hand over the phone.

"Get the car. I'll settle the bill and meet you out front."

Douglas loped downstairs, neck and neck with a photographer who had been listening to the radio on headphones. Both men hit the lobby at a dead sprint. The valet tipped the bill of his hat and waved Douglas's car ticket at a pomaded man in black slacks.

Yesterday, at a flea market in southern Budapest, Jodie and he had bought a used VW Bug from a man who trafficked in antique hunting rifles, Herend china, and toy SS soldiers. Prior to the purchase, she'd called Chubbs, who had recovered from being sore about her long absence after she filed him an interview with the famous author Sandor Kis, and explained the deal to him. No rental car agency would lease an automobile to anyone bound for Romania, and besides, most of the rental cars had already gone to journalists traveling around other parts of Eastern Europe. The editor wanted a story out of Romania pronto, so he okayed a sum of four thousand marks for a vehicle and told her to charge it, if she could.

She did. The Bug, an aquamarine model made in Mexico circa 1986, tooted into view. The driver hopped out. Douglas opened the trunk, which happened to be under the hood, and laid his things in a corner. Just as he was slamming it shut, he sniffed an unmistakably expensive perfume.

"I'm coming with you," said Pansy Buckner.

Douglas kept the hood open. She peered at him in the darkness.

"Caravan, you mean."

"No, Douglas, I mean in the car."

"Really?"

She nodded. Douglas didn't know what Jodie would say, but he considered it a bad idea. What if Pansy somehow stumbled across the truth about him? Maybe she already had.

"But won't you be going with Mr. Stamps or Ms. Strogar? This is such an uncomfortable little car."

Pansy moved a step closer. "I have no means of transportation. Okay? Ham is in Bonn, trying to get an interview with Helmut Kohl, but he called me thirty minutes ago and told me to get to Bucharest as quickly as possible and begin setting up the bureau. The only problem is, I can't, because Anna the superbitch already took off with the *New York Times* car that I purchased. She didn't even call to tell me. She just left me behind."

"I'm sorry," Douglas murmured.

"If I go by plane or train," Pansy went on, "it will take me a day or two longer to get there, and that would be a total disaster. I have to be there before Ham. You better help me, or so help me God—I have done some nice things for you two—"

Douglas gestured at the car. "It's small—"

"Fine."

Pansy removed wrapped sandwiches from a Gucci traveler, then gave the travler to Douglas, who packed it. Jodie came out the door. Pansy waved.

"I thought you'd be in Romania by now."

Pansy retold her story and added that, according to Fibys reports, the border could shut the next morning. It was settled. Pansy climbed into the back seat of the car. Douglas took the wheel. Jodie strapped herself in.

Douglas didn't have much experience with a stick, but gave it a game tug. The Bug fought at first. Its shift operated by idiosyncratic rules. But he coaxed and cursed, and soon the Volkswagen climbed up onto the ramp of the southern bridge, up above the plane trees and oaks, above the friendly, buttery lights of the Mohacs, and with a last spate of exhaust, hardly worthy of the moment, as Douglas gazed back with yearning, its wheels carried them away from sanctuary.

2.

A T SIX A.M., dawn just glimmering, the Bug made the eastern lip of Hungary. A unit of troops had arrived on the Romanian side of the border. In the dark, the movement of men could be clearly discerned.

They had driven through the night, six hours across the Pannonian plain—the *puszta,* as Esperanza self-importantly pronounced; one stop for gas and three for micturition. Douglas put the car into neutral, turned off the engine. Beside him, Jodie hadn't spoken in hours, though she hadn't slept.

Suddenly, she asked Douglas to pop the hood.

"I'll be right back," she said.

"What's she doing?" Esperanza applied lipstick.

Douglas swallowed the last chunk of fruit. At the flea market, in addition to the car, Jodie had purchased ten cartons of Kent cigarettes. They were unofficial currency in Romania, unlike the Marlboros still in Jodie's bag. She returned with two cartons to use as bribe material.

"Kents!" Esperanza exclaimed. "God, I meant to get those too."

Jodie smiled and tossed her a carton. In the early-morning hours, by the dim light from the dashboard, Douglas had caught Jodie stealing glances into the back seat at the body flopped over on its petite airline pillow. She seemed to be pondering the woman, and Douglas wondered if she suspected anything about Pansy's intervention on her behalf. If she did, she didn't say so. She popped the plastic sheen around the carton and plucked out two packs.

Douglas tried to get news on the radio. He switched dials between the BBC and Radio Free Europe. Both programs broadcast in Hungarian at that hour and were incomprehensible. The darkness dwindled. In the half-light, soldiers fanned out on either side of the checkpoint and positioned themselves betweem buildings and on rooftops.

Esperanza rustled in the back seat. "Can you roll down the window please?"

Douglas did so. He put the car back into gear and rolled forward. Soon, the Bug reached the checkpoint. A customs agent in ashen blue stepped to their window and gazed down. Esperanza and Douglas handed over their passports. Jodie checked all her pockets while the customs agent implacably watched. She pounded open the glove compartment, said "shit, shit, shit" so the customs agent could see her panic, dug out the innards of her pockets. Now she was rifling through papers, banana peels, and cigarette packs on the car floor. The customs agent was tapping the other documents against a palm. Douglas could see him glance over the car at someone else, at a soldier. Twice, three times, Jodie sifted through the mess at her feet. She asked Douglas to pop the hood again. He did it. Alarmed, the customs agent gestured at the soldier.

Then Douglas remembered. Her passport was at her belly, cradled in her travel pouch.

The confusion was cleared up. The customs agent took the documents into his rabbit hutch. After all the borders he had crossed in the last month, Douglas should have been indifferent to this latest. After all, crossing the Czechoslovak frontier into Austria had been simple enough, and Austria into Hungary a breeze. But he couldn't help himself. No other border mattered like this one. His escape at the East German bridge would mean nothing if the Romanians refused to let him in now.

The customs agent returned. He pointed Douglas to a parking spot. The passports had not pleased him. He did not indicate why. Maybe it was a visa problem. Jodie had obtained hers at lightning speed from the Romanian embassy, thanks to the efforts of Anton Olestru of the Information Ministry in Bucharest. Douglas had given her the name, saying that he was a friend of Stuart's, and when she called the Romanian press office in Bucharest, she was overjoyed to find he was an employee there and wanted to show Jodie how peaceful things were in Romania.

They found themselves in an office smelling of lye, cigarettes, and cornmeal mush.

"What now?" Jodie whispered to Douglas. She was too pale. He feared another slip into unconsciousness.

"Maybe nothing."

Soldiers smoked cigarettes and scrutinized them, particularly Pansy. One of them wanted to know if the pearls at her ears were real. He reached for a lobe to indicate his question. Pansy slapped his hand away.

In the next room, which shared a common wall, Douglas saw two men inspecting the documents. If he wasn't mistaken, they seemed to take special interest in his. One of them sat in a chair behind a desk and wore the ashen blue uniform of the customs agent, who had returned to his post, while the other paced around the room in a violet and lavender jogging suit. The latter was agitated, interrupting the otherwise silent inspection of the documents with remarks in Romanian. He would be Securitate, if Douglas was not mistaken.

Above the two men, large and festive, hung a portrait of Nicolae Ceausescu.

The man in the jogging suit gestured to them. When a seat had been found for each and coffee was served, he cleared his throat and spoke English.

"You are here because of Timisoara, yes?"

Jodie took charge. "Partly."

"And you?" He was addressing Douglas.

"Business."

"Of what nature?"

"I'm to lecture in Bucharest on the subject of pesticides."

"Why sneak into my country over this border? Surely it is easier to fly."

Douglas cleared his throat. "Sir, you are aware of the changes in my country now. Everything is a mess. *Alles Chaos.* Do you understand?"

"Chaos?" The man gave him a wary, frigid smile. "Yes, I understand chaos."

"Because of this chaos, I was unable to fly. I took the train to Budapest, a most unpleasant journey, and this young woman, who was staying at the hotel, was kind enough to offer me a ride—"

He nodded at Jodie. The jogger put out his cigarette. "I see. But she is a journalist. Do high-ranking members of the East German scientific community travel with the press, even in such times as these? Though I suppose if you are more than friends, that would account for it . . ."

Jodie's face remained hard. Douglas blushed. The jogger acted neither amused nor disappointed. But he did seem satisfied. He turned then to Jodie.

"Why are you so nervous?"

She crossed arms over her chest. "I'm not nervous. I'm ill."

"Are you a Jew?"

Jodie swallowed.

"Jews write lies about us, even though we protect them since the war. Maybe you are all Jews."

Jodie swallowed but didn't answer.

"I was in Timisoara," he continued. "No dead. No wounded. There was a scuffle with hooligans and chauvinists. But you will not be able to see, because the city is closed. Do you understand? No people get in. No people get out. It's a precaution so no more violence occurs—"

Jodie interrupted. "We don't care about Timisoara. We're going to Bucharest."

The man shook a forefinger in disbelief.

Jodie insisted. "My good friend Anton Olestru told me it was all lies in Timisoara. That's why he wanted me to come to Bucharest. So he could show me the truth about Romania."

"Olestru?"

Jodie leaned forward in her chair with a look of threat in her eyes. "Of the Information Ministry."

The man seemed startled and a little upset. "I shall call him."

"Please do." Jodie fished a piece of paper from her wallet and handed it to him. He sliced his palm at them, gesturing to wait, and stood up. "Write your name for me, please, on this paper."

Jodie did so.

"More coffee?"

He ordered three more cups, then left the room. The customs official watched them. Coffee arrived. Pansy tapped on the floor with her left foot, removed the pearl earrings from her lobes. Her green irises glittered. The jogger returned, handed the piece of paper containing the phone number back to Jodie.

"I reached Mr. Olestru at the ministry. He says to let you through. But—" The man's eyes burned, and at that moment, Douglas could see right into him, into a hatred as deep and swift as the Danube, never to be extinguished until the world sank in fire. "Do not write any more of your Jewish lies about us. If you do, neither Mr. Olestru nor anyone else will be able to save you."

CHAPTER TWENTY-SIX

Nester was right behind them. But he came too late to the Romanian border, which had closed.

It took five hours to get back to Budapest, where Green Men introduced him to members of the Transylvanian underground railroad, Hungarian patriots who smuggled books, guns, and people in and out of those portions of Romania inhabited by their brethren, whom they considered as lost as the Hebrews under Pharaoh. The dictator Ceausescu, a rapacious but inconsistent nationalist, had made criminals of Hungarians in Romania. Their Magyar language, their Catholic faith, and their ancient folk traditions had become a provocation against the regime, an obstacle to some surreal version of modernity, in which the People's Leader slipped on Mickey Mouse ears and vampire fangs while razing five-hundred-year-old Hungarian villages.

An unnamed quartet of young men, blond as Germans, drove Nester to the Romanian border just south of Oradea, where Douglas had crossed. They were met by a darker man, half Hungarian, half Gypsy, with a thick bolt of mustache and a wavy crest of hair. Nester was bundled into the trunk of this man's car—a Dacia, the Romanian national vehicle—and carried with bumps and bashes, by way of dirt roads, riverbeds, and fields, over the border into a poor Romanian farming village. Another Dacia was found. Nester was fed, clothed, and well bedded, and at dawn on the nineteenth, a sack of cold Debrecen sausages beside him on the passenger seat, he entered the legendary province of Transylvania on a lukewarm trail.

His first stop was Cluj, the region's capital, where he had a close call. A thug followed him to his hotel room, and in a drunken stupor, waving a switchblade, demanded Nester's money and documents. Nester did not know what else to do. He struck the man, who fell against the sink and hit his head. Nester got out of there, driving through the night to reach Sighisoara, a city within a day's drive of Bucharest—or Bucuresti, as the little red batons on the side of the road spelled it.

In Sighisoara, Nester decided to buy a gun. He didn't know exactly why. He had not been in possession of a weapon since his earliest days in the military and didn't know what good it would do him now. His enemies outnumbered him by thousands to one. If they wanted him dead, he would be.

At sundown, the city's generators shut down. Sighisoara had an odd, grubby, airless quality, as if it had existed in the bottom of a trash can for hundreds of years, undisturbed even by rats. Brüderlein came from here, and Nester tried to take comfort from that. He found a restaurant in the Gothic hall where, supposedly, Dracula had been born in the sixteenth century and, by candlelight, ate a meal of unidentifiable meat fried in inscrutable batter. Afterwards, buttoned up against the dark cold, he snooped around for someone—anyone—who might sell a downtrodden black American a sidearm. It was an impossible task. Most of the shifty characters in the streets looked like Securitate. Everybody honest had turned in. At last, when he'd almost run out of options, he found a haberdasher, a cavern-eyed man in a worker's blue smock who hawked boyar caps, French berets, and Turkish fezzes in the deep shadows beneath the clock tower. It was past nine o'clock. The shop was officially closed, but flame light spilled out. The haberdasher let him in and uncorked a demijohn of tzuica.

Nester saw a votive candle, a sleeping cat, a wall of caps, an icon of Saint Clement. The shop appeared authentic enough. He took a swig of the tzuica, which he didn't like. Then he pantomimed—bang! bang!—a finger pulling a trigger and put a hand over his eyes, like a salute, to show he was searching. The haberdasher meditated. Then he shrugged and lifted a machine gun from beneath the counter. He gave the gun a lush caress and pushed it toward Nester.

It was a rarity, a Romanian Orita, the only contribution made by the local weapons industry to the Cold War. The Orita resembled a plesiosaur, with a long neck, a small head, a few odd fins, and a snub tail. It was as deserving of human pity as a gun could be, and, under the influence of the alcohol, Nester chuckled with it, not at it.

He took the weapon in his arms. What a joke it was! By the mid-1970s, the Orita had been mothballed, except for a few factory guards and reservists, the last line of defense in case of an invasion. The haberdasher must be an old reservist, one of those aging patriots who long for the moment when they can once again do a good deed for the state. Nester indicated his admiration of the weapon but returned it with a rueful shrug. It was more than he needed. The Orita disappeared back beneath the counter. Undaunted, the haberdasher hoisted up a wooden box. He pulled out excelsior. Beneath it lay an arsenal.

The haberdasher raised a finger, checked out the windows of the shop, and made clear to Nester that he had always liked Americans, knew them to be very rich and fond of guns. He shambled back into the shadows beyond the candle and resurfaced with several boxes of cartridges. Meanwhile, Nester surveyed the merchandise. The old man stocked damn near every sidearm made in central Europe since 1938. There were shards of a Walther P38, the Nazi's pride and joy and the gun of a thousand cheap propaganda films; a single Polish Radom; Makarovs and Tokarevs of different issues, detritus left in the wake of strategies that no longer mattered, insignificant as dead spiders in a web; and finally, happily, high-quality stuff from Brno, Czechoslovakia, handgun capital of Europe. Most of the Bulgarian stuff was in pieces, and besides, Nester was reminded, neither the Makarov nor the Tokarev had parabellum chambers, so they'd be no match for whatever the Romanian Securitate packed these days. In the end, for fifty marks, he chose the moldering C75, and the haberdasher showed him how to work it. For a further ten marks, he bought a box of cartridges.

Thanking the man, already nervous, he hurried out, but not before a crawfish pair of fingers pinched a node of his black skin. In pidgin French, the haberdasher explained to Nester that he'd never seen *"un homme noir"* before.

2.

A GUN GAVE NOTICE; he would not go down without a fight, or that's what he told himself as a fist rapped three times against the door of his hotel room, a stinking, frozen cell with a bed made of lint and nails. He raised the pistol from the pillow beneath his head.

The knock came again. He checked his watch. It was three in the morning. He loosened the safety, as the haberdasher had shown him, and aimed the barrel at the vague outline of the door.

"Qui est la?" His French was rusty, but it would get him farther than English in this Francophilic backwater.

No one answered. Nester regarded the pistol for a moment. It was too big for his hand. The magazine showed signs of rust. No professional would have tolerated it.

On the other side of the door, he heard whispering. Whoever they were, they were about to break down the door, break it down and murder him in cold blood in the middle of the night. Though the room was cold, he perspired. Nothing happened.

"*Parlez-vous français?!*" he called.

Silence garroted his words. Nester's arm grew sore from holding up the gun. The haberdasher had informed on him. The creep was Securitate. Everyone was.

"Stand back." Nester reverted to John Wayne English. "Because if I hear you again, I'm going to shoot."

He heard feet shuffling away, couldn't be sure. Might have been a noise from the street. Thank God for the pistol, though. His right hand shook. If a boot had kicked down the door, he would have sprayed half the room with bullets.

An indeterminate time later, he woke again. There was the knock, this time even more insistent. Nester left the safety on the gun. For all he knew, the caller wanted to have sex with him for hard currency, and all he needed was a dead prostitute on his hands.

"Show yourself! *Répondez-vous!*"

The knocking ceased. The doorknob rattled, telling him something he already knew. Whoever it was could not open the door. He had locked it. There was a moment of relief. He could presume a few things at this point. If the knocker had been a detail of Securitate, he would either be dead or in custody by now. Those guys didn't have to knock.

He could also presume, with some certainty, that whoever knocked could as easily be an enemy as a friend. Maybe it was somebody from the Verein Albacete, armed with a silencer. But, he reminded himself, getting out of bed, a silencer could catch him in a dozen more convenient ways—on a street at night, in a restaurant, in a hotel lobby—without having to resort to a midnight call, announced by a loud, angry knock.

Nester stepped into his pants, gun trained on the door. He buttoned up his shirt with great effort. The knocks did not resume, but the human presence remained, a suggestion of breath and heartbeat just beyond the fragile wood. Nester pulled the curtains over the windows, released the safety catch on the pistol, and steeled himself to shoot. Staying out of the path of the door, he reached through the darkness, found the bolt, and jacked it back. He slunk into the far corner of the room, to a place between the sink and the flimsy plyboard walls cloaking the dung-choked toilet.

"It's open."

A few seconds went by. Nester's heartbeat pounded in his temples. A drip of sweat fell from his nose to his lower lip. The door creaked open. No light entered from the hall, but he could make out a human form slipping into the small square space, hands gently shutting the door behind.

"Now step forward."

The stranger obeyed. Evidently, he understood English.

"The string attached to the light switch is in the middle of the room. Walk forward, and it'll smack you in the face. When it does, pull on it. Keep your other hand in the air."

A step sounded, featherweight. The person was relatively slight anyway and appeared to be alone. One or two steps more, and he should turn on the light. Nester made out fingers reaching for the string, grasping here and there until they wrapped around it.

"Pull."

There came a click. The darkness remained. Nester almost fired. He had been dumb, dumb, dumb to let this happen.

"You're trying my patience—"

A familiar voice cursed. "No lights anywhere in this shithole! Not at night! And you know it, Cates."

For the sake of illumination, Nester drew the curtain back from the window.

"Give me one good reason why I shouldn't kill you."

"Because," Styles said, a burst of moonlight from behind a cloud revealing a mouth as craggy as a Carpathian peak, "I'm here to save you."

3

STYLES REFUSED TO TALK until they were out of the room, which, he said, was bugged and monitored, like all hotel rooms in Romania. Downstairs, the receptionist had ducked into her office to make a phone call. Styles and Nester snuck past the front desk with loud, echoing creaks. At that hour, close to four, there was only one inconspicuous place to go in Sighisoara, and they made for it. The city, an ancient abode of the Germans once known as Castrum Sax, rose like a missile on the cradle lands of Transylvania; it was a hill surrounded by eight crumbling defensive towers. Through the rutted streets, they climbed, up toward the Saxon church that crowned what had once been a fortress at the summit and toward their destination, the graveyard flung down Sighisoara's southern slope like a cape.

They reached the church, which was locked and under construction, and found the gate to the graveyard. No one was around, so Nester smashed the lock on the gate with the butt of his weapon. It didn't respond.

Styles pulled a locksmith's master key from a pocket and inserted it. The lock opened, and they trod upon the first stones of a sprawling hill of the dead, an endless downward sweep of tombstones that constituted an entire community, a tiny history of central Europe scrawled in the words *"Ruhe sanft"*—"Sleep softly"—the same phrase, Nester reflected, inscribed on thousands of Jewish tombstones in the same part of the world.

There were no benches in the cemetery, so they wandered down a stone path. Cold stars, just visible in the cracks between cloud banks, lit the countryside stretching away beneath the brow of the hill, south toward Bran Castle, the Brasov pass, and eventually Bucharest. Plane trees reared overhead, branches rustling in advance of a cold front. Styles leaned his back against a tree. Nester pointed the gun at his mouth.

"Put that thing away. You don't need it."

Nester ignored him.

"There's going to be trouble in this country," Styles informed him, as if this news were a revelation.

Nester lowered the pistol an inch.

"Military is at odds with the First Directorate. Civil war. You were right about that. Just got the country wrong."

He rustled in his pocket, and Nester raised the gun again. Styles rattled a pill case in his coat pocket. "My dose."

"How did you find me?"

"Easy. The same people who carried you over the border helped me too. Your contacts aren't very discreet, Cates. Might want to reorganize."

A plane tree creaked. Both men glanced nervously. Moonlight vanished, dimmed by a wing of cumulus. A brittle rain began to fall. Nuggets of ice pattered and tapped against the gravestones.

"What do you want?"

"Actually, that's what I'm supposed to ask you." Styles chewed on a pill and winced. Bits of white fell from his mouth. "I'm here to make a job offer, retroactive to November first."

Styles brushed the pill crumbs off his coat and buttoned up. "I am authorized by Langley to offer you gainful employment. We are going into Panama, and all hands are needed on deck. That's one thing. Secondly, the agency is now seeking out new areas for study, including extraterrestrial visitation, or what passes for it, and that makes you the man of the hour."

Nester fingered the catch on his gun, careful not to set his index on the trigger and accidentally add to the dead. "This is a bribe."

"Not really," Styles went on, eyeing Nester's gun with a smug condescension. "A week ago, an emergency session of the UFO Working Group convened. Security leaks were the topic. If the press got wind of a governmental intelligence team dedicated to resolving once and for all the question of extraterrestrial life, the group would be finished. You understand. During the course of the meeting, your name came up as a possible source of leakage. You are loose now, cut off from the army, with no reason to keep quiet about what you know. In your tenure with the group, you have amassed a wide intelligence, let's face it."

It was true enough. Nester had funneled the most sensitive of military documents, been debriefed on stealth technology in its embryonic stages, participated in tests at Groom Lake, where few other intelligence operatives had ever been allowed, and seen God knows what other classified material cross his desk.

"So word went through certain channels to Langley," Styles went on, "and through Langley, I was authorized to 'find' you and make an offer. Naturally, they don't know all about our little venture here, but they are aware that you've been taken out of military ops and put under a rather secret special section, run by me. So here we are, and if you want my advice, this new job is the simplest solution to your problems. You will head a task force within the Company to address the issue of UFOs and international stability, blah-blah-blah. Just yesterday, approval came through. Meanwhile, the Company can use you in an advisory capacity on Panama."

Snowflakes fluttered down.

"What else?"

Styles came to the point.

"Abort the trip to Bucharest."

Nester's wrists began to pulse.

"You're going to sweep them all away, aren't you?"

"What do you care? Glemnik fucked you over. What do you care if he and his whole cabal get it in the neck?"

Styles was impatient. He checked his watch. He peered upward at the impending silver. He had anticipated gratitude. Nester expressed none. The owl sighed.

"Listen," he said. "Not that it concerns you, but I may not need to sweep anyone away."

"Meaning?"

"Meaning that the Romanian government, without any prompting from me, has arrested Stuart Glemnik for espionage. He's in jail and unlikely ever to get out again—"

"And his brother?"

Styles crossed his arms.

"Tell me."

Nester marveled at himself. Why *should* he care? But he did. The sense of responsibility returned with maniacal force.

"Far as I know, the man you call Douglas Gleaming—the man I believe to be Jiri Klek—is bound for Bucharest. When he gets there, he'll be arrested too, and since he's believed to be responsible for the downing of a Tupolev plane a few years ago, they'll put him against a wall."

"You are . . ." Nester formulated the words with a great effort, because he knew that if he spoke them, he would not be able to say later that he hadn't known, hadn't understood. "You are truly here to save my life."

"Yes, Cates. If you go, you will be killed. That's a guarantee. Our old deal is off, because you now have a new and better one. Forget everything, take the job, and the hard drive will be yours, as security. No one will ever connect you to Coogan's death. I'll make sure of that. But if you go, you are saying to me and the Company and everyone else that you are against us. And that's treason. Klek is no longer your concern."

Styles had won then. By a grim coincidence, the Romanian government would execute the death sentences on Douglas and Stuart for him. Operation Second Home would fade like an unheard whisper. Only Nester and Tunt would ever know the truth, and they would both belong to Styles.

"I'm going to be sick," Nester said. He knelt and heaved. Nothing came up. It was something else, not just responsibility to Douglas. He had been betrayed by his own country, then pulled back at the last minute, and now they expected him to love them unconditionally for the rest of his natural days because they had plucked him from their own cauldron. He was disgusted with himself, with desperately wanting that job at the CIA, with wanting to be safe from the howling wind, with wanting to have Styles as an ally rather than an enemy.

As he knelt, he sensed the dead, and they, he was sure, sensed him. Their surnames were everywhere, like signals snatched out of the night, encoded phrases containing his destiny, and he clung to one of them, as if to a rope.

Franz Teutschlander
Born August 13, 1815. Died November 9, 1902.
Imperial and Royal military doctor
in the army of Radetzky.
RUHE SANFT

From 1902 through 1989, he had been right here, underground, sleeping, and softly, through the archduke's visit to Sarajevo, the Great War, the Great Depression, World War II, the Holocaust, the A-bomb, the Cold War, Coltrane, Malcolm, through Communism and its end, through *this*—he had been right here. What power, to be so immovable. Nester hung on.

Sleep softly.

"You've got an hour," Styles said. "And since you can't possibly trust me, I've brought someone along who may talk a little sense into you. You two can talk, then I'll be back. One hour. You hear me?"

Styles's feet crunched away on gravel. The gate rattled behind him. Snow sushed in the naps between graves. He was alone among the trees, alive among the dead. The Germans could not help him.

Nester knew nothing. He knew neither why he was here nor how he had come nor what he would do. Footsteps approached, lighter than those of Styles. At first, he thought he was imagining them. He looked up.

"*Du.*"

Waltraud smiled and winked.

"*Na?*"

The sight of her filled him with a silent reverence, even if he understood now that she was an owl. For the moment, the cold air had stopped blowing, and a still winter brilliance shone upon her. He could not speak. Waltraud reached out for him, and though he wanted more than anything to fall into her arms, to be relieved, at last, of himself, he raised the gun and said, "Your weapon."

4.

WALTRAUD UNZIPPED HER JACKET and revealed a small pistol tucked into her blue jeans. He found he could not aim his gun. Instead, he used it as a kind of shield.

"Don't come any closer."

She stopped. "May I sit?"

He put a hand over his eyes. She could kill him if she wanted. He didn't care.

"Styles is a fool," she said, seating herself on a cherub's head. "Don't you know that?"

Nester found one of the plane trees and slumped against it. His pistol dropped into the snow. He had an hour, a lifetime, to decide whether to die. He took sudden offense at the notion that he might be executed and buried here, next to Teutschlander. The one German he had loved had betrayed him, and with her, the entire country, the language, these dead.

"I was a talent spotter," she murmured, "that's all."

For the first time in her life, she sounded ashamed.

"You're his, *Schatz,* one way or another."

Waltraud crouched, looking across the flagstones at him. "One of his people came to me before you and I ever met. A young black man. He told me that the American government was looking for someone to be their eyes and ears in the neighborhood, and they were willing to pay money. He told me it was nothing much. I was just to keep tabs on my customers and one day, maybe, they would come to me for advice. It was good money, so I took it. Now and then, just to earn my keep, I sent them an envelope with the names of a few people. What could it hurt?"

Nester looked at her face. He had never known that a woman could be so beautiful. Among all those bones, she was spirit. Her bones moved, her eyes sparkled like the snow, her lips formed mist and words, and he could stop all of that with a single bullet between the eyes. It seemed like the profoundest of riddles.

"After I met you, I became nervous. I told the contact I wasn't interested anymore. I refused money, and that made someone curious. A new man came to me, and this man told me that I couldn't get out of the bargain, and if I tried, he would go to West German counterintelligence and tell them I was a spy for the East Germans. He said it would be very easy for an American agent to convince them of this, and I believed him. So I went along."

Against his will, Nester had begun to listen.

"What could I do? I agreed, but I stopped giving them names, and for a while, they left me alone. And then, one night three weeks ago, just after you left Berlin, he turns up again for the first time in almost a year. He tells me he can buy my way out of our deal if I do him one last favor. I never knew that this man and your Styles were the same person until that moment."

Nester lifted a handful of ice to his forehead. He gazed at the Czech pistol as if it were a hand thrust from one of the plots.

"He said it was the last thing he would ever ask from me. It was a minor thing, not very important. He told me he knew I was involved with you, and that he needed me to be on his side for just a little while. He said he needed something from me, and if I gave it to him, he might be able to save your life."

Nester bowed his head. "What did you tell him, Waltraud?"

"I told him about Bucharest. I said both the brothers would probably be going to Bucharest. I told him what you told me over the phone, that one of the brothers might already be at the Intercontinental, and that the other one would arrive in Bucharest around December fifteenth."

"Oh *goddamn,* woman! Didn't you realize that was a death sentence? Styles probably gave that information right to the Securitate."

She shook her head. Tears streamed down her face. "I didn't care. I don't give a fuck about Glemnik. I don't care whether he lives or dies."

"What did you tell this man about me?"

She came to him, reached out to touch his face, but he pushed her fingers away.

"I told him you were incorruptible. I told him you would die before you would ever hand a friend over to certain death."

She wiped her eyes. Nester picked up the gun. He made her back away from him.

"You don't know what you've done, Waltraud."

Just then, the wind picked up. The cemetery gate rattled. Had it been an hour?

Nester put the point of the gun barrel under his chin. It was the only way. Waltraud tried to snatch the gun from him. He put the ball of his ankle into her abdomen and kicked her away.

"Oh please God no—Nester—" she moaned, and it was like the dead calling to him in their sleep.

"Flieh!" He remembered an insignificant little quote from Goethe that had once filled him with yearning to go to the ends of the earth, to see and experience everything, and now made him want to die. *"Flieh!"* he cried again, replying to the dead. *"Auf! Hinaus in's weite Land!"*

A voice in his mind repeated the words in his own tongue, as if English alone could turn them into action. "Fly! Up! Out into the wide land!"

Waltraud looked at him as if he were insane. She didn't know the verse. Or if she had once learned it in school, as he had, she had long since forgotten it. And anyway, she did not care. Like most Germans, she did not give a damn about Goethe anymore. I am more German than the whole bunch of you, Nester thought with despair. I am the only German here.

The voice came again, more insistent this time. "Fly! Up! *Out!"*

He thumbed off the gun's safety. At that moment, he heard Styles come shambling down the hill. He saw the man navigating between dark parabolas and realized one piece of business had been left undone. Nester lowered the barrel from his chin. Waltraud watched him, and he eyed the gun in her waistband. If she tried to stop him, he would have to shoot back. She would give him no choice.

Styles stopped and folded his arms.

"Well?"

He seemed happier than Nester had ever seen him, as if he'd reunited two old lovers and had done something good for once in his life. His back was to Waltraud.

"I've made up my mind," Nester said.

Styles nodded. "I thought you might."

Nester jerked his arm up. The pistol quivered a moment in his fist. Styles's eyes widened in horror, but before Nester could squeeze the trigger, his foe lurched forward into the snow, struck by the butt of Waltraud's gun. She dropped the weapon and raised her hands. Steam blew from her mouth.

"Bucharest?" she asked.

CHAPTER TWENTY-SEVEN

1.

DOUGLAS WAS A FRACTION above timberline. The Volkswagen had died. Mounting switchbacks, the cold of the Transylvanian Alps, and the labor of crossing hundreds of kilometers of central Europe had finished it off. Pansy fiddled with the battery.

"Catastrophic failure," she muttered into valves.

Douglas and Jodie stretched their legs on either side of the VW Bug, which had chosen the hairpin curve before a Romanian war memorial for its final resting place. From that vantage point, their choices were stark. In the direction they had come, the road descended to another hairpin curve, five hundred yards or so below. Ahead, it rose around a bend. Douglas could not imagine a more inappropriate spot for a breakdown.

The memorial was a bicuspid against a half-mooned sky. Anchovies of cloud gusted out of the south. From time to time, these fish wisps obscured the moon, and everything went dark.

What wasn't sky was rock. Around the three of them, peaks loomed, great blue scrawls of stone clutching at the clouds. Douglas heard the crash of a distant waterfall and the shrieking of high winds on the other side of the curve. Here, a shoulder of the mountain provided a windbreak, but the minute they rounded the curve, they would be exposed to fury, to the high currents that could be seen driving the clouds. He had seen the sign for the waterfall a few kilometers back. If he was not mistaken, there was also a hotel: Casa Cascada. A sign had said so. Douglas wanted to leave the car at the war memorial and hike to the hotel. In the morning, perhaps with the help of the proprietors, they could return for the vehicle. By the light of day, it might be saved. Pansy protested. She didn't want to go any farther into the mountains.

"We're going to have to do something, Panse," Jodie argued. "We can't stay here."

The shortcut had looked easy. Turning south after Sibiu and taking the highway down a long valley, they should have reached Bucharest a day early. On the map, the highway was a thick red line, signifying, Douglas thought, wideness and importance. And by Romanian standards, the road was wide and important. There was a war memorial, after all, and a waterfall. But a great drawback had become clear in the last hour. The Moldavian, a spike rearing to heaven, separated them from southern Romania, from Bucharest. In the desolation of their spot, the mountain looked ethereal, as if the bicuspid of the memorial, caught by moonlight, had cast a shadow a thousand times as big. But it was real enough.

The weather changed. From beyond the stone shoulder, wind whistled through dead rocks and scattered dust tasting of ice. According to their travel guides, the Moldavian was the highest mountain in the country. Its passes were closed from November through May, due to the elements. Unfortunately, Douglas hadn't checked the advisories at the end of the travel guides until light had faded from the sky, until thousands of feet above sea level lay behind them.

"This is not my fault." Esperanza held a conference call with herself. "Ham can't blame me, the *Times* can't blame me, I did everything I was supposed to do, everything. If they blame anyone, it should be Anna Strogar."

She circled the VW in consternation. Douglas was sorry for her.

Jodie tried to calm her down. "It's nobody's fault, Panse. It's just a fact, and we have to deal with it."

At the back bumper of the VW, Pansy stopped, spun on a heel, and faced Jodie.

"You don't know the people I work with!" she snapped. "Everything is someone's fault!"

Then she went to the back of the car and slammed down the engine's lid.

"Can you help me out, please, Douglas?"

Douglas nodded.

"We'll try an old-fashioned method," Pansy went on. "Get in the car, and I will push. Jodie, please help me. With just enough momentum, the engine will juice, and we can get back down this mountain."

Jodie stopped Douglas from climbing into the driver's seat.

"That's dangerous. It's a steep drop."

Pansy crossed her arms. Wind tossed her hair across her eyes. She took a step toward Jodie. "Please."

Before Jodie could answer, Douglas climbed in. He buckled himself into the seat and put the VW into neutral. The two women got into position. He released the emergency brake. Esperanza counted three. With twin grunts, the two women pushed the car off the slight plateau of the curve. The VW started to move of its own volition. Douglas kept the passenger door open.

He twisted the ignition and saw a brief jack-o'-lantern flash of light in the dashboard. So there was a little life in the old Beetle, after all. His spirits lifted. He twisted again; it almost juiced. If they could get her started, the car would take them all the way back to Sibiu, where it could die if it wanted. Most of the road was downhill anyway.

The road was azure in the moonlight; pretty, he thought. He did the ignition again—almost, almost. Jack-o'-lantern lights flashed again, darkened again. The key was cold. It had bent a little in his hand. The road switched back three hundred yards ahead. Plenty of space to work with—four, five, six . . . Each time, the moment of ignition came closer, maybe because he was gaining speed. He gave a seventh twist of the ignition. He didn't want to take the curve at that pace, not without power. The VW might flip. He mashed the brake. The car didn't slow, which didn't make sense. There shouldn't be anything wrong with the brakes.

The curve was coming, a hundred yards ahead. He could turn, yes of course, it wasn't impossible, but what if something went wrong? Suppose the wheel didn't go far enough, suppose it stiffened up like the brake. The Beetle was old and unreliable. He had no margin for error.

He counted to three, jerked the ignition, and then an impossibility occurred. The key tore away. He beheld its butt in his fingers.

Jodie and Esperanza shouted in the distance. There was no more time to turn. He undid his buckle, grabbed the bag with the passports, as if it were a parachute, then rolled out.

He somersaulted into grass and gravel. The moon broke from behind cloud. Light flooded the road. The Bug seemed unsurprised. Its tires spoke. They uttered a flat, sad, receding statement of denouement, drowned, finally, in the hiss of far winds. Douglas sat up in the grass. He opened his mouth to say, "Stop!" The Volkswagen plunged out of sight.

2.

"Damn you!"

Pansy was upon him, beating him with hard small fists, painful as stingers.

"Everything went black!" Douglas shivered on the shoulder of the road. "No brakes!"

He looked down at what he had grabbed—the bag with the passports and, incongruously, a woman's black sock. The sock gawked on his digits like a finger puppet. Jodie's computer lay in the gorge, in the deep, dark gorge, with her cartons of Kent cigarettes, her beloved red shoes, the microcassette recorder and a journal of notes about Stuart. Douglas could see the shock on her face. She was overwhelmed. Transylvania had sucked her career down its gullet.

"You've *ruined* me!" Pansy shook with rage. Her eyes closed, she knotted bone-white fists. Tears ran down her cheeks. Jodie went to the edge, where the Bug had vanished. She peered down.

"I can't even see it." She let out a horrified giggle. "My God, Douglas, you really fucked up this time."

Now, in the shadow of the Moldavian, after kilometers of restraint, Pansy cut loose against both of them.

"I've had it with you. With *both* of you."

She walked down the slope of the curve, as if planning to follow the VW into the abyss. But she stopped after a few paces and came back up, her shadow unfurling dramatically behind her.

In a quiet voice, she spoke. "Why am I here? Because you were stupid enough to get beaten up in the demonstration in Prague."

She glared at Jodie.

"Because I saved your career and invited you to Ham's very exclusive party and then, God help me, I needed a favor in return. That was my mistake. Believe me, I've paid for helping you tenfold in the last forty-eight hours. If I'd known how incompetent you were—I mean, who buys a piece of junk like that . . . that Beetle? Who goes to Romania without knowing how to reach the capital?"

Jodie's eyebrows knit. She took a few steps forward. "Excuse me. What are you talking about? Saving my career?"

"I wrote your cover story, dear."

Jodie eyed her warily. "What?"

"Ask him."

Douglas listened in numbness. He had lost the car.

Jodie asked him to verify what Pansy had said, and he did with a single nod. He should never have asked Pansy for the favor, but what did it matter? They were stranded. They could die.

"It's true," he said.

Jodie was silent. The two women eyed each other in the cold and the darkness. Pansy wiped her eyes, and the tempest passed as quickly as it had come. Everything had been said. Nothing remained. They were alive, at least. That was something. There had been a temperature drop. Douglas could feel it in his bones. They would have to find some kind of shelter, if only in the lee of a rock. He was especially worried about Jodie. Caught up in her emotion, she looked as if she might black out again. She was still silent, staring at Pansy in doubt and anger and remorse. He hoisted their one bag over his shoulder, pocketed the black sock, and steadied her. She didn't resist. He guided her back up the hill toward the war memorial. Pansy soon followed.

They had no choice but to round the corner of the memorial and face the wind. It smacked them hard and cold. Douglas prayed for the headlights of a vehicle, something to carry them out of the night. But it never came. They trudged up and up. The memorial sank back into oblivion.

After an hour's ascent, they reached a covered piece of the road. It was not a tunnel, but rather a concrete slab resting upon a row of columns; between the columns shone stars. Grass and weeds growing on top of the slab thrashed about. Jodie and Douglas debated spending the night in a nook of rock at the center of the covered stretch, but after a few minutes, the spot grew too cold. The stone was worse than the night air. Douglas suggested they walk a little farther; then if nothing turned up, they'd come back. Jodie agreed. Pansy didn't speak.

It was a lucky decision. Ten minutes later, at the next curve in the road, they saw Casa Cascada, an utterly lightless edifice perched on the edge of a cliff. Beyond tumbled the waterfall, a thread of pale vapor suspended from the Moldavian. They were saved.

3.

WITH THE HELP of Pansy's French and a fifty-dollar bribe, the hirsute giant who ran the establishment was persuaded to give them a room. Officially, Casa Cascada was closed. Most of the time, he told them, very important people stayed there. Last month, the heads of the shipping collective in Constanta had come. There had been a conference and many prostitutes. He laughed. But now, with all the trouble, the government had closed the hotel down. No travel allowed. No movement. He held a candle in one hand, and with the other, waved. He shook his head. No, no, no! It wasn't a luxury hotel for tourists!

Eventually, seeing their distress and the money, he gave in. They entered a dark place that had a peculiar moist quality, as if the hotel had not been built out of wood or metal, but had congealed, like aspic. And there was a smell; homemade tzuica, pinecone, fart, and a stench more distant, as if the chicken in the aspic had spoiled. A large pinecone sat on the registration desk. The giant asked for passports, opened a vault in the wall behind the desk, and produced a sign-in book and a cashbox, into which he placed the money. He introduced himself as Viktor and shook each of their hands. When he came to Douglas, he peered for a long time, as if something had struck him. Jodie showed him why. Signing the book, she had come across a name and a date.

"Douglas," she said. "Didn't you tell me your brother was going by the name Sven?"

Douglas read: "Sven Karst," then an East German passport number, and a date, "November 15, 1989."

It was definitely his brother's handwriting. Douglas counted back. The night Jodie and he had met on the train, Stuart had been right here. An awe flooded him, as if he had sighted an angel. It was the first clear, crisp evidence of his brother's life in weeks. A month ago, anyway, Stuart had been alive and well and more important, secure enough to write his assumed name into a hotel register. Beside the name, Douglas saw, stood a room number. He made a mental note of it. Stuart had been in room 12.

"Hey." Jodie pointed at something else. "It's the name of your contact at the Information Ministry. Anton Olestru. He was here the same night."

Viktor eyed them. Douglas explained they knew Sven Karst from East Berlin. Viktor shrugged. He didn't want to know. Yawning through a thatch of beard, he indicated it was bedtime and led them to a double room with two single beds. Nothing else was made up. This room was for a famous poet. He booked every December, Viktor explained to Pansy in French. He liked the solitude. Once, the poet had written an ode called "To the Viktor of the Mountains." But this year, because of the trouble, the poet wouldn't come. The three of them could have his room. Viktor made a perfunctory gesture at airing the place out, slapping pillows, rustling curtains. Sorry, he indicated, no maid. Then he left, and his footsteps, heavy and loud, threatened to bring down the entire building.

No one fought over the bathroom. They were too exhausted. After turns in the toilet, they slipped off their shoes and crawled under the covers. Esperanza took the bed closest to the door. Jodie and Douglas shared. He lay next to the window and reveled in the warm skew of limbs around his body.

He tried to sleep, but couldn't. He was thinking of room 12. Ever since Vienna, when Nester questioned the authenticity of his brother's letter, suspicion had gnawed at Douglas. Nester had thought that Bucharest might be a trap. At the time, Douglas was too worried about Jodie to delve into the notion. But the more he thought back on what Nester had said, about the possibility that Stuart's old allies—his "flesh and blood," as he had written—had turned on him, the more concerned he became. And now Nester himself had disappeared. With the number Stuart's friend had given him, Douglas had tried to call Waltraud several times, but the line had evidently been disconnected. No question about it, he must get inside room 12.

Beside him, Jodie sighed and opened her eyes. She whispered.

"So I owe Pansy Buckner the high point of my career?"

He touched her lips with a finger.

"Don't think of it like that. If it weren't for her, you might not even have a career. Whatever her motives, she did do you a favor. She did me a favor."

Jodie pondered his words awhile.

"You know, it's funny. A month ago, the idea of this would have tormented me. But now? I don't know. Something has to be said, of course. But I guess I just . . ."

She let the thought trail off for a moment.

"It just pales somehow."

She clasped one of his legs with her thighs, which were bare. She had slipped off her pants under the sheets and was using him as a hot-water bottle. The bed was damp as a grotto. Wind made the walls groan. Under the least influence, Douglas felt, the hotel might slip over the precipice.

They kissed but resisted lovemaking out of consideration for Pansy. Just before she faded off, Jodie spoke in a drowsy voice. "I'll deal with it."

4.

TWO DAYS AND NIGHTS PASSED. The road remained empty, and the weather worsened. Sleet flags purled down the gorge. The waterfall could no longer be seen. From the troubled rotary phone in the hotel lobby, Jodie tried Olestru five and six times a day, got a ring but no answer. Meanwhile, their host Viktor, a Carpatho-Russian, came in and out of a tzuica-induced stupor. His wife had left him. She had taken their boy and run away with an engineer who had stayed at the hotel. For breakfast, the four of them ate cold cabbage leaves together and drank hot tea. At night, they had no light, and the candles were running out.

Viktor's radio emitted high, sharp whistles but little else. On the morning of the third day, he began to show signs of nervousness. He had expected to hear from someone about the political situation in the country, but no news had arrived. His food stocks were okay for the moment, but by the end of the week, the cupboards would be bare.

Douglas took advantage of his distraction to get into room 12. When Viktor descended to the basement to do inventory on his dry goods for the fifth time in a day, Douglas snatched the room key off its hook. Before he went up, Jodie stopped him. "There's something we have to talk about," she said.

"Not right now," he replied, kissing her. "I have to check Stuart's room while there's a chance. Keep lookout for me?"

There was no electricity, of course. The bed was stripped, the chairs draped in canvas. Rain beat against the windows. To his dismay, Douglas's feet drew loud creaks from the floorboards. He would have to hurry.

The first odd thing he discovered, to his shock, was a deceased scorpion in the corner of the bathroom behind the toilet, a creature necklaced by a smattering of sand. Douglas jabbed the scorpion with a cigarette butt he found in the sink. It was definitely of the order Scorpionida, of the family Iuridae, by the evidence of its stinger, which had no spine, and looked to be a cousin of the Giant Desert Hairy Scorpion, but what was it doing here? By Douglas's calculation, the thing had been dead for at least a week, if not longer. Presumably, someone from a desert clime had visited Casa Cascada and not too long ago. The scorpion had traveled in a shoe or at the bottom of a suitcase, scuttled out, and discovered it wasn't in Cairo anymore.

Douglas scooped the sad beast up in a wad of toilet paper and thrust it into his pocket. For a moment, he listened. He tried to imagine what he would say to Viktor if the man found him snooping. No excuse would really do. Douglas would have to trust Jodie's watchfulness. More quickly now, he searched the rest of the room.

Under the bed, his fingers came across something hard and small. Even before he examined the object, he knew what it must be.

Peering up at him like a sprite's eye was the stone that his brother had worn around his neck, the chip of basalt from the ancient city walls of Diyarbakir. Through the hole bored for the leather thong, Douglas could see the skin of the palm of his hand.

He hurried out of the room, raced down the stairs, and returned the key to its hook. The lobby was quiet. Laying down a volume of the collected works of Elena Ceausescu, the dictator's wife, Jodie told him that Viktor had returned from the basement a few minutes ago, thrown on a raincoat, and without explanation, headed into the storm. Douglas thanked her and asked her what she had wanted to tell him. Jodie shook her head. Pansy emerged from the kitchen, where she had been boiling water for tea and brooding. In the last forty-eight hours, she had stopped attacking them. In fact, she had stopped talking altogether. But now she spoke up.

"I think he's watching us," she said. Jodie gave a grim nod.

"Either of you plan to tell me why *exactly* he might be watching us?" At first, Douglas and Jodie pretended not to know what she was talking about.

"Oh please." She addressed this to Jodie, who looked startled. "You still don't want to enlighten me? After all we've been through?"

Pansy did not give her much time to reply.

"Fine. I made a deal with Douglas before. Now I'll make one with you." Jodie glanced at Douglas, crossed her arms, and waited for the terms.

"You have your own reasons for concealing the truth about your traveling companion. Maybe you're working on a big, hush-hush story together. Maybe there are other less mysterious explanations." Jodie began to blush. "Fine, whatever, *I don't care.* What I do care about is guilt by association. If he's involved in something shady, I don't intend to be a part of it. I *can't* be a part of it. What I mean is, I don't want you to tell a soul about me being here. Ever. If and when I want my presence in this hotel and my connection to Douglas known to anyone outside the three of us, I will say so. In exchange, I will mind my own business, and if anyone at my newspaper asks, if anyone of a more official nature should ever inquire, you can be sure I'll say nothing. *Entendu?*"

The women shook on it. An hour later, Viktor returned. He didn't bother to explain his absence.

That night in their bedroom, by candlelight, Jodie and Douglas examined what he had found beneath the bed in room 12.

"*This* belonged to my brother." He displayed the rock in his palm. "I think maybe he dropped it on purpose. As a warning."

Pansy sat on the adjacent bed, her back against the wall, her legs extended in perfect stillness before her, and her eyes fixed on the door. A cup of hot tea steamed in her lap, but she didn't drink.

"On purpose?" Jodie shook her head. "But he couldn't possibly have known you would be here."

Douglas kneaded his chin with his fingers.

"But he wouldn't have just left it either, Jodie. He wore the thing around his neck."

"You think he could have lost it in a fight?"

Douglas remembered again what Nester had said about a trap. "Maybe."

He glanced at Pansy. She was still watching the door, listening.

"Anything?" he asked. She shook her head. Her eyes did not leave the door. She lifted the cup of tea to her chest, as if to warm herself, but still did not drink.

Douglas took the black sock he had saved from the car and buried the rock in it. He stuffed the sock into his pants pocket. As an afterthought, he went into the bathroom and flushed the scorpion down the toilet. Jodie had asked him what he thought about the creature, and he hadn't known what to say. A memory of a disembodied head returned to him. His skin prickled. A mirror hung above the sink, and Douglas experienced a sudden certainty that if he looked up from the toilet bowl into that mirror, he would see the head staring back at him, staring in a dead-eyed way from a cloud of subterranean darkness.

Avoiding a look in the mirror, Douglas rushed back into the bedroom.

The next morning, Jodie and Pansy helped each other wash clothes. In a tub of frigid water, with a dull pink gob of Romanian soap supplied by Viktor, they cleaned everything in their possession. Wrapped in blankets, Douglas watched. After the clothes dried, in the same tub each took a bath. Douglas came last, and when he was finished, he dumped the tub in the parking lot. Above, stars were coming out, and the waterfall reappeared. It was time for them to get out of there.

That night, Viktor did not join them for dinner. Pansy explained that she had discovered something from him. Viktor had a brother who ran a kind of restaurant and lodge at the top of the pass, and this brother owned a truck. For a sum of dollars, provided the weather was good, the brother would take them over the Moldavian and on to Bucharest. Douglas and Jodie agreed. The sooner they got out of the Casa Cascada, the better. Viktor was notified, and he made the arrangements.

At the crack of dawn, a weather-beaten truck wheezed into the parking lot, and the three of them jumped aboard. Viktor did not come. He was sick, he said, *très malade*. He waved goodbye and slammed the door of Casa Cascada behind him.

On the way up the mountain road, his brother, Constantin, didn't talk much. Here and there, he pointed—at the cascade, at the switchbacks lying ahead, at the savage knife of the peak overswiping the pass. Soon, the waterfall dwindled behind them, and its source trickled beneath their tires. They ascended through cloud. Debris littered the road, snakes of rock from a cataclysm. There were no road shoulders, no rails. Back in the gray rift between mountains, far down, invisible, sat the Casa Cascada with its flushed scorpion corpse and drunken Viktor.

Eventually, they came to the pass, an ice-locked lap ending in a dark hole. Somehow, Douglas had expected them to go over the peak, not into it. Constantin parked at the entrance to the hole, gestured for them to wait a moment, then ran up steps to a desolate rectangle of concrete, a building even more godforsaken than Casa Cascada.

The tunnel yawning before them didn't resemble any Douglas had ever seen before. In his experience, tunnels were clean and well lit, with telephones on the walls in case of emergencies and catwalks for the stalled.

This tunnel offered no such solace. It looked like the aftermath of a mutilation. A claw had gouged into the Moldavian and ripped out its single eye. Douglas walked to the edge of the hole and looked in. The light died after a few yards. For all he knew, beyond that point, the road gave out in a bottomless chasm. It seemed not to go through the rock, but to plunge down into it. There would be no lights, no telephones, no walkways, and if a vehicle came in the other direction, they would have very little warning.

Constantin returned. Pansy asked him what he had been doing up there. He lit a cigarette, switched on the ludicrously dim headlights, and started the truck. He grinned, and nodded at the hole. Douglas took Jodie's hand. She squeezed it and seemed to want to tell him something. Douglas put the other hand in his pants pocket and clasped the black sock with its rock as if it were his own talisman. Pansy's eyes were fixed on Constantin. He had not answered her question. His lips were wet with tzuica. They entered the tunnel.

CHAPTER TWENTY-EIGHT

1.

VIKTOR WAS AN AGENT. Jodie knew that even before they entered the tunnel. Constantin too. How could they not be? Their hotels were too strategically situated in places of importance along a road that had probably been built for the military, so it could move rapidly over the mountains. They were agents and had been in contact with Bucharest.

An escort of three dark sedans met them in the valley on the other side of the tunnel. Pansy had asked Constantin what he had been doing up in the building at the pass, and Constantin had not answered. Why should he? The answer would not have helped them. They came out of the black mouth into Wallachia, into the Oriental East, as the guidebooks had it, descended a slippery road past a smashed bus and a crumpled gondola in a ravine as merciless as a vise. They skirted the edges of a great reservoir that went on for miles and miles, lowering itself slowly into trees and uninhabited hills until it ended at a dam where the sedans waited.

Before reaching the dam, Jodie had been thinking about how her period had not come; how it usually arrived with the punctuality of a Prussian train, and it should have come three days ago, when they crossed the Romanian border at Oradea. But it had not.

She thought of the fecundity she had seen in Transylvania. Piles of late-picked, ochre corncobs lay before doorsteps, set ablaze by the sun of an endless autumn. Dried red peppers curled down like leaves from the eaves of farmhouses. The last of the autumn pumpkins, swollen to orange bellies, mooned at her from wagons drawn by old women.

Explanation: She had simply passed her period by, like driving past a mile-marker at night. Or it hid in the dark, waiting until the overall danger to her reproductive organs dwindled, until Securitate, bad roads, massing armies, agents, and contaminated blood supplies no longer posed a general threat.

But there was a more probable explanation. It was partially her fault, Jodie realized. In her hurry to get to West Berlin, she'd forgotten to refill her birth-control prescription. Many times, she had meant to call Aunt Rachel, who had always helped her with these matters, and have her doctor send a new supply of pills. But she'd forgotten, and until Douglas, it hadn't mattered. Afterwards, he had bought some cheaply made East German condoms at the Hungarian flea market, and like every other aspect of the system, they had failed. Jodie had tried to broach the subject with Douglas at the Casa Cascada, but he had been preoccupied with his brother. Now it was too late.

Men in drab winter coats and slick boots stepped out of the sedans. A few of them cradled machine guns. Constantin lit a cigarette and told them to get out of the truck.

Pansy exited first. She didn't raise her hands. She didn't look at Jodie. She straightened her sweater and strode down the slope.

Constantin pushed Jodie and Douglas out of the cab of the truck. Pansy reached the first man in the blockade. His eyes were hidden by sunglasses. As she approached, his head tilted to one side, and a glimmer of a smile crossed his lips. A man cradling an automatic rifle joined him.

"I'm Esperanza Buckner of the *New York Times*." Jodie could hear her voice, a little too high but very firm, and realized, to her surprise, that she had grown fond of it. Pansy raised her identification in front of the man with the sunglasses. She seemed supremely confident, even contemptuous, as if she had walked into a newsroom in Podunk and demanded to see the editor. Jodie became terrified for her.

"Pansy!" she screamed.

Pansy glanced back. She gave Jodie an annoyed arch of her eyebrow. The man in sunglasses nodded. The butt of the automatic rifle swung up and caught her on the side of the head.

"Oh," Jodie heard Douglas say. "Oh no."

Pansy tumbled to the ground. The *New York Times* pass fluttered from her fingers. Wind off the water ruffled her hair. The assailant slung his rifle over his shoulder, knelt down, and took Pansy in his arms.

"Stay calm," Douglas whispered into Jodie's ear.

The man in sunglasses waved at Constantin, who turned his truck around and wheezed it back up the reservoir road toward home. Arms raised, Douglas and Jodie walked down the slope. Chips of concrete crunched beneath Jodie's feet. She felt detached from all of this. Would they be shot?

She couldn't conceive of it. After what she had endured, she could not conceive of dying. Pansy was carried to the first of the sedans.

Jodie was led to the hindmost car. She looked back for Douglas. She caught his eyes and wished she'd told him what was on her mind, just so he would know. A hand clamped the top of her skull and pushed her down into the car.

Inside, a burly man with a beard smoked a cigarette and held a gun against his belly. Jodie squeezed into the spot beside him. Another man, thin and bald and sneezing, climbed in too. The door slammed, and the car leapt forward.

"Anton Olestru?" she inquired.

Neither answered. They didn't even acknowledge her question. All the way to Bucharest, the burly man smoked, and the bald man sneezed. Neither said a word.

2.

THEY TOOK HER into the lobby of a hotel in Bucharest, the Intercontinental, she guessed. Tourists were everywhere. Judging by the labels on their steamer trunks, most were Greek and Israeli. Pale and heavy, dressed in beach colors, they bobbed around a desk in the middle of the lobby. It seemed a little late in the year for pastels, she reflected, even for Mediterraneans. She glanced around the room for anyone who might be Anton Olestru.

In Pitesti, the last big city before Bucharest, the other two sedans had been left behind. Now she was alone in this lobby with all these men. One of her escorts spoke to the man behind the counter. There seemed to be some kind of emergency. Jodie wondered what had become of her passport, her money, her American Express card. The man in the sunglasses had taken everything before pushing her into the sedan.

The desk clerk made a phone call.

Before long, a gray-haired man in an oatmeal-brown tie entered the lobby from the direction of the elevators. Could that be Olestru? He brushed off the front of his suit and ambled toward the tourists.

The desk clerk gestured to him. He walked across the room, nodding toward the desk. An odd calm descended. The tourists gazed at her. They didn't smile, didn't speak to each other, and didn't possess an ounce of tan among them.

The man wore a pair of glasses with thick frames and a suit that had been cut in the early seventies. His hair was an unkempt silver, his teeth gray. He made a slight bow.

There, at long last, stood Anton Olestru, who was supposed to take her into the bowels of the Romanian government and show her the truth. He shook her hand and spoke in perfect English.

"Jodie Blum, I believe."

She nodded.

"What kept you?"

A response caught in her throat.

"Allow me to introduce myself," he said, extending a hand. "Colonel Anton Olestru, Interior Ministry."

The tourists lifted machine guns from their steamer trunks. There must have been twenty of them.

"Where, please tell me, is Nester Cates?"

"Who?"

"The Negro soldier."

Jodie shook her head in disbelief.

"He was with your party in Vienna, was he not?"

Jodie's mouth went dry. She was too scared to ask about her friends. She didn't know what to say. He held her in his gaze for a long time.

"Very well then," Olestru finally said. He massaged his forehead with nervous fingers. A rage came into his eyes. "Very well."

CHAPTER TWENTY-NINE

1.

THE MOTION OF THE CAR finally ceased. Doors opened on both sides of Douglas.

He was marched through an underground garage to a pair of metal doors. Cars had leaked oil on the ground. There was a smell of standing water. One of his escorts pressed a red button, and the doors clicked open.

Escorts walked on either side of him, thin young men with aggressive strides. Once inside, they were joined by a third, who pinned the point of a weapon into the small of Douglas's back. On either side of the corridor were steel doors resembling the entrances to hospital coolers.

Douglas came to a paternoster, a sort of elevator in constant motion, and reared back. Paternosters scared him. For one, they had no doors, and yet within the frame they moved, creating an optical illusion. One car went down, one ascended, followed by another, and another. His escorts wanted him to descend. The next one opened at his head, yawned wide, fit into the space between floor and ceiling.

He lurched in and banged his forehead on the back of the paternoster. He was plummeting. Butterflies bubbled in his stomach. Two floors down, bare arms pulled him out. Another pair of escorts, these indistinguishable from the last, marched him down another, warmer corridor.

The doors here were narrower, with tiny hatches at eye level and numbers. Douglas sensed life beyond the doors, but could hear nothing. The corridor went on forever, a grim reminder of the Euclidean geometry lesson where two lines travel ever closer in parallel but never, throughout infinity, meet. The space between the two lines was lit at intervals by the same yellow bulbs he had seen in the East German barracks, and he saw, here and there, signs of irregularity in the stone, as if a great many spaces had been slammed together at high speed to create one.

The guards halted at one of the doors. Soon, a salt-bearded man in overalls scuttled up. He swung a key ring from a three-stubbed hand. The door resisted. It stuck like a piece of old gum to the wall. Finally, the key hit the right groove. The lock gave way, and the door creaked open. An effluvia of feces and ammonium smote Douglas. A gun butt poked. He stumbled across the threshold and glimpsed in that brief moment a human body beneath what looked like a suspended tree root. The door slammed behind him. The key turned in the lock. A single dim thread of light cut through an observation hole in the door. The rest was darkness.

2.

BY WHAT DOUGLAS HAD SEEN in the instant of illumination, the cell extended about six feet back and could not have been more than four feet wide. He stepped forward, inch by inch, until his toes struck what must be extended legs. With his fingers, he reached out and touched. It was wood, but very old and dry. What appeared to be the three tendrils of a root extended away from each other. To explore the rest of the cell, he edged around two of the tendrils. There was the faintest noise of breath, but it could have been his own. He continued a few more feet before his hands found the back wall.

He sensed the ceiling just above the crown of his head. Its bricks secreted a tepid liquid. He turned to the right and almost put his foot down a hole. A reek of waste came from it. His cellmate must be terribly sick. Breath went on whispering in the cell.

"Hello?"

Douglas crouched down, placing his fingers on the floor. It was a surface of moist excrescences, dank as the ceiling. He inched back the way he had come. When he thought he heard exhalation in front of him, he stopped. He sensed the root just over his head, and it unsettled him, as if a dragon had fallen asleep with its claw dangling down a pit.

"Are you alive?"

A reply came out, barely audible.

"Shhhhhhh—"

It sounded more like a death rattle than an answer.

"Hurt?"

"Sick." The voice belonged to an English-speaker.

Douglas could smell spoilage in the breath.

"Who are you?"

The breath hit him again. Douglas recognized his own fate. By this time next week, he too would be an odiferous wraith.

A finger brushed his nose. He froze. Another joined it. Before he could jerk back, an entire hand fastened upon his skin. The digits masticated as if eating fruit. He tried to tear himself free, but the stranger's hands were stronger than he would have believed possible.

They dropped away. The body slumped back. The cell was cold. Douglas clasped arms around himself. How long had this poor soul languished in the dark? Did he know that change crashed upon the world above, sweeping all before it? Had he heard about the Berlin Wall, Prague, Timisoara?

Douglas stood up and returned to the place against the back wall, careful not to step in the hole again or knock his head against the root. His eyes began to adjust. From that slight distance, he could see the outline of the body. It weighed nothing. It was bones and hair. Around it, like a coffin, was the cell, an oblong of ancient stone. Douglas could smell its earthy antiquity, and he recalled having read how Ceausescu had plowed under central Bucharest in order to build a new city. The root might be all that remained of a tree on a once pleasant avenue.

"What an awful place this is," he said aloud.

"Oh Lord," the voice of the stranger whispered.

The man's limbs began to shake. He started to sob. Then Douglas knew. He knelt. He leaned forward and touched his brother's head.

"I'm here, Stuart."

"That's not what I wanted—" The words dissolved into a sob.

His brother's body was naked but for underwear. It had been here, in this place, a long time; ever since November 17, Douglas guessed, the day after Stuart had been taken forcibly from the Casa Cascada. His "flesh and blood," as he had called them in the letter, had come for him in room 12, and there he had lost his talisman.

Stuart had once possessed the body and bearing of a soldier. Now he was a human desert. Disease and hunger had dried his flesh. The microflora of the body, the teeming stuff of health, had been laid waste by a drought and left Stuart bare. Or perhaps he was more like that anoxic sea he had been so fond of using to describe himself. Life still simmered on the surface, but within the depths, all was dead.

"Doug?"

Douglas's own name, spoken in this place, sounded like a judgment. He reached into his pocket.

"Where are you?"

"Here, Stu. Right beside you."

Douglas pulled out the black sock and dug inside. There, at the bottom, was the talisman.

"Give me your hand."

Stuart did. Douglas took the cold fingers and put the stone inside it.

"This is yours. The stone from Diyarbakir. Hold it close."

At that moment, Stuart's sickness became aggressive. Douglas got out of the way. Still clutching the stone, Stuart detached himself from the wall and spidered on all fours to the other side of the cell. He squatted over the hole. Douglas heard hands fumbling at an elastic strap. A smell of wet death emerged.

"Oh God, I've shit myself again."

His brother's breath quickened.

"They put poison in the food. I do nothing but vomit and shit all day."

He finished and crept back to his old spot. Then he lifted the rock to his eyes. He murmured so low that Douglas couldn't hear him.

"What, Stu? Talk to me."

Stuart raised his voice but talked so fast that the words flowed into a single long slur, like a chant broken here and there by gasps for breath and explosions of vehemence. Douglas caught eddies of sense. He made out the names of Günter and Diyarbakir. Then, just as it had begun, the murmuring stopped.

"Douglas?" His brother clutched the rock to his gut. His body convulsed. He tried to vomit. The convulsion passed.

"Douglas?" Stuart called again. "Would you hold me?"

Douglas lowered himself to the floor, into the moistness, and took the frail body under his arm. Its military strength, that which he had admired and envied when he first came to Berlin, had evaporated. For the first time in their lives, Douglas was the stronger of the two. He wiped his eyes.

Stuart placed his mouth to Douglas's ear, and this time, Douglas understood the sense of his words.

"Listen to me—" Stuart stopped for a second to get his breath. "Listen, and I will tell you everything."

Stuart's body was terribly cold. Douglas rubbed the tendons of his arms, the knobs of his bony legs, the brittle clock of his chest. He pulled his brother close.

"I'm listening, Stu."

Stuart took hold of his hand and squeezed it.

"I was a soldier for the Revolution."

Douglas nodded.

"Yes, Stu."

Stuart swallowed.

"On the day before I joined the United States Army," he continued, "I beat our father within an inch of his life. I was down in Oak Cliff, visiting a friend, and there he was, sitting at a table in a diner with a woman, a gaudy old spic wearing a wedding ring on her right finger. I didn't say anything. I just walked up, and I hit him. Now that I think about it, I do remember yelling out, 'Mother-mother-mother-fucker!'"

Douglas stared up at the dangling root, no longer a claw, but the udder of the universe, close and humid.

"At that moment—I'm telling you this for a reason—at that moment, I became capable of murder. I became a revolutionary."

Douglas bowed his head at these words. At last, Stuart was ready to tell the truth, but Douglas needed a moment before he could hear it. He must prepare himself. "Quiet for a minute, Stuart. Just be quiet."

Within seconds, his brother was snoring in his arms.

3.

TIME PASSED SLOWLY. Someone slid a plate of bread, mush, and water into the cell. Stuart hovered on the brink of consciousness.

At last, after an indeterminate stretch of minutes or hours, Stuart woke again. As if he had never ceased talking, he asked, "Are you ready now, Doug?"

And Douglas replied, "Yes, Stu, now I am."

Stuart coughed and took a deep breath.

"Operation Second Home was a covert training exercise, a rehearsal of an infiltration conducted between a rogue agent of the Central Intelligence Agency, Styles, and a rogue counterpart within East German counterintelligence, Mundung, without the approval or knowledge of either the American or East German governments. It was a small, unobtrusive little matter between minor officials on both sides of the Wall, and it was perfect for the Albacete Association—for us—for me."

The memory of a distant day came to Douglas, a gray morning in an East German village, when Herr Mundung had told him about cooking pigs in Albacete and about the Spanish Civil War.

He squeezed his brother's hand. "Go on."

Stuart's head lifted, and he looked into Douglas's eyes.

"I came slowly to the cause of world revolution, Doug. It didn't just happen. It took Günter, who died in my care, an old man with lung cancer, spitting blood into the sand beside his cot. It took Mundung, who took me under his wing after Günter died. It took the Turkish army slaughtering women and children before my very eyes. All this lasted years, Douglas, believe me. I read Marx and Lenin. I read Mao and Bakunin and the rest of them. It wasn't the books that did it, though. The books alone are nothing."

Douglas recalled his brother's apartment, the shelves full of German literature. "In the end, it was the examples of other people that finally convinced me, the examples of men I admired," Stuart went on. "Before he died, Günter told me something. He told me how his turning point came after he bombed a rebel village in Spain, when he flew back over the village to see if there were any survivors. He saw one: a little girl with her legs blown off. He landed the plane and put a bullet between her eyes. Out of mercy. And that was it. His days with Hitler's army were over. He returned to the air base, stole a truck, and escaped to Madrid. He joined the Republican side and started his life over—"

Here Douglas interrupted. "Have you bombed villages, Stuart? Have you killed little girls?"

Stuart pondered this question, but didn't answer. "Come on," Douglas urged. "You can't tell me that what you did to our father even remotely compares to those things. Please tell me that's not why you became involved with these foul people."

His brother's voice rose as emotion welled into it. "I knew that Jiri Klek had done terrible things, Doug. I knew he had killed innocent people. I wasn't under any illusions about that. And at first, I didn't want to join him and his colleagues, but I did, you see, because there had to be some corridor, some way of getting back to a first principle, even if it was a bloody corridor. Mundung and Günter, these men believed in something. They had gone off to war, they had *volunteered* in the first blush of their youth, to die for the Revolution. If the Spanish Civil War had been going on in the 1980s, I would have joined the International Brigades too, Doug, as they had. But it wasn't."

Douglas put a hand over Stuart's mouth and placed his lips against his brother's ear. "You haven't answered me, Stuart. What did you have to answer for? What crime?"

Stuart gulped once, as if he had been underwater. Douglas could feel tears dampening his shoulder. "Christ, Doug. I helped those Turks clear out the villages. Haven't you been listening to a single fucking word? My own government pimped me right into the Turkish intelligence effort against the Kurds. We were allies, man! I tracked Kurdish rebel formations, and the government erased them. And when I went to the villages afterwards, my God, my God—"

Douglas became aware, as his brother talked, that a new animation was entering the tortured body. Stuart had become energized, as if the act of revealing his obscene secrets had revived him.

Douglas squeezed his brother's hands again. "Okay, Stu. Okay. Go on."

Stuart seemed to take umbrage at this insistence. He pulled his hands away. Douglas could see his eyes shining between the strands of his hair. Something like anger seemed to be brewing in his brother's head. Stuart spoke again, this time in a faintly hostile, even accusatory tone. "For a while, all I could feel for myself was a tremendous loathing, a sickness in the heart, like I was one of those Turkish whores, all mouth in a corrupt body. I felt I must do something. I felt I must act. I didn't care for myself. I didn't care for anything except finding that first principle, that pure cause, and serving it."

Douglas felt a surge of pity for his destroyed family. For a few Christmases after Stuart resurfaced in Turkey, his mother, Stuart, and he had spoken over the telephone. They had talked of small things, of insignificant memories, like any family. They had made plans for reunions that they all knew would never take place. In retrospect, Douglas realized, Stuart had been as insubstantial as a spirit guiding their fingers across a Ouija board. He had given them sentences from the other side of the grave, and they had been happy.

Stuart rose into a crouch now. He was pointing at Douglas with a long, bony, trembling finger. "You were an example to me, Douglas."

This roused Douglas out of his sadness. "Me, Stu? How could I possibly have been an example to you?"

His brother's finger came close. The anger continued to build. It filtered into the cell like gas from a hidden vent. "The way you work, Doug. I studied you from the minute you came to West Berlin, and I saw something lacking in myself. I saw the way that you walked into a room and gathered intelligence on the goddamn insects. You had a look in your eyes. You were beholding the invisible world, judging it. Do you know what a strength that is? To shut out everything else in the whole chaotic world and concentrate on one thing in it? God, I have envied that quality in you. That quality makes you a revolutionary too, brother. That very quality."

"I am no revolutionary." Douglas's heart had begun to hammer with pity and indignation.

"Yes you are, Doug!" Stuart spat back. "When you put on your extermination outfit, you become a revolutionary. You concentrate on one thing, and that thing has very clear limits and very simple goals. What is necessary—what tools will I need? What methods will I employ? How much time is required?—to utterly sanitize this room?"

For an instant, Stuart paused. He seemed to want a nod of agreement from Douglas. When he didn't get one, his temper exploded.

"That's revolutionary, I'm telling you!"

Stuart's elbows had been resting on the knobs of his knees. Now his hands dropped to the ground, and he leaned forward on them, like a cat preparing to pounce. His voice sank to a whisper.

"When Klek told me he wanted to blow up the Amerika Haus, I looked the thing cold in the face, and I said, yes. Absolutely."

Douglas put a hand up to his brother, as if to keep him back.

"Oh Stuart. Please don't tell me that."

His brother glared for a few seconds in the dark, and then he spoke a familiar sentence very slowly. "We all have a second home . . ."

"No, Stuart—"

"Where everything we say . . . everything we do . . . is innocent."

"No, Stuart! I do not accept that!"

Stuart snatched Douglas's hand in his own. Tears glistened again at his eyes. His emotions were racing up and down like the temperature from a fever. "We were going to blow it up on the fifty-first anniversary of the pogrom against the Jews, November ninth, in the middle of an anniversary event. It was Klek's idea. The West German foreign minister was planning to attend, and so were the American and Soviet ambassadors. It would have been our way of announcing to the world that we despised both East and West. The real revolution wasn't dead, but renewed, Doug. Renewed at the moment of death, renewed in hell itself, like Christ already crucified!"

Words began to tumble from Stuart's mouth now. He would not let go of Douglas's hands. "We knew Styles was in West Berlin. We knew he hated Klek. We knew he was sitting in West Berlin, half out of his mind, watching the East, waiting for a chance to get himself—or one of his people—into East Berlin to pursue his obsession. So we came up with Operation Second Home. That is, Mundung did. We knew Styles would not be able to resist the idea of the rehearsal. We made one bet, Doug—can you guess what that was? We made the bet that Styles would come to me, that I was the only man for Operation Second Home, and we were right. But I never imagined all of you would be sucked down by it, I never thought you and Nester and Uta would be swallowed in this thing—"

"Liar!" Douglas wrenched himself away from the hands, now taken up by his own wrath. "How could you not have known? You planned to murder dozens of people in cold blood and didn't think your friends and loved ones would be affected?"

Stuart shook a finger, like a mathematician differing over the meaning of an equation.

"I'm sorry, Doug, but we couldn't simply blow up the Amerika Haus ourselves. That would have been too dangerous. A few years ago, some government or other would have protected us. That was one of the perks of the Cold War for your average terrorist. Someone always had an axe to grind with someone else. But that couldn't work for us, not in this instance. We were enemies of both sides, and that made us extremely vulnerable. Once the job was done, we could count on no protection. So we had to create an artificial act of espionage, and an artficial cast of characters, namely you and Uta and Grams. By the time our enemies had figured out that neither you nor Uta nor Grams had anything to do with the real plan, that is, with the bombing, we would have been safely away—"

Douglas experienced a shudder. "Uta and I were decoys?"

Stuart threw himself on the ground before Douglas. He writhed in the shit like an animal caught in a trap. Then he lurched up, and in an attempt to rise from the floor to the ceiling, slammed his head against the tree root. He wailed. His head began to bleed. Douglas could see the black liquid seep down his nose. As if the root had punched him in the face, Stuart struck back. He appeared to be trying to tear the object out of the ceiling, and Douglas, cowering from this show of madness, had an awful vision of his brother battering at death itself.

And then he was struck by a realization. "I saw him, didn't I? Down there in the shelter?"

His brother paused.

"Yes."

"He was down there the day that Styles confronted me, wasn't he?"

Stuart didn't need to confirm it. Douglas could see the disembodied head before him, as if the confrontation had only just occurred. He had been face-to-face with Klek, but had possessed too little information at the time to make the right connections.

"Styles *wasn't* insane. My God, I should have told him right then and there, when he confronted me in the cafe, I should have told him what I had seen. Klek was down there, planting charges, or trying to plant them anyway, and it would have worked if Styles hadn't stumbled across *me*. My God, Stuart, you would have murdered all those people—"

Now his brother erupted again. "And then the whole thing went to hell!" he cried. "All to fucking hell!" His hands boxed again with the root. This time, he cut himself across the knuckles, and the pain wrung a howl out of him. He spun into the corner of the cell next to the door, then began to slam the bloody fist against the wall. His howl ascended to a shriek.

"Styles saw you and went out of his mind! I mean, right fucking over, man! The resemblance wasn't *that* close, for God's sake! He shouldn't have reacted *that* way. None of us foresaw it. None of us foresaw how far he would go."

Another horrible truth came clear to Douglas. He saw his brother leaning over the corpse of a human being in the darkness of that same accursed air raid shelter.

"You killed Grams, didn't you, Stuart? It wasn't Styles, like you said. It was you."

Douglas tried to grab his brother by the legs, to stop him from thrashing around, to stop once and for all his long evasion of the truth. Stuart kicked his hand away, but his wild movements ceased. His voice lowered, and he sounded ashamed.

"He discovered the dynamite. He dismantled it. I had no choice. He was going to the police."

Douglas shook his head in dismay. "Why did I have to be there, Stu? Why did you have to involve me in all this, for the love of God?"

Stuart calmed down and cleared his throat. "I'm going to tell you, Doug, but you have to give me a chance. Last Christmas, you and Mom sent me a picture of the two of you standing in front of the Christmas tree, and I put the picture in my wallet. One night, over a beer, Mundung sees the picture. He sees the mark on your face, and he makes a mental note. I have never seen Klek before, but he has, and he makes a mental note. Follow?"

Douglas nodded.

"Now, at about the same time, this was last February, Klek shows up in East Berlin. He has just been to see Olestru, and Olestru has been talking to Mundung, and the three of them have come up with a plan to blow up the Amerika Haus as a statement against *perestroika*. Your picture filled in a final piece of the puzzle. Still with me?"

"No," Douglas said.

"Christ, Doug. You're supposed to be the smart one. The plan is very simple. Mundung's friend Grams has a cafe not far from the Amerika Haus. Okay? Mundung knows that in the subbasements of this cafe, there are old ducts running to the Amerika Haus, and Klek can use these ducts to plant the explosives. Grams never suspects that we are planning to bomb anyone, of course, but he is a fellow traveler, and so he does whatever Mundung tells him to. So Mundung hires you to exterminate ticks in the basement. And do you know why?"

Douglas did. He didn't want to, but he did.

Stuart nodded. "That's right, bro. Klek is one of the most wanted men in the world, which makes it dangerous for him to set foot in West Berlin, where he knows there is at least one madman watching for him already, Carlton Styles. But he is also a perfectionist, and he insists on laying the charges himself. And that's where you come in. Mundung told me they needed a *Doppelgänger*—you know, Doug, a twin—to come and go from the cafe in the basements on a regular basis. That way, on the day Klek plants the bomb, he walks right into the cafe, goes right downstairs, and no one thinks anything about it. Got me? Afterwards, when investigators are sifting through the debris, looking for clues, the people in the cafe recall a bug exterminator with a mark on his face, and that leads them to you. And if they need anything else, then we give them a call and tip them off to Uta. For all they know, you are the saboteurs—and by the time they realize the truth, we are all safe and sound in Bucharest—"

"And Operation Second Home?"

"I told you, man. That was all part of our cover. It kept Styles off our backs, and if Mundung's superiors discovered it, he could confess that he was involved in a pointless little operation that hurt no one, and even if East German intelligence got its nose out of joint, it wouldn't matter. They would be too outraged at the fake operation to ever imagine the existence of a real plan aimed against their own policies."

All that movement, the confession itself, seemed to have broken something inside of him. Blood welled out of his mouth. He put a hand to his lips, drew it up to his eyes, and stared. His voice trembled as he went on.

"We were almost there when Styles turned up in the cafe and identified you as Klek. After that, I knew he would have to kill you, Doug. Only that would satisfy him. That's what I told Olestru. That's what I told Mundung. You weren't supposed to die. I mean, *my* life? Fine! But not yours! Okay, under our plan, you might have had to spend some time in prison until everyone figured out you were just a patsy, but I could live with that. Prison wouldn't have killed you. Might have even made you a better man."

Douglas could not fathom it. His brother had been willing to see him go to prison, but drew the line at unintentional fratricide.

Stuart's body began to shake. "And then, oh Christ almighty, if that wasn't enough . . ." He doubled over, sick again, heaving more blood, and then went on. "As if that wasn't enough, the butt-fucking Berlin Wall had to fall. On that night of all nights!"

Finally exhausted, Stuart slumped back against the wall opposite Douglas and put his ear to the door, listening. "They'll be coming for you soon."

Douglas started to rise, but Stuart gestured for him to stay seated.

"There's not much more to tell, brother." Stuart wiped his eyes, then covered them with a hand. His breath came in gasps. "I grabbed you and Uta, in order to keep that bastard Styles from executing you. I loved Uta, Doug—I know you may not believe that, but it's true. Mundung sent me to that country-western dance class to win her over, but I fell in love. To him, she was just cannon fodder for the aftermath of the bombing, but I never really accepted it—"

He was losing strength, and with it, consciousness. "After I defected, and the Amerika Haus job was a wash, Mundung and the others were furious with me. But like I told you in the letter, they swore to stick by me, to help get me out of Europe. When I saw Mundung in that village in East Germany, he told me not to worry. Everything would be fine. He would take care of you. And I had to believe him, Doug, because I had no one else. So I made my way down here, and the whole time, I saw what was happening in Czechoslovakia and Bulgaria and East Germany, and I understood that we were all finished—that the cause was just—over—"

Douglas wanted him to stop now. He had heard enough. He reached for his brother, but Stuart would not budge. He stayed in the corner, as if he were holding up the wall.

"Let me finish, Doug. Just let me do this one last thing, okay?"

Douglas prepared himself for some other terrible revelation. "Okay, Stu."

"When I got to the Casa Cascada, they were all waiting for me: Mundung, Olestru, Klek, one or two others. They told me I'd betrayed them. Do you believe that? Because I had defected and blown their plan to destroy the Amerika Haus, all of a sudden, they saw the hand of conspiracy. They wanted answers. They asked me to admit to being a spy. They said they knew about Nester's mission to infiltrate and expose them. They knew that I was Nester's agent, that he was connected to the highest intelligence levels and had planted me next to Günter as a spy. The sooner I confessed, the better. Can—can you believe that fucking shit?"

Stuart mustered a final laugh.

"Do you know what I told them, Doug? I asked them, what is a revolution, in its essence? They looked at me like I was insane. I said, a revolution, by definition, is that which passes away."

At this, Stuart's legs gave way. He sank to the floor. His hands covered his face.

"I realize something now." Stuart spoke into them. "I mean, I knew it when I killed Grams, but now I'm sure. All along, I thought it was revolution I was after, that revolution would solve all my problems, clear my conscience. But it wasn't revolution, Doug. Not at all. It was something else. Something truly linear. Truly clean. I felt that when I held Grams in my hands, as I watched him die. A first principle . . ."

He paused. His hands dropped from his face to his lap. The talisman rolled out of them, across the floor, and into the latrine. His eyes remained open, but his breathing stopped. Douglas closed his eyes. He would allow his brother this last chance to slip away for good.

4.

ATER, HOURS LATER, breaking into the endless twilight, the door swung open. Numb, Douglas let go of those precious limbs, which had lain warm beneath him in bunk beds or beside him in station wagons for so many years and cold beside him at the last. Douglas was not yet thirty, but felt he had lived a century. Hands reached in for him. He was blindfolded, hoisted out by arms and legs.

Around him he heard confusion. People were running. Intercoms crackled. Conversations sounded tense. At one point, off in the distance, he caught echoing gunfire.

He was carried a certain distance, dropped against concrete, stripped. The blindfold was ripped away. Above him loomed a shower head. Before he could grasp what was happening, water blasted out. Bristles raked his face and legs. He was extracted from the shower by what felt like tongs, searched, and given a set of filthy clothes.

He was blindfolded again, carried another chaotic stretch, then seated in a chair. Someone approached. The blindfold was removed again. Douglas blinked.

At first, all he saw were their eyes, then his comprehension widened. He faced two men and a woman seated at an oak table. The men wore military garb, the woman a dress. Behind these three, standing against the wall, were several guards, guns in their arms. To his left was a door, and an old oak podium stood next to it. There were others in the room. Douglas glanced right and saw the rotund, sickly Herr Mundung, the pursuer from Budapest, still wearing the cross around his neck, and a skinny but deeply tanned man of indeterminate age in a brown woolen coat seated together on a bench. On the face of the tanned man, on the left cheek, appeared a black dot, the powder burn. Douglas nodded. The same eyes that had once stared at him in the shelter gazed at him without response now. It was, at long last, Klek, the desert specter, who had left behind the dead scorpion like a turd shat in the Casa Cascada; the man for whom he had been mistaken. He had the coldest eyes Douglas had ever seen.

He became aware of movement behind him.

"Douglas," he heard Jodie whisper. He whipped around long enough to see her and Pansy seated next to each other, overseen by guards who looked familiar from the bridge at the reservoir. Pansy's head was bandaged. Like him, both of them were wearing soiled clothing.

"Quiet," warned the man who appeared to run the show, a gray-haired fellow occupying the middle seat at the table. He dragged on a cigarette and sifted through a voluminous pile of paper handed to him by the woman.

"This session of the Romanian People's Tribunal, Directorate One, in the matter of a conspiracy to destroy the Assocation of Albacete, and in effect the Revolution, is now called to order."

He put out the cigarette and addressed Douglas. "You're all here," he said, "but one."

Douglas remembered what Stuart had told him. These men had all succumbed to a wicked nonsense. They believed themselves betrayed by Stuart on behalf of Nester. In their ignorance and fear, in the solitude enforced upon them by their own delusions, they believed the Americans gathered in their hands were their destroyers.

The man before him, Douglas guessed, must be Anton Olestru, the one who, ultimately, had killed his brother. A vicious certainty flamed in Olestru's eyes. He knew his enemies, and he wanted vengeance. But he needed something, evidently, before he could begin to exact it.

The ashes of his cigarette spilled over the tabletop. Its smoke curled up in the still air of the room. Douglas's hand was hanging at the edge of the seat. From behind, Jodie grasped it. The slender, warm fingers dimmed the horror of Stuart's confession and death for an instant and gave him the courage to speak.

Jodie let go of his hand, and Douglas pointed at Olestru. "I hold you responsible for my brother's actions. For the murders he might have committed, for one he did commit, and for his own."

Olestru ignored the comment.

"We don't have much time, which makes it all the more important for our witnesses to offer quick, incisive accounts of themselves," he announced. "Representatives of the People and of the People's Association of Albacete have already briefed the witnesses in private and are apprised of the essential points of their testimony."

Mundung spoke up.

"Where is Cates?"

Olestru cocked his head in Mundung's direction, piqued, it seemed to Douglas, at being challenged.

"In Bucharest," he said. "Our people will apprehend him soon enough."

Mundung seemed impatient, but he nodded, as did his companions, the cross-bearer, and the man Douglas supposed to be Klek. Douglas found in the latter's thick, gray eyebrows, the browned skin, the tangled dark head of hair, and the gloomy, unreadable eyes a memory of his own origins, a distant collusion between geography and genetics. When he grew older, he might look like this man. On the other hand, to Douglas, the powder burn looked nothing like his own housefly.

These thoughts were shattered by gunfire. Beyond the door behind his back, automatic weapons rattled.

"The People intend to prove the following," the head of the tribunal shouted over the noise. "That Nester Cates set a trap for the Men of Albacete, in effect the revolution, using these conspirators; that he infiltrated the revolution with the help of Stuart Glemnik; that Glemnik stopped an action that was to be carried out by and for the revolution, namely the targeting of an American-Zionist cultural gathering; that the conspirators have each contributed in their own way to the revolution's betrayal and are worthy to be sentenced to death for said contribution—"

The force of an explosion could be distantly felt. Douglas's chair moved.

"First witness!" the speaker cried.

One of the guards left the room. He returned a minute later, one step behind Uta Silk.

CHAPTER THIRTY

YET AGAIN, Uta was on her bicycle in Marburg, pedaling down the steep road, down, down, down from the castle to the St. Elizabeth Church at the bottom. As she cycled, she squeezed the brakes on the handlebars to keep from going too fast. The sun shone through the leaves of thick dark oaks. Friends waved as she reached the central market square, Herr Mundung and Tante Greta and Stuart and Douglas and Renate and Nester. She built up speed coming around the corner where her mother's best friend ran a tea shop, and just there, she squeezed on her brakes and watched in horror as, in her tightly clenched hands, the brakes snapped away. They turned to razors and tore her fingers off. The waving people began to scream. Her father emerged beside her, on his own bike, mud smeared on his pale blue lips. He emerged from a door and raced after the tumbling fingers. There were dead children everywhere. She held the bleeding stumps against her breasts, felt the bike gaining in speed, moving faster and faster down the narrow cobbled lanes of the old city. Then, as the St. Elizabeth Church came into view, with the saint herself in a field of red petals on the tympanum above the door, waiting patiently, beckoning to Uta, she crashed through the church doors and into a storm of light. She didn't scream. She laughed. Church bells pealed.

Then she woke and realized they weren't church bells at all. Something was happening beyond the walls of her cell. She wiped tears from her eyes.

Herr Mundung appeared. He was weary, fat, and old, like his doctrine. He described her dream in anti-Capitalist terms, wiping the sweat from his brow, his face pale as that of a corpse. In his interpretation she was trying to cycle away not only from her father's influence, but from the overwhelming shadow of the castle, which stood for centuries of German warmongering that had culminated in National Socialism. Deep inside her, Herr Mundung said, were the Nazi and the Capitalist, keeping her from a break with the past, but the force of history had already swept her in its embrace. She could no more resist the momentum of Marxist-Leninism than she could turn the bicycle around and pedal back up the castle. History ripped her fingers off. Finally, he explained, the collision with the church was obvious, and Uta's ironical imagination had chosen an apt symbol for free-market hypocrisy in the figure of Saint Elizabeth, an exploiter of the people who appeared to represent the generous and compassionate qualities of the Christian but, in fact, represented the lies Americans and others told themselves in order to continue their brutal rape of nine tenths of the world. By the way, he concluded, tell me about Nester Cates.

She pondered his words and knew, for the last and final time, that he was a fool. Not that it mattered. God was coming, and she wished to see Him. She had made a decision, and it was a good one, as all decisions, in one way or another, are good, as all suffering, in one way or another, is good. Of course, the direct reasons for her suffering bordered on the absurd, but that lay in the nature of things.

Once, she had seen Stuart. She had been asked to denounce him in some kind of tribunal. In answer, she knelt and kissed Olestru's feet. They had fed her some awful stuff, overcooked cabbage rolls. Diarrhea was killing her.

Her father had made her memorize every line of Graf Helmuth von Moltke's last letter to his wife, every line, and now its words came back to her with the force of a prayer. Uta visualized the aristocrat Moltke sitting before the Nazi judge, and she heard the judge's question as if it were addressed to her in her cell.

"Who do you take your orders from?" the judge asked Moltke. "The Eternal Hereafter or Adolf Hitler?"

Olestru had gone to great lengths to spin lies around her. First, he had played her friend. He insisted on showing her a few old German churches in Transylvania. He bought her a nice lunch in the old square of Brasov, a pile of Transylvanian sausages on a bed of Hungarian peppers, and plied her with questions about Stuart. Did she have a certain kind of relationship with him? *Eine Beziehung,* he asked in German. Not anymore, she had told him. Now she loved Stuart with a great Christian love, as Saint Elizabeth had loved her husband, who died during the Crusades.

When they arrived in Bucharest, she was placed under arrest. At first, she thought it had something to do with the visa, but no. She was accused of espionage. Olestru produced a file. She was a Fascist, he said, under the orders of Nester Cates, who had laid a trap for the Men of Albacete, and when she guffawed, he flew into a rage. His manners dissolved into red foam. He said they had sent an agent to Budapest, and this agent had determined that Stuart Glemnik's brother was involved in the plot as well; soon, he would be in custody, and all of the conspirators would face a firing squad. Denunciation might save her life, Olestru hissed.

But he didn't understand. Uta had settled her earthly affairs. In Marburg, she had taken leave of her family. She had kissed her mother goodbye and buried her father. In East Berlin, she had said farewell to the political convictions of her youth, accepted their defeat, and tried to help in their final destruction. In her apartment, she had tried to subtract from her own flesh what had been taken from others; from Douglas, from Grams, from the dog at the checkpoint. But God had stopped her. Life was no longer hers for the taking. Though she was ready and even eager to die, Uta had left the possibility of suicide behind. She had come to Bucharest to be sacrificed.

Olestru had threatened to have her torn to pieces by German shepherds. He had told her to stand against a wall. Uta had risen and awaited her executioners. It had been a bluff, of course.

A dwarf entered the cell and assaulted her with a jet of water. Shit flew across the stone, ran down the gaping hole at the back of the space.

Goodness is born in a woman when she dies to the world. That's what she had been taught. And she had died in that bathtub in West Berlin. At long last, she was good. She was prepared.

For what?

For God's revolution. It had not abandoned her, after all. It had been searching. She heard its fingers scratching at her coffin lid, digging down into this prison. Through the walls of the cell, she heard its great nails bending back steel and concrete. She was not deceived this time, and she was not guilty.

Her father had murdered children and died in peace. So be it. That was finished. It was done. She could do no more about it. What had Meister Eckhardt said? If a man gives you a hundred marks and you lose forty of it, do you think of the lost forty or do you make use of the sixty?

The sixty, she replied.

Richtig!

The three-fingered jailer brought a plate of food, which she did not touch. It would only make her sick. And what did food matter now? In her heart, she had loved death and sin and brutality. In her heart, she had loved murder, but not anymore. That too was finished. It was past. The pure eye sees color, Meister Eckhardt had said. Life and death were shades in the spectrum.

She felt a power tumescent within her. She was aglow with the revolution, not the fake one of Herr Mundung, all words and empty gestures, but the real one, the thing beyond description. It was trying to be born inside of her, just as it was digging above. Outside and inside were the same. She could hear panic. Men were running. They were screaming. Fear was in the air, the delicious fear of bullies and cowards.

At last, someone came for her. She was blindfolded, pried like a snail out of her shell. Still she heard the revolution. Its fingers had broken the skin of the earth.

She began to smile. It was coming. She had the most tremendous urge to laugh. She was riding her bike without brakes, sailing past the sun-dappled roofs of Marburg, where she had grown up happy. They brought her to a room. She could smell others. They removed her blindfold, and she saw a tableau of her past before her. She might have been in the marketplace of her dream. There sat the faithless Herr Mundung, fat and lost to the last. There was the fiend Olestru, and the innocent Douglas, who signaled something in the air. Behind him were two women she didn't know, and she pitied them, because they looked scared and shocked and sad.

She smiled at them all. Olestru put out a cigarette and yelled. He wanted her to speak.

"Is this man part of your team?"

He pointed at Douglas. She ignored him and listened to the approach of God. He was just down the corridor now, just a bit down the way, hurling Himself in their direction.

Suddenly, a man rushed in. He went to Olestru and whispered something. Olestru jumped up. With her pure eyes, she saw color—the sheen of rose across the gray of the ceiling, the strain of gold in the black of the gun, the deep blue sea in the pink of her flesh. God was descending, descending, yes, just a few hundred meters away.

Olestru called out in Romanian to the guards. Men took her by her arms and carried her through the doorway. Douglas and the others were taken too. They were herded into a long, dark corridor. Behind her, she heard Olestru speak in German to Mundung. "Let's get them to the alcove in the west corridor, I'll get what I need from her and have them shot. It's all we have time for. This place is no longer safe. *Einverstanden?*"

Men careened past them. There were screams, rattles of gunfire, wild lights. They came to the alcove, and the four of them—she, Douglas, and the two women—were placed with their backs to the wall. She was the closest to the darkness on their right, but she wasn't scared at all. The darkness felt good and alive. She wished to dive into it.

"Now, Fascist," Olestru said, taking an automatic rifle away from one of his guards, "answer me. Do you know this man as a counterrevolutionary assassin?"

Douglas was beside her.

"They killed Stuart," he whispered, his voice broken.

Uta refused to cry. The thought of his death filled her with sadness, but also joy. He had suffered, and now his suffering had ended. He had found his way home. These men could no longer touch him.

"Very well then." Olestru ordered the remaining guard to stand beside him. Mundung and two other old men drew pistols from their belts. All five leveled their weapons. Uta stared into Olestru's eyes and saw the end of things there; hers as well as his.

"I pronounce you traitors to the revolution"—Olestru checked the chamber of his pistol—"and sentence you to death. Turn around, all of you, and face the wall."

No, she thought. There was a sound down the corridor, a stampede of human beings. Olestru hesitated, glanced to his left. She turned to the right, to the darkness, thrust out her arms, and the darkness ripped away, as if it had been a curtain. The sky overhead became the clearest, finest northern German blue. Her hair became long and unfurled in the wind. She was about to enter the church. With a wave of her hand, she called forth all the buried energy within her, all those brightnesses dwelling like insurrection within her blood. She reached out for revolution. She summoned Him forth, and with an explosion of fire, a din of metal, a last wild pealing of bells, in the unexpected shape of Nester Cates, He arrived.

CHAPTER THIRTY-ONE

1.

NESTER SAW A PINK DOT with gray hair on the first-floor balcony of the Central Committee Building. A voice roared across the Square of the Republic. It was the dictator, and he had organized a rally on his own behalf.

The day was gray and cold. Romanian flags, red, yellow, and blue pierced by hammer and sickle, wiggled in a mild wind. A host of people had gathered, tens of thousands of them. They thronged the square. Nester could barely move.

Which were Securitate? That one with the mole? The avuncular, smiling priest? The pregnant Gyspsy in front of him?

Some of them probably thought Nester looked suspicious, a tall black man in bifocals, his mouth hidden by a scarf, his skull capped with red wool. They would imagine him an Arab mercenary, one of those killers allegedly hidden by Ceausescu in deep Carpathian vales. He must watch himself. He must not attract attention.

Placards had been handed to factory workers, the usual procedure at such rallies. The placards praised the party, the leader, the leader's wife, and were toted by people with reddened eyes, men and women who lived in abject fear, went hungry, lived without electricity or heat, and were confronted every day with some new vicissitude of arrant power—relocation, dislocation, prison.

Nester's guide, Ion Voicu, a short, heavy man with an eye patch, bore a placard too. Voicu was chief among Nester's Romanian Green Men, a biologist disgraced by his involvement in a religious cult centered on an extraterrestrial creature named Strigoi. He spoke excellent English and had surprising connections for someone of his metaphysical leanings. The two men had met in 1985 at an international science fair in Frankfurt and become covert pen pals.

Voicu had insisted on coming to the rally. As strange as he might seem to the majority of his fellow citizens, on this day he was one of them. On television, he had learned about Berlin, Prague, and Sofia. He knew the Wall had fallen. He knew democracy had returned to Czechoslovakia and freedom of the press to Bulgaria. That's why he'd come. That's why they'd all come.

Nester could see it in their eyes. They knew what had happened within their own borders too. They knew about Timisoara. And yet there was Ceausescu on his balcony, on the same spot where, a mere month ago, he had been cheered and applauded by a mass of terrorized mannequins. He had invited all these people who hated his guts to the very center of the city.

They screamed insults at him. Forced chants of solidarity drowned in outrage.

"What are they saying?" Nester took his friend by the arm.

"They have just called him a liar and a murderer," Voicu replied, a thick black mustache trembling around his lips, one dark brown eye welling forward from a soft hollow. The other eye had been lost in a laboratory fire.

"He's trying to tell us that irredentists were responsible for Timisoara."

Ceausescu's voice ceased. Even from this distance, five hundred feet from the balcony, the dictator's shock at the crowd's reaction could be registered. This was being filmed live for television; it would be witnessed by millions of Romanians. He had to be aware of the significance of his sudden silence, of what must be interpreted by all those distant eyes. He backed away from the balcony edge.

Nester tried to count the Romanians visible from his vantage point. A hundred thousand workers from all over the city had supposedly been transported to this place, the Square of the Republic, to hear "the genius of the Carpathians" speak. They had been arriving by bus for hours. Others had come of their own volition, streaming in from offices, homes, factories, and libraries. Up close, invisible to the eye of the camera, which would no doubt show them as a colorful, enthusiastic mass, these people conveyed rage, or an emotion preceding rage, something deeper, less predictable. That emotion, whatever it was, had brought them to this place and would not let go. A number of grease-spattered men close to Nester, mechanics by the look of them, clutched banners declaring *"Ura Partidul."* "Long Live the Party." Beneath these words, the men glowered. They appeared to be losing their tempers, as if the banners insulted them with every flap of the wind.

After a while, Ceausescu edged back up to the balcony and tried to speak again. His words had lost a measure of stridency. He went on for a few minutes before booes rose from the crowd.

"He's offering wage increases now," Voicu explained to Nester as a new round of catcalls and whistles burst around them. "It's a bribe, you see. It means he's losing his nerve, and the only thing he can think to do is buy us off."

In answer, one of the mechanics lowered his placard to the ground, placed the tip of a brown work boot on the *P* in *"Partidul,"* and ripped the word in two.

2.

I T TOOK AN HOUR to get clear of the square. Once they had, they ran, Voicu taking the lead. Behind them, shots rang out. Wind sent a whiff of tear gas through the begloomed streets. Students were setting up barricades.

After a few blocks, they slipped inside a university building. It turned out to be the biology faculty.

Voicu made a phone call. Soon, they were met by one of his people. Word had come. Ceausescu was meeting with Polexco, his politburo. The scene at the square had enraged him. He wanted an all-out assault. Already, troops were moving. Armored cars had been deployed. By nightfall, Securitate and military units would occupy the center of the city. There would be a fight.

Their informant had also heard, but could not confirm, that the defense minister had refused to move against civilians, that Ceausescu and he were at odds. Voicu didn't buy it.

"That could be a trick, to fool us all into thinking they won't use force."

There was more. Voicu's people had thought it better to get Waltraud and Styles out of the Intercontinental. For the moment, the hotel was safe, but who knew what might occur in the next few hours. The two were safe in a dormitory not far away. As before, Styles was under guard. Nester asked the messenger if he had actually seen them, and he said he had. For the moment, Nester told himself, he must be satisfied with that. Against his own instincts, he had trusted Waltraud alone with Styles. He had no choice.

"We must alter our strategy," Voicu declared.

Earlier that morning, he had set up a simple business deal. His connections within the Interior Ministry, who, as always, were short of cash, had agreed to hand over the Glemnik brothers in exchange for hard currency. As it turned out, the head of the Interior Ministry didn't even know the brothers were in his possession. When it came time to do the deal, in a field on the road to Ploesti, several thousand dollars would change hands, the Glemniks would go free, and the affair would quietly end. It had stood a reasonable chance of success.

But events at the rally had changed things. No one at the Interior Ministry could be trusted, not even for money. Tomorrow, for all they knew, Anton Olestru might be the new interior minister.

"Of course, this may work in our favor." Voicu bummed a cigarette off an attractive young woman who had been listening to them, someone who could have been Voicu's lover, could have been his daughter, could have been a member of the Strigoi cult. Nester didn't know, and Voicu didn't care to explain. "If the army sides with the protestors, then some of the Securitate will break away too. It stands to reason. If that happens, we may be able to use the chaos to break your people out. We may not have to pay a dime."

A flock of ragged kids skittered through the door of the faculty and up a flight of stairs. Bullets kicked after them. Window glass shattered. Everyone ducked. Voicu put his arm around the young woman. He whispered something to her, and she spidered off on all fours.

Voicu was right. They had no choice but to move with the events. Nester peered into the street. Waltraud would be happy, at least. It was her money they would have had to pay, a few thousand dollars borrowed from her bar's vault. A thunder of motors could be heard. Nester smelled fuel reek. Down the stairs, grinning like monkeys, crept the boys. He marveled at them. As they came running, he'd seen the same grins on their faces as if they were playing at kick the can. But then, insurrections were intoxicating, else why would people throw themselves headlong into them? It was the pulse at the temple, the reek of cordite, the sound of one's own war cry. Isn't that what he had always read between the lines of Malcolm's sentences, within the rhythms of Schiller's prose, that very excitement? Hadn't Du Bois traveled in these regions with some hope of insurrection in his heart? Nester had never felt so close to those guiding spirits, so in touch with their minds, which seemed to hover in the smoke of battle.

Voicu handed out the pieces of chocolate Nester had given to him earlier. Close by, more bullets cracked. When it was quiet again, they ventured onto Magheru Boulevard. Shadows were deepening. In Berlin, brown coal flavored the air. Here, the taste was oil, a suggestion of dilapidated refineries to the north. Nester wished he could see Waltraud, make sure she was safe, ask her one more time for the truth. He hoped he hadn't made a terrible mistake entrusting her with so much. If he had, it was too late. The final mistake was accomplished.

Swelling numbers of young people, university students mostly, loitered at the intersection known as kilometer zero, the end of the line for all roads leading from the periphery of Romania to its center. The closer one came to Bucharest, the smaller the number of digits, until one arrived here, at the navel of things, a nondescript traffic circle shaped in the form of a zero, bound by chunks of nineteenth-century architecture on one side, overshadowed by the massive headstone of the Intercontinental Hotel, Europe's largest, ugliest spook haunt, on the other.

The spot didn't provide much cover, although, if one could get to them, subway entrances on all four sides of the intersection might do as shelters. Looking up, Nester could imagine at least a dozen ideal nests for snipers. If the Intercontinental fell into the wrong hands, no one on kilometer zero would be safe.

Near at hand, a corpse twisted against a curb. It had been a man. Blood slashed down the asphalt. The legs had burned. He thought momentarily of the charred programmer from Bad Aiblingen, a Cassandra corpse if ever there was one. Nester wondered aloud who had killed the man in the street. Voicu shrugged. He didn't know, didn't want to know. Wouldn't be the last, his squinting eyes said. Wasn't the first.

The young woman returned. Voicu pumped her for information. Nester searched the facade of the Intercontinental, a series of balconies rising to the heavens. Supposedly, the thirteenth floor belonged to the Securitate. He counted up to thirteen but saw nothing, not even a light. The hotel was grim. Its facade yawned inward, so that its sides, capped on every floor with reinforced concrete, resembled the jaws of a mouth opening wide for a bite. In front of the building was a strange monument, a kind of stylized medieval axe. It was the least compelling version of a luxury hotel Nester had ever seen, devouring all hope of comfort.

As the sun faded, a red glow settled upon the balconies.

"We'll keep moving," Voicu told him.

3.

IT SEEMED IMPOSSIBLE to Nester that they had only arrived in Bucharest on the previous day. He remembered gazing at the city in those first few minutes and feeling somber, as if in the presence of something great and deceased. He had never expected to see Bucharest in person. As an army brat and then an American soldier, this place had been as inaccessible to him as Pluto. It had been an abstraction, a relatively insignificant piece of the geopolitical puzzle with some picaresque nineteenth-century history thrown in for fun. It had been aerial photographs, minority problems, armament treaties, Ceausescu at Disneyland.

Now that he was here, he felt like Neil Armstrong walking on the moon. His former notions about the place seemed as distant as childhood.

The Dacia had driven down eerily wide avenues, past outsized triumphal arches and empty Orthodox churches, around unfinished masses of construction and orphaned blocks of scaffolding. At first, it had all seemed a field of bones, an ossuary where an ancient country had been buried. Soldiers like ghosts guarded every square inch of it, as if positioned at the gates of a gauche hell, and yet their presence had a superfluous quality. Bucharest seemed dead beyond need of restraint. But as he looked more closely, he saw pieces of life: an old Orthodox woman crossing herself beneath the arch of an exquisite little church; elements of style through the doorway of a woman's hair salon—a *coafor,* as the Romanian had it, a nice, lively, Latinate word; a tough sense of romance in the stride of a young man in black market blue jeans. Beneath the stone, what seemed dead was alive, and that became more apparent with every passing hour.

At dark, they entered an apartment a few blocks from the traffic circle and found Waltraud drinking tea with Styles.

"Maus!" She gave him a hug.

Nester glanced over at Styles, who scowled, but remained silent. He was escorted into another room by Voicu's men. Waltraud blinked at Nester. He didn't have much to say to her, and she was hurt by his coldness, but he couldn't help it. He had not yet made up his mind about her.

Voicu wanted them to stay put awhile. He'd be back soon, he promised, after he figured out what was going on. Nester didn't like the idea. He wanted Voicu close by, but the man would not be persuaded. He posted another guard on Styles and reassured Nester. Should anything happen, should the government undertake massive reprisals, his people would get Nester and Waltraud out of the country or die trying. In addition to being a religious sect with a deep, apolitical faith, they were now a militia and had just acquired an armored car.

With that bit of information, Voicu left. Moldavian choirs sang on television. Waltraud switched channels in disgust. Nester fell asleep.

4.

H E WOKE ON THE FLOOR beside the couch and didn't know how he'd gotten there. Waltraud's head came over the edge of the couch. "What the hell was that?"

He shook his head. Voicu burst into the room, trailed by men with guns. "Wake up!" he cried. "We're going! Now!"

Someone ran into the other room to fetch Styles. Mortars had struck the building.

Nester threw on his coat, checked the pistol at his waistband. Soon they were all gathered in the hallway.

"He's coming with us," Voicu explained, indicating Styles. "I don't want him creating any mischief at my back."

His men looked exhausted, as if they'd been running and fighting for hours. Nester didn't want Styles along, but there was no arguing with them.

Voicu laid out the situation. Sometime in the night, Securitate units had joined the revolt. No one knew how many. Other units had stayed loyal to the government. Snipers were everywhere. They would have to keep their heads down. That was one.

Two, the Intercontinental had fallen into the hands of the students. So had most of the area around the university. For the moment, they had a secure field for their operation, and they must take advantage of it, because who could say how long security would last?

Three, the loyalties of the military were still an open question. Individual soldiers, even whole units, had begun to defect to the uprising, but if the rest of the army sided with Ceausescu, the rebels would be outnumbered hundreds to one.

"There is a civil war going on," Voicu concluded, "and we must use it."

"Now?"

"Now or never," Voicu replied.

They headed for kilometer zero.

5.

T HE FIRST THING Nester saw there was a wheelbarrow heavy with severed heads. As he moved closer, the heads became spoiled pumpkins. A vendor lifted a mealy one with a fat man's jowls and called out a price.

"Special Romanian pumpkins." Voicu thumped one on his way past. "At midnight, they turn into democracy."

Beyond the gourds were tanks. Candles flickered on their lids. Students climbed onto them and offered sandwiches to the commanders, many of whom had tied white ribbons around their arms. Here and there, carnations bloomed from the ends of Kalashnikovs.

The pumpkin vendor lofted a specimen to a tank officer, who passed it back like a basketball. The thing split apart in the vendor's hands. They made their way around the vehicle.

Gypsy kids scuttled underfoot. They had become a kind of unofficial scout network, pausing now and then to ask for baksheesh and food before scampering off down dark alleys to count the dead, case the streets, sniff the wind. They returned with grain and information. A few bread shops in the vicinity of the university had opened their doors and were handing out their wares to the insurgents.

"We wait here for our guide." Voicu snatched a loaf from a passing kid. "When he comes, we'll go underground."

He pointed at an entrance to the subway.

"Where the hell can he be?" Voicu fumed.

Down one alley, Nester saw flames lick out of a shop, heard their faint crackle. How could anyone tell an enemy from a friend in this city? The soldiers all wore the same uniforms. A few identified their loyalty to the new cause by wearing white ribbons, but anyone could do that. The Securitate could be anybody. They could pretend this and be that. Nothing was fixed. Nothing stood still.

Tracer bullets skizzed red and wild out of the darkness, and Nester crouched. A few yards away, a young man lit three candles on the sidewalk. There were more corpses, and he was mourning. Voicu offered bread.

They heard all kinds of rumors. The Ceausescu government had fallen, they heard. Then a bomb went off from the direction of the subway, and the idea seemed ludicrous. The Securitate had taken back the Interconti-nental and were only waiting for an order to massacre the crowds below, which expanded minute by minute. The students had taken over the televi-sion station. The city of Cluj had burned to the ground. Ceausescu had appealed to the Iranian government for a small army of mujaheddin.

"This boy wants to be blessed by a priest," Voicu said, returning with the mourner in tow. "Then he wants to come with us. Snipers killed his sister."

They walked a couple of blocks down the boulevard, staying in the shadows as much as possible, and came to a small white church with five arches. A fence surrounded it, but the padlock had been broken, and people were streaming inside.

"This church was burned by the Turks," Voicu told them. "It's all black inside. I'm an old atheist, so I'm going to wait outside and smoke a cigarette."

The mourner went inside, and out of curiosity, Nester followed. The entrance smoked with fire from votive candles, which cast the only light. Back in the recesses, gold glinted. Saints' eyes beheld him. It was mostly a dark place. He could not see the priest. People murmured softly and crossed themselves. A few knelt. This church had been closed for a decade, Voicu had told him, and now it was open. Nester couldn't say why, but it scared him, the way the story of Lazarus in the Bible had always scared him. He said an uneasy Lord's Prayer and backed out, bumping into a one-legged beggar on his way in.

Finally, their guide came. He had been below, in the tunnels, and he had seen Americans in custody. He didn't know if they were the ones, but he thought maybe so. Anyway, there was no time to waste. They had been carried to some makeshift tribunal where summary executions were expected. All night, Securitate units had been battling each other in the neighborhood of the tribunal, but for the moment, the fighting had moved elsewhere.

Voicu pressed down his mustache and buttoned his jacket up to his throat. He adjusted the patch on his eye and gave Nester a nod.

Waltraud drew Nester aside. She asked to see his gun. He handed it over, and she did a quick inspection.

Her Polish husband had been a gun dealer. For fun, on weekends, they had gone to Tegel Forest and blown away beer cans. She could handle herself with a gun. "No matter what else happens, *Schatz*," she whispered into his ear, "we get out alive. Even if it means leaving those two Glemniks. *Einverstanden?*"

He decided he would trust her. It was the only way to go on, and if she betrayed him this time, he would be dead and nothing would matter anyway. She kissed him. They were ready.

6.

EVERYTHING HAPPENED FAST. One minute they were in the subway, headed through a smoke haze for the train platforms, then they were leaping over a door that still smoldered from explosion, rushing down a hall that branched off from the trains into darkness. An old intelligence question had been answered. The rumored Securitate tunnels did, it appeared, connect to the subway system. To his right and left, Nester perceived stone walls.

"We must make two kilometers in twenty minutes," Voicu called over his shoulder.

One hall gave way to another. They leapt down steps, took a right, hung a left. Upon the initial descent, Nester had counted ten people in their party, men and women. He did not know who they were, did not know their names or what functions they served. He was not sure Voicu knew. One way or another, they had entered the tunnels as a group of ten. Now, behind him in the dark, Nester heard what sounded like a much greater number. It might have been an echo. It might have been more distant groups running in other directions. But as they hurried, he was almost certain that their own number had multiplied, that a body of some size coalesced around him.

All of a sudden, he bumped into someone who had stopped. It was Voicu.

"Look at this," he mumbled.

Before them lay a ghastly trash heap. A man in brown uniform had been shattered by a tide of machine gun fire. His remains had tumbled back on a bier of glass shards and what smelled like dried fish. Voicu picked up a piece of the stuff and bit into it.

"My God." He handed it to Nester. "It's dried abalone. Three hundred dollars a pound. This must have been a private stash."

Nester tossed the thing away.

"Thousands of dollars' worth here."

Voicu crouched. The pieces resembled blackened ears. The Romanian stuffed his pockets. Behind Nester, Waltraud pushed. "Let's keep moving. I don't like it here. There's something coming up behind us."

They left the abalone and ran again. It seemed to Nester they must have come at least a few kilometers when they hit a wide intersection of corridors. As soon as they crossed the gap, an invisible party opened fire from their left. He threw himself into the nearest recess. Voicu took him by the shoulder.

"Are you hit?"

"Where's Waltraud?"

"Are you *hit?!*"

"No!"

Waltraud called from the other side of the intersection. "Have you got Styles?"

So she had lost him. More shots rang out.

"We must go on," hissed Voicu. "There's no more time."

Nester refused; after all this, he would not lose Waltraud, particularly not with Styles on the loose. Voicu grew incensed. Someone up ahead handed back an automatic pistol. Voicu counted three, jolted around the corner into the intersection, and slammed three bullets into the darkness.

"Come on then!"

Waltraud and one other crossed.

"I was next to him with my gun in his ribs," she panted. "Then I lost him."

They hurtled off again. Behind them, a grenade ruptured. He felt the heat of it on the backs of his legs. Shrapnel thunked into the walls. They ran on.

He closed his eyes and jogged with a deep rhythm. When he opened them again, they were surrounded by strangers, all moving at the same tempo, all headed in their direction. The corridor had widened, so three could move abreast.

"Who are they?" he called ahead to Voicu.

"Who knows? They haven't killed us yet, so they must be on our side!"

They passed scenes of carnage. In one office, a secretary's head had been removed and impaled on a decapitated lamp. In another, a blood-drenched hunting knife had been balanced on the mouth of a toilet seat. The hallways rang with the clamor of boots, the thud and crack of gunfire, the heaving of human breath. Voicu and the guide wrenched to a stop at an intersection. An eerie silence descended. Then, as if out of a hole in the earth, they heard a voice, speaking in an oddly worried tone of a death sentence.

"That's Olestru!" one of the guides exclaimed.

Nester leapt forward, Voicu and Waltraud one step behind him, followed by at least twenty men armed with automatic weapons. These men knew nothing of the Glemniks. They were on a mission to waste enemies and didn't much care who the enemy was. They would never stop to sort out bodies.

Nester had to arrive first, and he did. Suddenly, in the darkness, he came face-to-face with Uta Silk, her hands uplifted, her mouth opened in laughter. Douglas stood beyond her, guns turned on him.

"Drop your weapons," Nester had a chance to say.

Voicu hurtled into him.

"In the name of the people of Romania—!" the cultist cried.

Nester threw himself at Douglas. For an instant, he saw Uta Silk reaching out to him.

"Get down!" he called.

She laughed. He lost sight of her.

CHAPTER THIRTY-TWO

BODIES FLEW. Douglas didn't see the man who first opened up. He didn't see a gun. He watched Uta's eyes grow wide, her left hand fly up. She reeled back. He heard himself call her name.

He fell. The four men before him blew back, as if in a gust. Olestru shrieked and fired at the ceiling, knocking out all but a single lightbulb. Blood spat out of him. He hit the ground. For an instant, Nester was there, landing on Douglas's forearms. An acknowledgment passed between them, a flicker of human connection, then he sprang away, searching, perhaps, for Stuart.

The last lightbulb flickered out. Suddenly, Douglas could see nothing. From behind came the thud of rifles, the clatter of ejected shells. Clash-crash, he heard, between the walls of the corridor—a slamming together of trash can lids. Fire flashed. He closed his eyes, reached out for Jodie, who clutched back, telling him all he needed to know. She was alive.

He had a sensation of absurd physical chaos, then opened his eyes. The bullets could not be seen, except, by association, when they blasted matter; for all intents and purposes, they didn't exist. All he perceived was disturbed air, and within the air, a theoretical demise, and though he wanted to stay out of its way, he felt a certain assurance. Time and again, death had proven inept at finding him.

Boots stamped away in the darkness. Suddenly, the barrage stopped. A flashlight switched on. Douglas found himself staring across the corridor at Mundung and his old companion, the desert soldier who had never once opened his mouth. It was a horrific sight. Evidently, Mundung had found the flashlight in the fingers of a dead man and switched it on before he pried it loose. Now he tried to break the fingers, which held tight to their last possession, and this made the light dance around. Mundung mumbled curses while his colleague tried to reload.

Both men had been shot. Both bled. Both looked gray in the flashlight beams, as if cut from dirty ice.

"Cates!" the East German cried. "Where is the *Schwein* Cates?"

The fat man finally obtained the flashlight, but his weapon seemed to have jammed. He pounded its grip with the palm of his hand. The Dalmatian was silent as he glanced around. The cross-bearer had been shot; his cross could be seen gleaming nearby. Douglas wanted to crawl away from the Albacete men, but he realized that Jodie and he were partially obscured from their sight by corpses. If he moved, he might draw attention to himself, and Jodie would be exposed.

Nester had vanished. Arms tightened around his waist. He looked down. Jodie was there. He put a finger over his mouth. They must be quiet until Mundung and his companion either expired or departed.

The lull continued, though Douglas heard breathing and the sound of reloading. Then two shots were fired—he could smell the gunpowder. The shots made an echo. He was sure they had not been fired at him. Someone groaned. Far away, a voice called his name. He looked up. There was Styles, approaching to the right across a heap of shells, heads, guns, and fingers. His mouth dripped, his eyes rolled in his head, but he managed to stumble forward, checking each body to see if it might be an adversary. Evidently, it was he who had fired the two shots, and now he did it again, into a prostrate body. Soon, the lunatic would reach Douglas. He lurched through a curl of his own smoke.

A movement caught Douglas's eye. It was Mundung again, a few yards from Styles, crawling away from him. "Please don't kill me." The fat man's body slid. "My mother was a Jew."

Styles stopped. He lifted the pistol and fired a bullet into Mundung, who did not speak again. A white haze obscured Douglas's vision, and then he was staring right into the eyes of the diplomat, who thrust another round into the butt of his pistol.

"You," he said. "Klek."

"No."

"You've hacked me away, piece by piece. My face, my work, my sanity. Hack, chop. Look at me, Jesus. Would you ever think I graduated summa cum laude from Princeton. Would you? Well, I didn't."

From the far left, startling Douglas, Nester spoke.

"Put the gun down, Styles."

Douglas peered into the darkness, but could not see him.

"That you, Cates? You Teutonic black bastard?"

"Don't move, Styles. Not another step."

Across the corridor, where Mundung lay, a man stood. Douglas didn't see him, but sensed his presence, as he might sense a fish beneath the surface of a pool. This was the man from the desert. The others were dead. Douglas wondered how he had come here, if he had known Stuart, if he was indeed a terrorist or some bureaucrat, like Mundung, or just a man, like Douglas, caught in a spoke. Styles lowered the pistol toward Douglas, but turned a moment to see who was behind him. And in that instant, the man fired, and Douglas saw the top half of Styles's face go blurry. A single white eye went sailing, a red-rimmed coin, hot as a spark. Styles collapsed. The assassin ducked out of the flashlight beam, and Douglas could hear him slinking away. A silence fell.

Now Jodie was untangling from him.

"Where's Pansy?"

"Here."

The reporter was hiding a few feet away behind her own pile of dead. Douglas sat up. Nester arrived, kneeling before him. Douglas looked around.

"Uta?"

Nester pointed to the far corner of the alcove where they had been standing. She had crumpled in the angle. At least three bullets had passed through her body. Douglas took her hand, checked the pulse. She was alive. He took off his shirt and stuffed it into her wounded abdomen. Nester gave him a hand.

"Where's your brother?"

"Dead."

Nester drooped.

"It's the Gleaming luck. He was damned from birth. So were we all."

Douglas looked down at Uta's face. He remembered the night they had stumbled across that little fire in Kreuzberg, when she had struck him as the most exciting woman on earth. It seemed impossibly long ago, that fire, a detail from the distant past, but in his memory it had a vivid purity, as if the Uta Silk burnished by its gleams were the real one, and the dying woman at his fingertips an impostor. She was not yet twenty-three years old, not yet out of university. Her father had lived to be an old man, and she was shattered. A madness lurked in things, a brain as fevered and sorry as the one inside Douglas's brother.

Her eyes were wide open, but focused on some internal astonishment. Douglas reached out and cupped her cheeks in his hands.

"Uta?"

Her eyes flickered in his direction.

"You can hear me?"

She didn't nod, but Douglas saw she had registered the question.

"I'm sitting here thinking about that fire in Kreuzberg. You remember the one?"

She managed a twist of lips. Blood seeped through her teeth and down her chin.

"The whole building would have burned down if we hadn't called the fire department."

He squeezed her hand and thought of something his brother had once told him, a thing he had imagined so many times that it seemed to him he had witnessed it himself. In his mind, he saw the two of them, Uta and Stuart, approaching each other in the crowded gym of a West Berlin community college. Around them spun Germans in a Texas two-step. In their ears played a song—what had it been? "If I Ever Fall in Love with a Honky-tonk Girl." Douglas had never heard it, but he was sure it must have fiddles and a pedal steel guitar, like all of those old songs. Uta made the first move. That's what Stuart had said. She put out her hands. He took them and, slowly at first, they started to dance, mimicking the steps, turning and turning, mixing in now with the others, smiling at each other in embarrassment and gratitude. His brother said they had danced poorly, but in Douglas's mind, they moved in perfect two-four time, turning and turning, forever.

"It's going to be all right," he said.

She smiled then. Her eyes shut. And, like that, she died.

HOME AT LAST

CHAPTER THIRTY-THREE

1.

ON CHRISTMAS DAY, 1989, the Romanians executed Nicolae and Elena Ceausescu. It was great television. Jodie picked up the telephone and called Dick Chubbs. She was staying at a ski resort called Poiana Brasov, a place once frequented by the dictator, and thus one of the few locations in the country with decent international phone connections.

"Blum? Where the hell have you been?"

It was early Tuesday morning in New York.

"In prison. Dodging bullets. I hear we invaded Panama."

Chubbs thought about this for a moment. "You okay?"

"Yep. Want a story?"

Chubbs was steamed, but he listened. She had three ideas for him. First, she would write a longish piece on the Romanian revolution and how it cast a shadow across what had gone before in East Germany and Czechoslovakia. The revolutions had begun peacefully in East Berlin, turned a little more violent in Prague, then burst into open bloodshed in Bucharest. The latter should not be used as an example in Yugoslavia, and so on. He jumped on it, told her to keep it to two hundred lines. They had great pictures. She already had plenty of good material, including an interview with Petre Roman, a leader of the provisional government.

"Now you're makin' me happy, kid."

She suggested a short sidebar on what it was like to be a prisoner of the Securitate.

"Have you seen the *Times* piece yet? One of their people wrote about that already."

Jodie suppressed her indignation. Finally, and she brought this up with a lump in her throat, she had something else, a wild sort of story that involved American and East German spies, the terrorist Jiri Klek, a bug exterminator, and a West German student revolutionary. She didn't know everything yet, but enough to write a book, if she wanted to, and *Probe* could have first crack.

Chubbs stopped her.

"You sure it was Klek, by the way?"

"Why?"

"Well, apparently, he's dead. Shot in southern Lebanon. Israelis got him a few years ago. Turns out his real name was Yusuf Khan. Seems he was a Palestinian. All that stuff about the war and the partisans, complete bullshit. Made up. A cover. Now *that's* a story."

She objected, but he wasn't interested.

"Let's stick to the story we got. The story of the revolution. Maybe you can write a book about this other stuff. Doesn't sound quite enough for *Probe,* at this point. You know what I mean, kid? For all we know, it's the usual old hugger-mugger in the back alleys of Berlin. Not anything too spectacular. Not in light of recent events. Right?"

"Right."

"Just give me revolution for now."

She would.

"Just give us the news analysis, and we'll get that National Magazine Award for you yet."

Jodie had one last question for him. Pansy Buckner had written Jodie's cover story while she was out cold, so Jodie was now in the awkward position of owing her career to the woman. Fine. But she had to know the truth. Swallowing her pride, she asked: "What did you *really* think of that Eastern European piece?"

"Nice. Not as good as the Berlin stuff, but perfectly nice. This ain't the time to rest on your laurels."

Jodie hung up. She was disquieted. The image of the dead Ceausescu refused to leave her television screen, even when she turned it off.

2.

PANSY KNOCKED ON THE DOOR. She had set up the temporary bureau for Ham Stamps, then requested leave to go home. Jodie offered a mineral water and a plate of soda crackers. Pansy accepted. She sat. The dictator's dead face stared from the television screen.

For the first time, Pansy actually looked beat. Arriving at the Hotel Intercontinental to discover there was no bureau, Stamps had exploded. After getting out of the Securitate tunnels, Pansy had been escorted by Voicu to the Intercontinental, where her boss had chewed her out, accusing her of costing the *Times* a big story and lots of money. When she told him what had happened, he changed his mind, apologized profusely, and saw to it that her account of her beating and imprisonment made it onto the editorial page of the *Times*—a coup. Certain details had been left out, she reassured Jodie. Meanwhile, one of their reporters had been shot near Timisoara. For seventy-two hours, everything was chaos; then Pansy bowed out.

Jodie and she had shared a car up to Poiana Brasov. The next morning, Pansy would drive on to Hungary. She didn't trust air transportation. During the worst of the fighting, one plane had been shot down on the runway of Otopeni airport, and she wasn't about to take her chances.

Jodie told Pansy that she was on deadline. There wasn't much time to talk.

"So you're staying?"

Jodie lowered her hands from the console of a laptop borrowed from the Associated Press. She nodded.

"Can I give you some advice, friend to friend?"

Jodie shrugged. Why not?

"This story is hot now, but it won't stay that way. If you can, get the Middle East or the China bureau. Those are perennials. And don't stay abroad too long. It's so easy to get stuck in a rut."

Jodie sighed and rubbed her forehead. A somberness had been growing all evening, and it overwhelmed her in that moment. "You know, Pansy, I'm not sure, but I have a feeling this has all gone right to my heart. Do you know what I mean? It's like it's not really *news* anymore, all this. It's more than news. If I just thought it was news, I'm not sure I would even be able to write about it. I might just crawl into my bed and go to sleep."

Pansy shook her head. "Well, it's news to me, and old news at that. Panama is the hot thing now. Ham keeps talking about how this is a sea change in American foreign policy, and he may well be right."

She pulled auburn bangs back from her eyes, revealing for a moment the gun butt bruise on her forehead. "I expect we'll run into each other in some exotic capital one day."

Jodie nodded, staring down at her console keys. "Could be."

"And if that happens, then maybe you'll call me Esperanza, because that's what my friends use. Not Pansy. Not Panse. I hate those names. I'm Esperanza."

"Esperanza."

Jodie extended a hand. "See you in one of those exotic capitals."

3.

THAT NIGHT, she filed. She slept for a day, then left Poiana Brasov by car. But for the driver, she was alone. Snow was falling. A blizzard had sprung upon Romania on December 26. The entire country had vanished under ice. Nester had arranged for a driver to take her to the Hungarian border. Another car would be waiting on the other side.

The trip passed without event. She wondered briefly if a peasant woman in Transylvania was wearing her rose-red shoes. She hoped so. They had cost enough.

She wished Douglas had come. He had stayed in Bucharest to make sure Uta and Stuart did not end up in unmarked graves, or so he said. Jodie had offered to stay, but he didn't want that. He wanted to be by himself. She resented this desire, but understood.

Three days after Christmas, Jodie reached Margaret Island. Photos of the dead Ceausescus had gone around the world. They were everywhere. She went for long walks along the Danube, watched the news, read newspapers. Her story came out in the United States, and radio stations wanted to speak with her about her analysis.

Morning sickness began. Sooner or later, she would have to go to a doctor and get a medical confirmation, but that would keep till she returned to Berlin. She waited a couple of days, but Douglas never came. In the meantime, she made small talk with other correspondents who had covered Eastern Europe over the last few weeks. To her surprise, their acquaintance came easy. She could hold her own with any of them, had as many good stories. She was part of a club, and it gave her a kick.

Sometimes the knowledge of her state dampened her spirits, though at times, the feel of it in her breasts, in her very blood, caught her by surprise and gave her joy. Once, she tried to find the thermal pool where she thought the baby had been conceived, but it had vanished.

On the day before New Year's Eve, Dick Chubbs called.

"Sit down, kid."

"What is it?"

"Are you sitting?"

"What is it, Dick?"

"Good news. It is my privilege to make you an offer."

The number two correspondent for *Probe* in Moscow wanted to go home. His wife had run off with another journalist, and he was distraught. The magazine needed somebody there pronto.

"A staff job?"

"Bingo."

Jodie accepted. Chubbs told her she could have a few days off, if she liked, but wanted her in Moscow by the second week of January. That didn't give her much time. She packed her bags, left a note for Douglas at the front desk of the Mohacs, and raced to the airport. By that evening, she was on her way to Berlin.

On the plane, sorrow came over her, and she began to cry. But it wasn't all sorrow, she thought, more a mixture of elation and deep grief, as if she were in mourning and celebration at once. She couldn't eat her food. Out the window, cirrus purpled. Stars could be seen, high and white. Down below, the last of the sun caught mountain peaks and steeped them in vermilion. She wiped her eyes and wondered how she would ever tell her parents she was never coming home again. Home was below.

CHAPTER THIRTY-FOUR

1.

FOR TWENTY DOLLARS, Douglas hired a man to build two coffins. They were plain things, made of planks from a smashed wardrobe. The day after Christmas, Uta and Stuart were laid to rest in the snow of Belo cemetery, with those who had died in the name of the revolution. It was not the happiest of fits. These two probably belonged outside the cemetery walls, along with all the other poor souls who had fought on the wrong sides, defected at the wrong moments, made the worst possible choices at the least optimal seasons, but what did it matter? The dead were the dead. Douglas stuck the national colors and a carnation on their cross. Unaware of their contents, a monk from Snagov Monastery sang over the graves. After the service ended, Douglas went to an Orthodox chapel and lit a taper in their honor. For now, it was all he could do. One day soon, he would return and take them home.

Meanwhile, Nester and Waltraud left, headed for Berlin. Douglas thanked them for everything. He apologized for what his brother had done, but knew it wouldn't help. Nester would never hear the name Gleaming again and smile.

On his last night in Bucharest, Voicu invited him to a party at a new little cafe called La Bolsha Vita. There was a Ginger Bathory look-alike contest, lots of abominable Moldavian champagne, pistol firing, and a feast of mutton and french fries.

Douglas sat in a corner and thought about his brother. Despite his dying words, his discovery of some awful first principle in the murder of Grams, Stuart had been decent. Douglas could not believe otherwise. He simply could not. Those words were a confusion brought on by Stuart's own fading consciousness, the beginning of a thought never consummated. No, Douglas thought, his brother had not discovered the joys of murder, he had merely died believing he had done so, and there was a difference. How very Glemnik!

The truth about him lay elsewhere—not in his own actions, but in his odd capacity to inspire the actions of others. As far as Douglas could tell, Stuart's misguided sense of mission had created the entire debacle, as if he were a chemical that had driven everyone else insane. Thanks to Stuart, the Albacete Association had believed it could bomb the Amerika Haus. He was their cover, and without him, the risk would have been too great. Klek would never have ventured into enemy territory. Douglas shook his head. Styles was no better. He too had been captivated. Stuart had allowed *him* to think he could infiltrate East Berlin and nab Klek. Without Stuart, a man seemingly agreeable to any purpose, Styles would never have embarked on Second Home. And the rest of us succumbed as well, Douglas thought. Stuart had offered something to each of them: to Uta, he had presented the irresistible combination of love and revolutionary activity; to Nester, he had appeared as a one true friend; to Douglas, a family. But in truth, searching for some irrevocable, last reckoning within himself, Stuart had only assumed the shape of these things. He could not have *been* them, because he had never understood that they were real, that there *were* such things as comrades, patriots, lovers, friends, brothers, and yes, murderers. In that sense, Stuart had betrayed no one. How could he?

An American businessman wandered into La Bolsha Vita and asked the bartender for directions to the Intercontinental. Douglas overheard. The American was the representative of a consortium of investors, looking into the possibility of a joint venture in the energy sector. After drinking a lot of wine with someone named Bela from one of the ministries, he forgot which, he had gotten lost in the snow and darkness. The bartender did not understand a word of this. Douglas downed the last of a glass of vodka. He zipped up his jacket, took the drunken American by the arm, and with a last wave to Voicu, led him home.

2.

BY THE TIME he got to Margaret Island, Jodie was gone. Douglas read her note about Moscow. She'd forgotten to leave him her address in West Berlin, and that sparked a jealous fear. She had left him behind. A new life was beginning.

The hotel manager begged him to stay. Laszlo the croupier pleaded. The meal moths had returned. Rats, cockroaches, and ticks were worse than ever. Douglas thought about it, but in the end, he simply couldn't. Much as he liked the idea of clearing the Hotel Mohacs of infestation, he would be reminded of Jodie. He would drink himself into a stupor, and the arthropods would multiply.

He wrote Jodie a letter, care of Waltraud, at the Narkose bar, telling her how he felt. If she didn't want him, he would understand. He would not make trouble. He was resigned to her answer.

With money she had given him, he flew to West Berlin and took a taxi straight to the Narkose. It was afternoon, and the place had filled with East Germans, friends of Waltraud's cousin Dagmar, who had been made a full partner and was counting money in a corner. Nester was out, but Waltraud fed him and gave him Jodie's address. She had come by every day and asked after Douglas. She was leaving for Moscow soon, Waltraud told him, so he'd better hurry.

He found the apartment in Schöneberg, and to his horror, discovered from an American neighbor that Jodie had left for the airport an hour before. It was New Year's Eve, the neighbor said, and Jodie didn't want to spend it by herself in a city she was leaving, so she had decided to go to Moscow early. The neighbor gave him another letter she had left behind. He tore it open.

If you ever get this, Douglas, then you should know two things. I am pregnant, and I still like you. Hmmmm, he says, eyeing the letter. That's interesting. You're damn right it is. Get your ass to Moscow! JB

Douglas caught a cab to the airport. By the time he got there, the plane had taxied away from the gate. Tegel had an observation platform, and he climbed it.

Jodie's jet was a sleek and beautiful thing, and he watched it take off with a newfound admiration. She was in there. She was pregnant. The jet's engines rose to a roar. The machine moved down the tarmac, lifted off the ground. He watched it rise into the pearl-bright sky, swing up, and curl around. It was making a circle, turning first west, then back in the other direction. All of Berlin, its two halves, stretched beneath its belly. She wouldn't be able to see him, but he waved arms anyway. The plane ascended, became small, a piece of sunfire bound east. The East, he thought. Surely the East needs exterminators.

CHAPTER THIRTY-FIVE

ON NEW YEAR'S EVE, 1989, without much fanfare, Nester officially resigned from the United States Army, and on the same day, received the official job offer from the Central Intelligence Agency. He told them he'd have to think it over. Waltraud lobbied in favor, his conscience against. What would Stuart have advised?

Outside the Narkose, fireworks split the night. Church bells pealed. Even within the bar, the heavy glamming and clanging of metal could be heard. The din had reached a fever pitch by ten o'clock, and normally, Nester would have been out in front of the bar shooting bottle rockets with everyone else, watching German punks throw black cats at each other while their parents got drunk on *Sekt* and listened to *Die Fledermaus* on the radio. Berlin was celebrating its recovery that night; for the first time in decades, East and West could ring in the new year together.

In honor of it, Waltraud's new business partner, cousin Dagmar, had brought over her ex-husband, his friends and relations. She had made a move on Nester, which he had gently rebuffed. Now they were all outside together, but he couldn't bring himself to join them.

After Bucharest, the noises set him on edge. They reminded him of the echo of gunfire in the chasms between apartment blocks. They conjured up the dead man on his pile of abalone.

And so, at the stroke of midnight, he was alone at the Narkose bar, happily sipping a mint tea as everyone else watched the night sky explode, and curiously for a skeptic, he was thinking about the existence of extraterrestrial life, something which had never much interested him before, certainly not during his stint at the UFO Working Group. Now that so many dictators had fallen, however, he was willing to rethink his position. Brüderlein would applaud.

Hell, he thought, Eastern Europe was an unidentified flying object, a chariot of fire hurtling across the stars. Some it struck with terror. Others it filled with rapture. It had come to earth and abducted Communism. It had abducted him too, and Stuart Glemnik and Uta Silk. It had whirled and danced before the eyes of men and was now, as he sipped his mint tea, about to return to wherever it had come from. The visitation was over, and the human race would be left in shadow again, forced back on the weak stuff of memories, ideology, and religious faith. Germany might be reunified. The Soviet Union might fall. Other enormous changes might occur, but not this, not what he had witnessed, this rush of light through the tunnel of madness.

The door of the bar banged open. Bells and bursts filled his ears. The door closed again. Two men approached, one of them hidden from view in a cavernous parka and hood.

The one in the hood extended a mitten. Behind him, sheepish, stood Jerome Tunt. Nester took the mitten without squeezing.

"Quite a party they're having," Tunt said.

"Yep."

"Makes you feel proud to be an American, doesn't it?"

Nester gestured at stools.

"Have a seat."

The men declined.

"Me and Carl are headed down Panama way." Tunt reached into his coat pocket for something. "Care to join us?"

"No thanks."

The owl found what he was looking for. He laid a diskette on the counter.

"As promised."

Nester eyed the obscene piece of information. A man had died for it.

"Get it out of my sight," he said. Then stopping himself, he picked up the diskette. "On second thought."

Better not to let these two men have anything that could incriminate him. Before anyone could come into the bar and see the object, he thrust it into his pocket.

In truth, exoneration no longer really mattered. After being rescued from the tunnels, Carlton Styles had been stitched back together, but the separate parts barely made a whole. In the gunfight, he had lost an eye. His larynx had been damaged as well. Nevertheless, he kept moving, whittled, bitter, wordless. The CIA had finally done itself a favor and pensioned him off, but he refused to become inactive. With Tunt, who had quit the army, he had evidently formed a lasting alliance.

"Tell me something, Jerome," Nester said. "Just so I understand what I have here in my pocket."

The ex-corporal peered into the depths of the hood, secured some approval, and looked back at Nester.

"Why keep a log of this operation, if it was supposed to be so secret?"

Styles nudged Tunt, who gave a sheepish answer. "There was a time when we thought—when we believed, honestly, well, when Major Coogan, especially, believed that Operation Second Home might win him favor at Fort Leavenworth, you know, as a kind of innovation in our relations with enemy intelligence. If things had happened differently, Carl here figures, we could have all been given some sort of covert Congressional Medal of Honor maybe, for services rendered. There would have been promotions all around, Carl figures. Unfortunately, it didn't go down that way."

Nester stifled a horrible urge to laugh. "Yeah."

"Anyway, Coogan insisted on the log. He was on the verge of giving it to the Pentagon when we caught up with him. He'd have given us all away, so we did what we had to."

Tunt peered back into the hood, as if waiting for further instructions. Nester had not forgotten that these two men were murderers. But he saw what awaited them. Their doom lay just around some approaching turn, and did not need his help.

"You be careful, Jerome," Nester said, experiencing a flash of pity.

"Yessir."

Tunt stared at the floor. Styles leaned against him. Nester was repulsed and touched by the sight. The door banged open again. Waltraud came running into the bar.

"*Maus,* you must come see."

"Waltraud—"

She ignored the visitors and tugged at his arm. *"Bitte, bitte, bitte!"*

He gave her a long hard look. She stopped tugging. They both knew she had no right to ask anything of him, not even this. But it was her city. On its finest night, he could not deny her.

"If you'll excuse me, gentlemen."

Her arm twined around his, they went outside, joined the men dressed as Hell's Angels. The fume of Polish cigars filled his senses. The sky might have been made of bells. Near and far, they reveled. Light crashed against light. Darkness glowed. Despite himself, despite everything, Nester gasped. It was a wondrous sight.

CHRONOLOGY

1917

November 7—Bolshevik revolution in Russia (the Russian Revolution).

1936

July 18—Outbreak of the Spanish Civil War.

1945

February 7—Yalta conference of the Allied Powers during World War II, unofficial beginning of the division between East and West in Europe.

April 30—Adolf Hitler commits suicide in his bunker.

May 8—VE Day, end of World War II in Europe, beginning of the division of Berlin and Germany into four occupied zones: French, British, American, and Soviet.

1948

July 24—The beginning of the Berlin airlift, first real skirmish of the Cold War. Soviets cut off access to French, British, and American sectors of Berlin, and Allies fly supplies in.

1949

April 4—Founding of NATO alliance of western countries, primarily against the Soviet Union.

May 23—Establishment of West Germany as an independent country, still occupied by Allied powers.

October 7—Establishment of East Germany as an independent country; Soviet military government replaced by Soviet control commission.

1953
March 5—Stalin dies.
June 17—Soviet Union sends tanks and troops against 30,000 East German rioters.

1955
May 14—Founding of the Warsaw Pact, military alliance of the Soviet Union and its satellites, in the wake of West Germany's entrance into NATO.

1956
November 4–14—Soviet forces put down Hungarian uprising.

1961
August 13—Closing of the border between East and West Berlin; beginning of the construction of the Berlin Wall; mass flight of refugees to the West.

1965
March—Nicolae Ceausescu becomes premier of Romania.

1968
August 20–21—Invasion of Czechoslovakia by hundreds of thousands of Warsaw Pact troops; the invasion puts down a popular cultural, social, and political movement known as the Prague Spring.

1969
September 28—Czechoslovak reformist leader Alexander Dubcek ousted from the Communist Party.

1981
August 31—Solidarity movement in Poland wins the right to strike and to organize trade unions free of Communist Party control.
December 13—General Wojciech Jaruzelski declares martial law in Poland; suspension of Solidarity movement.

1985
March 11—Mikhail Gorbachev becomes general secretary of the Communist Party of the Soviet Union; beginning of the era of openness (*glasnost*) and reform (*perestroika*) in the Soviet Union.

1988

June 16—In Hungary, small demonstrations on the 32nd anniversary of the execution of Hungarian reformist Imre Nagy.

1989

January 15—20th anniversary of the death of Jan Palach, who burned himself alive in Wenceslaus Square after the Warsaw Pact invasion; 4,000 people defy a government ban and gather at the site of Palach's suicide.

March 31—In Romania, ethnic Hungarian pastor and political dissident Laszlo Toekes is ordered by the government to leave the city of Timisoara. He refuses.

May 2—Hungarian border guards begin dismantling the cement, barbed wire, and barricades along the Austrian border; East Germans begin to escape over the border to the West.

May 31—American president George Bush calls for the end of the division of Europe, the tearing down of the Berlin Wall, and the introduction of free elections throughout Eastern Europe.

June 4—Chinese government puts down student revolt in Tiananmen Square in Beijing; in Poland, first quasi-democratic elections in decades; Solidarity wins, ending one-party rule in that country.

June 7—East German government under Erich Honecker expresses approval of the Chinese reaction.

June 16—Reburial of Hungarian reformist Imre Nagy on 33rd anniversary of his execution by Communists, attended by more than 200,000 people.

August 24—Tadeusz Mazowiecki becomes first non-Communist leader of parliament in Poland in decades.

September 4—1,500 East Germans gather in Leipzig, East Germany, to protest government policies; first of the Monday-night demonstrations.

September 11—Hungary officially opens its border with Austria; East Germans begin to leave for the West by the thousands.

September 25—In East Germany, 8,000 demonstrators gather in Leipzig.

October 2–10—10,000 demonstrators gather in Leipzig, singing "We Shall Overcome" and "The Internationale."

October 7–8—40th anniversary of the founding of East Germany; Gorbachev visits East Berlin. Small protests in East Berlin broken up violently by police.

October 9—In the wake of Gorbachev's visit to East Berlin, tens of thousands of East Germans take to the streets in cities all over the country, 70,000 in Leipzig alone.

October 16—Monday-night demonstrations crescendo in East Germany, 120,000 demonstrators in Leipzig alone.

October 18—Hungarian parliament passes amendments to the constitution; the word "People" is dropped from the People's Republic of Hungary; the values of bourgeois democracy and the rule of law are formally recognized. East German Communist Party ousts its leader, Erich Honecker, and replaces him with Egon Krenz.

October 23—In Hungary, 33rd anniversary of the 1956 uprising; existence of a new Hungarian republic is proclaimed by the leader of parliament. In East Germany, Monday-night demonstrations continue, with 300,000 people taking to the streets.

October 26—First official meeting between the East German opposition movement, known as the New Forum, and a high-ranking government official.

November 2—In Romania, ethnic Hungarian pastor Laszlo Toekes is assaulted in his home in Timisoara by members of the government security force, the Securitate.

November 7—Under pressure from mass flight and demonstrations, the East German cabinet resigns.

November 9—Opening of the Berlin Wall.

November 10—Bulgarian dictator Todor Zhivkov, in office since 1954, is ousted; in East Germany, the border between East and West falls away. Thousands of East Germans cross into West Berlin. West German chancellor Helmut Kohl arrives in the city.

November 17—In Czechoslovakia, students organize a ceremony in Prague to commemorate the 50th anniversary of the murder of a Czech student by the Nazis; 30,000 people gather, and the riot police attack them.

November 18—Vaclav Havel and other Czechoslovak dissidents gather to form an anti-government front, soon to become the Civic Forum political movement.

November 20—Romanian dictator Nicolae Ceausescu tells Communist Party Congress that Romania will not follow other Eastern European countries along paths toward democracy or capitalism; in Czechoslovakia, hundreds of thousands of people gather in Prague to protest the government.

November 28—West German Chancellor Helmut Kohl proposes a ten-point plan for the confederation of East and West Germany.

December 1–2—American president George Bush and Soviet premier Mikhail Gorbachev meet in Malta.

December 10—In Czechoslovakia, the first non-Communist government in decades takes power.

December 15—In Timisoara, Romania, demonstrators form a human chain around home of Laszlo Toekes, trying to prevent soldiers from forcibly removing him.

December 16—Thousands more demonstrators join them.

December 17—Government forces attack the demonstrators; thousands are rumored dead.

December 18—Romanian borders are closed.

December 20—100,000 Romanians gather in the Square of the Republic in Bucharest to hear a speech by Ceausescu; afterwards, they refuse to leave the square. Protestors take over parts of central Bucharest.

December 21—Some government forces defect to the side of the protestors; Ceausescu and his wife, Elena, flee by helicopter from Bucharest.

December 22–26—Civil war in the streets of Bucharest.

December 23—The Ceausescus are captured.

December 25—The Ceausescus are summarily tried and executed.

1990

October 3—Reunification of East and West Germany.

1991

August 18–21—In the Soviet Union, a coup of hardline Communists against Russia's first democratically elected president, Boris Yeltsin, is attempted and defeated.

1992

January 1—Dissolution of the Soviet Union.

ACKNOWLEDGMENTS

I could not have finished this book without the help of a number of people. I want to thank my parents, John H. and Sally, who gave me support and a laptop when I most needed them; my siblings, Tolbert and Molly, who have always believed in me; my tireless, patient, and wonderful editor Cindy Spiegel, as well as Susan Petersen and Cathy Fox at Riverhead; my agent and friend Gordon Kato; friends and family whose support, advice, and help over the years have been indispensable—Dale Sherrod, Edward Serotta, Tim Whitby, Harriet Davison, John Tagliabue, Paula Butturini, Christian Caryl, Darrell Dellamaide, Veronika Hass, Peter Slevin, James Hynes, Doug Wright, Allan Gee, Jack Simons, Patricia Peart, Doug Stott, Barbara Wojoski, Mark, Reba, Steven, Robin, and Scott, Sharilyn, my dear Madeline and thoughtful Ruby; my editors and colleagues at *US News & World Report* during my years in Europe, including Steve Roberts, John Walcott, Jeff Trimble, Brian Duffy, David Lawday, the generous Robin Knight, and the best chief of correspondents I could ever hope to have, Carey English; also Jim Fallows, who gave me time off for revisions; and friends at the *New York Times* who gave me help and encouragement to go over to Germany in the first place, particularly Phil Taubman, Maureen Dowd, David Binder, Janet Battaile, Barclay Walsh, Earl Smith, Victor Homola, David Rampe, and Von Alston. Special thanks to Nate Irwin at the Smithsonian for talking to me about bugs and to Joseph Knott for advice on extermination, and for their insights into East Central Europe and Germany, Alan Ashburn, Jan-Peter Boening, Lisa Schmitz, Fred Kempe, Marc Fisher, Brooke Unger, Debra Wise, Katie Hafner, Peter Green, Brenda Fowler, Nomi Morris, Jeff Schneider, Fritz Hahn, Michael Klipstein,

Danny Benjamin, and several former members of the HVA who probably prefer not to be named. I fell in love with the German language thanks to the late Erich Heller, and owe a debt to the authors Gale Stokes, Timothy Garton Ash, Joseph Rothschild, Martin Rady, Hannes Bahrmann, Christoph Links, Bernard Wheaton, and Zdeněk Kavan for their histories of this part of the world. Finally, endless thanks to my wife, Debra, without whom this book, quite literally, could never have been written.